MW00569465

GLITTERING SAVAGES

A brutally strong hand reached out, grasped her neck and drove her back. A fleeting look from a pair of dead eyes compounded her sudden terror, before she felt a mouth clamping onto her throat. The teeth scissored through the skin and into the sinews and flesh beneath.

Jennifer screamed. 'No! *No!* Please God! *No!*' The words never passed the hand which slapped across her mouth. She struggled as best she could, fighting the horrifying sensation in her neck, the stinging heat of the flood. Her attacker sucked everything she possessed through the wound.

She was drained of all her talents and desires, her will to live, her most animal instincts. Even her pain was stolen . . .

Also by Mark Burnell

Freak

About the author

Mark Burnell was born in Northumberland in 1964. He has since lived in Brazil and travelled extensively throughout South America before returning to England and a job in the City. He is now a full time writer, living once again in his home near Corbridge, Northumberland.

Glittering Savages

Mark Burnell

NEW ENGLISH LIBRARY
Hodder and Stoughton

First published in Great Britain in 1995
by Hodder and Stoughton
A division of Hodder Headline PLC
First published in paperback in 1995
by Hodder and Stoughton

A New English Library Paperback

10 9 8 7 6 5 4 3 2 1

A CIP catalogue record for this title
is available from the British Library

ISBN 0 340 61783 7

Typeset by Keyboard Services, Luton, Beds

Printed and bound in Great Britain by
Cox and Wyman Ltd, Reading, Berks

Hodder and Stoughton
A division of Hodder Headline PLC
338 Euston Road
London NW1 3BH

For Julian Alexander

Prologue

1963

He was in the dark, listening to the storm. The wind drove icy rain against the fragile walls of his motel room. The only light was provided by the flickering red neon sign that hung above the mud pool which passed for a parking lot. It tinged him with a dull crimson. The door opened and a rush of freezing air brought a shower of rain into the room. She stood in the doorway, barely visible from where he sat, stewing in his fear.

"I wasn't sure whether you would come," he said, his voice trembling with anxiety.

"Nor was I," she replied, before stepping into the room and closing the door. "You can turn on the lamp, if you like."

He did and when he turned back to face her, he recoiled. She was naked. Her voice was as chilling as the weather outside when she murmured, slowly, "And I thought you'd never notice."

"Why . . . why are you . . . *like that?*"

"Why not? I felt like it."

"In the freezing rain and wind? I don't understand."

"No, I don't expect you do. Now, are we going to talk about my minimalist dress sense, or have you something more urgent to discuss?"

He nodded and reached for his notes, which were lying on the desk beside him. Little pools of water were forming on the worn carpet around each of her feet. She wasn't even shivering. She moved over to his bed and he tried not to stare, but found his gaze instinctively drawn to her glistening body. She had an animal muscularity that he found quite beautiful.

He asked, "Why did you have to pick these people? After all, they've got enough problems without . . . without *you*."

She smiled. "I know. It's laziness, I suppose. They're really too easy, but . . ."

Her voice trailed off, so he prompted her. "But what?"

She cocked her head to one side, still smiling. "They scare wonderfully well. Haven't you felt it? The silent hysteria."

Dr Andrew Martin sat up straight on the frail wooden chair. His cold fingers were stiff and moved the pen clumsily. The scrawled notes were untidy and inadequate. Outside, the November rain continued to savage Burrows, a small mining town in the Appalachian Mountains of Virginia, not far from the border with West Virginia.

"And sensing this terror – this silent hysteria – somehow sustains you, does it?"

"No. It's preferential, not essential. The nervous eyes and the secretive whispers . . . you must have noticed them. It's exquisite," she told him, permitting herself a satisfied smile. "Fear is a delicacy."

Marilyn Webber sprawled across his bed, soaking his sheets. The motel was located at the south end of the road which ran through Burrows to the rest of the world. There was nowhere else to stay, giving Frazier's Motel a monopoly on accommodation in the town. Competition might have raised the standards, but who came to stay in a place like Burrows, Virginia, anyway? Even one motel seemed like excess.

He wondered why she'd agreed to see him. He pictured her moving naked through the trees which carpeted the mountains that loomed over the dismal town. From there, she watched and waited, oblivious to the hostile conditions, selecting with precision before the stalk and slaughter.

"Poor communities almost always scare the most easily."

In his experience, this was true, but Andrew Martin said

nothing. Arriving in Burrows had been an unpleasant shock. It was hard to believe that he lived in the same country as the inhabitants of this town. Where he came from, life was about having a car the size of a whale. It was about white picket fences and barbecues. Coming to this part of Virginia was like a journey to another world; backward and broken, the people were foreigners to him, aliens in an unfamiliar country. He knew it and they knew it, peeping out of their crumbling wooden homes at him, while he strolled through the rain, all of them knowing his thoughts: Burrows was coal, and without it the community was dead, which might have been a blessing. There was no profit in mining for those who cut the face. They were alive, but not living. And now they had Marilyn Webber.

"How did you come across Burrows?" he asked.

"By accident. I was driving up from New Orleans to New York City, meandering here and there. I stumbled across this place and all the elements were right: a secluded, poor community, forgotten by outsiders. It's bleak here. The inhabitants are slaves to superstition and that makes them ideal."

Martin thought about it. The leaden skies and the silver rain. The dead eyes in the faces blackened by dust from the mines. The mountains that rose like a dark threat over the fragile collection of tiny homes and threadbare stores, which huddled together and called itself Burrows. A cursed community.

"I'm glad I stopped here, Dr Martin. You see, I'm drawn to desperation."

Not just drawn to it, he thought. She was feeding on it, preying on the fear she created.

The hopeless state authorities were mystified. It started with the disappearance of several of the town's inhabitants. No trace of them was ever found and the police tried to stem the rising tide of rumour by suggesting that those concerned had moved on, gravitating towards the big cities, which was a natural instinct for anyone living in a place like Burrows. But that was before people started becoming ill.

The victims faced weight loss, a draining of facial colour, a lack of focus in the eyes – as though concussion were present – and a decline into crippling exhaustion. In the later stages, a crop of mental disorders flourished. One victim had been caught trying to commit suicide by tearing out his throat.

Those who escaped the illness, were not immune from the fall-out. The community was turning on itself, making pariahs of those who became infected. And they in turn, being ostracized by the mainstream, were turning on themselves as they disintegrated. They were dying in miserable isolation, petrified by their illnesses until mental infection, mercifully, spared them the horror of reality in the final stages of their decline.

"Are all of you drawn to this type of desperation?"

Marilyn Webber shrugged. "I couldn't say. I wouldn't presume to speak for the others."

"So why are *you* drawn to it?"

Marilyn looked over at the window. Through the persistent rain she could make out the neon sign, which misleadingly claimed Frazier's Motel was a place of comfort and hospitality.

"It's time for me to go," she said.

He looked up. "Will you do it again tonight?"

She raised an eyebrow, and said, "Maybe."

He sat back, listened momentarily to the rain pounding the cracked tarmac, and then asked, "Do you know what these people would do to you, if they found out?"

Marilyn shook her head, as she rose from the bed, looking serious for a change. "What *they* would do? It's what *I* would do that counts, believe me."

Martin tried not to let his anxiety show. He had so much to ask and it looked as though his time had run out.

"Can I see you again?" he stammered.

She smiled. "Dr Martin, are you falling in love with me?"

"I have so much more to ask."

Marilyn thought about it. "I'll be in New York soon, for three or four days. Then I'll be gone. For good. But I might have a little time for you . . . perhaps."

Dr Martin's face brightened. "You could come out to my

house. That's where my work is stored. I could set up equipment for . . ."

The idea seemed to amuse her. "Where do you live?"

"Connecticut."

This amused her even more. "Not quite Burrows, I expect."

He shook his head. She stood up straight. Her perfect skin was still damp. She stepped forward, just inches from his face, and pushed her fingers through his hair before tugging his head back, so that he looked up at her. He felt her naked flesh against his body. He was too scared to move, or even utter a word in protest. She said, "You're still not sure what I am, are you?"

"No," he croaked.

"Well, you'll see. I promise."

Everyone is supposed to remember what they were doing on 22 November 1963, when they heard that President Kennedy had been assassinated. Darryl G. Cummings certainly never forgot. He was being treated in hospital for severe shock.

He was the first police patrolman to enter the Martin house in Connecticut, early on that morning. He climbed through the shattered living-room window and what he discovered on the floor scarred his memory like fire scars skin.

Chapter One

Ever since she discovered her husband's infidelity, she wondered what an affair would be like. His numerous indiscretions were casual physical encounters which left no emotional trace. Wet press-ups was what he once called them. *Wet press-ups!* She shook her head sadly at the recollection of the tasteless phrase and how amused he had been by it.

Jennifer Colson stepped out of the shower, splashing water across the tiny tiles of the bathroom floor. They were mosaic size. She dried herself with the thick hotel towel and heard a gentle knock at the door. It was Room Service with a tray of Earl Grey tea. The miniature Oriental who carried the tray had as good a command of English as Jennifer had of Cantonese. Their communication consisted of hand signals, before she ushered him out of the room with a generous tip.

She returned to the bathroom and stepped out of the dressing-gown. Naked at thirty-six and looking good on it, she thought. Jennifer was five seven tall with pale skin and straight dark brown hair. It was cut in a short, boyish style which, allied to the glasses she usually wore, not to mention her clumsy dress sense, made her far plainer than she need have appeared. Few people gave her a second glance. Certainly, David Colson had long since forgotten how attractive she was and she had become disinclined to remind him.

She pulled on a loose-fitting dress, which hung awkwardly from her shoulders. It had a bold floral print. Against the heat of the day, the billowing cotton felt cool on her skin. Jennifer poured herself a cup of tea and wondered where her husband was. With another of his lobotomized conquests? Probably. But it didn't matter any more. It no longer hurt.

She cast an eye around Room 114 of the Cadogan Hotel. The greyish-blue carpet had a quiet raspberry design running through it, which matched the large vases of the lamps on the low tables at either end of the sofa. They had broad cream lamp-shades. Jennifer sat on the edge of the bed and pictured the two of them, locked together with their limbs in a knot. The idea of it brought a quiver to her stomach. It wouldn't be long now.

She lit a cigarette and moved over to the window, peering down onto the junction of Pont Street and Sloane Street. She felt like a spy, booking in under a false name. The faint possibility of detection heightened the sense of mischief. Jennifer almost longed for it, just so she could see David Colson's face when he discovered that his wife had been unfaithful to him. Not only that, but how would he cope when he learned that she had fallen in love with a man barely half his age?

Of fame's many prices, Jennifer had discovered that none was more taxing than lack of privacy, especially where marital decay was concerned. As her husband's theatrical and cinematic success blossomed, so the more prurient sectors of the press kept an increasingly watchful eye on his private life. Jennifer had long since accepted that fidelity was not one of David Colson's talents. On the other hand, she also believed that the papers had hastened the disintegration of their marriage and had certainly made it seamier than it need have been. Some gossip columnists wrote admiringly – or was it jealously? – of his perpetual adultery. Jennifer, when she was mentioned at all, was usually portrayed as some emotionally retarded homemaker who preferred to live in ignorance. The fact that she was a world-class cellist was often overlooked entirely. Although a little ashamed at entertaining such thoughts, she couldn't deny that she felt a thrill as she contemplated how news of her own adultery might be reported. Would David Colson's colossal ego ever recover?

His infidelities ended up in diarists' columns, or with David booking into clinics for furtive check-ups, or delivering brown bags of banknotes to pay for discreet abortions for girls who should have still been at school. Jennifer's one infidelity had ended up in love, a real passion.

André Perlman was a twenty-four-year-old genius from Montreal. Like others burdened with the tag of "genius", he had a reputation for emotional volatility. It might even have been justified when he held a violin in his talented hands. But when he held Jennifer, he was like she was at that moment: intoxicated and enslaved, a servant to the heart. They were sick with longing when apart and passionate to the point of distraction when together.

Jennifer sucked on her cigarette and tapped some ash out of the window. They hadn't seen each other for three weeks. André was on his way from Berlin to Chicago, to sign a contract to perform with the Chicago Symphony Orchestra. This would be their only night together, but he would be back from America in three days. Then they planned to break the news about their affair and their future. In four days, David Colson would be stewing in the hot juices of humiliation. Not before time.

Jennifer pictured André on a Boeing 747 the following day, slumped in his First Class seat, too exhausted to respond to the cabin crew's polite enquiries. Tomorrow, she would be tender between her legs and every irritation would remind her of how it had been so exquisitely achieved.

The minutes crawled. Jennifer poured herself a second cup of tea and turned on the television. It was the first week of Wimbledon and she watched Steffi Graf putting some unseeded player to the sword on Centre Court. The commentator's voice was muffled by the chorus of traffic which rose up through the window from the sizzling street outside.

When the phone rang, Jennifer was across the bed and holding the receiver before the second peal.

"This is reception, Miss Ross."

Ross was Jennifer's maiden name. Considering the nature of her liaison with André Perlman, she enjoyed using it as she checked in.

"Yes?"

"Mr Goldman is here."

"Mr Goldman?" she replied, failing to suppress a giggle. "Please send him up."

She replaced the receiver on the cradle and skipped into the bathroom. She applied the lightest touches of scent to her throat and wrists. Adjusting her dress so that a good portion of her cleavage was on display, she opened the door to him.

A brutally strong hand reached out, grasped her neck and drove her back. A fleeting look from a pair of dead eyes compounded her sudden terror, before she felt a mouth clamping onto her throat. The teeth scissored through the skin and into the sinews and flesh beneath.

Jennifer screamed. "No! *No!* Please God! *No!*" The words never passed the hand which slapped across her mouth. She struggled as best she could, fighting the horrifying sensation in her neck, the stinging heat of the flood. Her attacker sucked everything she possessed through the wound. Her control was evaporating, all her memories were fading, everything she'd ever known was vanishing. Hot streams of blood were dribbling down her neck, over her chest, staining the dress she was wearing for André.

She was drained of all her talents and desires, her will to live, her most animal instincts. Even her pain was stolen. Her protest disintegrated into limp surrender. She was a hollow soul when she felt several points of staggering pressure across her chest. The sound of cracking filled her astonished ears. That was the last thing.

Moments later, André Perlman strolled into Room 114 of the Cadogan Hotel and had just a slither of a second to spot the carnage before powerful fingers dug into his throat and yanked him forward. He tried to yell but the fingers which took him by the neck silenced his cry before it could escape from his gaping mouth. Out of his burning eyes he caught one brief glimpse of

Jennifer's ruined body. The wall was streaked with a monumental explosion of her blood. She lay face down in a purple pool. On the bed was . . . *was what*?'

He was being propelled too fast to see it properly. It was lumpy and crimson, slick with the blood which clashed shockingly with the bedspread. It looked like . . .

André Perlman heard the thick splash of hot blood on the coffee table and tea tray, without ever having time to realize it was his. He was tumbling forward as something seemed to erupt inside his chest.

A minute later, Jennifer Colson and André Perlman lay side by side in the hotel room, completely broken. The third inhabitant of the room was sliding towards the floor, submitting to the ravages of the blissful rush.

Chapter Two

The year was 1915 and it was her only trip to Russia. St Petersburg proved to be quite breathtaking. The gift was a gold statue recovered from treasures discovered in a small tomb that had been concealed on one of the many agricultural terraces outside the ancient Incan capital city of Cuzco.

"I had no idea that you had visited Peru."

"Yes, in . . ." Sophia checked herself and then said, "A few years ago."

Tsar Nicholas seemed quite taken with the gift. He turned it over in his hands, letting his eyes roam over the glittering gold carving. Alexandra sat to his right, her hands playing gently with the beautiful pearls that cascaded from her neck and pooled in her lap. Tatiana had been laughing with Alexei while the parents looked on lovingly, but they were led away when the beautiful stranger entered.

What Sophia had seen so far only confirmed the rumours she had heard: the Tsar was happier running a family than an empire. He was a private man. Often, when they laughed, it was at remarks and looks which could not be construed by outsiders, leaving them awkward and isolated.

"Would you dine with us this evening?" he asked, looking up at her and then at his wife.

Sophia looked at Alexandra, who smiled warmly, but said nothing.

Early the following morning, Sophia stood by the open window of her bedroom. She looked out over St Petersburg's beauty and felt filled with an emotion that left her in conflict. Elation and despair battled for the heart. The evening had been a beautiful, appalling revelation. The family unit, threatened by custom and duty, held together by blood chains. All of it, every last glittering detail, was beyond Sophia's reach. It made her envious and self-pitying. They had what she longed for. Her fruitless searches left her heart aching and heavy.

The wind had sharp teeth and savaged her skin. She looked up. The swirling clouds were a sea of turbulent pearl. She reached out and watched her hand glisten in the cold, silver rain.

Rachel Cates awoke with a start. Her eyes were already open, but they suddenly regained the power of focus. There were tears spilling from the swollen ducts.

Her bedroom had a high ceiling. Tall french windows opened onto a generous first-floor balcony. On hot nights, she left them ajar. The slightest breeze would ruffle the curtains, but on that night it was so still they might have been carved from stone. Through the narrow cracks came the muted sounds of a city trying to sleep through an unnatural heat. Sirens sang in the dark constantly, like some hideous aural wallpaper, and occasionally a distant drunken shriek or the squeal of brakes from a speeding car would provide an ugly alternative.

She lay naked on her back, spread across her broad bed, staring at the ceiling. There were white lilies in a tall vase, perched on a small circular table. Their large brilliant heads hung sadly from their thin necks. Her dress lay on the floor in a lake of its own blue. She'd left the heavy gold choker on the thick slice of marble into which the bathroom basin had been sunk.

The dreams alarmed her. They were so vivid. The detail was so precise. Everything had a correct history and order. This was *real* Virtual Reality.

She sat up and wiped the tears from her face. The lilies were beautiful in the fragile darkness of early morning. Day was just beginning to force night into retreat. The oppressive humidity of London gave the air a bitter taste. It wasn't a city designed for heat. She sighed and felt the leaden weight of sadness inside her.

Why should she wait? As far as she was concerned, she'd already waited for too long. She'd displayed more self-control than was necessary. Now was the time. There would be nothing to gain by waiting any longer.

Rachel got off the bed and walked over to the window. Night's departure was signalled by the lilac traces in the sky. The glass panels of the french windows felt surprisingly cool to the touch. A taxi cruised slowly around the crescent of Lennox Gardens, looking for business. Up above, she saw the bright pinpoints of an aircraft's lights as it moved across the purple sky, dipping towards Heathrow. It would be daylight by the time the passengers left the terminal.

She nodded to herself, confirming her own conviction that the time to act had arrived. To delay would be pointless and painful.

It had been a sweltering night, as Robert Stark and Laura Keillor made love. He ran his fingers across her, carving through the perspiration on her skin. Tiny drops of sweat meandered in peculiar patterns across the geography of their bodies. They moved in the dim light which spilled down from the street into Robert's basement flat. Robert lay on his back and looked up at Laura, who sighed. Her fabulous copper hair tumbled down her back. In the strange half-light of his bedroom, it looked more blood-coloured than copper. Their skins were wet and burning.

They collapsed back onto the sheets in a soggy heap, waiting for the gentlest breeze to come and blow away some of the heat from their scorched bodies. Their fingers touched, slowly twisting and turning, tying themselves into friendly knots.

"I can't stand this heat," she sighed, lighting a cigarette and moving over to the window, where she was washed in weak light. "So much for London being cold, grey and wet. This feels more like Florida."

"Except they have fresh air in Florida."

A car murmured as it passed slowly by.

Laura said, "My skin is tingling."

"Well, I try."

She flicked some ash out of the window and turned round, grinning, as she said, "Oh, you wish, Robert." She rummaged through a pile of cassettes and put on "New York" by Lou Reed.

"What do you suppose would happen," she wondered, "if either of us fell in love?"

"With each other?"

"Maybe. Or with someone else."

Robert shook his head and said, "I'm not sure."

"Do you think we'd resent the way we're behaving now?"

"I know I wouldn't."

She waved a finger at him.

"You don't know that. You just like to think you wouldn't."

Robert looked at their clothes which were strewn across the floor. They were tangled together, just like Robert and Laura had been moments after they cast them off.

When Laura finished her cigarette she came back to bed and lay down beside Robert. She kissed him on the shoulder, the neck and then the mouth.

"So," she murmured, breaking into a sly smile, "are you too damaged for what I've got in mind?"

"That depends, doesn't it? If handled with care, I'm sure I could..."

"Oh, I will be careful. I promise," Laura assured him. "But you have to remember the old maxim: if it isn't hurting, it isn't working."

"I've never been a fan of the 'no pain, no gain' theory."

"You will be."

Afterwards, she drifted into sleep. He pulled a single cotton sheet over her body and gently ran his fingers over her flesh, watching the material move as his hand glided beneath it.

Sometimes, when they were walking down the street, Robert enjoyed watching other men watching her, with their eyes nailed to her body and their tongues stapled to the pavement. She made women jealous and hateful, and she enjoyed that especially. Laura had no time for frail and precious girls who worried about diets and cracked fingernails. She could be a classic bitch when she wanted to and he supposed that was part of the attraction.

It was just after six when Robert awoke. The temperature was already rising, leaving the seasonal average in its wake. He made a cup of coffee and returned to the bedroom as the alarm went off.

"Oh God! Turn it off, Robert! *Please!*"

He reached down but his clumsy fingers nudged the clock off the bedside table. It clattered onto the floor.

"Please, please, please!" she protested, burying her head beneath a pillow.

Robert hit the switch. She poked her head out into the daylight and blinked furiously.

"I'm shattered," she sighed through a yawn. "I'm going to look like a bloody tramp today!"

"And so you should, having spent the night behaving like one."

"Robert Stark!" she cried, throwing the pillow at him. "How dare you! I swear if there weren't parts of you I enjoyed, I'd cut them off!"

"It feels like you already have."

"I need a cup of coffee."

"I'll get you one."

Robert was in the kitchen when Laura appeared, wearing one of his shirts and nothing else, running two hands through her rich hair. He handed her a cup as she sat on the table and asked, "Is it immoral for us to behave like this?"

"You ask me that, at this time? How should I know? Why should I even care?"

Laura loved the games Robert and she played. Jack Clark once said she behaved more like a man than a woman, with regard to her attitude towards Robert. Jack was stuck so steadfastly in prehistory, it wasn't worth even trying to explain it to him. As for behaving like a man, Laura didn't care if she was behaving like a robot, so long as it felt good. If that put her in a minority, so be it, but that was how it was with her.

Robert lived in the apartment block which stood on the corner of Lennox Gardens, at the northern end, just by St Columba's Church. Since there were only four proper apartments in the building, they hardly required a full-time, uniformed porter, so Robert was the caretaker. In return, he received rent-free accommodation in the small, dark basement flat and a meagre salary. His free time, of which there was plenty, was devoted to his never-ending novel. The manuscript was a rainbow: no matter how far he progressed, the end was never any closer.

The ground-floor flat was the smallest in the building but, by any standard in London, it was still large. Godfrey and Mary Peake lived in it. He'd been a merchant banker in the days when gentlemen still existed in that profession. The first-floor flat was the finest in the building and belonged to Rachel Cates. As caretaker, Robert had never got further into it than the entrance hall. Her privacy encouraged gossip.

Above Miss Cates lived the Lorenzos. Vernon Lorenzo was a native New Yorker who worked for his bank's London office. Robert knew he was thirty-nine because Cassie, his ridiculously healthy wife, kept saying how worried her husband was about his forthcoming birthday.

"Vernon's losing sleep – not to mention hair! – over the big four-oh," she would say.

Vernon and Cassie Lorenzo had two children and a dog. Kevin was ten and Melissa was eight. The pug was called Nixon.

Charles and Agatha Sandberg lived on the top floor. They liked to sit in their grand drawing-room and look down onto the private gardens that formed the centre of Lennox Gardens. Agatha sometimes used binoculars to check who was strolling on the lawns or sitting on the benches. Looking down from the

Sandbergs' flat, the cars, which were parked with their bumpers to the garden's railings, looked like brightly coloured metallic petals fanning out from a large verdant core.

Vernon Lorenzo stepped out of the building and into the humid morning, sniffing the air with relish, as though it were alpine pure. He wore an immaculate suit. It must have been handy for his tailor that he was always in perfect shape, thanks to the jogging and the tennis, not to mention the squash and swimming. Cassie fed him on bean sprouts and yoghurt, washed down with fresh fruit juices.

His hair was oiled back. It didn't look to Robert as though he was losing much of it, no matter what Cassie said. As for worrying about being forty, he barely looked thirty. His shirt was allergic to creases. He wore a blue tie with small white dots. A gold tie-pin kept it in place. He turned to Robert, who was polishing the brass intercom plate.

"Happy?" he asked.

"What?"

Lorenzo squinted at him.

"What the hell are you doing here, Stark? Why don't you get a proper job? Haven't you heard? People aren't reading any more. They watch films and take drugs. *Jesus!*"

Then he was gone. Robert shielded his eyes from the sun with a raised arm and watched Vernon Lorenzo striding towards his corporate car. The man never missed an opportunity to treat Robert like something that had just navigated a passage through a dog's digestive system. Robert still didn't know why that was.

Rachel's fantastic dreams still haunted her, leaving a trace long after the event was finished, the way the smell of burned toast lingers in a kitchen. And because the images still bothered her, so did the sensation of sorrow which accompanied them, no matter how hard she tried to focus on something else.

She stepped out of the bath and chose not to towel herself down, heading straight for the large, spotless kitchen. The television was on and a weatherman with a charisma bypass was talking about drought. She passed through the kitchen and walked to the window of the drawing-room. London was dying. The stench of decay hung heavy in the lowered sky. Under the claustrophobic, dirty, yellow haze, millions of people wheezed and sweated through days of heat and humidity. A sky of brilliant blue still existed, but for Londoners it was a memory. As for rain . . .

Rachel permitted herself a wry smile at the weatherman's talk of drought. Drought was a word she associated with disasters on a biblical scale, usually in impoverished, disease-ridden African countries. It had nothing to do with bans imposed upon the lawn-sprinklers of Kent.

When she was almost dry, she pulled on a tight-fitting green dress. She stepped outside the front door to the apartment block. The heat spilled onto her shoulders. The sun was struggling gallantly to burn through the slice of dirt which was the city's ceiling.

Robert appeared, climbing the tradesman's steps with a collection of bulging black bin-liners slung over his left shoulder. Rachel watched him as he dumped them with the others on the edge of the pavement, ready for collection.

She surprised him, saying, "Nasty work."

He spun round and saw her standing by the railing. He wiped a film of sweat off his brow with the back of his hand.

"Not as nasty as leaving them down there. The dustmen are threatening to go on strike. This might be the last pick-up for quite a while."

"This city!" exclaimed Rachel.

A collection of sirens filled the air. The emergency services were trying to carve a passage through the rush-hour traffic. Robert felt hot and agitated and noticed how cool she looked. His gaze fell over her instinctively, taking in the body beneath the tight dress. Self-conscious of the feelings this aroused, he looked away.

"Is everything all right, Miss Cates?"

"What do you mean?"

He cleared his throat. "Are you settling in all right?"

"Yes, fine, thank you. What about you?"

Robert frowned and said, "I'm sorry?"

"What about you? Are you all right?"

He smiled awkwardly and nodded.

"I was referring to your writing," Rachel explained.

"How do you know about that?"

"I've got ears."

This exchange went against the received wisdom. Rachel was supposed to be a cold recluse. No one in the building had yet had any kind of conversation with her. It was normally quite an achievement to get "hello" out of her.

"Is it going well?" she asked.

"Yes."

"Really?"

He smiled and said, "Well, actually, no. It isn't. But that's the way it is with writing, sometimes."

"I wouldn't know," she confessed. "What's it all for?"

Robert wasn't sure what she meant.

"Fame or fortune?" she said.

"Both would be nice. Neither is very likely, I'm afraid. But I've always fancied . . ."

His voice trailed off.

"Fancied what?" she prompted him.

"I don't know. A reputation. A name."

"A little slice of immortality?"

"Exactly."

Robert tried to imagine Rachel filling her days by organizing charity-balls and other fund-raising events for worthy causes. The picture was totally wrong. What else did an heiress do with her endless empty days? Did she entertain armies of lovers? Did she better herself with literature and art? Was she reduced to being a senseless shopping addict? Was *haute couture* her religion? Robert doubted it.

"So what do you do?" he asked, hoping she wouldn't be offended by his enquiry.

She allowed a smile to spread slowly across her lips. The look embarrassed him. But instead of averting his gaze, he looked at her and tried to guess her age. Twenty-five? Thirty? She had an ageless face and he could easily imagine that when she turned fifty, few would believe she was forty.

"Why, Robert? You don't mind if I call you Robert, do you?"

"Of course not. I was just wondering, that's all."

She said, "I don't think so."

He squinted. "What?"

"You think I don't know how they speculate? You think I'm oblivious to the guessing game that *all of you* have been playing?"

Robert shrugged and said, "Like I said, I was just wondering."

"Sure you were!" she said, with a sly smile. "Anyway, I'm not going to tell you. I'll leave it for you to find out."

Chapter Three

The stewardess cut a careful passage back towards the galley. The 747 rolled like a ship on a sea of heavy swell. She used the tops of the aisle seats to steady herself. Some passengers hadn't managed to sleep at all, sitting in the dark with frightened eyes, their fingers gripping arm-rests with a painful intensity. Drawn faces peeped at her from the gloom, seeking reassurance. She wore her warmest smile for them and hoped it helped. A few cones of light fell upon those who chose to try to read or write. Her eyes were drawn to a passenger sitting in an aisle seat, three rows from the back of the aircraft.

His eyes were closed and he was shaking. The stewardess reached over and touched him on the shoulder. Before she could withdraw her hand, his fingers grasped her wrist and squeezed tightly. He looked scared. They stared at each other for a second. Then he let go of her.

"I . . . I'm sorry."

He was shifting his large body in the small seat, trying to mask his embarrassment. The anxiety was still evident in his apology.

"You all right?" she asked.

"Sure, I . . . a nightmare, I guess, or something," he replied, avoiding eye-contact and searching for the pack of cigarettes she could see were in his breast-pocket.

"Can I get you something?"

He looked up at her, finding a little composure now. He shook his head. "No. It was just a dream. Thanks, anyway."

She used her smile again, the one designed to calm and reassure. Once she moved on, the passenger rose from his seat and moved to the rear of the aircraft, where he shut himself into one of the diminutive washrooms. He splashed water over his face and looked at his reflection in the mirror. The fluorescent light made him look ill.

The bad dreams preyed on him, staining his thoughts. He tried to purge them, but it wasn't possible. Sometimes he could sideline them, but not for long. Chris Lang stood straight and dried his face with a paper towel. He was tired. First, there had been the doubt of whether he would be allowed to go. He'd had to fly down from Seattle to Los Angeles, to speak to Josef Koptet himself. And once the old man had given Chris his blessing, he'd been in a rush to leave for London before anyone changed their mind.

He stepped out of the tiny washroom and walked into the rear galley, housed in the tail of the 747. The stewardess saw him coming. She rose from her seat and said, "You okay now?"

"Yeah. Just getting cleaned up. Any chance of a drink?"

"Sure. What would you like?"

"Just water or something."

She nodded. He was tall and broad. No wonder he looked so uncomfortable in his seat. The designers at Boeing obviously assumed economy passengers were midgets. His hair was thick, curly and dark brown. There were the slightest flecks of grey over the ears. The stewardess wondered whether he was a member of the well-preserved forties or the burnout thirties. He wore a washed green twill shirt, with the cigarettes still bulging in the breast-pocket. He was quite heavy-featured, she thought, with a straight nose, a broad mouth and a chin with a one-inch vertical scar on it. His brown eyes looked dull and weary. As a long-haul stewardess she'd seen *that* look a million times.

She poured him a Perrier. He took the glass and nodded graciously. "Thanks. How far gone are we?"

She looked at her watch. "We'll be waking everyone up and

serving breakfast in about twenty minutes. After that, we'll be on the ground in an hour or so."

"Good. I'm not sure my legs can take much more confinement. They should have a section for us."

"They do. It's called First Class."

She was grinning. Chris nodded and smiled. "Working on the principle that the more you are, the more you pay, I suppose?"

She shrugged and seemed faintly amused by the idea. "Maybe. I might suggest it and see if I get a bonus through the employee incentive scheme."

Chris returned to his seat and smoked a cigarette. The Institute had been reluctant to sanction his trip. It wasn't simply a matter of money; it was a question of credibility. They were in no hurry to jeopardize the excellent reputation they had earned. Chris understood that but felt frustrated by their timidity. That was why he'd eventually had to detour via Los Angeles, to see Josef Koptet. Persuading the old man had been the easy part.

He examined newspaper clippings covering the double murder of the world famous violinist, André Perlman, and the equally talented cellist, Jennifer Colson. Some reports had tactfully avoided the question of what the two of them were doing in a hotel room together. Others had not shown the same restraint. When it came to documenting the actual killings, the lack of detail fascinated him, the sense of something concealed. Journalists at a press-briefing got nothing concrete from the officer leading the murder hunt. They had no inkling of the extent to which they were being kept in the dark. He could feel it in their writing. At least, he thought he could. After all, he was acting on a hunch, not on firm evidence. But if he was right...

The 747 touched down at Heathrow fifteen minutes late. The airport was choked with incoming flights. It took him an hour and a half to clear Immigration and Customs, and to find the Underground to carry him into the city.

The carriage began to congest as the train headed towards

central London. His journey coincided with the morning rush-hour. Funereal faces filled the train, squeezing themselves into the metallic coffin. When he changed stations, he had to wrestle his case out of the compartment, through the cheap suits, slim briefcases and monstrous backpacks, which belonged to the invading army of young tourists who laid siege to the capital every summer. He breathed heavily on the asphyxiating clouds of cheap scent and summer sweat. He escaped from the Underground at Victoria, where – he had been assured – he would find plenty of hotels that sacrificed civility for economy. The Monarch Hotel on Belgrave Road was cheap enough in every sense.

Chris dumped his case on the bed and moved over to the dirty window. People hung around in the early morning sun, sitting on steps or leaning against railings, chatting casually, smoking cigarettes, reading the back pages of the tabloids.

His bed was a ruin. The springs were shot and the lumpy mattress was too narrow. The walls were peeling badly. A small hand-basin jutted out of the wall at a precarious angle. An oval mirror was tacked to the wall above it. There was a threadbare carpet, whose edges had been nailed into the creaking floorboards a couple of inches short of the skirting board.

It was hot and humid. He unpacked slowly, putting his clothes in the small chest of drawers that stood in one corner. He lit a cigarette and spread out several pages from the file across the bed. There they were; reports on the Colson–Perlman slaughter lying next to reports of other incidents in Munich, Chicago, Tokyo, Buenos Aires and New York City. There were plenty more of them, spanning many years, and all linked by one factor: the method.

Katherine Ross turned the key and half-expected to find the lock had been changed. The heavy door opened and she entered the unfamiliar flat; it had been two years since she had last been there and she knew that it had been redecorated less than six months before. The front door swept uncollected mail against the dark green wall. She hit the light switch and small halogen bulbs set in the ceiling cast puddles of light on the Iranian carpet and marble floor.

Why on earth had Jennifer gone to the Cadogan Hotel when she had this apartment? It was a ten-minute walk away. Was she afraid that David Colson would make an unscheduled visit? He was supposed to be busy shooting a film in Hamburg, so she should have been safe. Maybe she didn't want to give the neighbours a chance to see her and Perlman together. Whatever the reason, it was now buried with them.

Katherine shook her head slowly. Of all the people she knew, her sister had been one of the least likely to have an affair. It was almost as hard to accept as the slaughter itself. Katherine shut the front door behind her and moved deeper into the flat.

She had picked up the keys to the apartment the previous day, when she drove out to Oxfordshire at David Colson's request. She arrived shortly after nine and was ushered into his study. He was seated behind his desk, a cup of coffee steaming by the phone, a bottle of whisky, four-fifths drunk, by his elbow. His eyes were rubbed red and raw. When she stepped into the room, he looked up at her and said nothing at all. He opened his mouth, but no word emerged. Instead, he swallowed hard and lit a cigarette, another to add to the mountainous pile in the ashtray.

Katherine had never liked Colson. Her sister had been a perfect wife to him and he had been a perfect bastard to her; a drunk, a womanizer and a liar. But during that first moment in his study, she came close to feeling pity for him. Normally, his self-confidence shone. He wore his arrogance with burnished pride, delighting in his success and ensuring those around him were aware of it. Now he appeared pathetic, a feeble wreck. Katherine guessed his misery was due not only to the fact that Jennifer was dead, but also to the circumstances of her death. She had been cheating on him when it happened. Given his adulterous reputation, there was a sickening irony in that.

People would never forget it and that would really matter to David Colson.

"How are you coping?" she had asked him.

He grunted and then mumbled, "A bit . . . you know."

He pushed a set of keys across his desk and Katherine said, "What are these for?"

"The flat in London. Her things . . . I thought you might want to . . . personal things . . . I thought it might be better this way."

So now she was alone in their flat and she felt as though she was about to commit a burglary. In the drawing-room, she passed by a set of photographs on a circular table. Three images of the happy couple set in solid silver frames. *The happy couple.* David and Jennifer clutched each other tightly and beamed saccharin smiles for the camera. A honeymoon snapshot, perhaps. From Katherine's perspective, Jennifer's marriage had been a shambles. How many sorrowful calls had she received in the middle of the night? How many tearful lunches had she been summoned to? How many adulterous outrages had she been forced to hear about? And yet never a word about André Perlman.

Katherine felt a little bitterness mixed into her grief. She had shared everything with her sister. Not only that, but she had *done* everything for her too: never once had she flinched from a desperate request . . . and there had been plenty of them. Jennifer should have told her about Perlman. Katherine deserved to know. Jennifer *owed* it to her.

Katherine felt guilty about her bitterness but could not deny its existence. Similarly, she couldn't suppress her anger. Decency suggested grief was the only emotion she should be experiencing, but that was not how she felt.

It went further than simple hate for an anonymous killer. She felt furious for what the slaughter had done to her parents. She herself had been robbed of her only sister. All her relatives had been wounded. All her friends had been shattered. The orchestra had been devastated. The public had been outraged. The tabloids had been in clover. All these things fired

Katherine's rage. And that there seemed to be nothing she could do only made it worse.

On a bedside table she came across a photograph of their parents, Alfred and Mary Ross. Tears began to blur her vision. Mary Ross was still so shocked she could barely speak. Alfred Ross had been required to identify the body and the impact of that duty had crushed him. Katherine wasn't sure what he had seen, but what he had said made the horror evident.

"Your mother wanted to see Jenny one last time," he told her, the day after the identification.

Katherine had nodded. "I can understand that."

"But I couldn't let her."

She met his weepy gaze. "Maybe you should have."

He shook his head. "I couldn't, Kathy."

His voice unnerved her. "Why not?" she whispered.

"Because there . . . there wasn't . . . she didn't look like . . ."

Katherine was truly speechless. She watched the tears spill from her father's eyes as he struggled to control the shaking that ran through his bony body, while a selection of the most hideous images filled every corner of her mind.

Eventually, he said, "I had to lie to her."

"Don't blame yourself, Dad. *Please.*"

"The most important thing I ever had to say to her and it was a lie. You can't imagine . . ."

His voice faded away. The trouble was, Katherine *could* imagine. It was too easy. Since first hearing the dreadful news she had done little else but imagine. It was impossible to prevent it. Every waking moment was haunted by appalling visions, and sleep, when she could get it, was just as bad.

Why kill them? Katherine couldn't find an adequate answer for that question. The police had asked her if there was anyone she could think of who might be prepared to go to such lengths. The notion was laughable. Nobody she knew held a grudge against her sister. Perhaps some militant feminist groups resented her for sticking by David in the light of his well-publicized infidelities, but would anyone have a reason for killing her? Absolutely not.

Maybe the motives for the crime lay with André Perlman. After all, he had earned a reputation for emotional volatility. Perhaps in a heated moment he had outraged somebody sufficiently to compel them to commit murder. But the police who had spoken to Katherine had implied that no one could identify a reasonable explanation. She instantly recognized the line they were promoting: the slaying was a one-off, perpetrated by a killer who acted without reason or discrimination. Everyone had an opinion and no two were the same. The newspapers offered many possible theories, nearly all of which were more ludicrous than Katherine's wildest guesses. The truth was that nobody seemed to know a thing.

In her soul, she felt there was a motive, although she had no idea what it might be. She didn't know the vile details and the police were not about to disclose them to her, but she instinctively resisted the explanation they were offering. This was not the product of a chaotic mind acting at random. She just knew it wasn't.

David Colson had left two large suitcases by the double-bed for Katherine. She went through the cupboards and drawers, removing all of Jennifer's clothes. Whatever failings David Colson had as a husband, financial provision was not one of them. On the other hand, Jennifer had never been a great spender of money, or even a great admirer of fine clothes, so Katherine supposed that she bought the garments to please her husband, not herself. That would have been typical of her.

Katherine caught her reflection in the bathroom mirror as she passed by the door. She stopped and stepped closer to the reflection, reaching for the light. Her fatigue showed in the pale skin and the grim smudges beneath the eyes. Everyone always said they could tell they were sisters. Katherine had never seen it herself and now she never would. She would age, but Jennifer would stay the same in her mind, never looking any older than she had on the last occasion they were together.

Being in the bathroom reminded Katherine of the moment Jennifer broke the news of her engagement to David Colson.

In those days, she and Jennifer had shared a flat. It was about seven in the evening, during the middle of the week, and Katherine was soaking in a steaming bath after a taxing day's work. She recalled Jennifer bursting in, her face coming out of the steam, coming into focus. Her eyes glittered like the rock on her finger. She said nothing at all, just thrust the gem towards Katherine for closer inspection. From somewhere deep inside herself, Katherine had summoned a sincere-looking smile and words of congratulation. Even then she had disliked and distrusted David Colson.

But Jennifer had never seen what kind of man he was. She was besotted and you can't argue with true love. At least, that's what Katherine had been told. How would she know?

She drifted back to the present. Her drawn reflection was crying so she turned away from it. She wandered through the apartment like a ghost. The stillness was eerie. The distant grumble of London traffic only served to underline the creepy tranquillity of the flat. Somewhere out there a killer strolled free, perhaps preparing for a repeat. Who could say? Not the police, it seemed. The man in charge of the investigation was a rotund detective called Harold Daley. He had already interviewed Katherine once and the word which sprang to her mind was "clueless".

If there was something she could do, she would have done it. She hated her passivity, but what was the alternative? What active role could she possibly have? She gazed out of the window and allowed her mind to drift back to a distant summer, an Italian sunset, a family holiday, a happy time.

Chris awoke just before four, stained by the damp, dirty air of the city. Jet-lag still taxed him. He took a cold shower and then sorted through the papers he'd dumped on his hotel room floor.

Detective Chief Inspector Harold Daley was the man he'd seen on CNN, back in Seattle, and his was the name that cropped up in most of the newspaper clippings he'd collected. Daley was running his investigation out of Kensington Police

Station, on the Earls Court Road. Chris left his grotty hotel and walked back to Victoria to catch the Circle Line on the Underground. The sun was a fuzzy yellow disk in a beige sky. Its clarity might have been diminished, but its heat wasn't.

The woman on the desk was tough-looking, her sandy hair gathered tightly at the back, tensing her skin. It made her look like a cheap cosmetic surgery victim, her skin stretched back like a face caught in a G-force tester. Her gums jutted out of her mouth when she opened it. She had broad shoulders and a burdensome bust which protested against the confinement of her uniform shirt.

"I'd like to speak with Detective Chief Inspector Daley."

"You and the rest of the world," she sneered, looking back at the papers on the desk. "He's busy."

"Well, I might be able to help him."

She looked dubious. "You want to tell me how, sir?"

He smiled and shook his head. "I'm afraid not. I'd rather speak with him in person."

"Thought so," she said. "Like I said, he's busy."

"I'll bet he is. Searching for leads and getting nowhere, right?"

"DCI Daley can't see you," she insisted, flatly.

"Then I'll wait."

"It might be a long time."

He smiled politely. "That's my specialty."

Chris took a seat and rummaged through a copy of *The Times* which he had brought with him. He smoked a couple of cigarettes. He knew the form well enough by now. In the end, an audience came sooner than expected. Eighty minutes wasn't bad. Harold Daley presented himself, appearing from behind the duty officer.

"Maggie tells me you insist on speaking to me. Says you got that determined look about you, like you'll still be here next week unless we hear you out."

Chris rose from his seat and cleared Harold Daley by several inches. He extended his hand.

"That's right. I'm Chris Lang."

Daley looked surprised. "Maggie never mentioned anything about you being American. Not that it makes any difference, of course. Where you from?"

"I live near Seattle these days."

"Seattle? Never been there. Went to Orlando in Florida once. The wife wanted to go. Not really my style, to be honest. Anyway, what do you want?"

"Could we talk in private?"

Daley looked a little overweight but Chris knew plenty of people with a similar bone structure who would have made him look slim. His hair was thin, especially on top where he was almost bald. He had a thick neck, supporting a bowling-ball head with a definite red tinge to it.

"We'll use an empty Interview Room," he said.

Daley couldn't be bothered to go back to the AMIP – the Area Major Investigation Pull – building, on the other side of Earls Walk. In fact, he was glad for an excuse to be out of it for a short while. He seemed to have spent an aeon in there since the Colson–Perlman investigation began.

Detective Inspector David Smith was making himself milky coffee in a Styrofoam cup when Daley and Chris passed by.

Daley said, "Coffee, what a good idea. Oh, and Dave, you could join us. This gentleman says he has something to tell us."

Smith was about the same height as Chris, but half as wide. His cheap suit looked even cheaper hanging from his curved shoulders. The charcoal grey came close to matching his skin. He pushed his hair out of his face, pressing it down across his pointed scalp.

"So, Mr Lang," said Daley, making himself comfortable in an uncomfortable chair, "what's on your mind?"

"You're in charge of the investigation into the case concerning André Perlman and Jennifer Colson, right?"

Daley nodded, while he cupped his hand round a match, as the flame touched the end of his cigarette.

"You haven't released any details of the killing yet. You didn't say how they were murdered, did you? You wouldn't say whether it was a shooting, or a stabbing, or whatever."

"So?" retorted Daley, defensively. "I'm not obliged to."

"I'm sure you're not. But in this case, isn't the reason because you don't know what killed them?"

Daley and Smith both stiffened. Chris had a good idea of what was running through their minds. This wasn't new territory for him. In which case, he expected . . .

"I can't discuss details of the case."

. . . both of them to clam up. Daley's words earned a rueful smile from Chris. "I understand," he told them. "I know the position you're in, but let me tell you something about Colson and Perlman and see if it sounds familiar, okay?"

Daley pouted indifferently. Smith leaned against the wall and blew smoke out of the corner of his mouth. His trousers were three inches too short, his shirt collar was at least an inch too large.

"Before you get into that," said Daley, rubbing his chest, "perhaps you'd like to tell us how you fit into all of this. Your address, what you do, where you were when Colson and Perlman were getting . . ."

Chris cut him off with a raised hand. "Certainly. Anything you want. But first, just hear me out."

Daley shrugged in a noncommittal fashion.

Chris said, "Going back to Colson and Perlman, I'd say they both sustained massive chest wounds. There were other injuries, including some lacerations that resembled bites, the only problem being that none of them have yielded saliva for forensic examination. Any of this getting close?"

Smith looked a little less casual, no longer leaning against the wall. Daley was still sprawled in his seat, but his eyes were focused clearly on Chris, who continued. "Instead of saliva, there were traces of a substance which no one has yet been able to identify."

Smith looked towards Daley for a lead. Daley took a deep breath and drummed his fingers on the table. The American was spot on with his information and there were plenty of questions that Daley wanted to ask, but he wasn't about to give everything away just like that.

"I hope you haven't been badgering the staff at the Cadogan."

"Of course not. Besides, they wouldn't know about the lack of saliva and the substance found in its place, would they?"

That was true. Daley and Smith were two of only four men who knew the results of the saliva test. The other pair were Bryon O'Sullivan, who had performed it, and his assistant. Daley knew the other three well enough to know they'd keep silent.

"Okay, Lang, are you going to tell me how you've reached your conclusions?"

Still being cautious, thought Chris. "Because it's happened before."

Now Daley looked genuinely interested. "Where?"

"New York City, for one."

"What's your connection?"

"I was involved in the New York case."

"How? You from the NYPD?"

"No. I'm not a policeman. I work at the Koptet Institute in Seattle. And for your information, that's where I was when André Perlman and Jennifer Colson were killed. Check it out."

Daley and Smith looked at each other. "I will," said Daley. "What's this institute got to do with anything?"

"The Koptet Institute researches blood. It looks into the properties of it, the genetic make-up, as well as carrying out pioneering research into diseases like leukaemia and haemophilia."

"So how come you ended up in New York?"

"The institute offered its expertise to help with the investigation."

Daley detected an economy with the truth. He said, "And because of this, you just jumped on a plane from Seattle, or wherever, and flew over here to . . . to what? To have a look? To help us out?"

"More or less, yes."

The answer was not the one Daley expected. He raised his eyebrows. Smith had something to say. "Why, specifically, was the – What was it called?"

"The Koptet Institute."

"Yeah, right. Why was it called in to the New York investigation?"

"There were irregularities with the blood that the on-site forensic team couldn't fathom."

"Whose blood? The killer's or the victim's?"

"The killer's."

"But you've just implied that you knew we didn't find any attacker's blood on our victims."

Chris nodded. "That's true, but in this particular case in New York there *were* traces which were found and we established that there were irregularities with the blood that were very important. Regular testing never came up with a suitable explanation. We did."

"And what was that?"

Chris considered this. Smith crushed his paper cup and dropped it onto the edge of the table. Daley was smoking his cigarette, trying to look relaxed.

"Well, we established that the killer has a very rare blood disorder. A simple blood test would prove this conclusively, if ever he were apprehended."

"What kind of disorder?" asked Daley.

"One that might have a severe impact on his behaviour. It might be a fatal disorder, without precautions."

"Sort of like diabetes?" suggested Smith.

"Not entirely dissimilar, in that sense," agreed Chris. "But it's something far rarer."

Daley was nodding to himself. It was the behavioural aspect which interested him. "You think this might be a mood thing? A loss of control during violent changes of temperament?"

"Not necessarily," said Chris, "but that's not really my field, anyway. I just do blood."

"Nevertheless, you suggest it could affect his behaviour?"

"It's a distinct possibility, yes."

A uniformed officer appeared in the doorway and knocked on the open door.

"Excuse me, sir. Your meeting . . . they're waiting for you."

Daley took out a pen and piece of paper. "Give me a number where I can contact you."

Chris gave the number at the Monarch before a young uniformed officer showed him out. As they were walking to the meeting, Smith asked Daley, "What do you reckon?"

"I'm not sure. No hack could have got hold of Bryon's saliva tests, could they? Not in such a short time and with only the four of us knowing about it?"

"No chance."

"I want him checked out thoroughly, Dave. And find out where he was when Colson and Perlman were getting stiffed, all right? I'd feel a lot better if he really was in Seattle."

Chapter Four

Miss Ferris, Alexander Rock's secretary, pointed towards the double doors on her left and told Laura, "They're waiting for you."

The conference room stretched before her. One wall was a vast window of smoked glass, which dimmed the outrageous sunlight. The table was a large oval that could seat two dozen in comfort. Laura helped herself to a cup of coffee from the sideboard and peered down onto the rush-hour throng that filled Victoria Street. She felt curiously hollow and it was something to do with Robert.

"Right," said Alexander Rock, "as some of you are no doubt aware, we have been invited to tender a bid for the design of the new municipal sports stadium in Marseille."

Laura loved the time she spent with Robert. How many other people could enjoy the relationship they had? Precious few. She knew there would be no nasty surprises. There was no need – no room, even – for bitterness or suspicion. But something was bothering her.

Robert and Laura were long-term friends, but had grown particularly close in the aftermath of Robert's last affair, which had ended so calamitously for him. Laura recalled quite distinctly how painful it had been to watch him suffering the agonies of his crucifixion. She understood the pain well, having been a victim herself more than once, but she was never burned as badly as he was.

Robert was a curious creature, she often thought. He was an isolationist who loved to socialize. He said solitude drove him crazy, but imposed it upon himself more than she believed was necessary. Sometimes, it seemed, he suffered for no other reason than to service some ascetic streak in him.

Maybe that was why he got shot down in flames in such spectacular style. Laura had watched him lay himself open for it, declaring love for the girl in such an open-hearted way that it hurt to watch. His naïvety had been sickening. It was like being a child at the pantomime; Laura wanted to scream at him, "There! Behind you! *Watch out!*"

She recalled going round to see him, when she first heard the news, about forty-eight hours after the event. For an entire afternoon, she talked to him, or rather, *at* him. All she got back was a catatonic stare through a dense fog of cigarette smoke.

Laura herself had come to find outright commitment and emotional intensity very hard to handle. The stifling jealousies of past lovers left her cold and there was the constant fear of finding another lover with a violent streak. One, she figured, was more than enough.

Robert and Laura had one grim thing in common: they both fell too hard for deeply unsuitable candidates. Robert's merciless lover used his heart as a football, while Laura's used her body as a punch-bag. Yet, for all that, she'd been in love with the cretin. No, *she* was the cretin, she decided. She must have been, in order to lose her heart to Fraser, a Scot who did nothing to ameliorate one of the rather ludicrous stereotypes ascribed to that country's males. He was a Neanderthal who could only express himself on a rugby field.

It was such a relief to be rid of him. Since then, the very thought of Fraser made her shudder. She marvelled at how spineless she had been. The abuse she had taken was astonishing to her now. Those nights when he staggered round to her place, drunk to hell, were awful, but at the time, she had tried to convince herself that there was some romance in there . . . somewhere. Her insanity then was now a source of bitter laughter.

The other men she'd known had all fallen by the wayside for

one reason or another. There were the unfaithful, the boring, the dishonest, the weird. There were the ones who made an impact at the time and who, when contemplated in retrospect, turned her cheeks red and forced her gaze onto her shoes. And then there was Robert.

The main difference with Robert, of course, was that she wasn't dating him. They slept together, it was true, and in many of their friends' eyes, this meant that they were going out together. But they weren't. In that sense, sex was merely incidental. As Robert had once put it, "We just get on, which occasionally means we just get off."

That was exactly right, except that "occasionally" was beginning to turn into "regularly", but Laura wasn't complaining and neither was Robert, she noticed. Last night had been their fourth in a row together.

They ate out quite a lot, usually at Laura's expense, since he was most often penniless and she was increasingly well paid. They went to watch films a lot, sometimes walking out if they got bored, which was often enough. Laura couldn't see the point of suffering two hours of misery when you could cut it short.

Robert and Laura did all the things that best friends do, and a few more that they generally don't. She had come to the conclusion that the benefits of a single life outweighed the penalties, especially when Robert took care of those aspects of a committed relationship she might otherwise have missed.

For Laura, the arrangement was perfect. And, as far as she knew, Robert felt the same. He always said he did.

". . . Wouldn't you agree, Laura?"

They were waiting for an answer. The gazes were faintly hostile, except for the one coming from Alexander Rock. She was the star on the team. That's why she walked into meetings late and said, "Hi, Alex. How was Barbados?" instead of, "Oh God, I'm so sorry I'm late."

"I was explaining how this stadium was to be more than just a functional construction," he said. "They want something that makes a statement about the city it represents. I think we'd all agree that with Marseille's rich cultural mix there will be plenty to draw upon."

"Oh, quite," agreed Laura, shifting in her seat. "They've done a beautiful job with the Delle Alpe in Turin, for instance. If they want a work of art and are prepared to be imaginative, we can give it to them. We'll make those swanky North American stadia look like fifties council flats. The Astrodome? A box with a tacky lid on it. Have you seen Arrowhead Stadium in Kansas City? It's charmless! And as for the Georgia Dome in Atlanta . . ."

She rolled her eyes in exaggerated exasperation and then drained her coffee cup before addressing Alexander Rock directly.

"If you're going to build something on this scale, you might as well make a statement as well as a stadium. It's not necessarily going to cost any more except, perhaps, in the imagination department."

Most often, Laura worked in a large open-plan office, a communal arena for Harding Rock's brains trust, but she also had a small, private office. After the meeting, she retreated to it, closing the door behind her, lighting a cigarette and sitting down to stare at the rusty world outside. A mountain of untouched files rose like a tower-block on her desk.

She couldn't quite shake the hangover from Johnny Stainger's birthday. A dozen of them had celebrated at the Middle Kingdom, a Chinese restaurant in Bayswater. Afterwards, she and Robert had returned to his flat. She figured her corporal ache had more to do with fatigue than alcohol or cigarettes. They'd barely slept. They slumbered in the city's oven and when the heat roused them from their dreams, they made love. She smiled a little, feeling good.

She was happier now than she had ever been with any man she'd actually dated. The relationship was a little unusual, perhaps, but it worked. She had to admit that the way they executed their friendship wasn't universally admired. Kate Friedland once told her, "It's no way to live, Laura. It'll only bring you unhappiness."

That was easy for her to say. She was married. Anyway, it had brought her nothing except pleasure so far. Could Mrs Friedland say the same for her marriage of two months?

Sunlight ignored the pathetic shield of the tangerine and lemon curtains. Chris Lang lay on his back and felt his heart booming. He swallowed and looked at his watch.

Outside, someone was trying to start their car. The engine wheezed pitifully and died. Chris rose from the bed. His mouth felt dry. Once again, bad dreams had fractured his sleep. Anything less would have been a surprise.

He dressed and stepped out onto the landing, softly closing the door behind him. It was quiet. The noise level hadn't dropped before two in the morning. The drunks were comatose now, the hookers were laid and paid and recuperating. Chris came down the staircase, treading carefully on a carpet which once used to be held in place by stair-rods, but was now secured by a random collection of twisted tacks. A mongrel sat on the worn chocolate and lilac carpet in the lobby. In one corner, a small counter had been installed as a reception desk. It had a cracked Formica top. Behind it, there was a narrow door leading into some sort of office. A small black and white portable television flickered on a desk, surrounded by several cartons of a half-eaten Chinese takeaway and an empty two-litre plastic bottle of beer. There were a couple of overloaded ashtrays by the pair of boots that rested on the desk by the telephone. They belonged to the obese, sleeping figure who was slumped in a wooden armchair, in front of the TV.

Chris strolled in the early morning, watching the groggy city trying to shake off the night. The Belgrave Road was largely empty, except for the occasional speeding taxi. There were two drunks slumped against the railings of the gardens in Warwick Square. One of them was sitting in a pool of his own urine. He crossed the Eccleston Bridge, which arched over the railway lines that came out of Victoria Station and snaked their way south through the suburbs and on to the coast.

He found his thoughts drifting back to the girl and the leather restrainers. The vivid scars, the syringe scabs in the crook of both elbows, where the staff pumped her full of drugs to keep her under control, turning her into a malleable zombie. She had to be protected from herself. And the staff had to be protected from her too. The keys croaked in the locks again. Hard heels made a discordant click against the gleaming floors of countless, endless, gloomy halls. The muted cries of the bewildered and wretched echoed through the labyrinth. The corrupt stench of the disinfectant in his mind overpowered the real odour of London's filth. He grimaced and flicked his cigarette butt into the road.

Chris shivered despite the warmth of the morning, when he thought about the surgeon's needlework and the delicate wrists, the scissors and the slender neck.

Robert left all the doors and windows open, in a futile attempt to encourage a breeze. The fact that not one of the hundreds of sheets of paper which covered the floor had moved even fractionally was testament to the deadly stillness of the morning. He was praying for one large gust, but not because he needed cooling. One outburst from the wind would wreak havoc to the chapters that fanned across his sitting-room and it would provide him with hours of organization. That would take his mind off the fact that he'd come to a complete standstill. He found it hard to believe that after five hundred pages he could be so completely lost for direction.

What the book needed was some serious discipline. Robert had allowed himself to stray and the book had become fat and loose in the process. The thought of cutting up his beloved manuscript so offended him that he hadn't yet been able to bring himself to do it.

On good days, he considered the novel to be his passport to immortality. On bad days, he regarded it as the concrete overcoat he'd be wearing when he eventually jumped into the sea of absolute failure.

Rachel Cates watched Robert for more than two hours. She

stood in the shadows near the front door, absolutely motionless and completely silent. He never knew she was there. Even when his eyes were briefly cast in that direction, he never saw her in the gloom. She saw the pain of his struggle and felt it herself. She wept softly for him.

Chris stepped out of King's Cross and consulted the sheet of paper with the instructions. The Euston Road was completely blocked. Drivers peered into the shimmering brown exhaust fumes which rose from the vehicles in front. According to Richard Elmore, it was only five minutes' walk from the station, just off the Caledonian Road.

It was too early in the evening for the whores' parade, he thought. The pubs were crowded. Most of the punters spilled onto the pavement, making them as congested as the roads. They drank beer and soaked up the remains of the stale sun. The police were trying to run a diversion at the top of Pentonville Road which seemed to be making the traffic worse. A couple of skinheads in spray-on jeans and torn T-shirts were taunting the owner of a kebab takeaway.

Richard Elmore had a flat in a small, two-storey, converted terraced house, on a street that came off the Caledonian Road. Chris rang the bell and heard the splintering grind of a wooden window being levered open.

"Richard Elmore?"

"Maybe."

"I'm Chris Lang. I believe Josef Koptet spoke to you about . . ."

The head disappeared. A minute later the front door opened. In his prime, Richard Elmore had probably been six feet tall. But age had shrunk and crumpled him. His handshake was still firm enough. His bulky nose divided two piggy eyes, which were well recessed beneath the ledge of his forehead. His red cheeks seemed to be weighing down the rest of his face. The down-turned mouth was almost a scowl. His thick, silver hair was like wire, erupting out of his scalp in a design all its own. He wore an old shirt, rolled up at the sleeves, and a pair of tatty grey flannel trousers that just coped with his impressive girth.

He looked Chris up and down and then muttered, "Yes. Very much as he said. Come in, Mr Lang."

Elmore started to climb the stairs. The hall was dingy since there was no bulb in the uncovered, overhead socket. A spicy odour drifted from the doorway on the left. Elmore closed his own front door and led Chris into his sitting-room, a small rectangle connected by a crumbling arch to the kitchen.

"Can I offer you a cup of tea?" he asked.

"Thanks, yes."

Chris looked around the sitting-room. It had a permanence to it. He wouldn't have been surprised to learn it had looked the same thirty years before. A couple of gadgets here and there might betray the era, but little else. There were two deep, worn armchairs either side of a small iron fire, set in a Victorian grate.

"How is Josef?"

Elmore was in his cupboard-sized kitchen, filling a whistling kettle from a dribbling tap.

"He's well. A little frail, physically, but he's lost none of his lucidity."

Elmore chuckled. "He sounded as sharp as ever when he rang me. I hadn't spoken to him in over a year, perhaps eighteen months."

It was curious to picture Koptet and Elmore together. Elmore was scratching his way through life, surviving in a hole of a flat, clearly without money. Meanwhile, Josef Koptet's accommodation problems ran only as far as having to choose which of his fabulous properties to stay in.

Elmore lit a ring on the gas cooker and a blue flame danced for him. He put the kettle on. Chris leaned over a collection of framed photographs on a small table by the dirty window. There were two of a handsome woman with a stern stare, taken perhaps fifteen years apart. Another photograph showed Elmore in the same shot as the woman. There were others of Elmore abroad, in different attire for different climates. One caught Chris's eye in particular. He picked it up from the table and held it to the dying light coming through the window.

It showed a youthful Richard Elmore standing next to Josef Koptet. They were flanked by several armed men. Some of their clothing was military, some civilian. Chris guessed they wore just as much as they could lay their hands on. The snow was knee deep. The men's faces were gaunt and dirty, but they were all smiling.

"One of the most exhilarating times of my life," murmured Elmore. "Scared to death and elated."

"The Second World War?"

Elmore nodded. "Yugoslavia. Fighting the Croats and the Nazis. That's where Josef and I first met."

Chris put the photo back in its place. Outside, the sky was going orange, with red creeping in at the corners.

Elmore was looking down at the shot of Koptet. "Yugoslavia was where it all began. When we weren't fighting the Nazis, we were stealing medical supplies. Bandages, equipment, drugs, anything. The black-market had an insatiable hunger. Medical supplies brought big profits. Always."

Chris couldn't picture the Josef Koptet he knew as a thief. His Josef Koptet was an elderly billionaire with a penchant for Chablis and Impressionist paintings. He wasn't a guerrilla with a penchant for black-market trading and killing Nazis.

The kettle started to whistle. Elmore shuffled back towards the kitchen with a broad grin on his sagging face. Chris lit a cigarette and leaned against the doorway. "You worked with him after the war?"

Elmore was selecting a tea-pot. He smiled. "Not to begin with. By 1945, Josef had a very healthy network of contacts right across Europe. He milked them mercilessly in the following years and that was the bedrock of his fortune. He started running Western drugs and medical equipment into Eastern European countries. There was a mountain of money to be made, but not by anyone. You had to have the leads and Josef seemed to have a monopoly on those."

"So he was selling drugs they couldn't get elsewhere?"

"As well as drugs that *were* available elsewhere, but which he was undercutting on price. Even when the network was in place and running smoothly, and there was no need for him to be involved directly, he would often choose to run these consignments in personally. That was not forgotten lightly. They all appreciated the risk he was taking, even though they knew it was making him a wealthy man. He played it very shrewdly."

Koptet had long since shed his dubious past like a snake sloughs its skin. Now he was revered in his adopted homeland as the founding father of Koptet Pharmaceutical and the sole sponsor of the Koptet Institute, an organization he funded entirely.

Elmore poured the tea and they returned to the sitting-room. The old man rested his cup and saucer on a table and reached for a leather-bound photograph album from the bookshelf. He handed it to Chris, who flicked over a couple of leaves until he came to rest at a black and white photograph of a young boy. He was lying on the frozen ground, one shoulder exposed from a shredded shirt. There was a chunk missing from the upper shoulder, at the base of the neck. He looked at the next shot. There must have been a dozen faces staring back, as white as the snow around them, drained of life, looking into the lens with shark's eyes. He'd never seen such a cadaverous group of living people.

"When did this all begin?" Chris asked.

"In the late forties, early fifties. Actually, the roots of it lay a little before that, when we were in Yugoslavia together, fighting the Nazis. We lived in the mountains, constantly on the move. Every now and then, we would stumble into a small village and find people like this," he said, looking down at the photograph. "These two were actually taken in Romania, I think. Around 1951 or 1952."

They were pitiful. Parents clutched their withered children with skeletal hands. They were barefoot in the ice.

"I suppose we saw it in only two or three places, out of the hundreds we went through. But where it existed, it appeared to have decimated the local population. We suspected it wasn't necessarily terminal, but that once contracted the victim's deterioration was so general that without healthy assistance they were unable to care for themselves, thereby ruling out recovery."

Elmore reached for a tobacco tin and some rolling papers. Chris offered him one of his but the old man declined.

"It looked like a cross between the harmful effects of interbreeding and severe malnourishment. They were the most lifeless people I've ever seen, rotting before they died. Even the fleshy ones, those who appeared to be relatively well nourished, were suffering. They were sometimes so weak they couldn't even speak properly. They wandered around aimlessly, apparently unaware of what they were doing, of our presence, of anything at all.

"I'd never seen people so hollow and considering what I *had* seen during the war, that's saying something. It really scared the shit out of all of us. Where it occurred, it seemed like an entire community under a curse. But then we'd move on to the next village, which was usually some distance away, and everything would be fine. But they'd know what we were talking about and none of them would go near such a place. They'd sooner butcher someone from a cursed village than talk to them. They were that frightened. But like I said, it only happened on two or three occasions.

"In the end, we put it down to a variety of things. A virus that got out of hand, lack of supervision and drugs because of the war, lack of diet, that sort of thing. I think we knew it wasn't any of those things, but we were busy, so we were happy to leave and to forget."

Chris could understand that.

"After the war, Josef began running his drugs and equipment into Eastern Europe, making a fortune for himself. He started coming across more tiny communities that seemed to be afflicted in the same way as the two or three we'd seen in Yugoslavia. There were two things which he couldn't understand. Firstly, the condition itself. Nothing he was trading could make an impact on it and he hadn't heard of anything similar in the West. Secondly, no one wanted to know. From the inhabitants of the nearest neighbouring village right up to governmental level in the capital cities. There, it was just a case of indifference towards the least fortunate members of society. But on a local level, it was a hysterical fear of the infected. A sort of plague mentality.

"Josef discovered some common ground between the cursed communities he came across, in whichever country they appeared. The settlements tended to be small, rural and isolated. The inhabitants were poor and ill-educated, but not necessarily undernourished or initially unhealthy."

Chris had digested the facts off a printed page before now, but to hear it first-hand was a chilling experience, especially given some of the cases he'd witnessed.

Elmore sighed and finally lit the rolled cigarette he had been preparing in his lap. "Josef, for all his love of material things, was always a man of compassion. I say this not in a sycophantic way, but as a fact. In this case, though, it was more than compassion which drove him to investigate. He contacted me because I had been one of those who saw the Yugoslav villages with him and he recalled how upset I had been by what we discovered. I jumped at the chance to work with him again simply because I was stuck in a rut in London, looking for a way out.

"We travelled out there on a morphine run and went to a couple of places in eastern Hungary and, for me, it was just like being back in Yugoslavia. The same kind of people in the same kind of state. Decaying and terrified, shunned by all outsiders as surely as lepers used to be. They were on their feet – some of them – but they were as good as dead."

Chris would have preferred whisky to his cup of tea. As Richard Elmore recalled the past, there were moments when his gaze suddenly cooled, as he drew up another image which had probably been dormant for years.

"Anyway," he continued, a little wearily, "we discovered something new here: the incredible power of superstition. It was rife. Over a period of two years we drifted through the whole region, taking in Hungary, Poland, Czechoslovakia, Bulgaria, Romania. Everywhere we went, the infected communities were ravaged by disease and savaged by fear. Superstition and myth had these people in a frenzy. You couldn't blame them, of course. They were ill-educated and abandoned. Nevertheless, a lot of their troubles were self-inflicted. As you and I sit here now, it's hard for me to convince you quite how destructive myth can be, but I've seen the evidence. Families turning in on themselves, killing each other according to legend. Community lynch mobs fired by terror and ignorance. It was appalling and it was happening, right in the middle of the twentieth century, right on our doorstep.

"These stories, these fears, all had a single strand which bound them together. From Poland down to Yugoslavia and Greece, there was one element which ran constantly through all the fear."

Chris said, "Vampires."

"Yes. Vampires."

"And you laughed, I suppose. Who wouldn't?"

Elmore chuckled. "Exactly. We were sceptical, certainly. On the other hand, we were prepared to be open-minded. We were ready to expose ourselves to ridicule, if there was a chance it might lead us closer to the truth. Now, neither Josef nor I were expecting to find Bela Lugosi in a smart black cape, dressed for dinner. However, it soon became clear that when all the myth was peeled away, there was still something left. Something hard and factual. That was how it started. As for what's happened since then, I expect you probably know more than I do."

Chris shook his head. "I doubt that. So how come you two parted company? Josef never said."

Elmore smiled limply and placed a hand over his chest. "I fell in love," he said. "With Maureen. We married here in London in 1957. She wanted a settled life and so that's what we had. Josef was disappointed, I know."

Chris nodded. "He's said that much. More than once, too."

Elmore seemed pleased by the guarded compliment. "I was a teacher at a school not far from here."

"You've always lived here?"

"Since we got married, yes. It was the only home Maureen and I ever had together. That's why I'd never move now, apart from the fact that I'm too old to change," he added, with a throaty laugh. "As for Maureen, she passed on in 1977 and since then . . ."

He looked around the room at his collection of old things.

"She's still here?"

"That's right," said Elmore, nodding slowly.

He looked downcast for a moment, glancing through the window at the fading day. Then he put his memories aside and said, "I understand your facilities are wonderful."

Chris nodded. "Especially the leukaemia division. In many circles, it's considered the world leader in its research."

"And in your division?"

"Well, we're not up against much opposition. One or two bodies, as you know, but none of them have the resources we have."

"And have you found my information useful?"

"Definitely. Especially when we were putting together the directory. I was studying it before I came over." Chris cleared his throat. "So, what do you think about the Colson–Perlman killings?"

Elmore pinched the remains of his crumpled cigarette, inhaled deeply, and then dropped the butt into a clay ashtray. He sat back in his leather chair, stretching his feet out before him.

"I don't think it's relevant, if you want my honest opinion."

"You do know that we've uncovered other similar killings, close to the focal points of previous research?"

"Yes."

"And you're saying that's a coincidence?"

"I'm saying I've seen too much to rule out anything."

Chapter Five

"Where is it?" asked Harold Daley.

"Fourth floor," replied David Smith, "and the lift's buggered."

"Wonderful!" huffed Daley, flicking his cigarette butt onto the pavement. "Who is she?"

"Sarah Reynolds. Twenty-six years old. Unmarried."

"She live with anyone?"

"Another girl. Mary Birch. Apparently, she's on holiday in Greece somewhere."

"What the fuck does she want to go to Greece for? She could have stayed here to eat crap and drink ouzo. You ever been to Athens?"

"Never. The wife won't fly."

"Well, don't. It's a fucking dump. If you want to see run-down buildings and unshaven Greeks, go to Tottenham."

By the time they reached the fourth floor, Daley was sweating profusely. Heavy clouds hung over the city, promising a monstrous rainstorm that never came. The humidity reached intolerable levels, thunder rumbled, but not a single drop of rain fell.

Detective Constable Malloy was smoking a cigarette in the doorway as Daley and Smith arrived.

"Put that out, Kevin," said Daley. "What's it like in there?"

"A bit colourful, sir. One or two of the lads are a bit . . . you know . . ."

Daley turned to Smith. "Who found her?"

"The cleaner. A Portuguese woman. She comes in once a

week. Has her own key. Apparently, the two girls are usually out at work when she calls."

"She here?"

"In the kitchen," confirmed Malloy. "WPC Marsh is giving her a cup of tea."

Daley and Smith moved into the crowded flat. They caught a glimpse of Rosie Marsh consoling the cleaner in the small kitchen. There were dirty plates stacked by the sink and two empty bottles of wine on a scrubbed wooden table.

A team of forensic experts were already sifting through the scene. Daley thumbed through a pile of letters that were on a small table in the hall. Reynolds obviously wasn't the sort of girl who worried about bills until the final warning. By a framed Robert Doisneau photograph, a uniformed officer in his early twenties stared blankly at the carpet. The hot, humid air carried a bitter taste which made him grimace.

"You all right, son?" asked Daley, putting a hand on his shoulder.

He nodded weakly. His skin was almost as pale as Smith's.

"Where is she?"

"The living-room, sir."

"Tell you what, why don't you go downstairs and give the lads outside a hand, eh?"

Daley's nostrils picked up the first traces. It was an appalling, acrid odour.

"Jesus Christ!" muttered Smith.

Daley winced but there was no escaping it. In his experience there were certain sights to which you could build up a partial tolerance, but there was nothing you could do to conquer the smell. It was sour and strong and once you inhaled it, you were infected for as long as the memory of that first breath lingered. The buzz of flies was a vile presence, a ghastly reminder of how the cleaner came across the body; she probably heard the greedy hum before she ever saw the corpse. Sarah Reynolds' left leg was partly trapped beneath her body. She lay twisted into an unnatural pose, as though rigor mortis had stiffened her instantly, freezing her in a fatal second. Daley looked around.

Bryon O'Sullivan was kneeling over the body, examining it closely. The ceiling light reflected off his balding scalp. His bushy moustache was almost touching the blackened blood on her shredded clothing. He waved away the flies when they got too close to the major wound.

"Harry," he said, acknowledging Daley's arrival without looking up at him, "this is something special."

"Smells like it."

O'Sullivan peered into the crater where Sarah Reynolds' chest had once been. Some fragments of bone had been hit so forcibly they were almost dust. To Daley, it looked as though something inside her had exploded outwards. He'd mentioned this on the first occasion and O'Sullivan had disagreed.

"No way, Harry. If it had been something inside her exploding outwards we'd be seeing damage to the spine."

The crater in the girl looked larger than the wounds found on the others. Daley had seen murders where the victims had been mutilated in unimaginable ways, but in this case it was simply the scale of her wound which left him momentarily speechless. Apart from the two at the Cadogan Hotel, he'd never come across anything quite like it.

There were men crawling all over her flat searching for leads, but Daley was filled with a cold sense of doubt. They'd turned up nothing from Room 114 of the Cadogan Hotel.

"Any ideas on the weapon?" he asked O'Sullivan.

"Not yet, but as you can see, the wound looks the same as the other two. A little larger perhaps, but the same design. Sort of flower-shaped. As you know, we didn't find a thing on the other two."

"What about the heart?"

"Walters found it."

"Which one of you is Walters?" Daley asked the collection of officers in the living-room.

Smith patted Daley on the shoulder. "He was the pale-face you sent downstairs for fresh air."

"Damn nearly stepped on the thing!" said O'Sullivan.

"Found it by the sofa. Looked like he was going to puke, so I sent him out."

"You're all heart," muttered Daley.

"Which is more than can be said for Miss Reynolds here."

"Hilarious, Bryon. Any bites on her?"

There had been bites on Jennifer Colson's throat and on the back of André Perlman's neck, but they had been too messy to provide any useful information. They hadn't even yielded saliva for examination.

"Yes. At least one." He held up the girl's left hand. There was a deep, dried laceration on her wrist. "She doesn't look to have anything under the fingernails, so I'd guess it was a mismatch. She never even scratched him."

"Perhaps she couldn't. How long since she was done?"

O'Sullivan shrugged. "I'll give you a closer time later but, for the moment, I'd say about five or six days."

"Smells like a fucking fortnight!"

"No, it doesn't," O'Sullivan assured him, looking up with a face darkened by that particular experience.

Smith spent ten minutes with Oliveira the cleaner. Her pidgin English was bad at the best of times, but it was virtually non-existent in her current state of shock. He rejoined Daley in the living-room and summarized.

"Her name is Maria Oliveira and she comes from Estoril. She's been cleaning here for two years and comes once a week for three hours. When she arrived this morning, she found the body and called us. That's her story. She's basically ga-ga."

"I'm not surprised," said Daley. "It's one thing cleaning dirt off a bath, but it's quite another when you've got to start hoovering hearts off the carpet."

Smith said, "Apparently she told Rosie that the door was locked as normal. I've had a look at it and it seems fine. No forced entry, it seems."

"So she knew him, perhaps. Talking of forced entry," said Daley, turning to O'Sullivan, "any signs of it on her?"

"Doesn't look like it. Again, we'll wait for further tests, but there's nothing obvious."

Daley played the answer-phone. There were five messages on the cassette. There was a leather-bound address book by the phone. He flicked through a few pages and then looked up. The pattern of the bloodstain on the outer door reminded Daley of a Chinese fan: crimson struts spreading out from a central point. Arterial spray, perhaps. He took a deep breath and listened to the blaring horns rising up from the street outside. He felt sweat dampening the collar of his shirt and he longed for a cigarette. Anxiety swelled within him. They now had three victims and what did they know about the killer? Firstly, he was immensely strong and, secondly, he was using a weapon that they hadn't yet been able to identify. He was a biter too, although not, as yet, a "salivator". And that was it. The total findings of their frantic investigation.

The bathroom was chaos. The shelves were filled with half-empty shampoo bottles, facial scrubs and tubes of toothpaste that had been squeezed in the middle. Tampons spilled across the floor from a cardboard carton on its side. Sarah Reynolds wasn't a tidy person. Her clothes littered the bedroom floor. On the bedside table there was a photograph of a young man – probably the boyfriend – set in a brass frame, a glass of water, a clock-radio whose green digits winked at him and a packet of contraceptive pills. Daley examined the days marked on the back. Assuming she'd taken one on the day she died, O'Sullivan's estimation of the murder time would prove to be about right.

He went through her drawers and cupboards. Clothes frothed over the edges when he pulled the drawers open. He found an envelope of photographs in the bottom of a drawer full of underwear. He flicked through them. There were several of Sarah herself. A real head-turner, thought Daley. You would never have guessed it, judging by the lump of meat and bone next door.

He returned to the living-room and wondered out loud, "Anyone know what she did?"

"Legal secretary," said Malloy. "Worked for a firm in St James's. Foster's down there now."

Daley stood in the doorway and turned to O'Sullivan, who was peering down at the body.

"She's all yours now, Bryon. No point in keeping her here, so you might as well get on with whatever you're going to do to her. And tidy her up, for Christ's sake. Someone's still got to come and officially identify her. It'll probably be her parents, when we get hold of them."

"Poor bastards!" muttered O'Sullivan.

"Exactly. She looks like something out of *Alien*. Make sure someone does a good job on her, will you? It'll be enough of a shock for them, without having to see her like this."

Robert Stark jammed a fire-extinguisher against the heavy front door, to keep it wedged open. It didn't make the hall any cooler, as he'd hoped it would. He ran the vacuum-cleaner over the carpet, a tedious ritual he repeated three times a week. He caught sight of himself in the large mirror. His T-shirt was damp with perspiration. The slight gloom of the hall made him look darker in the reflection, but also made the whites of his eyes seem brighter. His cheekbones seemed sharper than normal, casting deep shadows over the lower half of his face.

". . . discussing today's news in detail. And what about the revelation that the Home Secretary is having an affair with an Egyptian acrobat? Should the press be allowed to . . ."

The portable radio was on the table. Robert tuned it and found a golden-oldies station, where Louis Armstrong and Ella Fitzgerald were singing "Summertime".

Vernon Lorenzo trotted down the staircase which wrapped itself around the iron grille lift-shaft. His hair was oiled back, as always. Robert thought he shaved with a laser; his chin was usually smooth enough to shine. When he passed by, his expensive after-shave stained the air.

"Turn that goddamned radio off!"

Robert shackled his temper and wondered what the man's problem was. Maybe Lorenzo was like that with everyone. Then again, maybe it was because he came from New York.

That city had a reputation for rudeness. Robert watched him disappear down the steps. How did Cassie Lorenzo put up with that? She was always so sweet-natured. He left the radio on, as a news bulletin marked the hour. As usual, none of it was good. The dustmen were striking and it looked as though London Underground would follow suit. The traffic was abominable already. Robert was sure that an Underground strike would paralyse the capital once and for all. The city was disintegrating in the summer's oven. Tempers exploded, tolerance evaporated like rain on the baking tarmac. The stench of decay permeated everything. London seemed to be a city stewing in the fetid juices which seeped from its own rotting body.

"Hello."

Robert was coiling the vacuum-cleaner lead around two plastic spools. He looked up and saw Rachel Cates in the doorway, holding a small package wrapped in plain paper. She wore a chocolate-coloured knee-length dress. Her hair was gathered at the back.

"My dish-washer doesn't seem to be working properly," she said. "Everything's dirty. Maybe it needs the engineer. I don't know, I'm useless with machines. I was wondering whether you'd take a look at it, in case it's something really simple."

Rachel Cates had a magnificent flat. The drawing-room had tall french windows which opened onto balconies, overlooking the almond-shaped gardens below. It was a large, airy room, predominantly dark blue and green. She had fabulous Persian carpets. By one door, there was a fluted column which rose six feet from the floor and supported a marble bust of a full-faced man in military uniform. There was a large stone fireplace that was pleasantly abrasive to the touch. Robert saw a silver drinks tray, on a sideboard, beneath a large oil painting in a heavily gilded frame. It showed a lakeside village under snow, surrounded by bleak woodland. The villagers congregated around an enormous fire at the ice's edge.

On another table, there were three gold figurines with

details picked out in turquoise. In one corner, there was an unfinished oil painting on an easel, which depicted a group of men crowded around a banqueting table, dressed in their finest clothes.

"Do you like it?" asked Rachel, who was standing behind Robert, close enough to be his shadow.

"It's very impressive."

"Thank you. I haven't finished it yet."

Although unfinished, Robert had assumed from the content and style that it was an old work. Both the canvas and the paint seemed to have aged.

Robert turned to her and said, "You did this?"

Rachel smiled and then nodded.

"Really?"

"*Really.*"

"I didn't mean to be rude. It's just . . . well, it looks just like . . . like . . ."

"Like the real thing?"

He blushed.

"Don't be embarrassed. It's meant to. I suppose you'd call me a forger." She smiled at the suggestion and toyed with her hair. "Only for fun, though."

"It's very convincing."

"It should be. I had an excellent teacher. Jacob Eckhardt. He taught me everything. His technique was unequalled. As you can see, he even showed me how to prepare and age a canvas."

Rachel led him out of the drawing-room across the hall and towards the kitchen. He caught a glimpse of her dining-room.

"You have a wonderful flat," he told her. "I had no idea . . ."

"You must have been in it before."

"I never got past the entrance hall until now," he admitted.

"Really?"

"*Really.*"

She ushered him into the kitchen. The microwave and oven were built so neatly into the wall that they were easy to miss. There were two fridges – one for liquids only – and a two-tier freezer the size of a tall man's coffin. Running along the tiled wall were two sinks and more spotless marble worktop than most chefs dreamed about. There were racks of herbs and spices. Robert saw gleaming ladles, vast serving spoons, lethal carving knives, giant pasta claws, painful looking nut-crackers and a fancy garlic crusher with ornately carved handles. It looked like a show kitchen, not a real one. It was surgically clean.

She dropped her package onto the marble worktop and started to unwrap it. It contained several large, bloody chunks of fillet steak. She prodded each piece. Blood oozed across the cool marble.

"The dish-washer's right beside you," she told him, looking him straight in the eye, while she licked her bloody finger clean.

Robert sank to his knees, pulled open the machine door and peered inside. The filter was blocked. He could see that straight away as he dipped his hands into the cold grey water.

"You want a cigarette?"

"No."

"How long since you gave up?"

Robert retracted his body from the machine and looked up at her. "Maybe I never smoked."

"Maybe, but I doubt it. You look the type."

"And what does that mean?"

She shrugged and said, "I thought it was almost compulsory for writers to smoke."

Robert returned to the task of plucking grim morsels of food from the bottom of the machine.

"So, when did you give up?" she wanted to know.

He took a deep breath and said, "If you must know, it was after I split up with my last girlfriend."

"That seems a peculiar time to kick the habit."

"Well, it was a peculiar time in my life."

"That's usually when most people take it up again."

"Not the way I was feeling."

She frowned. "And how was that?"

Robert sat back, shaking water off his hands. "Sick. After we split up, I felt like sh . . . *ill*. So when I got my head together again, I gave up boozing and smoking."

"You don't drink, either?"

Robert smiled ruefully. "I eventually took up drinking again, although not to the same extent. All the same, one out of two isn't bad, wouldn't you say?"

She remained straight-faced. "You didn't split up."

Robert wasn't sure he'd heard correctly. She was still leaning against the marble worktop.

"I'm sorry?"

"You didn't split up," she told him.

"What do you mean?"

"She dropped you."

There was an awkward silence. Awkward for Robert. Rachel looked completely unfazed.

"And how do you know that?"

"It was a guess. I mean, if you slipped into such a serious decline, that would tend to indicate that your separation wasn't a mutual thing."

Robert was not convinced. "Not bad," he said, coldly. "Is there anything else you'd like to take a stab at?"

Rachel seemed amused, her mouth turning up marginally at the corners. She thought about it for a moment and then nodded, saying, "Sure. Why not? I'll bet the cigarettes you used to smoke were Marlboro."

Robert considered this. She was right. Most of the time he smoked Marlboro, or, occasionally, Winston. "A percentage chance," he said.

Rachel looked annoyed. Robert turned back to the dishwasher. She said, "This girl you split up from, when you gave up smoking . . . did you ever blindfold her when you were making love with her?"

He slowly turned his face up to her again. Her look of severity had gone. Robert was dumbfounded. She said, "Not all the time, of course, but every now and then. Was it something you did on occasions?"

He wasn't sure whether he was shocked, upset or angry. He suppressed the desire to react and, instead, turned back to the machine. He couldn't fathom her intent, her apparent delight at his confusion, or his own feelings of embarrassment and unease. He focused on the dish-washer, buying himself time to claw at scraps of composure.

Why had she asked him up to the apartment? It had nothing to do with the dish-washer. Just by sticking her fingers into the dirty water at the bottom of the machine, and by withdrawing the few offending pieces of food, she could have solved the problem herself. He shut the dish-washer door and stood up, his face a calm façade masking the turmoil in his head.

"That's all it was," he assured her, icily, ignoring her previous enquiry entirely. "The filters were clogged."

She said, "Thanks. I would have looked an idiot if I'd called out the engineer for such a trivial job."

He nodded. "You would have, yes. In fact, I don't think . . ."

"Was I close?"

"What?"

"About the blindfolds?" she wanted to know. "Was I close?"

Robert looked at her. What was this? *Who* was this? His bewilderment was gradually transforming into anger. He watched her finger prodding the bloody flesh on the marble, squeezing blood across the smooth surface. She ran her finger through the scarlet puddle. He thought about her painting, her forging, as she called it. The canvas filled his head. The details, the colours, the cracks that come with age. She wiped her finger clean this time.

Rachel took a couple of steps towards him. "What about the blindfolds, Robert? Do you like that?" she asked him, before placing a hand on his neck and kissing him on the cheek.

The thrill surged through his body right down to his toes. He didn't move at all, paralysed by uncertainty. His heart fluttered and his confusion was absolute. Rachel withdrew her lips from his cheek and stepped marginally back, so that their faces were just inches apart. She gazed deep into his eyes with a steely look in her own.

"You don't have to answer that," she told him, "if you don't want to. At least, not yet."

Then she broke away. The blood looked bright against the marble and beneath the sharp glare of the overhead light. She caught his eye and very slowly, very deliberately, tore a chunk off one of the blocks of fillet steak. She put it in her mouth and chewed slowly, never letting her eyes leave his.

He could have said something to her, but didn't. He was marooned between protest and intrigue, unable to decide which course to take. So, instead, he chose another direction altogether. He left.

Robert was desperately relieved to get out of her apartment. He felt like a drowning man allowed to surface for air at the last instant before submission. His confusion bordered panic. For all her more obvious attractions, he found part of her repellent. He felt bitter that she had made him so uneasy. It was unfair. It was against courtesy. It was hard to know whether he wanted to slap her or sleep with her.

The phone was ringing when he reached the basement. He didn't hurry to answer it. Whatever it was could wait. He strolled casually into the kitchen and picked up the receiver. The voice on the other end was urgent.

"Robert, it's Johnny."

Her figure featured heavily on his mind's screen. He said, "Johnny who?"

"Stainger, for God's sake! How many others do you know?"

A few, he thought. He tried to shake off her lingering presence. "Hi, Johnny. What's up?"

There was a long pause before Johnny said, "Oh Christ, you haven't heard, have you?"

"Heard what?"

"It's Sarah, I'm afraid, Robert. She's dead."

Robert didn't understand. "Sarah? Sarah who?"

"*Your* Sarah. Sarah Reynolds."

Chapter Six

Harold Daley tapped an inch of ash into an empty Coke can and picked up the report which O'Sullivan had brought him. He took it out of the plastic folder and flicked through the top two sheets. O'Sullivan's signature was scrawled across the bottom sheet.

The gash on the left wrist was now confirmed as a bite. Again, a test for saliva proved negative, but O'Sullivan found a substance in its place that they were still trying to identify. Daley had wondered whether it was something the killer was applying to bite-wounds in order to mask his saliva.

"It's possible," O'Sullivan had said, "but unlikely. I can confirm that it has animal origins."

"But not necessarily human?"

"Certainly not human."

"Then what?"

"I wish I could say. None of our tests have got further than confirming it's a mammal."

Evidence from both crime scenes was at a premium. The only material for examination had been a small selection of clothing fibres. They were mostly still being matched, but one early result suggested the killer was wearing a pair of Levi's, which hardly narrowed the field much. Since physical evidence was so sparse, Daley had ordered his men to interview more rigorously than ever.

In André Perlman's case, this was a limited exercise, since he had no family in the country and just a few colleagues and friends. Taking statements from those who knew Jennifer

Colson was a far more labour-intensive operation. Among those who knew her well, the shock of her murder was matched by astonishment at her infidelity. No one seemed more stunned by this fact than her husband.

"Jennifer? With . . . with . . . *Perlman*? There must be a mistake! She wouldn't have! She . . ."

Daley conducted that interview himself. David Colson appeared more upset by her liaison with the violinist than by her slaughter. This impression left its mark on Daley. "It could be a classic case," he'd told Smith, forty-eight hours into the enquiry. "Jealous husband, who fucks like a rabbit himself, suddenly finds the wife at it too. Can't take that at all – an insult to his manhood – so he decides to top not only her, but the lover too!"

Smith had thought about it for a moment. "Doesn't work."

"Why not?"

"If he's so upset about her shacking up with this musician, he'd want to keep it quiet. So he'd hardly do it while they were together in a London hotel, would he? He'd wait until they were apart and then take them out individually, so no one would ever know they were shagging each other."

As it turned out, Colson was choked with sound alibis. At the time of his wife's death, he was working on a film in Hamburg. Daley was upset at having to scratch him off the list of prime suspects because his was the only name on it. Anyway, now there was Sarah Reynolds. Even with the most malicious will in the world, there was no way to realistically tie Colson to her.

Jennifer Colson's parents, Alfred and Mary Ross, had been useless interviewees. Their shock and discretion prevented them from saying anything about their daughter that deviated from their perfected ideal of what she had been. Katherine Ross had been a little more forthcoming in the initial interview and had now agreed to face a more detailed set of questions. He hoped the interview with her could be concluded quickly.

Since the Colson–Perlman investigation began, Daley had barely seen Alison. "I'm your wife!" she had screamed at him, a few mornings before, as he edged towards the front door with his fried eggs untouched on a plate in the kitchen. "I'm not just some passing convenience you can visit when you have the occasional spare five minutes, Harold!"

Daley was used to that charge. Alison had spent years chiding him for his excessive dedication to the job.

"Please," she had cried that morning, as he prepared to leave after a fitful four-hour sleep, "please come home early tonight. I'm worried for you. I'm worried sick."

He could see she really was and so Daley decided he was going home early tonight. He had nearly ten minutes of blissful solitude before a uniformed officer showed Katherine Ross in, as he was finishing his coffee. He rose from his chair and dropped the paper cup in the bin.

"Miss Ross, come in. I'm sorry about the mess."

Katherine looked around the rectangular room. There were two boards on the far wall with messages made by coloured marker pens. There were computer terminals on tables. The shades were down over the windows. An amber glow tainted everything. She sat in the seat he was pointing at and began to fiddle absentmindedly with her glasses. The frames were thin black circles.

"Thank you for coming here, rather than making me come to see you. I'm rushed off my feet at the moment, so any . . ."

Katherine found herself on the brink of her own breakdown. She resisted the bleak invitation because of her father. The strain of her mother's disintegration was already too weighty a cross for his fragile shoulders to bear. By sheer force of will, Katherine wouldn't allow herself to add to his burden.

One urge was constant and strong: the desire to escape. It had been there before Jennifer was killed and in the merciless gloom that followed, its appeal grew stronger. But she couldn't abandon her parents. She found their situation so depressing that it was sometimes the strongest element in the force which pressed for her exodus. And at the same time, it remained the one thing – the *only* thing – stopping her.

"Coffee, Miss Ross?"

She shook her head.

"Cigarette?" he asked.

She surveyed the smoke-filled office and said, dryly, "Hardly necessary, I think."

Daley smiled limply and then consulted a pad of paper. "Now, you've already stated that you couldn't think of a person who would want to do this to your sister, or a reason for it. Correct?"

"Yes."

"And now you've had a little more time to . . . to reflect on things, do you still feel the same?"

"Yes."

"You're sure?"

Katherine bristled with irritation. "Of course. Besides, Jennifer never knew Sarah Reynolds."

Daley perked up. "You know that for a fact?"

"Naturally."

"How?"

"Jennifer and I were very close. We discussed everything. If she'd been friends with Sarah Reynolds, I would have known."

"So you knew about your sister's affair with André Perlman?"

Katherine nearly snapped, but caught her tongue just in time. It was an unfair question. "No. No, I didn't."

"I'm not trying to be a smart-arse, Miss Ross. I'm just digging in the dirt for anything, any possible connection between the two scenes."

"Maybe there was a connection between Sarah Reynolds and André Perlman?"

"Maybe," he conceded.

"Meaning that you haven't got a clue?"

This time it was Daley's turn to bite his tongue. But the blank expression on his face confirmed what Katherine had suspected: he knew nothing. The man looked exhausted.

"My father saw Jennifer," Katherine told him. "He had to

identify the body. And when he saw what this . . . *bastard* had done to her, he had to lie to my mother. That was a new experience for him."

Daley couldn't tell whether he was looking at sorrow or anger.

"I want to know how she was killed. My father *needs* to know."

He replied, in a lethargic monotone, "I'm not at liberty to discuss those sort of details. Not in this case."

Katherine took a slow, deep breath, aware of a trembling she found hard to suppress. "Well, what can we discuss?"

Her icy sarcasm set Daley on edge. "Perhaps we could go back to this issue of people and motive. If you were to think hard – very hard – is there anyone, anyone at all, who might provide a starting point for us? Something they did, something they said? It might have been a long time ago, it might have been . . ."

"Think very hard?" muttered Katherine, removing her glasses. "What do you think I've been doing? Ever since it happened, every minute of the day, my mind is filled with possibilities. I haven't thought about anything else, for Christ's sake!"

"Please, Miss Ross, be reasonable."

"Be reasonable? *Be reasonable?* My sister was gutted by some monster and you want me to be . . . *reasonable*? My mother is having a nervous breakdown! She has to take drugs to stop her from killing herself. My father has to cope with his own grief while he looks after this woman who he's loved all his life, and who's suddenly disintegrating in front of his eyes. Can you imagine what that's doing to him? Have you any idea at all? They have to contend with their daughter being carved up in a hotel room, while her reputation is carved up in the tabloids and *you* . . . you have the audacity to tell me to be reasonable!"

She didn't burst into tears, as Daley half-expected she might, and she didn't ask him what he thought about her accusations, either. She just looked down at the glasses in her hand, cleaned a lens on a handkerchief and then put them back on.

"I don't expect to speak to you again," she said, "unless you have something important to say, or something serious to ask me."

And before he could get in a word, she was heading for the door. He rose from his chair and followed her out. The corridor outside was hot and congested, full of swaying, sweating bodies blasted on drugs and drink, the product of a bulk arrest just off the Lillie Road.

"Miss Ross, wait! *Miss Ross!*"

Daley was struggling to pull himself through the human tide. She seemed to sail through with ease. Suddenly, the American appeared. Chris Lang. The name flashed in Daley's mind and the body filled his vision.

"You said you'd get back to me and you didn't."

"Not now!" barked Daley, trying to edge past him.

"And now there's another one dead."

"And you could have prevented that?"

Chris said, "Not necessarily, but . . ."

"As I thought. Now get out of my way!"

Some of the drunks were singing a terrible version of "*Fairytale of New York*".

Sinatra was swinging
All the drunks they were singing
We kissed on a corner
Then danced through the night.

An officer who yelled for silence was universally ignored. Daley shouted, "Wait, Miss Ross!"

She was by the door now and turned round, her face still set in bitterness. She mouthed the word "What?" and planted her hands squarely on her hips.

"You're not to talk about this case with anyone. You mustn't discuss any details of our conversation or . . ."

"*What bloody details?*" she screamed, incredulously.

"Why didn't you get back to me?" Chris asked.

Daley was watching Katherine, who was glaring at him from the door. He was too tired for manners. He turned round to Chris.

"Because I checked on you, like I warned you I would. Dr Richard Cook's the guy who runs your institute, isn't he?"

"That's right."

"Well, he wasn't overjoyed to hear you've been making a nuisance of yourself. It seems you're not exactly a novice at this sort of thing. But that's not all, not by a long shot. As an additional measure, I checked out your New York story."

Chris felt his stomach seeping into the soles of his shoes. Daley saw the look and felt encouraged.

"I spoke to Captain Eugene Ferraro of the NYPD. Does that name ring a bell?"

Chris nodded.

"I thought it might!" crowed Daley. "He sends his regards, by the way. Apparently you two know each other quite well. According to him, he arrested you for obstruction. Is that right?"

"More or less."

A few of the drunks cheered.

"He suggested I do the same and I have to confess, I'm sorely tempted, but I'm tired and I promised myself I was going home early tonight, so I won't. But . . ."

"Ferraro's completely unreliable."

Daley was momentarily speechless. Chris watched sweat drops sprouting on his rosy forehead. Two of the drunks were squabbling by the desk.

"Shut up, Lang! Just shut up and listen! Who the hell am I supposed to believe, eh? A respected captain in New York's Police Department, or some wacko who thinks he's a vampire-hunter?"

A partial silence descended upon the tightly packed congregation in the corridor. Daley looked around and milked his sudden audience.

"That's right! A bloody vampire-hunter!"

Chris took a deep breath of the sour air which infected the hall. "That's not correct, Daley, and you know it."

"Oh what? Don't nit-pick with me!"

Chris said, "Your killer has a . . ."

"A pair of pointed teeth? Get the fuck out of here, Lang!"

Some of the drunks were giggling, holding onto each other for precarious balance. A young girl with raven hair was having a fit in the far corner. Two officers stepped in to prevent her bouncing off the walls. She babbled incoherently as they marshalled her towards a detention cell.

"He'll do it again, Daley."

His patience with the American was gone. The fact that the killer was a biter was not public knowledge, but if it ever became so, and if Lang was still around to spread his ridiculous stories . . . Daley shuddered at the prospect.

"Get this man out of here!" Daley ordered two officers, before addressing Chris directly. "If I see you here again, I'm going to take a leaf out of Captain Ferraro's book and arrest you. You got that?"

"You'll be sorry!"

"No. You'll be sorry because you'll be banged up!"

"I'm telling you, Daley, he'll do it again."

"I don't know what you get up to in Seattle, but we don't have vampires here, okay? We're looking for a monster, yes, but we're not looking for some weird fictional creation from Eastern Europe. Do you think you can grasp that? But in case you're right," he sneered, "I've got your number and I'll give you a call and ask you to come round with your wooden stake, your crucifix and your garlic. Now fuck off!"

The sun had set but it was still hot. Exhaust fumes and humidity conspired to make breathing dirty. Chris turned away from the entrance to the police station and looked down the Earls Court Road.

"Hey, you! Wait!"

He turned round and saw her on the pavement behind him. It was the woman who had been arguing with Daley before

Chris barged in. She had dark, piercing eyes, behind her circular-framed glasses.

She said, "I saw what happened."

Katherine had watched from the doorway, as they argued in front of the alcoholic crowd. Daley had lost sight of her in the mad congregation. She had almost been knocked down when Chris was manhandled out of the station by two policemen.

"Is it true?" she asked.

Chris glanced away for a moment and then looked back at her. "It's a private matter."

"It didn't sound very private."

He smiled wryly. "No, I don't suppose it did . . . but it is, all the same."

"You know something, don't you?"

"You saw what he thought."

"So what? They don't know everything. In this case, they don't know anything."

"What are you?" he said. "A lawyer? A journalist?"

She smiled. "If that's what you think, I'd better change the way I dress."

Chris smiled too. "No, don't do that. Just change the questions you ask."

"Will you tell me what was going on? I *need* to know."

"How come?"

"I'm Katherine Ross." The name passed Chris by. "I'm Jennifer Colson's sister. She was Jennifer Ross before she married David Colson."

He recalled the cellist's photo in some of the newspaper clippings he had. There was, as far his memory could confirm, some physical affiliation with the woman standing in front of him. The dark eyes, the straight, dark hair, the pale skin. But his caution remained.

"I see," he murmured, without much conviction. "Be that as it may, I don't . . ."

"Please. I have to know. You owe me an . . ."

"I don't owe anybody anything," he interrupted firmly. "Let's be absolutely clear about that."

She looked hurt. If it was an act, it was first-class. She avoided eye-contact with him. "The police won't tell me a thing. Not a word."

"They have to be careful."

She scoffed. "Why? In case they let slip the secrets they don't hold? They won't tell me anything because they don't know anything."

"And you think I do?"

Katherine shrugged and brushed a few strands of hair out of her face. "I don't know. But I'm willing to risk it." She paused for a moment, before adding, wearily, "I'm that desperate, Mr . . ."

"Lang. Chris Lang."

She nodded. "I'll listen to anybody, Mr Lang. I've got to try every possibility . . . no matter how crazy."

"You wouldn't believe me."

"I said, no matter how crazy. I might not believe you – you're right about that – but I'll listen and I'll be open-minded. You should let me be the judge. If I don't go for it, I'll tell you and leave you alone. That much I can promise."

His battered sense of instinct said she was legitimate and sincere. It would have been easier to reject her, but he took a chance. "You want a drink?"

The look on her face was not pleasure, but relief. She sighed and nodded. "Yes. Yes, I would. Very much."

They found a small pub, where most of the customers drank outside, catching the last of the day's heat and light. Chris and Katherine took a table inside, tucked away in a cool, secluded corner. She had a Bloody Mary and he ordered a beer.

Once they were seated, she said, "I heard that buffoon Daley shouting that you were a vampire-hunter. What did he mean by that?"

Chris offered her a cigarette, which she declined. He lit one for himself.

"It's not true, is it?" she asked.

"A vampire-hunter? No, it isn't true."

"I thought it sounded too ridiculous."

"I work for the Koptet Institute in Seattle. We're into blood, professionally speaking. We deal in every area of it, from disease research to synthetic manufacture. Anything you can think of."

"And what do you do?"

"I work for a small division which investigates new or unknown diseases. We look into the causes and see if they're blood-related. If they are, we try and identify the problem so we can nail the complaint."

"It sounds interesting. Rewarding work, I'll bet."

"Most often it's fruitless and frustrating. There's a lot of footwork for precious little return."

"So you don't spend your days sticking needles in people's arms and taking blood tests."

"Not personally, no. I pass my time considering the circumstances and environment of these illnesses. For instance, has a similar-sounding disease appeared before? If so, where? What type of community did it afflict? Is there a link in the diet, or the climate? Is it specific to gender or race? Is it prevalent among the poor or is it indiscriminate? Is it specific to humans? All those sort of issues need addressing and the fact is, it's painstaking work."

"But somebody has to do it, right?"

"Right."

Katherine's expression lightened into a smile. "Well, it sounds as though you, more than most, would know about vampires, if they existed."

"I would and they don't. At least, not outside Hollywood movie studios. The myth of the vampire, on the other hand, remains strong in certain pockets around the globe. But that has nothing to do with the creature being a reality. It's simply the by-product of fear and ignorance, an explanation where there isn't one. Something concrete to hold on to. A false idol. I've come across such communities in my time and it's never vampires that are to blame for their plight. It's just disease."

Katherine finished her Bloody Mary. Coins were spilling out of a fruit machine into the collecting dish. The player took a handful of them and started to pump them back into the slots.

Chris said, "Would you like another drink?"

"No, thanks." She felt hungry. "Have you eaten yet?"

They found an Italian place round the corner. A tacky crooner's ballad trembled out of cheap speakers. The walls had framed photographs of Tuscan countryside. The tables sported red and white chequered tablecloths and candles sticking out of green, wax-coated wine bottles. An over-attentive waiter with a barrel-sized gut brought a bottle of bad house red. Chris took a sip. It was bitter and purple.

"So what happened in New York?" she asked.

"There was a series of murders, all linked by the way the victims were being killed. Anyway, some of the killer's blood was found on two different bodies but there was something wrong with it. Conventional testing failed to provide an answer. The Koptet Institute was asked to run its own tests and see if it could come up with anything. We did and we'd seen it before. I went to New York to follow it up but, as it turned out, I needn't have bothered. The NYPD weren't having any of it."

"Like Daley today."

"Exactly. Except in New York it was a turkey called Eugene Ferraro. *Captain* Eugene Ferraro. He wouldn't even consider what I had to say because every time I opened my mouth he had this picture of Bela Lugosi in his head. He entirely missed the point I was trying to make."

"Which was?"

"They were looking for some psychopath – with a brilliant mind, it has to be admitted – who just *happened to be* infected with a highly unusual blood disorder. The fact that the killer was carrying the disease was entirely down to chance. But having established that, it did narrow down the possibilities dramatically. Any suspect turning in a positive blood test would almost certainly be guilty. The probability of two virus carriers falling within the scope of a single police investigation is so minute it can barely be computed. But Ferraro wasn't listening. He ignored me to begin with and then arrested me."

"So why are you here?"

"There are other similarities between the cases. The method of killing, for example. Also, in each New York murder the victim was an expert."

"In what?"

"Acting, economics, architecture, surgery, nuclear physics, athletics, whatever. And that's the same as here, isn't it? Your sister was a leading cellist, Perlman was a top violinist."

"What about Sarah Reynolds?"

Chris took a deep breath. "That is a little confusing, I have to confess. She's the first not to fit the pattern, but I'd still go with the general theory."

Katherine refilled her glass. Concern spread across her brow. "Are you saying the New York killer is here in London?"

"I'm saying it's a possibility."

"So the New York one was never caught?"

"No. They never even got a trace of a scent."

Katherine looked gloomy and asked, "So, how was Jennifer killed?"

Chris shook his head. "There's no need to get into that and I'll tell you why. I don't have any proof of how she died. Anything I'd say would be speculation and would just upset you."

"I'm already upset."

Chris leaned back in his chair and sighed. The waiter came and cleared away their plates. He asked if they wanted anything more and they ordered coffee.

Chris lit a cigarette. "Do you believe what I've told you?"

"I'm not sure, but nobody's offering anything better."

"That's all very well, but I'm not . . ."

"I was her sister, for God's sake!"

Chris considered this. Katherine took a sip from her coffee. She put her elbows on the table and held the cup with both hands, taking tiny sips of the steaming liquid. She said,

"Please, Chris. I want you to tell me how you think Jennifer was killed, even if it is speculation."

"Katherine, I'd rather..."

"I'm probably going to find out sooner or later, so it might as well be now. *Please.*"

Chris saw the determined look in her eyes and said, "It's not nice. Are you absolutely sure?"

She nodded firmly. "Absolutely."

"Okay," he murmured. "Put the cup down."

Chapter Seven

The sun was shocking so Robert slipped on a pair of sunglasses. He heard the buzz of bees floating around a bush by the low stone wall. He felt a trickle of sweat slip down the side of his face, just by his left ear. Johnny's head was bowed so low his chin was almost on his chest. Mary Birch, Sarah's flatmate, was shaking, as she tried to tighten the rein on her sobbing.

Sarah Reynolds came from Devon, and that was where she was committed to the soil. Robert first met her in a crowded, steaming airport terminal in Istanbul, where they were both waiting for a delayed flight. She had been on a cultural tour of Middle Eastern ruins and Robert had been on a fortnight's drinking binge in the sun. By the time they stepped off the Gatwick Express at Victoria Station, eighteen hours had elapsed from the moment they first met. That was enough for a start.

Robert fell deeply in love with Sarah. Although they never lived together, they rarely spent a night apart when it wasn't absolutely necessary. As time passed, he began to wonder whether they might marry. In the early days, they discussed it in a light-hearted fashion, but once possibility began to look like probability, it seemed dangerous to joke about it.

Robert looked at her coffin, as it began to be lowered into the dusty trench that had been carved out of the parched soil for her. He found himself wondering what she looked like beneath the lid of the wooden casket.

He'd stumbled onto her infidelity quite by chance. If it had been on the screen, the audience would have laughed at his misfortune, his absurd humiliation. It was so basic, culled from the very best tradition of the bedroom farce.

They had keys to each other's flat and, on the night in question, when he opened the door to her apartment, he discovered a stranger walking out of Sarah's bedroom, clutching a small towel around his waist. The stranger was Anthony Baker.

Robert shivered in the scorching afternoon sun. The memory of it was horribly vivid. He remembered telling her that he forgave her and that he didn't want to dwell on it any more. It was finished. They'd had a great past and they would have an even better future, he'd assured her. And Sarah had simply looked at him a little sadly.

"It's not going to work, Robert," she said.

His disbelief had been obvious. "What?"

"Us," she confirmed. "It won't work. I'm in love with him."

The low that followed was deep and long-lasting. When the sadness subsided, as it inevitably does, a permanent strand of hate remained. It wasn't a fire he needed to stoke artificially; it burned continuously, fuelling itself on an inexhaustible supply of bitterness.

Ever since Johnny Stainger broke the news of her murder to him, Robert had felt emotionally dead. He watched the reports on the TV, heard the news on the radio and saw the headlines in the papers. It all left him cold. Now that she was dead, everyone seemed to be treating him as though they were still in love. Everyone kept asking if he was all right, how he was coping with the loss. He wanted to tell them that Sarah was an irrelevance, a bad memory. He was only at the funeral because her parents, who had been so kind to him, had asked him to attend. While others mourned, Robert felt guilty because he was unable to conjure up any great sense of sorrow.

Robert and Laura strolled along the Chelsea Embankment. The sky was a pink haze. Car exhausts belched ceaselessly along the choked traffic lanes. It was low tide on the Thames. Robert and Laura stopped and leaned against the stone wall, peering down onto the broad river. At the water's edge, the banks were dark and muddy. Robert saw rusting cans, oily ropes, discarded shoes, yards of abandoned nylon net and plastic sheeting that was green with slime.

"I read that the Thames was the cleanest of Europe's major rivers," he said to Laura.

"It makes you think."

"It makes you sick."

Laura leaned away and arched her back, sighing slightly. "How was it?"

"Depressing. Like funerals should be, I suppose."

Robert shook his head and gave what Laura took to be a bitter smile. She said, "What is it?"

"I was just thinking how glad I am that it's all over. Ever since Johnny phoned me up with the news, I've had to put up with everyone treating me as though she was my wife."

Laura gasped, "God, Robert! Do you have any idea how callous that sounds? You must have felt something."

"Oh, I did. But it wasn't sadness. I kept remembering how she ditched me and everything that I felt in the aftermath. I used to wish that something really dreadful would happen to her. Then it did. And today, while I was standing over her grave, I really couldn't bring myself to feel any sorrow for her. I can't say I was glad, or that she deserved it, but I just felt utterly numb. It could have been anyone in the coffin, a stranger."

Laura took a cigarette from her crumpled pack and lit it. She, more than anyone, had seen the damage that Sarah Reynolds had inflicted upon him. It had been frightening to witness his decline and it had been difficult to drag him back to normality. Laura had seen first hand the extent of his love for Sarah. She could never underestimate the strength of that feeling. Even now, it made her wince to recall his anguish.

Later, as the funeral passed into memory, Robert and Laura made love in the dark, moving slowly and silently. Robert's head was empty. He lost himself to physical sensation, holding Laura close to his body as she wrapped her limbs around him.

Laura had always played it cool with Robert. Even though he denied it vehemently, she reckoned Robert would have taken Sarah back, if she'd changed her mind. This fact alone would have stopped Laura from making a move on him, had she had a mind to do so.

They rolled over her unmade bed and Robert sighed softly. She clutched him tighter than before, her head filled with pictures of him, like a collection of moving photographs. She pushed harder against him and dug her fingers into his shoulder blades. Her lips sucked the skin on his collarbone. Robert needed good company tonight and she would provide it. She'd make love to him like he'd never known before and then she'd look after him so well he'd never want to let her go.

Laura had to admit that when she heard about Sarah's murder her sense of shock and horror had been tainted. While Sarah was alive, Robert had been out of reach.

But she was gone now, turned to dust.

Isabelle stood by the window and pressed her fingertips against the glass. It was icy to the touch. The sky was grey and turbulent, spilling thick snowflakes. It was the heaviest fall she had seen in years. She looked down onto the Rhône and saw a fragile boat navigating a precarious passage from one bank to the other, over choppy waters. She could barely make out the buildings on the opposite bank. Their marvellous architecture had been reduced to grey blocks of smudge that were only just distinguishable against the background of steel snow and sombre sky.

When she had been outside, a few minutes before, it had been bitterly cold. The thick snow completely deadened the sound of Lyon. She could have been in a ghost town.

She turned away from the window, leaving it partly open, and looked across at the large four-poster bed. The thick, burgundy curtains were drawn back and she gazed upon the man who lay there, pale and shivering. A hearty fire crackled in the grate, full of bloody orange health, but it made little impact on the coolness of the room. There was a small elegant table with a circular top, which stood next to a deep chair. Upon the table stood a decanter and two wine glasses. One still contained the claret that had been poured into it the night before.

She moved over to the edge of the bed. The shadow she cast over him seemed to pluck the man from his fitful sleep. He opened his eyes and managed a frail smile.

Isabelle looked down at him with a mixture of pity and relief. A week ago he had been a man in his physical prime, a colossus compared to those around him. He was a man of honour and education. He was intelligent and compassionate and universally respected. And by midday, he would be dead.

Isabelle knew it was unfair. But while she felt sad, there was also a sense of relief.

"Isabelle," he sighed, in a voice weakened to a whisper. "Lie beside me."

She lowered herself gently onto the bulky mound of sheets and blankets.

"Everyone is afraid to be in my company, in case they should catch the illness which has taken me. Everyone except you. Why are you not afraid?"

"Don't speak. Save your strength," she told him.

"For what? We both know where I'm headed."

Isabelle looked over to the window. Small flurries of snowflakes blew through the gap she had left. She could just make out the soft blows of horses' hooves clipping the snow-coated cobbles of the street below. She leaned over him, kissed him lightly on the lips and closed her hands around his throat. Since illness had infected him, she had hoped to avoid this, but now she saw that it was appropriate. His immense power had completely left him. His fingers grabbed her wrists but his strength was no greater than a baby's. The body protested meekly and Isabelle cried for both of them.

"Marcel!" she gasped.

Rachel could hear people arguing in Lennox Gardens. Their voices were loud but their words were indistinct. She rose from the bed and felt drained by the dream. She made a fist and pressed it firmly to her chest. She wished they would stop, but they never did and, she supposed, they never would. She knew that while other people might dream frequently and vividly, none of them were tortured by the visions she had.

Rachel took a cup of coffee onto the bedroom balcony. There were an old couple arguing by the railings around the gardens. They jabbed accusatory, arthritic fingers at each other to back up their flawed arguments. A red helicopter passed overhead, the thud of the blades temporarily drowning out every other sound. Directly below her, Robert appeared, wearing a pair of jeans and an old white T-shirt with a faded black and gold Simple Minds logo on the front and a list of tour dates on the back. He was barefoot, carrying a bucket full of foaming liquid and a plain, wooden scrubbing brush. He started to run the brush over the stone steps in front of the apartment block.

She watched in silence as his arms flicked back and forth. She could see his shoulders pumping beneath the worn cotton of the T-shirt. Why him? She didn't know.

Robert was thinking about Rachel. It would have been easy to believe she was a professional painter, had she not specifically said she wasn't. She had the beauty of a model and the composure to be a fine actress, but he knew instinctively that she was neither of these. His thoughts were interrupted by the arrival of the police. Detective Constable Kevin Malloy was accompanied by WPC Rosie Marsh, a petite woman with pinched lips and freckled skin. They came to ask questions about Sarah Reynolds.

"We're talking to everyone who knew her," explained Malloy. "It's routine, but it's urgent. I understand she was your girlfriend a while back. Is that correct?"

Robert gave them a potted account of their affair and answered a list of basic questions. He was sure that none of his answers were of any use. They thanked him for his time and asked him to get in touch if he had any ideas for them.

"We need all the help we can get," said Malloy. "He's a maniac and if we don't catch him soon, he'll do it again."

Robert frowned as Malloy and Marsh headed for the door. "How do you know that?"

"Pardon?" replied Malloy, standing in the doorway.

"How do you know he'll do it again?"

Malloy looked embarrassed and Robert knew why.

Robert knocked on her door and waited. The lift coughed into life and rattled, as it descended in its iron cage towards the ground floor. The packing case was enormous. She opened the door and her eyes brightened when she saw it.

"You were expecting this?"

"Yes. Oh my God, yes!"

"What is it?" asked Robert, as he manoeuvred the case off the trolley and onto one of the Persian carpets.

"A cello."

"I didn't know you played."

"I've only recently taken it up. Along with the violin."

"The violin too?"

"Yes, but it's this I prefer."

She produced a knife to cut through the straps which secured the case. Robert held the box as she reached inside and withdrew the cello. It looked old. The wood was stained and beautifully polished.

"Isn't it magnificent?" gasped Rachel, letting her eyes roam over the instrument's body, as she held it by the neck. "Quite exquisite. Worth every cent."

Robert cleared some of the protective packaging off the floor and stuffed it back into the box.

"I bought it at auction."

"Really?"

"Yes, in New York."

"And this is what you're learning on?" he asked, clearly surprised.

Rachel looked at him coldly and Robert wished he'd kept his mouth shut. It was her money and none of his business. Rachel lost the hardness in her face but remained solemn.

"I heard what happened," she said.

She caught Robert off-guard. "About what?"

"Your girlfriend. I'm very sorry. It must be a horrible shock."

"She was my ex-girlfriend."

"Still . . . it must be a traumatic time for you."

She looked truly upset.

"I didn't enjoy the funeral," he confirmed. "But I haven't felt as shattered as everyone keeps thinking I should."

"Really?"

"To be honest, she had no place in my heart."

Rachel considered this for a few seconds and said, "You must have felt something for her, surely? After all, if you once loved her . . ."

"Well, I suppose so. But . . ."

He didn't want to pursue the subject, but she seemed keen. "But what?"

"My predominant feeling was curiosity. I just wanted to know what happened to her."

"That's understandable."

"Or maybe funerals and I just don't get along. I wasn't upset at my father's funeral, either."

Rachel picked up the cello and took it over to the window, where the light was clearer. Robert wheeled the trolley to the front door. When he returned, she was still bent over the instrument, running her fingers and eyes over the gleaming wood.

"Thanks for bringing this up," she said. "Would you like a drink?"

"Well, I . . ."

"Have a drink," she told him, resting the cello on the floor and walking away from the window.

"Okay."

"So, when did he die?"

"Who?"

"Your father."

"A couple of years ago. Heart attack."

"What about your mother? Is she still around?"

"Yes, she's alive and kicking, as far as I know. She divorced my father when I was a kid. She's onto husband number three now. Or maybe he's number four. I'm not sure. Poor bastard!"

"You don't get on with her?"

"I don't know her well enough to say that, but I wouldn't like to be anyone's fourth husband. He's some psychiatrist in Los Angeles. A real fruitcake. If ever anyone needed analysis, it's him. What about you?"

Rachel looked offended. "What about me?"

"Any brothers or sisters?"

"No. I'm an only child," she said, before turning away from him and murmuring softly, "a lonely child."

It may have been quiet, but Rachel had ensured it was loud enough for Robert to hear.

"What about your parents?"

"No. My mother died giving birth to me."

"I'm sorry."

"There's no need to be sorry."

She headed for the kitchen and Robert followed, the hum of the television set growing louder as he approached.

"I didn't mean to . . ."

"Like I said, there's no need to apologize. Do you have any brothers or sisters?"

"No."

"So we're both lonely, only children, aren't we?"

Robert's attention was distracted by the news bulletin on the television screen. The report switched to a press conference where a row of plain-clothed policemen sat behind a table groaning under the weight of microphones pointed at the mouth of the man sitting at the centre. His name flashed up on the screen. Detective Chief Inspector Harold Daley.

"Was this a sexually motivated attack?" asked an anonymous voice, just audible over the clicking cameras.

"There is no evidence to suggest that," said Daley. "We can't rule that out of the motive, but the victim was not sexually assaulted."

"Have you any comment to make about stories in this morning's papers linking this murder with the killings of Jennifer Colson and André Perlman?"

Daley shifted uneasily in his seat and cleared his throat.

"I'm afraid that's pure speculation."

"But you can't rule it out?"

"It's not based on factual evidence and that makes it a scare story. Under the circumstances, I find it distasteful and completely irresponsible. That's all I wish to say on the subject."

"He's lying," muttered Robert, recalling his exchange with Kevin Malloy earlier in the day.

"How do you know?" asked Rachel.

"I just do."

Daley was now addressing the cameras directly.

"Although this heinous crime was committed in a private flat, there must have been plenty of people who saw the killer. I'd ask everyone who was in the area at the time to cast their minds back and think. Did they see anyone acting unusually? Was there anything that seemed out of the ordinary? Any information at all . . ."

Rachel shook her head and said, "They're not going to catch him, are they?"

The TV's glare cast a sick pool of light on the marble worktop. Rachel looked at Robert, fascinated by his apparent lack of emotion. This was something she hadn't expected. He really didn't seem upset. Not only that, but surely the manner of death ought to have stirred some sentiment within him? There should have been outrage and a sense of protest, but there wasn't. There appeared to be nothing more than curiosity. Even that was mild. She reached into the fridge and withdrew a chilled bottle of Sancerre.

"Is wine okay?"

"Fine."

Rachel poured two glasses, handed one to Robert and led the way into the drawing-room. She took a silver box from the mantelpiece above the stone fireplace and flipped open the lid.

It was filled with cigarettes and she offered one to Robert who shook his head.

"Of course," she said, acknowledging her mistake. "You've given up, haven't you? I nearly gave up too. In the end, I decided just to ration myself. Nowadays, I just have the odd one, usually on special occasions. I always try to make it an act of pleasure, not desperation. It's nice."

"Well, I don't have that self-control. If I had one now, I'd be back onto two packets a day by this time next week."

"Don't be absurd, Robert. It's just discipline. It's easy."

"For you, maybe."

She replaced the box on the mantelpiece, took a sip from her glass and said, "How was your interview with the police?"

Robert looked up from the carpet. "How did you know about that?"

"I saw the police car," she told him. "I was standing on the balcony and I saw it pulling into the kerb."

That was perfectly plausible, except that Robert found he didn't believe her.

"I saw them going down to the basement, so I figured they were going to interview you about your girlfriend."

"My *ex*-girlfriend," Robert insisted. "Besides, how do you know that's what they came to see me for? It could have been about anything at all."

Rachel took a sip from her glass of Sancerre. Robert was by no means the most handsome man she'd come across. At first, she had found him almost unattractive, but the more time she spent with him, the more she liked the way he looked. His eyes could mesmerize her and she was careful not to be caught gazing too fondly into them. Not yet, anyway. She liked the high cheekbones, even if they weren't structurally perfect. She found herself attracted to all the little things that a purist would call flaws.

"I suppose they could have been asking questions about something else," she admitted. "But, realistically, what are the chances?"

Chapter Eight

"Hi, Ray. Not too busy tonight."

"Not yet. What are you having?"

"Oh, I don't know. Surprise me."

"Strong or very strong?"

"The strongest."

"You're evil, Karen."

"Thanks, Ray. You always say the sweetest things."

Stephen Abraham watched the girl called Karen lean over the bar and take a wallet of matches out of a glass ashtray. The front of the shiny black cover had Seven of Hearts embossed on it in a scarlet that matched Karen's shocking lipstick. On the back there were seven small hearts. She lit her cigarette and spun around so she was facing the tables, which were partially lost in gloom. Abraham cast an eye over the congregation; plenty of strangers, he noticed, even though it wasn't especially crowded. That was promising.

Ray, the friendly bartender, poured a double measure of tequila into the shaker. Abraham fingered his empty glass and put it down on the end of the bar. The girl hadn't noticed him yet, which was good. He preferred to observe unobserved; it appealed to his untamed voyeuristic instincts.

She was wearing a bright turquoise top and a pair of leather trousers with a belt that had a large, bright, silver star as a buckle. She had hazel eyes and mousey hair which she dyed blonde. Abraham would have preferred it if she'd left it the natural colour. The bartender slid a glass across the bar top to her and she took a sip.

"Jesus Christ, Ray! What have you put in this?"

"Something to pep you up."

"Something to blow me up, more like."

Abraham could see Karen loved Seven of Hearts. He imagined how exciting it was to her, by way of a stark contrast to what he assumed was the numbing routine of her day. She obviously liked the people who came here. He guessed they looked haunted and exotic to her. She was an impostor, really, and he enjoyed the faintly pathetic pleasure she clearly found in her surroundings.

Since she arrived, Abraham had stalked her, his eyes stapled to her wherever she roamed. He rarely emerged from shadow, choosing to melt into the inherent darkness of the club. The fact that she was unaware of his predatory gaze only served to excite him further. While he waited, he fantasized, imagining her daily routine and the ways in which she tried to add spice to her pointless life. And then he dreamed of the night ahead, the deceptions she would fall for, the horror of the reality overwhelming her when it was too late. The prospect made him shudder with exquisite anticipation. It was time to move.

Ray noticed Abraham making his way along the length of the bar. Their eyes met, but nothing was said. Karen only saw Abraham as he pulled up beside her. He stared directly into her eyes and she was startled by his boldness.

Abraham caught his reflection in the smoked mirror behind the bar. He wore a black suit with a navy blue shirt that was fastened by onyx studs right up to the throat. The studs were so handsome it would have been a pity to hide them beneath a tie. He had long, thick dark hair which was pushed back over the scalp and seemed to stay in place, when gravity might have invited it to fall about his gaunt face. He had good, Slavic-looking cheekbones and a pair of pale blue eyes.

He said, "I'm sorry. I didn't mean to surprise you."

"You didn't," she lied, clutching at composure.

"Could I buy you a drink? My name's Stephen."

She had overcome her shock and now permitted herself a

grin. Abraham liked Karen's sly smile. She looked up into his face, into his inviting eyes. She extended him her hand. "Karen."

"What would you like?" he asked.

"What would I like?"

"To drink."

She nodded and widened her smile some more. "Let me see. What would you suggest?"

"Well, I..."

Abraham froze. His heart felt like a ball of ice in a chest of icicle ribs. Somewhere out there something was glittering, a brilliant halo in a murky atmosphere. Karen's smile faded. He couldn't believe what he was seeing.

"You okay?" she said.

"I... er, you want... to drink?"

"Are you feeling ill? You don't look too good."

Abraham felt fear creeping up on him. It was hunting him, its bleak shadow already engulfing him. Panic's fingers wrapped around him, closing tightly on his mind, squeezing into a terrifying fist. He reached for the rail that ran along the bar.

Ray saw consternation on Karen's face and the way she was edging back from the stranger, almost falling off her stool.

"What's... what's *wrong* with you?" she spluttered.

Abraham looked past her, not hearing her. His brow creased and a shadow fell over his eyes, but the pupils seemed to blaze brighter than before. Karen knocked her cocktail glass over, spilling Ray's potion across the counter.

Abraham put his hand to his forehead and squeezed his eyes shut. The fear was howling in his head. The brilliance in the dark left him both terrified and intrigued. Instinct told him what it was but logic resisted. The urge to investigate grew hand-in-hand with the desire to flee. He looked up at Karen and his desperate appearance frightened her. She stumbled from the bar-stool and dropped her cigarette onto the floor.

Ray arrived. "Everything okay, Karen?"

She was staring into Abraham's eyes. They were burning, she thought. Ray was about to open his mouth when Abraham suddenly lurched away from the bar. In a moment, he was gone, lost in the crowd.

At the other end of the bar to where Karen had been sitting, Robert nursed an expensive, watered-down vodka and tonic. Laura stood beside him, caressing his shoulder.

"You want to dance?" she asked.

Robert didn't even want to be there. The evening was designed to take his mind off Sarah's murder, to cushion the blows his shattered emotions were supposed to be taking. He found the idea of dragging him out to some club to get smashed pretty perverse. It was a wake in poor taste, as far as he was concerned.

They went to Santiago, a Spanish restaurant on Frith Street, before heading into the West End's heart. Robert wasn't sure how many people had been at dinner. A dozen? Fifteen? They sat crammed around tables and shouted orders to waiters who were sweating and flustered. The food was terrible and Robert couldn't hear a word for the riot of background conversation.

Laura kissed Robert on the ear and lit a cigarette.

"Are you having a good time?" she asked.

He looked at her blankly and she tossed her head back and laughed. It made him smile.

"I've seen people looking happier in a dentist's waiting room," she said. "Look, I'm going to wander. I'll see you later."

"Maybe."

"If I get lucky, I'll call you in the morning and give you the gruesome details."

Robert meandered through the club on his own. The dance floor was seething. His friends had been swallowed by the sea of flesh which raged down there. A lighting rig swung low over the crowd, rotating fantastically, blinding people with brilliant spears of white light. Neon tubes highlighted the columns which ran down either side of the floor. Robert watched Laura drawing hungry glances from both sexes.

He'd never seen so many grotesque males fondling glassy-eyed girls who thought eighteen was old. Shadowy figures in sunglasses nestled in gloomy corners, clutching hideous psychedelic cocktails. Alcohol-sodden girls pressed themselves against strangers, their bulbous surgically-constructed breasts protesting at the confinement offered up by their bright dresses. Robert had blown his nose into handkerchiefs which had more material than most of them were wearing.

All the others who had been at dinner were out there somewhere. They had entered Seven of Hearts as a group and had dispersed like glass shattering on stone, never to be rejoined.

The club was an inferno. He'd thought it had been boiling at Santiago, but it was positively polar compared to Seven of Hearts. He pulled his shirt away from the slick skin of his body. He was surrounded by exotic and absurd animals, fired on drugs and drink. The music hammered his brain, the beat as persistent as a drill. He felt like an intruder, drifting through the freak circus and spying on all the pointless people in it.

"You're lost."

He barely heard her over the din.

"What are you doing here?" he shouted.

Rachel looked stunning. Her dress was black and simple, dropping to the knee. Her shoulders were bare. She had gathered her hair at the back, letting it fall in a pony-tail. With it drawn away from the face, it accentuated her fine features. Robert looked at her skin. Despite the heat, there wasn't even a hint of perspiration on her. Her eyes were bright. A slim watch was her only decoration.

"Watching you."

"What?" cried Robert, leaning closer towards her, assuming he'd misheard.

"I've been watching you."

He stood up straight and said, "Why?"

"I've been waiting for you."

He didn't understand. "How did you know I'd be here?"

"I didn't."

Robert thought about it for a moment. "You followed me?"

"Yes."

"All night?"

"Even when you were eating in Santiago."

"Where were you?"

"Waiting."

"Inside or outside?"

She smiled thinly. "Does it make a difference?"

Robert couldn't prevent a little smile himself. "I assume there's a reason for this."

She nodded. "Like I said, I was waiting for you."

Rods of white light danced over both of them. Robert saw the reflection in her dark pupils. The bass beat rippled in his stomach. The smile suddenly vanished from her face.

The stranger in front of her looked ill. His skin was white. His eyelids flickered and Robert saw panic in his face. The lips trembled as he opened his mouth to speak. At first, nothing came out and he looked like a fish. Then he said, "Are you . . . you are, aren't you?"

Rachel said nothing. He was wearing a blue shirt with beautiful onyx studs. Stephen Abraham was quivering. Robert wondered if he would pass out in front of them.

"My . . . *sister*!" Abraham cried desperately, as his hand reached out and touched her arm, his fingers pressing into the skin.

Rachel shuddered, a mixture of disgust and anxiety. She looked at Robert and then back at the stranger, before she shook her arm free of his wretched grasp.

"No!"

The denial brought a new look to his face. Utter confusion. He turned to Robert, staring deeply into his eyes. It unnerved Robert. Abraham looked back at Rachel. "Are you brother and sister? Am I the brother of one of you?"

She said, "Please leave us alone."

He was moving towards Rachel again and she looked

scared, so Robert stepped forward, sliding between them. He put a hand on Abraham's shoulders and saw no menace, just despair and . . . and something else.

"Take it easy," Robert told him. "Why don't you sit down and have a drink?"

"I can feel . . . I feel . . ."

"If you feel half as ill as you look, maybe you should have an early night."

Robert let him go. Abraham watched them retreat and made no further move. Rachel leaned forward and murmured into Robert's ear. "Thanks. He was beginning to . . ."

Robert said, "Who was he?"

"How should I know?"

"He knew you."

"Because he called me sister?"

Robert didn't answer. The noise and the heat were beginning to make his temples throb.

"I've never seen him before," she insisted. "Listen, he was probably drunk, or on drugs, or something. Who knows? Who cares?"

He smiled awkwardly and ran a hand through his hair. Rachel looked at him anxiously. He was sweating. Burning and nervous, she thought.

"Thanks for stepping in," she said. "I was a little worried he might do something . . . You know. Something stupid."

"So was I." He looked around and Abraham had gone, so he turned back to her. "Would you like a drink? I mean, I feel as though I could use one."

"Me too," she said, before adding, "but maybe somewhere else."

"Somewhere else?"

"Yes. Unless you want to stay here. I know you came with friends, so maybe . . ."

Robert pictured her spying on him in Santiago, as her voice trailed off. Where had she been? Peering through the window? Did she see his glum face isolated in drunken laughter? Could she tell him what he ate?

"Do you want to stay?" she was asking him.

Robert cast a dismissive glance over the crowd in Seven of Hearts and said, "Not really, no."

"Then let's go to another place."

His hand touched her wrist and she was as inviting to his fingers as she was to his eyes.

"Where?"

The question amused her and she permitted herself a little smile, when she said, "Come on, Robert. You can do better than that."

Stephen Abraham sat naked and cross-legged on the scrubbed wooden floor. The long tentacles seemed to reach for him, even though he knew they were static. The satin sheets rippled on the hot night breeze, making waves, an emerald surf.

He was in perfect isolation, the only one in the room, no one else in the house. Except for the rabid crowd inside his head. The dreams of the wretched coloured every thought he had. Sometimes they implored him to do normal things . . . working, eating, sleeping, fucking. And sometimes they didn't.

He looked down at his forearm and the series of parallel notches he'd carved on it. His fingers touched his shoulder and located the wound which wouldn't heal. The squatters in his skull wouldn't allow that.

Someone once told him that there could be little worse than sliding into insanity's abyss and being aware of it. At the time, he'd laughed it off without ever seriously considering it. Like bad car crashes, insanity was something for other people. But now he knew they'd been right. It was the most appalling revelation. No fear could match it.

And his decline had been alarmingly rapid. So far, he'd managed to mask it in public, only allowing the crowd to swamp him once he was alone and safe. But tonight, in Seven of Hearts, that changed.

Abraham cried harder and dipped both hands into a plastic bucket of old razor-blades. He withdrew a handful, squeezing his palms together, the rusty cutting edges tearing him from every imaginable angle. The blood was hot between his fingers and over his arms. Then he rubbed the metal slices over his trembling body like a moisturizing cream, wailing as they cut through his skin and into the haunted flesh beneath.

"Leave me alone! *Get out of my fucking head!* Who are you? What are you doing to me? Please! *What the fuck do you want from me?*"

Chapter Nine

Robert awoke and felt a moment of panic, as his eyes tried to acclimatize to the dark. The content of the bad dream faded, as though he'd pulled the plug on his internal TV screen. The twisted images and scrambled sounds had gone in a flash. He lay on his back.

Rachel was asleep next to him. He wondered how much it would cost to repair the tear in her black dress. He'd hardly restrained himself in the taxi, working his fingers between her thighs as she parted her legs and urged him on by holding his wrist and tugging it towards her. The driver's eyes had danced in the rear-view mirror.

They kissed in the cage-lift, their mouths clashing as clumsily as their bodies, rattling the ancient machine. And when they kicked Rachel's flat door shut, she dragged him down to the floor in the hall, just by the entrance to the drawing-room. Her dress was bunched up around her waist. When she grew bored of fiddling with the buttons on his shirt, she ripped it apart.

At first, Robert tried to wrestle the dress over her head, as she spread herself wider over the marble floor and pulled him deeper inside her. Eventually, she reached down and yanked the material upwards, crying, "Just pull it!" He did, and the thing tore.

Robert now sat up and wondered how long he had slept. The curtains were only partly drawn, allowing a dim slice of light to penetrate Rachel's bedroom. She lay on her side, facing away from him. The cotton sheet only covered the lower half of her back. Her thick hair flowed out across her pillow. She had pale skin, but everything looked dark blue in the night. Robert rolled onto his side and slid his right arm over her.

Her fingers found his and they locked together. Then she took his wrist and pressed his palm flat against her chest. He could feel the slight divide and swell of the top of her breasts beneath the heel of his hand. Her skin was warm.

For a few moments, she kept his hand securely pressed against her skin and then she slowly ground her hips back into him. He moved his fingers up to her throat and then down to her breasts. The palm of his hand ran over the nipples, rubbing softly, sensing the change. He slid his fingers across her stomach. He liked the way certain points made her tense. They started to rub in rhythm.

"Are you asleep?" she murmured.

"Can't you tell? I'm almost in a coma."

"I thought so."

Rachel allowed his fingers to creep spider-like into the undergrowth of her pubic hair. She sucked in the damp night air with a sharp hiss as he picked up the soft skin on the inside of the top of her thighs. He brought the fingers back again and felt her thumb digging sharply into the pulse on his wrist. Through the tangles of hair, he came across the warm flesh and its first slick traces. Rachel murmured something incomprehensible.

His excitement was stoked by the way she was sliding her body against his. When he was so erect that the aching hurt, she leaned forwards slightly so that her fingertips could guide him into her. He pushed, feeling himself disappear, enveloped by the wet, heated pressure of being inside her. His stomach muscles tightened as he drove deeper into her, as far and as slowly as he could.

The whole room was dark blue. The ceiling was covered in smudges of rippling shadows, painted by the curtains on the breeze. Robert heard the gentle clicking of a clock marking time. Their breathing sounded loud. Then Rachel disentangled herself. She rolled over in the bed and knelt at his side.

"Are you okay?" he whispered hoarsely, staring up at her in the blue darkness.

Rachel moved one leg over his body and delicately lowered herself onto him. She leaned forward, planting her hands on the pillows either side of his head. Their lips touched. Robert strained his neck forward and their tongues were like snakes, brushing, flicking and darting. She sat up straight and tossed her head back, sighing as he ran his hands over the flat flesh of her stomach and onto her breasts.

"Do it . . . do . . ." she gasped. "Do it . . . do what you want . . . whatever you want."

She was clawing at his arm without thinking, as she leaned back, straining him, testing him.

". . . What you want . . . anything you want . . ." she mumbled. "If you want . . . you can . . . hurt . . . you can hurt me . . . if you like."

"What?" croaked Robert.

Between deeper and deeper breaths she said, quite clearly, "You can hurt me, if you like."

He stopped moving and looked up at her, squinting in the gloom, as though that would help him see her face. It didn't.

"Don't stop," she sighed.

He lay there in the darkness, feeling her tongue playing with his fingertips. *You can hurt me, if you like.*

"What's wrong?" she asked, softly.

His tongue felt swollen inside his mouth as she brushed the back of his hand with her lips, licking the knuckles. She was still moving, her hips gently gyrating. Robert watched her swaying shape and wished he could edit her words from his memory.

"Please," she said, "tell me what's wrong."

"You don't know?"

"No."

"Why do you think I might want to hurt you?"

She stopped moving. His hand slipped from her grasp and she rose off him, collapsing onto her side of the bed. She curled into the foetal position. He sat up and put his hand on her shoulder. He expected it to be shrugged off, but it wasn't.

"I don't know what you must think of me," she said, quietly.

"Nor do I," he confessed.

"I'm sorry."

"For what?"

Rachel uncurled herself, twisting around so that she lay on her back. Robert was on his side, propped up on an elbow.

"I'm not sure," she admitted. "Offending you, perhaps? For thinking you might be like that?"

"I don't want to hurt you, Rachel."

She took his hand and turned her face slightly away. There was something wrong with someone who offered up physical pain as lightly as a kiss on the cheek. He leaned over and kissed her on the forehead. She turned her face up to his and placed a hand at the back of his neck.

"You're confusing me," she said.

"That's not my intention."

"I know. That's part of the problem."

She ran her palms over his ribs. He kissed her shoulders and neck, moving down to her breasts, letting his tongue and lips run over her nipples. Her fingers played with his face and then she turned his head up towards her and said, "Make love with me."

And so they did. They oozed all over the bed, a single unit of many limbs. They shone. The sheets creased and dampened as they held their breath at the painful bridges. They were glued together while they decorated each other's faces with hot kisses which lacked direction because they were too frantic to focus.

When Rachel had an orgasm, she cried out, as she tensed into marble before relaxing into jelly. When Robert came he was too choked to even gasp. He felt the sinews in his neck trying to tear through the skin.

And then they were in each other's arms, neither apparently breathing, as calm as a mirror sea. While he gradually withdrew, she kissed him on the mouth and he could see, even in the dark, the brilliance of her wet eyes.

"I never quite expected this," she said.

"Neither of us did."

"Things could get complicated."

"If we let them."

"They will, unless we go back to being strangers."

"That's what I meant."

"I don't want that, Robert."

He held Rachel in his arms and waited for the slide into sleep. But having her in his grasp was like being plugged into a recharging socket. He felt her breathing and how the blood came up to her skin in hot waves. She kissed his chest softly and drew patterns on his collarbone.

She told him, "I don't want to go to sleep."

"I can't go to sleep. I know I should. Part of me even wants to, but I can't."

She kissed his ribs and licked the skin. Robert could smell her on his fingers and on his wrist. The addictive scent of sweat and sex still lingered in the heavy, humid air. He inhaled the drug and was hooked and high before he'd emptied his lungs.

She made playful bites on his throat when they made love again. Sometimes she lowered herself so that her erect nipples brushed his body and sometimes she sat up straight, insisting he remained flat on his back. When she did this, she blocked out what little natural light there was and existed only in silhouette.

They sweated. It wasn't frail dew drops; it was streams. His hair soaked the pillow. He felt little rivers flowing over his lower stomach, dribbling through the groin and onto the bed. When she snapped her head forward, hot drops would fall from her face onto his body.

Rachel sat upright, moving her hips in a hypnotic rhythm which Robert hoped would never end. His eyes were only half open and he was floating, so he never really saw what happened.

Several burning drops splattered onto his stomach. She fell forward and kissed his face with renewed passion. She ran the fingers of her right hand over his forehead and through his wet hair. They were hot and left damp, smouldering traces across his skin. She picked out his temples and traced delicate patterns over his eyelids, before moving down to the mouth. The fingers were wet as she ran them across his lips, gently parting them. She purred pleasurably when he started to suck them. Then she sat up again, and held out her hands for him to hold. When he did, she gasped, "Sit up!"

He did and when they kissed she wrapped her arms around his shoulders and her dark hair fell over both their faces. Then she peeled away from the clinch and leaned over to the bedside table. She reached for something and Robert was dimly aware of a tiny jangle as she clutched something in her right hand. When she returned, he pressed his face against her wet breasts and his lips stumbled over her nipples.

She moved with blinding speed; Robert's eyes barely tracked it. There was a sharp tearing sound, followed by a tiny flash of metallic blue light which stood out against the night's gloom. Her right hand moved across the base of his throat and his left collarbone in one rapid sweep. A burning pain followed.

"Jesus Christ!" he protested, pulling away. "What the fuck is that?"

Rachel dropped whatever she was holding. It glittered in the dark as it fell onto the sheets. Then she rose up, circling his head with her reaching arms, and drove herself down onto him. She clutched him to her and then nuzzled his ear. "Don't be a baby, darling. It's nothing."

The pain on the collarbone flushed. Rachel pushed her mouth onto the source and ran her lips over the area, sucking it and kissing it. He could feel her sweet tongue licking the hurt, soothing it. She cried softly. From there on, she treated Robert so exquisitely he didn't care. He crashed back onto the bed. Rachel fell forward on top of him, tightly clamped to his body, working her mouth so intensely over the collarbone she seemed tacked to it. She killed the pain. There was a pleasurable fizzing sensation at the base of his throat.

As he came inside her, she held onto him, as though he were life itself, sighing, "Oh God! You're mine!"

After that, he slept.

Robert was in a huge room with little light. The hooks in his flesh were killing him. His agony was absolute. There was no gravity. He simply floated in the direction of the hook that pulled the strongest. There were pure, shining steel spikes in his shoulder blades. He felt them going in, splintering the bone.

He felt something scratching his chest. A metal mouth. It was cold, as freezing as the blades when they'd bitten into the flesh on his back. He felt it moving lightly across him and then felt patches of warm air, pooling on his skin. Suddenly the breeze blossomed into a scorching wind. It seared the centre of his chest, burning away the skin like rice paper under a blow torch. Then the cold steel jaws plunged into his chest. His nerve-endings ruptured under overload and he started to scream.

Rachel had both her hands pinned on his shoulders when his eyelids flicked open. She cried, "Robert! Robert!"

Inside his ribs, Robert felt pain and sickness. He slipped from her grasp and stumbled from the bed. His vision was impaired, his muscles burned with every movement. He swayed like a drunk as he lurched towards the bathroom, where he slid to his knees, grabbed the rim of the loo and threw up.

His knuckles paled as his grip increased, while the spasms in his stomach refused to stop. Long after there was nothing left inside, the contractions continued to curse him, wracking his body. Sad strands of bile hung from his mouth like vile stalactites. His eyes offered up more liquid than his guts could, tears streaming down his puce face. When the effort was over, his hands let go and he rolled onto the floor, too shattered to even maintain the kneeling position. His stomach felt bruised.

Rachel stood in the doorway and regarded him in a detached way for a few moments. Then she lowered herself to his side and wiped away some wet hair from his face.

"Come back to bed," she said.

"I need a drink," he whispered. "Some water."

"No," she assured him, "you'll just throw it right back up."

"But . . ."

"Trust me, Robert."

Rachel turned off the bathroom light. She offered Robert a hand, which he took, and pulled him slowly to his feet before leading him back to the bed. She laid him down upon the crumpled sheets. As he reached for the bedside light, she intercepted his arm and placed it back on the bed.

"No. No light. Relax," she whispered.

He found his muscles unknotting themselves, the tension falling away. The aching began to recede. So did his thirst.

"What are you doing to me?" he mumbled indistinctly, as Rachel continued to soothe and cool him.

His blurred words and childish demeanour brought a smile to her lips that was almost maternal.

"I feel . . . I feel . . ."

She hushed him and watched him tumble into a deep sleep. She could have left him if she'd wanted to, in the knowledge that it would be several hours before he awoke. But for a while, she chose not to. She continued to sit at his side, gazing upon him with a fascination which never diminished. After nearly two hours, the creeping sun hit the lip of a small gold bowl on her bedside table and a tiny, sharp star of reflection caught her eye and broke her concentration.

She showered and then stepped onto her balcony with a cup of coffee, a daily ritual she liked to observe when the weather permitted.

London was set to suffer another scorching day of intolerable heat and humidity. But that didn't make a dent in her mood. She was drunk on the essence of happiness.

He drifted into consciousness to music. It was faint and elegant. He lay on his back while his eyes adjusted to the light. It wasn't particularly bright since the curtains were still partly drawn. A fly buzzed annoyingly as it circled overhead. Robert couldn't see it. He looked for Rachel on the other side of the bed. She wasn't there.

There were dark stains on his pillow and on hers. There was blood all over the sheets. Sweat had diluted some of it into pink smudges, but where it had remained pure, it had darkened as it dried. There were a dozen or more drops on the shade of his bedside table lamp. It was even on the floor. He looked at himself and saw that it was on his skin, too. It wasn't just a few drops, either; it was all over him. Where it had dried, it had crusted. He scratched a few flecks off his thigh.

Robert made a recollection and instinctively touched his throat and collarbone. His fingers had no trouble locating the laceration. It was sensitive to touch, leaving his fingertips slightly pink and damp, still raw.

He climbed out of bed. The muscles in his legs quivered and he ached all over. He checked himself in the bathroom mirror. His body was blotchy where the stains had sunk into the skin. He splashed cold water over himself and rubbed the marks vigorously. He rinsed his mouth out and returned to the bedroom. The bed looked like a sacrificial altar. Robert saw the chain on Rachel's bedside table. He picked it up and examined it. It was silver and on the end of it there was a tiny blade in the shape of a cross. There was a miniature scabbard for the blade itself, which lay beside it. The silver was bloodied.

He pulled on a pair of trousers and went in search of Rachel, clutching the tiny blade in his hand. He found her in the drawing-room. She sat on an antique chair, by one of the open windows. Between her thighs was the cello's bulky body. Her right hand ran the bow and her left hand skipped up and down the neck. When he awoke, he'd naturally assumed he was listening to a recording.

Her skin was cream and her hair was clean, shining in the hazy sunlight that spilled into the drawing-room through the open french windows. Rachel saw him in the doorway, stopped playing and smiled. She wore a navy dress with white spots on it.

"I thought you were a beginner," said Robert.

"I am."

"But you could be a professional."

"Thank you."

"I'm serious."

"Well, I had an excellent teacher."

Robert frowned. "Like in your painting?"

"Exactly."

Robert knew he was missing something. She rested the cello on its side and came over to kiss him.

"How do you feel?" she asked.

"I feel . . . better," replied Robert. "Better and . . ."

"Confused?" she prompted him. "I know what you're thinking."

"You do?"

She took hold of the hand clutching the blood-encrusted blade and held it up between them. "Yes, I do."

"Can you blame me?"

"It's not a question of blame."

She ran a hand round his neck and through his hair.

"Listen, this isn't . . ."

"I had to have you," she whispered. "I had to taste you."

"*What?*"

"I had to taste you. Your blood. I had to. I . . ." Her eyes looked away from him and she was temporarily lost. The dreamy quality lingered for a few seconds and then vanished when she turned back to him. "Besides, it's only a scratch."

"*Only a scratch?*" spluttered Robert. "Have you seen the amount of blood on your bed?"

"That's not you. That's me."

She raised her right arm and there was a faint trace of a cut halfway between the wrist and the elbow. Robert was out of his league and he knew it. He just shrugged uselessly and said, "What?"

"We're both cut."

"All that blood from a tiny scratch like that?"

"I'm a quick healer. Believe me, it's deeper than it looks."

Like everything else she said or did, it seemed to make no sense. And yet despite it all, he was still there and in no rush to leave. "But why?"

Rachel said, "You had to taste me, too. I wanted you to. I *needed* you to, darling. You'll think I'm crazy, I know, but it was important."

He didn't understand. Naturally. He didn't even need to say so. She knew it.

"The fingers in your mouth?" she reminded him. "You ought to remember that. You almost choked."

"They were . . . ?"

"That's right. They were covered in it."

Robert just stood there with his jaw hanging down. When it looked as though he was about to speak, Rachel put a finger on his lips. "Don't say anything. Leave it."

Logic demanded that he run but Robert felt no danger. Nor even a particular sense of disgust. There was an overflow of curiosity, it was true, but there was no repulsion. He wanted answers and he wanted to stay.

When she offered him a shower, he accepted. He stood for several minutes under intense needles of hot water before cooling the temperature. He stepped out and wrapped a heavy towel around his waist. The face that stared back at him in the mirror seemed to have regained some of its vitality.

When Robert returned to the bedroom, he found Rachel drawing the curtains. She pointed at the bed.

"Look. Fresh sheets."

The sheets looked hotel crisp.

He said, "Tell me something. Why were you at Seven of Hearts last night?"

"Why were *you* there?" she countered. "You obviously didn't belong there. I could tell you were miserable."

"I was badgered into it. It was less hassle to go along than to make a scene about it."

"Well, you know why I was there. I was following you. I was waiting for you. You don't believe me, do you?"

Robert shrugged in frustration and said, "I don't understand."

"Not yet, but you will."

She moved away from the window and stood directly between him and the bed. Without a word, she drew her dress over her head and dropped it to the floor. She stood naked before him and allowed daylight to reveal her true beauty. Her skin was pale and smooth, really flawless. As for her dark eyes, they were utterly captivating. Her passport may have stated that they were brown but they looked more like tar than chocolate.

She stepped forward and laid her fingers on his stomach. He didn't believe she would harm him. Enslaved by what he saw, he believed her to be a risk worth taking.

"No knives, please," he murmured.

"No knives, I promise," she said.

She tugged at the knot of the towel and it gave way. Robert felt the coarse material brushing his legs as it fell to the floor. Rachel wondered how he would have reacted had he seen her in the dark, her mouth streaming with their mingled blood. She'd looked like an animal after the kill; her prey hunted, slaughtered, ripped and devoured. The sensation of their hot blood turning their skins slippery had been divine. The dark had concealed the truth. And she'd known that by the time morning came, it wouldn't make any difference anyway. She was in paradise.

Rachel kissed him and said, "Last night was the thrill of my life. Thanks."

Chapter Ten

They met at a café which would have looked better between two palm trees on the Nice waterfront and not between a branch of Boots and a closed travel agent's store in West London. Richard Elmore had selected a table near the back and was eating a croissant when Chris and Katherine arrived. The flaky pastry had spread across most of the paper tablecloth. He took a loud slurp from his cup of coffee and summoned a waiter whose surly attitude at least lent some French authenticity to the place.

Chris introduced Katherine before they sat down. Elmore rose unsteadily to his feet and said, "I'm very sorry about what happened to your sister, Miss Ross."

"Please call me Katherine," she said, shaking his hand and then sitting to his right.

"Has Chris told you about me?"

"A little."

Chris added, "I've also given her a basic outline of what we deal with."

"What *you* deal with," insisted Elmore, before lowering his vast bulk back to the sitting position. "He's a scientist, you see, whereas I am nothing more than a retired adventurer."

Chris permitted himself a wry smile. "I'm no scientist and I don't recall you ever retiring."

Katherine and Chris ordered breakfast and Elmore asked for more coffee. He paused until the waiter had retreated before speaking again, directing most of what he had to say towards Katherine.

"The important thing to remember about the people we study is that they have an illness. They are sick. That is the basic fact and it is useful to remind oneself of this when all the other information conspires to confuse. Now, I'm no expert in haematology, but I do know that the chemical properties of this disease are quite extraordinary; Chris's friends in Seattle would be able to give you all the data you could ever want. However, far more interesting to me are the symptoms and side-effects. Weight loss is common, as is a drastic drop in blood pressure. Most victims are anaemic and more than half of them have trouble digesting solids. Yet peculiarly, both vision and hearing tend to be dramatically improved, and often to levels beyond those we would normally consider perfectly healthy. Another symptom is a tendency towards emotional volatility; violent mood swings are commonplace."

The waiter reappeared with breakfast. Elmore sat back while the man pushed a basket of croissants towards the centre of the table, next to a fresh pot of coffee.

Katherine reached for a glass of orange juice and asked, "How is it contracted?"

"We have no idea. At least, I assume we don't, unless the people at Koptet have made some progress of which I'm unaware," he said, turning to Chris.

"No, we haven't."

"It's just as well it isn't contagious, otherwise we'd be in serious trouble. There is no cure."

Chris said, "Given what it does to the blood, we're unlikely to find one, either. At least, not in the near to medium term future."

Elmore poured himself another cup of coffee. "The strangest symptom of this disorder – by a very great margin – is the ability to detect it in others. Those who are infected by the disease can *feel* it in other sufferers."

"That's impossible," said Katherine.

"To our way of thinking, it is. But it's a reality nevertheless. Of course, the complaint is so rare that it would be quite possible – even probable – to go through life never encountering another sufferer. But when they do come across each other, they know."

"So who are these people? What do we call them? What is their disease?"

"It doesn't have a name," said Chris. "We only have a project reference number for it. But around my lab, the disorder is sometimes referred to as Elmore's Syndrome."

The old man smiled and had clearly heard this before. Katherine let their private joke slide. Elmore said, "There is a young man here in London who suffers from the complaint. Stephen Abraham, a sculptor."

Chris frowned momentarily and then nodded. "Yes, he's on our directory in Seattle."

"I should hope so," said Elmore.

"What about him?" asked Katherine.

"He wants to see me."

"So?"

"He's not the social type. I haven't had any contact with him for ages. So when he called me out of the blue and demanded to see me, my curiosity was aroused. It could be a coincidence of timing, but I very much doubt it. He sounded flustered."

Katherine shrugged irritably. "I don't get it."

Elmore nodded. "No, you wouldn't. To understand the significance of this, you have to understand a little about Stephen Abraham. He's a strange man with an over-active imagination and an inactive sense of humility. Panic is not something I would expect to associate with him. Even if he felt it, I'm sure he would usually make an attempt to disguise it. It's in his nature, and yet his unease was quite clear. Having said that, I have to treat Abraham with caution. It's important to be careful about taking him at face value. He is arrogant, self-important and quite often abusive. As often as not, he'll lie rather than tell the truth, simply because it amuses him to, or perhaps because he considers the truth boring."

"What did he want?"

"He wouldn't say, which is typical of him, I'm afraid. His

capacity for melodrama can be excessively tedious. Nevertheless, he is the genuine article and under our current circumstances, I think we should at least see him. So I have arranged a meeting."

"What are you expecting to learn from him?"

"I have no idea," he said, in a fashion which convinced Katherine that he did have an idea, but that he was not going to reveal it. "On the other hand, what have we got to lose?"

Laura picked Deep Waters in South Audley Street. It was her favourite restaurant and since she was taking Robert to lunch, she figured she might as well test the elasticity of her company expense account. A waiter brought a couple of Martinis and they ordered. Laura lit a cigarette and took a sip from her drink.

"God, I needed that!" she sighed, replacing her glass on the table.

"Nose to the grindstone?"

"Like you wouldn't believe. Did you know that in Marseille, there are . . . ?"

Laura spouted statistics and theories. Robert found his attention wandering. He thought about Rachel and how she offered herself up to him and how he accepted, gorging himself on her. And he thought about the vicious silver blade on the bedside table. He hadn't been aware of tasting her blood. By the time she forced her fingers into his mouth, his taste buds had been knocked out by a variety of heady flavours.

It was a perverted weapon; a crucifix as a blade.

She hinted she was a novice with the knife. Robert wanted to believe her, but she'd done him so expertly that he had his doubts. Maybe it was beginner's luck.

Rachel never spoke of family history and friends or, indeed, of any of her background. He didn't know how she passed her days. She could have been a top-class hooker, except no whore's purse could pay for her apartment at Lennox Gardens, he decided. She might be a mistress to a wealthy businessman, or a major criminal. But it wasn't her style. She wouldn't be a mistress to a criminal, no matter how successful. Similarly, she wouldn't be impressed by some flabby champion of global business. So who would she be impressed with? And what on earth was she doing with Robert? She could have had virtually anyone she chose. Instead, she took to bed the caretaker from her apartment block. It didn't make a bit of sense to him.

"Robert? *Robert?*"

He looked down and saw monkfish in a peppercorn sauce on his plate. Laura stubbed out her cigarette. "Have you listened to a word I've said?"

"Sorry. I was, I was . . ."

Laura was waiting for an answer. She sat back. All the diners at Deep Waters spoke with hushed voices, hunched over their tables. Most were discussing business.

"Look at these twats!" she complained. "They come here and eat some of the best fish in this city and they don't even notice. They don't taste, they don't relax, they don't even look at the bill, they just sit and talk percentages. Fucking maggots!"

"Laura!" protested Robert, under his breath.

"Oh what?"

Robert said nothing, hoping his look would explain.

"*What?*" she said. "I mean, why shouldn't I? Look at them. A dickless congregation, if ever I saw one. Incidentally, you look fucking dreadful. Are you ill?"

"You don't want to know the details."

"Maybe you should see a doctor."

"It's nothing serious."

"Have you looked in a mirror today? It *looks* serious!"

Laura paid the bill, saying it was a crime to charge so much, but since Harding Rock were paying, she didn't care.

Robert walked home in the searing heat of London's streets. The pavements were littered with overflowing dustbins and mountains of rubbish bags, all waiting for disposal. Everything smelt strong. The grass in Hyde Park was turning light brown. Green was fading from the city. He walked down

Park Lane, which was completely congested, and took a short cut through Wilton Crescent. Opposite the Berkeley, there was a tramp filtering through the trash that was vomiting out of a split rubbish bag.

He bought a copy of the *Evening Standard*. There she was. Sarah was still front page news, even now she was buried. The newspaper claimed there was a link between her murder and the double killing of Jennifer Colson and André Perlman at the Cadogan Hotel. He'd known there was something going on when he caught out Detective Constable Kevin Malloy. That had been confirmed by the obvious lies of Harold Daley, which Robert saw on the television.

He looked forward to returning to the sanctuary of his own flat. As it turned out, he barely recognized it when he stepped through the door.

Rachel must have been through the place in a raging storm. She'd done months of hard physical labour in a couple of hours. The kitchen was no longer a hygiene risk. Plates and cutlery sparkled in the drying rack. The sink was clean, the plughole clear of unidentifiable waste. She hadn't actually rearranged the contents of his kitchen cupboards, but she'd cleaned all of the poison out of the fridge. Robert usually prided himself on having a fuller fridge than anyone he knew. But now that the out-of-date milk cartons and the condensation-dampened plastic bags of rotting vegetables had been removed, it looked practically bare. The chilly beers remained, along with two lonely-looking packs of butter in the fridge door, but there was little else. She'd even got rid of the smell.

Robert's bedroom was a revelation. The carpet greeted him like a long lost friend. The clothes which usually denied its existence were either piled neatly on a chair, or hanging in his cupboard, or even folded in his drawers. His bed was made. The bathroom was as ruthlessly spotless as an operating theatre. The sitting-room was fit to usher people into. There were no crushed beer cans lurking in a corner, masquerading as abstract art. The overflowing bins of crumpled paper had been emptied. It looked like she'd used polish on the tables.

Where did she find that? In *his* flat? It was a mystery to Robert. She'd left him a note.

Robert –

it doesn't seem fair that you're the only one who has to clean up for others. I thought I'd show solidarity! I hope you don't mind the intrusion – it was done with the best intentions. Just being in your flat makes me miss you all the more. So when you feel the urge, come upstairs and put me out of my misery,

R.

Robert folded the paper carefully, even though it was nothing more than a scrawled note, and put it away in a desk, where he knew it would not be discarded absentmindedly. She was a strange girl. Strange but wonderful. Making love with her was definitely a slice of heaven. On the subject of slices, he had to admit that the knife had been painful at the time, but progressively exciting in retrospect.

She had been so beautiful in the morning, when bathed in daylight. He wondered where she had come from. What was she doing? She was inviting and enticing. And unnerving. When Rachel thrilled Robert, she scared him.

Richard Elmore wiped the sweat from his forehead with a sail-sized claret handkerchief. His jowls rippled as the cab bounced over the treacherous roads, all scarred by a history of roadworks. Katherine wore a man's cream coloured shirt, rolled up at the sleeves. Chris liked the way it looked on her.

The taxi was edging down the Portobello Road. A few small, fashionable bistros were already doing brisk business in the early evening, beneath a daffodil sky. Two antiques dealers were chatting on the pavement outside their neighbouring shops. There was an old woman with an accordion, propped up on a bench outside a pub. She was playing hideously.

Stephen Abraham lived just off the Portobello Road in a handsome four-storey house. He opened the front door, nodded at Elmore and said to Chris, "You must be Lang."

"That's right."

"So who the hell are you?" he asked Katherine, before turning back to Elmore. "You said just two. You and him."

"Does it make a difference?"

Abraham looked more emaciated than when Elmore had last seen him. He had lost some weight and this was most obviously reflected in his face, which had become progressively angular and gaunt. The skin, however, remained unnaturally clear. It was almost as if from birth to adulthood it had never been exposed to the harsh effects of sunlight or pollution. There were no signs of ageing, not a single wrinkle or blemish. It was so pale it had a blue tinge to it. Elmore noticed Katherine staring at Abraham and was not surprised.

When Abraham returned her gaze she snapped out of her daze and spoke up. "I have an interest. My name's Katherine Ross. Jennifer Colson was my sister."

The irritation disappeared from Abraham's face and was replaced by curiosity, and then excitement. He turned to Elmore. "Is this true?"

"It is."

He smiled. "Well, you'd better come in, then."

Elmore picked up on the mood swing. A couple of moments ago Abraham had been sufficiently agitated for Elmore to suspect he might ask them to leave. Now he looked like a six-year-old at a birthday party.

Stephen Abraham had a dark house. Lights were low and the decoration was gloomy. Dark greens, darker blues and the darkest reds. Shades were pulled and heavy curtains drawn. The first floor was given over entirely to his sculpture.

The climb up the stairs left Elmore breathless in the stifling heat. He reached for the wall and placed his hand against the navy plaster. Abraham peeled his gaze off Katherine and laid it upon Elmore. "You're not in very good shape, are you, old man?"

The closest sculptures were tortured: skeletons of twisted metal soldered together with ugly joints, draped in sheets of sapphire silk and emerald satin, which were stretched tightly over the frames and then strategically torn by barbed wire and rusting razor-blades.

Elmore saw the distaste in Katherine's expression and said, "As I was telling you, Stephen is a sculptor of some renown."

"Not enough," said Abraham. "But then they know nothing."

"What's it all for?" asked Chris, gesticulating towards the collection in his studio.

"It's a project which I'll be previewing next month. The title is Breaking Skin. That's the theme which unites each piece."

Chris couldn't see any unity at all. Some were plaster-moulded. There was a soapstone horse's head which had been finished to a beautiful, smooth shine. The wood carvings were crude, still sharp and chiselled. A bronze octopus-like creation spread its scarred tentacles over a third of the pine floorboards, out towards a section of the floor that was covered in dark blotches and the stellar-shaped explosions of single drops.

"Breaking Skin?" Chris queried.

Elmore glanced at Katherine and Chris before looking back at Abraham. The sculptor's weakness for an empty, dramatic statement remained undiminished. Evidently he milked some pleasure from the act, while he watched Chris mulling over the title and the pieces.

"I know, I know," sighed Abraham with theatrical weariness. "It's a little obvious for you and I, but to the public at large . . . who knows what they'll make of it? That's the delicious part of what I do: watching the so-called experts making fools of themselves trying to interpret the pieces. I expect some self-important arsehole will conclude that Breaking Skin is a metaphor for the collapse of Communism or the rise of neo-Nazism or some such nonsense."

"And it is, in fact, what?"

Abraham grinned. "It's the first instalment of my autobiography."

Elmore found his patience beginning to wear slightly thin. At least Abraham was being relatively civil. In the past, there had been meetings where he veered wildly from uncontrollable tantrum to whispered, trite confession, before embarking on another tantrum. As a rule, Elmore had found that the more colourful encounters were the least informative.

On one wall was a series of large portraits of a beautiful woman. They were done in charcoal and crayon, a variety of paints, ink and pencil. Different sizes, different poses, same model. In front of them stood a rough block of marble. She had only been half-released from the stone.

"I like that," said Katherine.

Abraham folded his arms across his chest and nodded sagely as he gazed fondly at the stone. "That's not part of the exhibition. That's a private commission."

They rose to the top floor, where there was a small roof garden. Inside, by the open windows, stood a wooden table with a tray on it. There were glasses and a bottle of champagne in an ice-bucket. Abraham popped the cork and poured for them. He wore black trousers and a black silk polo-neck. He pushed the sleeves up to the elbow. Katherine noticed the power in the forearms. It was an incredible structure of sinews, moving like a maze of mechanical cables, like some Heath Robinson cyborg.

They stepped onto the roof garden which overlooked the intersection between Abraham's street and the Portobello Road. The brightness of the warm sun was a welcome contrast to the studied gloom of the house's interior.

Elmore noticed Abraham stealing repeated glances at Katherine. He saw the hungry look in the sculptor's eyes. If he was right about Abraham, then Katherine's presence – she being the sister of Jennifer Colson – would certainly appeal to him. At the very least, he would find it a delicious irony and perhaps something more.

Elmore said, "You called this meeting, Mr Abraham. What's on your mind?"

Abraham looked out across west London and replied, "I could never go to the police. They wouldn't understand. It would just bring me trouble. That's why I had to call you. I need to be taken seriously, I need to be listened to."

"We've been out of touch for quite a while."

"Sure, but you know the truth. You probably know why I asked you here, otherwise you wouldn't have brought these two. Especially her."

Elmore felt a lurch in his stomach, a sensation that used to be commonplace but which had generally been absent during the blander days of his most recent years. Katherine looked tense too.

Abraham said, "Can I trust you?"

Elmore nodded. "Of course. And you can trust Chris too. He works on this subject in America. He knows everything about you."

This seemed to amuse Abraham momentarily, who turned to Chris with a sly half-smile. "Do you? Do you really?"

"I've studied your case. It makes fascinating reading."

This attempt to appeal to Abraham's ego seemed to hit the mark. Elmore had previously suggested that pandering to Abraham's vanity was likely to make him more amenable. On the other hand, there was an air about him which Elmore had not encountered before. From one extreme mood to another, the one thing that usually remained constant was his self-confidence. It was almost as if he viewed his rare condition as a mark of excellence, something that made him superior to the rest of humanity. But that arrogance was missing and although Abraham still strutted, genuine doubt seemed to lurk just beneath the surface.

Elmore said, "What's wrong?"

He looked across the neighbouring roof-tops and said quietly, "I know who killed André Perlman and Jennifer Colson."

Elmore resisted the urge to blurt "Who?" and instead

looked across at the other two, who were trading anxious glances. Abraham turned round to face his audience and let his gaze fall upon Katherine, as he added, "It's true. I know who killed your sister."

The silence was stunning, until Elmore asked, "And what about Sarah Reynolds?"

Abraham nodded. "Her as well, yes."

It was Chris who succumbed to obvious temptation and asked the vital question, "Who did it?"

Abraham pulled an anguished face. "That's the problem. I can't tell you."

"Why not?"

Elmore was intrigued by Abraham's behaviour. He had never seen the sculptor so unsettled. Katherine was too shocked to do anything but sit still and stare.

"Because something's stopping me."

Chris looked at Elmore who asked, "What is it?"

He looked up from his shoes and said, "If I tell you, I'm dead. It's that simple."

Chapter Eleven

Robert sat up in bed. He could still feel the heat of the puppy's blood on his fingers and the waves of fear coming from Laura. His threats were so vile. Robert felt Rachel's arms coming around his shoulders and hugging him.

"Don't worry," she said. "You were just dreaming."

"I know, but it was so real. I was at this party. I think we were celebrating Johnny's birthday, but it wasn't at the Middle Kingdom."

"The Middle Kingdom?"

"It's a Chinese place in Bayswater. It's where he had his birthday party recently. Instead, we were in some huge hall with a chequered floor, like a giant chessboard. It was crowded and we were wearing black tie. Laura was there and she wore an emerald dress which looked brilliant against her copper hair. She gave me a puppy as a present, even though it was Johnny's birthday." Robert stopped and looked up at Rachel. "Why did she do that?"

Rachel smiled. "I don't know. What happened?"

"I tore it to pieces."

Robert frowned while he thought about it, as though he were checking that the memory was correct. Then he nodded slowly. "Yes. I did and I promised to do the same to Laura."

Rachel wasn't concerned with the dog. "Who's Laura?"

"She's a friend of mine. And the look on her face . . . I don't know. Her fear was real."

Rachel tickled Robert's ear and ran her other hand

up and down his spine. She planted light kisses on his face.

"You're awake now," she said, softly. "You know it was a dream. It's natural."

"It wasn't natural, believe me."

She brushed her lips over his. "Don't worry, darling. It *is* natural. You'll get used to it."

Robert leaned slightly back and looked her in the eye. "What are you talking about?"

She took her time answering. Eventually, she said, "Now that you've had it once, it won't be such a shock if it happens again, will it? Nightmares – even vivid ones – are natural. Everybody has them, it's just that some people get them worse than others."

He nodded slowly and said, "I guess you're right."

Rachel said, "I know I'm right."

A thought occurred to Robert, but he dismissed it quickly. It was too paranoid. Rachel kissed his neck and throat. Her fingers left sensitive trails of excitement on his skin, the pleasure lingering like vapour trails across a cloudless sky.

"Kiss me," she commanded him.

Robert took her face in both hands and moved his mouth close to hers.

"Not there," she purred. "Lower."

The attack came without warning. They were down in his flat. He was showing her old photographs. Robert always found other people's photo albums a yawn-inducing experience but Rachel appeared genuinely engrossed, lapping up every detail in a fashion he found almost disturbing. She pored over every faded shot, asking questions and paying full attention to his answers.

It started in the stomach. A sharp pinpoint of pain which made him sit up straight. He caught his breath and it passed. He turned over another leaf in the album and Rachel kissed him on the cheek. As she cast her gaze towards the photographs, something erupted inside him. He would have screamed fully if his lungs had found the air to fuel such a noise.

"Robert!" exclaimed Rachel, as he slipped from the sofa to the carpet, squirming with every new twist of misery.

"Help me!" he muttered hoarsely, his teeth grinding against the burning sensation which fried every nerve.

"Where is it?"

"Everywhere."

"Where did it start?" she asked, kneeling beside him and cradling his flinching form in her arms.

"In the . . . in the . . . stomach." His breaths became shallower as the pain of breathing became greater. "A doctor," he hissed, "call a doctor."

Rachel rose from the floor and disappeared from the room. She returned brandishing a soaking tea-towel which dribbled water onto the carpet.

"Here. Hold this against your stomach."

"What is it?"

"It's a tea-towel I've wrapped around some ice cubes."

"Ice?" he protested.

"Just do it," she ordered him. "I know what I'm doing."

It didn't sound like it. It went against conventional wisdom, he thought. He held his breath as he pressed the icy, sodden towel onto the flesh of his stinging stomach. It made him wince. Rachel pressed her hand over the wet material to ensure contact was maintained. It didn't take long. The coldness seemed to draw the pain out.

"I'm beginning to feel better," he muttered.

"See? You should have more faith in me, Robert."

Rachel smiled and stayed with him. The aching ceased and his vision cleared. She fussed over him and he liked it. "What would I do without you?"

"You seem to have survived up to now."

"Ah, but you never miss what you don't know, do you?"

She moved her head from side to side. "Maybe, maybe not,

but you'd better be careful. Any more talk like that and you might start sounding like the settling-down type."

He smiled. "And would that be such a crime?"

"Not necessarily, but I'm not sure it would suit you."

"Why not?"

"Oh, I don't know," she said, casually, strolling towards the window. "I thought you might turn out to be the sort who wouldn't settle down until he was thirty-five and rich enough to have four mistresses, three houses, two boats and a plane."

Rachel looked across the room at Robert, who was slumped on the sofa. Part of her felt sorry for him. She wanted to put him out of his misery, but it was too soon for that.

"I used to think that," he confessed, "when I was a little younger and a little less practical."

"I see."

"Besides, the chances of me even owning a second-hand car by the time I'm thirty-five are no brighter than they were when I was twenty-five."

Rachel smiled sympathetically. "I'm glad you've changed your point of view."

"It sounds as though you're about to propose," Robert told her.

"Not yet!" she laughed. "A few good orgasms is hardly the basis for a permanent future, is it?"

"People have committed on less."

"And usually they've paid for it."

"True," he said, as she came and sat beside him.

They kissed.

Robert said, "I feel much better now. But then I always feel better when I'm around you."

She slapped him playfully on the arm.

"I'm serious," he insisted. "I feel physically better when I'm around you."

The humour vanished from her face. She considered his words and then simply said, "Good."

He was also slow to say anything. "You call that good?"

"Yes. If that's really how you feel, stay with me."

She was sincere. He took a deep breath and said, "What do you want from me?"

Rachel moved closer, put a hand on his cheek and let her mouth hover inches above his. She said, "All of you," before kissing him.

That was when Laura appeared.

"Robert, I came just as . . . oh!"

She stopped in the centre of the room as Rachel coolly detached herself from Robert and rose to standing. Robert scrambled to his feet and tugged at his untucked shirt. Rachel and Laura looked each other up and down. Robert could feel the instant mutual animosity. Rachel smiled politely, extending a hand.

"How do you do? I'm Rachel."

Laura shook hands, grudgingly.

Rachel looked so superior and composed, especially compared to Laura who was flustered and hot, having battled across half of London. Rachel's smile was kind. The power she exuded, which bordered arrogance, wasn't visible, but Robert and Laura both felt it, running through the hot air like an icy breeze. She turned to Robert.

"I have to go now. I will see you later."

The way she said it did not make it sound like a possibility or a hope. It was definitely a statement of irrefutable fact. Laura hardly waited for the footsteps to fade before asking, "And who is she?"

"Rachel Cates. She lives in the first-floor flat."

"What the hell is she doing down here?"

"What is this, Laura?"

She gave him her sourest look. "You don't know?"

"No, I don't."

She shook her head in a sad way. "Look at you, Robert," she sighed. "You're a mess. You're in even worse shape than you were the other day at Deep Waters. You look like bloody death and you're still going to tell me there's nothing wrong?"

"What's this got to do with Rachel?"

"I don't know. Maybe you could tell me."

He looked at her blankly. "I don't know what you're talking about, Laura. Honestly."

"Then you ought to see a doctor."

"There's no need for . . ."

"Yes there is! I don't know how you feel, but if it's half as bad as you look, you should be in intensive care."

"Thanks a lot."

"For Christ's sake, Robert! I'm worried about you. I've been worried about you since I last saw you. That's why I came over. You may be healthy enough to kiss what's-her-name, but that's about all, by the look of it."

"So that's what this is about," he concluded.

"No! *No!* It's not about her," Laura insisted. "It's about you, Robert. You've got to see a doctor. You've got to promise me."

He held his hands up in surrender. "I promise."

Although Laura had made him promise to see a doctor, she needn't have. He was sufficiently worried to make the effort himself.

"Well, I don't think there's very much wrong with you," was Dr Rebecca Foster's verdict, as she removed her glasses and sat back in her chair.

She was a big-boned Irish woman in her early thirties, with thick curly hair. She shared her surgery with three other doctors. It was full of tissue-thin carpets and plastic units in avocado and grey that were easy to wipe down.

"You do look very tired," she told him. "You should certainly try and get some rest."

"Of course I'm tired! I'm bloody exhausted! My body feels like it's made out of lead."

His appointment had been for nine-thirty and he'd been stuck in a waiting-room designed for midgets until ten past ten. There was no reasonable ventilation in there, so the sick could trade viruses with consummate ease. Even in winter, it was over-heated. Robert was positive that if he wasn't seriously ill when he arrived, he certainly would be by the time he left.

Dr Foster asked questions that were designed to deflect, not to probe. He listed all his symptoms and she wasn't even interested. Perhaps she thought he was a hypochondriac. She seemed to believe that sleep was the universal panacea. Robert didn't share her enthusiasm for this.

"And that's going to cure me, is it? If I came in here with a pair of shattered knee-caps, I suppose you'd give me a Band Aid and an aspirin, would you?"

"And what would you like me to do?"

"I don't know. A blood test, perhaps? Something."

"And what should this blood test be for? HIV?"

"How should I know? That's your job."

"Would you like an HIV test? Perhaps it might be a good . . ."

"I'm not interested in an AIDS test! I just want to know what I've got and get rid of it!"

Robert left the surgery exasperated by her lack of interest and sympathy. He walked back to Lennox Gardens, feeling low in the muggy morning.

Did Rachel know what was happening to him? That's what Laura was implying. Maybe she had a point. It didn't take a genius to see that Rachel was toying with him. When he was around her, he felt fine and as soon as they were parted, he began to deteriorate. At first, he thought he was imagining things, then he thought it was something psychosomatic, but now he didn't believe that, either. It was something more fundamental.

He still couldn't figure out where she picked up her information from. She knew things about his past that were impossible to know without actually being there. Sarah was the only possible key. But even if Rachel had known Sarah, which he doubted, there were things which Sarah wouldn't have confessed to anyone. He was sure of it. And without Sarah, what other access was there? At first, he thought he was being paranoid, but not any more. She had a route into his past.

She also had a route into his heart. Robert could put up less and less resistance to her. He knew it was ridiculous, but that didn't make any difference. He tried to keep a tight hold on the reins because the memory of a previous experience still counted for something. The more he allowed himself to fall for Rachel, the greater the risk of being shot down. Sarah Reynolds had taught him plenty about humiliation's excruciating properties and it had been a crushing experience.

He was coming down the stairs when he heard it. It wasn't loud but the sound was clear enough as he set foot on the second-floor landing. It was crying and soft whispers. The front door of the Lorenzo flat was slightly ajar.

He pushed the door open. Cassie Lorenzo was sitting on the floor in the hall, with her back to the wall. The two children were in attendance, their arms around the mother's shoulders. Even the dog, Nixon, seemed concerned, sitting attentively by her ankles. It saw Robert first and snarled softly. All three looked up at Robert. Cassie was wearing sunglasses, but Robert could see the tears on her cheeks.

"I'm sorry," he said. "But the door was open and I heard..."

She disentangled herself from her protective children and rose to her feet, trying in vain to smooth out the creases in her linen skirt. The apprehensive children continued to clutch her. Cassie addressed Kevin.

"Take Melissa into the sitting-room. Go watch some TV."

"No!" he protested.

"Go on, you two," she insisted. "I need to talk to Robert."

They departed, reluctantly. The pug stayed by Cassie, looking up at her.

"Mrs Lorenzo," started Robert, "I didn't mean to intrude but, like I said, the door was open. You could have been burgled and I thought..."

"It's all right, Robert."

He could see she was shaking slightly. She raised a hand and held the back of it against her forehead. Robert stepped forward and took her by the arm.

"Are you all right?" he asked.

"I just feel a little . . . light-headed. I need to get myself together."

He caught sight of their drawing-room. It was a mess. There was an armchair on its back and a broken lamp by the fireplace. They went into her kitchen. There was clutter, signs of a regular domestic existence. A notepad was tacked to the wall with a child's fragmented drawing on the top sheet. Scribbled reminders were pinned to the fridge door by magnetic tags. There was a Snoopy clock above the microwave and a picture of Kevin standing on a beach with a Chicago Bears cap sitting on his head.

As she moved around the kitchen, Robert saw what the glasses tried to conceal. She had a bruise around the left eye. It hadn't been there when Robert last saw her, less than twenty-four hours ago.

"What happened?"

She sat on a wooden chair and started to cry, still retaining enough composure to keep her sobbing quiet so that she wouldn't trouble her children any more. Robert stood above her and felt helpless. She looked ridiculous, cupping her face into her hands but still shedding tears into her sunglasses. Robert reached down and removed them. She regained control of herself and wiped her eyes with some kitchen towel which she tore off a roller. The bruise was vicious, a collage of purple and blue.

"I'm sorry, Robert," she said in a drained voice.

"Are you okay?"

"I will be."

"Who did it?"

She looked up at him and whispered, hoarsely, "Can't you guess?"

Vernon Lorenzo had made a habit of being thoroughly unpleasant to Robert, whenever an opportunity presented itself. As a result, Robert disliked him intensely. However, for some reason, Robert never suspected him of being anything other than a model husband and father. Maybe this was because Cassie and the children always appeared so sweet-natured and well-adjusted. Despite Vernon, Robert had come to regard the Lorenzo family as something approaching the perfect model.

"Why?" asked Robert, not really expecting an answer.

"He's having an affair," she sighed, wearily. "And when I confronted him ... well, we had a row and then the children were . . . it turned into a fight and then this."

She ran her fingers over the dark blemish on her face before flicking several locks of blonde hair out of her eyes.

"Where is he?"

"At work. As usual."

"Is there something I can do? I don't know, do you want the police or . . . ?"

"No!" she interrupted, urgently. "No way, Robert! You've got to promise you won't . . ."

"It was just a suggestion."

"It's happened before and we've always managed to . . ."

The look on her face showed how much she regretted letting the words slip.

"For how long?"

She shook her head, sadly. "Long enough for me to know how to cope with it," she assured him.

"But what about Kevin and Melissa?"

"They're protected. Mostly, it doesn't get that far." She looked up and there was determination in her face. "It's just the way it is, Robert. Besides, I'd never let him harm the children. So long as they're safe, then . . ."

"But it doesn't have to be like this, Mrs Lorenzo. You could . . ."

"No, Robert," she said, firmly. "You don't understand. You have to promise me you won't say a word about this to anyone."

"But . . ."

"You've got to promise! If it ever gets back to Vernon, he'll go mad. If you won't make the promise for me, then do it for Kevin and Melissa. Please!"

Robert shrugged. "Whatever you say. But if ever you need me, you call me."

Cassie looked up and managed to find a feeble smile. She touched him on the hand and said, "Thanks, Robert."

Chapter Twelve

Richard Elmore peeled the lids off several Chinese takeaway cartons. Katherine looked out of Elmore's drawing-room window. In the street below, someone was trying to turn an old Ford Capri's engine, using jump leads hooked up to a rusting lime Toyota.

Earlier in the afternoon, she'd met Caroline Taylor. Chris had asked her to speak to anyone – anyone at all – who might be able to point them in a likely direction. Caroline Taylor had been a friend of Jennifer's since they were children. Now she was married to a lawyer and had a pair of children of her own. Katherine hadn't really known what to ask her and Caroline had treated her with pity, which was embarrassing. But worse than that, Caroline Taylor knew about Jennifer's affair with André Perlman. She'd even met him.

"What was he like?" Katherine asked.

"Charming, Kathy. Absolutely charming. He was only twenty-four, but he had a sort of . . ." Her attention drifted for a moment. "An older man's calm and composure, I suppose. Jenny was completely infatuated with him. I'd never seen her so animated. I'm surprised you never met him."

"So am I," said Katherine, dryly. "I didn't even know about him."

"Really? I thought you and Jennifer shared everything."

Katherine smiled bitterly. "So did I."

"She used to say there wasn't a secret between you."

"That's what I thought. And she was in love with him?"

"Oh, yes. That was quite obvious. And in a way she never

managed with David. She was deliriously happy, Kathy. I'm not just saying this because of what's happened. She really was in love with him."

That, at least, made Katherine feel a little better. Jennifer never hurt anyone and her exceptional tolerance of David Colson remained a model of dignity in adversity. Even when his adulterous exploits were at their cheapest and seamiest, she never resorted to tabloid behaviour.

She turned round. Chris was pouring wine into three glasses. Elmore was in the kitchen fetching plates and forks.

She said, "So what's the idea?"

Chris handed her a glass. "Abraham comes along to see if he recognizes someone."

"And if he does, then what?"

Elmore, who had returned from the kitchen, said, "We'll cross that bridge when we come to it."

Katherine said, "Do we believe him?"

Elmore shrugged. "Like I told you, one has to be cautious about taking Abraham at face value. But this I can tell you: his behaviour was completely at odds with how he normally is. His customary self-confidence – his arrogance – was not there. True, there were a few occasions when he tried to put it on but it was a bad act. He was genuinely frightened."

Elmore had been impressed by Katherine's composure. Once Abraham had confessed to knowing the killer's identity, Elmore supposed that she wouldn't allow him to keep it quiet so easily. Maybe she understood what kind of creature the sculptor really was. She had not pressed him, unlike Chris, who had quickly become exasperated at Abraham's reluctance to share his secret. His fractious enquiries had only served to make Abraham less forthcoming than he was already inclined to be.

Katherine took a plate and began to scoop bean-sprouts out of one of the cartons. Elmore was spooning egg fried rice onto his cracked plate.

She said, "Do you think he really knows?"

Elmore didn't answer immediately, wanting to be careful

with his reply. "I don't think he knows for a fact. I think he has strong suspicions. But there's something else too."

"What?"

"I can't be sure. Somewhere in his mind there's a complicating factor, something which has created doubt. I mean, if he knew for sure, Abraham is the type of man who would boast to us about it, even if he had no intention of letting us know who it was. He would enjoy that advantage and he would exploit it. But you saw how he was, so I would guess that there is an unknown element in the equation."

"Like what?"

"Well, we know, for instance, that people with this disorder can sense others with the same illness. It seems clear that whoever he has in mind has the same condition as he does. *That* is the essence of his secret. He trades off the fact that he is different and that only he knows why, that those around him feel the difference but have no idea what it is. Their ignorance makes them fearful and Abraham feeds off that. But perhaps in this case, there's something more, something he hasn't encountered before, something he senses that is connected to the condition but which is actually alien to him, something unknown, something to scare him."

Chris said, "You got any ideas about what that might be?"

Elmore shook his head. "I'm afraid not. Not yet, anyway. What did you make of him physically?"

"Well, he's clearly at an advanced stage. He looks painfully anaemic."

"So?" said Katherine. "It happens to plenty of people."

"True, but not like him. We've seen this sort of thing before."

"Isn't it possible he's lying about everything?"

Elmore said, "It is possible, but highly unlikely. He knows things he shouldn't and doesn't know things he should. For example, he's right about the method of killing and since that's not been made public, we have to ask how he knows. I'd say we should give him the benefit of the doubt . . . for the moment."

"Chris said you've seen this before. Where?"

Elmore opened a book for her and she flicked through the black and white photographs. The living dead looked back. Their skins were white and their eyes were set in black patches, like macabre clowns. Stephen Abraham didn't look as ill as anyone in the album.

"I don't understand how these people – or how Abraham – could have anything to do with the person who murdered Jennifer."

Chris said, "Remember I told you how I researched the environment and circumstances of new and strange blood-related illnesses?"

"Yes."

"Much of my time is spent cross-checking with other cases, finding strands of similarity in the hope they'll lead us to a cause. There is a link between the ritualized style of killing and Abraham's condition."

"What is it?"

He shrugged. "We don't know exactly. What we do know is that the vast majority of cross-over cases tended to occur in small, impoverished and isolated communities. But there are exceptions. New York was one and this looks as though it's another."

"These photographs," Elmore told her, "were mostly taken in the fifties, when we pioneered research into the subject. The people suffered in just the same way as Abraham. These photographs simply show the decline at a more advanced stage."

She came across a photograph of a crowd outside a small, ramshackle church. The steeple was fat and fractured, the wooden slats blown away on one side. A pathetic gathering of dead trees stood either side of the uneven steps which rose to the entrance. The people in the shot were dressed in old clothes and tatty boots. Some were virtually in rags. They were crowding around a central man, who had his right arm raised and was clutching an unusual looking dagger. The blade was long, twelve to eighteen inches, and the end of the handle protruded from the bottom of his fist. Most weary eyes were fixed on the blade.

"What's this?" she asked.

Chris looked over her shoulder. It was a photograph he'd never seen before. Elmore said, "This was another of the 'cursed' communities that we came across. It was things like this which persuaded Josef to spend money on research that he knew nobody else would be undertaking."

Chris told Katherine, "Richard and Josef knew they'd stumbled across something which went beyond mere folklore and mythology, beyond a collective paranoia. The illnesses they came across were not psychosomatic."

"That's right," said Elmore. "We were aware of regional legends entwined with illnesses, but we wanted to delve deeper, to strip away the mythology and see if we could find out what was really happening."

Katherine looked back at the photograph. The man who held the dagger aloft appeared to be shouting something. Despite the signs of fatigue, malnourishment and disease, the crowd was animated.

"What's going on here?" she asked Elmore.

"It's fantasy interfering with fact. The knife is supposed to be special: an instrument designed specifically for killing vampires."

Katherine suppressed a smile. "Like the wooden stake in the films?"

He nodded. "Precisely. And just as ludicrous. They believed that by running this knife through a vampire's heart, you kill it. It comes from the same myth stable as all the other fancy stories you've ever heard. In some Hungarian backwaters, for instance, this weapon would have been used to dispatch werewolves. Same story from the same source, just regionally customized, like an accent."

"But they believed it anyway?"

"Of course they did. They couldn't understand what was happening to them. Fear and ignorance often give birth to hysteria. These people would accept any explanation, even if it didn't solve the problem. Just so long as they believed they knew what they were dealing with . . . there was supposed to be some comfort in that. Somewhere back in time, the legend starts and with the passing of generations, it's perpetuated and embellished."

Chris said, "The children are born and bred into the myth. That makes it hard to shake."

"That's right," confirmed Elmore. "They're cursed from conception, I'm afraid. To be honest, we never went into it that much. We regarded the subject as a quaint distraction and nothing more. But as I recall, the blade had to have special properties to combat the vampire's awesome strength! Or something like that."

Katherine's eyes ran up and down the weapon. "It looks expensive," she said, "especially considering how poor everyone around it looks."

"Oh, they were expensive," Elmore assured her. "The whole community would band together to pay for a single dagger. I suppose it was an exorcism of sorts. They had to make great sacrifices to meet the cost."

Katherine looked at the faces in the photograph. The dull eyes looked up at the blade with optimism shining through their misery. A very false dawn.

"And Abraham is part of this?" she asked.

"No. He shares the medical disorder, but he's removed from the mythology which infects backward communities like these. He's just ill."

Elmore put the book away and cast his eye over a list that Chris had drawn up of people he wanted to visit. He pointed at a name and said, "What does that say?"

Chris leaned over and peered at the writing. "Stark. Robert Stark."

"Who's he?"

"An old boyfriend of Sarah Reynolds."

"And when we go to see him, Abraham comes along too?" asked Katherine.

"That's right."

"What's going to happen to Abraham?"

"He's going to die."

"Does he know this?"

"Probably not. Anyway, it's not a problem."

"What do you mean?"

"Once his mental decline accelerates, as it surely will, he won't be aware of it. He won't be aware of anything at all, except for the chaos inside his head."

It was just after four in the morning when Katherine got up. She parted the curtains. Her street, which ran off the Bishop's Bridge Road, not far from Paddington Station, was quiet. She pulled on a silk dressing-gown. Jennifer bought it for her when she went to China with the orchestra.

There were no tears – she'd spilt enough already. Instead, her bewildered imagination tried to picture the scene. Was it quick? Did Perlman watch? Or did he go first and was Jennifer forced to play witness? Horrible, unanswerable questions. And above them all, one glittered more brightly than the rest: why?

Katherine stirred her coffee and took a first tentative sip. She sat in an old armchair, in front of the blank television screen. She thought about Chris and Elmore. The more she saw of Chris, the more she liked him and the more she couldn't understand his involvement. She found herself wishing he was doing something else. As for Elmore, there was something sad about him. He had an air of what-could-have-been hanging over him. It was in his eyes when he looked at the photographs or recounted some past adventure. It was as though his life had peaked and died before he ever knew it had begun.

Shortly after six, she got dressed in a pair of jeans and a pink and white chequer-board shirt. Then she left her flat and made her way over to Victoria. She reached the Monarch Hotel just before half-past seven. The beer-gut dozing behind Reception looked up at her with bloodshot eyes.

"Where's Mr Lang?" she said.

The man shrugged and slid the Guest Book across the

cracked Formica top. Names were sparse. She found his room and knocked on the door. He opened it, a towel around his waist and his face coated in shaving foam.

"Like your beard," she said. "Makes you look like Father Christmas."

"What are you doing here?"

"I couldn't sleep. I had things on my mind. I thought maybe you'd like to have breakfast, or something?"

"Sure. Why not? Let me . . ."

"I'll wait out here for you," she said.

When he reappeared, she looked into his cramped room and he noticed. "It's not the Ritz," he admitted.

"It's not even Holiday Inn. I think breakfast better be somewhere else, don't you?"

"Definitely. I don't think they even have a kitchen here. Probably just as well."

They walked up the Belgrave Road to Victoria and found a café near the bus station. Chris ordered coffee and Katherine opted for tea. They moved over to a table by the wall, beneath a fading photo of Henry Cooper.

He asked, "What was keeping you awake?"

"What you said about Jennifer."

He nodded, as though it were the answer he expected. "Maybe I shouldn't have told you."

"I insisted, remember?"

"Then maybe I should have lied."

She smiled. "Yes, maybe you should. But you didn't and I'm glad about that. I still can't come to terms with it, but I suppose it's unrealistic to expect to. At least, not yet."

Chris lit his first cigarette of the day. Katherine took a sip from her tea. It looked grey and tasted of nothing.

"What was Jennifer like?"

"Introverted. When we were children, she'd spend her spare time in her room, reading or practising her music. I always had more friends than her – I guess it looked as though I was having more fun than she was – but I was still intensely jealous of her."

"Why?"

"Because she was so bright and talented. Even at a relatively young age, I knew that. Plus, she was beautiful and nothing fuels sisterly jealousy quicker than the realization of beauty in the other!"

Katherine was smiling as she said it. She straightened her round, black glasses.

"Sibling rivalry," he said.

"Exactly."

The woman behind the cash-register tuned her radio to a new station. The blue lamp fizzed as another fly flew into its lethal light and fried. Chris rolled some ash into the foil ashtray.

"How did she get involved with a guy like David Colson?"

Katherine sighed and shrugged. "Colson was already famous when they met. He had two plays running in the West End, one of which had just been made into a film. Jennifer got taken to the London premiere of the picture by a nice man she was seeing, who had been an assistant editor on the film. She got introduced to Colson and hey presto!"

"Love at first sight?"

"Something like that, at least from Jennifer's point of view. Colson was this good-looking famous man and Jennifer saw herself as this plain-looking, average cellist, who was lucky to achieve anything. It wasn't true, of course, but that was how she often saw herself. Anyway, she was just so staggered that Colson could take an interest in her that she completely fell for him. Hook, line and sinker," said Katherine, bitterly.

"And you didn't like him?"

"No. But it didn't make any difference. Jennifer wouldn't hear a word against him. Rather than alienate myself from her, I learned to keep quiet."

Katherine was looking at the tiled floor. Chris ate some of his toast. The man behind the *espresso* machine was telling an old woman she couldn't bring her dog into the place. She pretended she couldn't hear him.

Chris nodded in sympathy with Katherine and murmured, aimlessly, "Those marital pitfalls."

She looked up. "Have you ever been married?"

"No."

"Haven't you ever been tempted?"

"Plenty of times, but not in reality. It was just wishful thinking, not a serious possibility."

"Why not?"

Chris drank half his cup of coffee and thought about it before answering. "Well, it just wasn't, because . . . because . . ."

That was his answer. Katherine said, "Because no one got that close?"

He nodded. "That's right. No one got that close."

"Why?"

"I just . . . I . . ."

He was struggling for words again and Katherine noted the troubled look. "Listen," she interrupted, "I'm sorry for being nosy. Don't answer, if you don't want to. I'll ask something else, something safe."

He smiled. "Thanks."

"What about your family? Your parents?"

"Long since dead, I'm afraid."

"Brothers? Sisters?"

"None."

"Well, that's clear enough. Where did you grow up?"

"I moved around a bit when I was a kid, but most of my childhood was spent in California. I wanted to be a football player. Not very original, is it?"

Katherine shook her head. "I wanted to be a ballet dancer or a nurse!"

"There you go. I had visions of myself as quarter-back for the San Francisco 49ers."

"And instead you ended up looking for new diseases?"

"That's right."

"How, exactly?"

Again there was another pause and this time Katherine got the impression he was formulating a deflective answer. "I guess I just drifted into it," he said. She knew that wasn't right, but recognized he wasn't going to divulge anything more.

"Listen," she said, cautiously, "why don't you check out of that dump of a hotel and move in with me?"

He looked up from the coffee cup. "I'm sorry?"

"Your hotel is a tip. I don't care how cheap it is. Whatever you're paying, you're being ripped off. You could stay at my place and save yourself the money. Plus, it would be more convenient."

"Thanks, Katherine, but I couldn't do that. It would . . ."

"Why not? I'm not proposing marriage! Besides, I feel I owe you."

Robert ran a foaming cloth over the baking roof of the white Mercedes. The car belonged to Godfrey and Mary Peake. It was eight years old and when Robert pressed his face close to the driver's window he saw there were only twelve thousand miles on the clock.

"Mr Stark?"

He looked up and slowly straightened himself, squinting in the bright sunlight. The man was tall, well over six foot, and broad to go with it. He said, "Mr Robert Stark?"

There were three people standing behind him. There was a fat man in a plain shirt with rolled up sleeves and a pair of grey flannel trousers. Next to him there was a girl in glasses with short, dark hair. She wore a pink and white chequer-board shirt. And to her left . . . Robert recognized the freak from Seven of Hearts. He wore a black, lightweight suit and a pale yellow, cotton shirt.

Robert turned back to the one who had addressed him and said, "What do you want?"

"My name's Chris Lang. This is Richard Elmore," he said, pointing at the fat one before sweeping a hand over the other two. "And Katherine Ross and Stephen Abraham."

The freak was called Stephen Abraham. They looked at each other and Robert wondered why the man wasn't saying anything to his friends, why he wasn't telling them they'd met before. He looked desperately ill, worse than Robert himself.

Robert said to Chris, "What can I do for you?"

"Miss Ross is Jennifer Colson's sister. You know I who mean?" Robert nodded. "And we understand that you were once Sarah Reynolds' boyfriend. Is that correct?"

Robert said, "Perhaps we should go inside to talk."

Abraham felt confused. He knew the face from Seven of Hearts, but there was something wrong. He wasn't feeling the same way about him now and yet he was feeling *something*. He was pretty sure that Stark knew who he was, but he hadn't said anything. Their eyes had met and silence prevailed.

Katherine said, "The police have been useless in my case. They won't tell me a thing about what happened to my sister."

"So who are the rest of you?" asked Robert.

Chris said, "We're helping Katherine try to discover what happened to Jennifer Colson."

"What's this got to do with me?"

"Haven't you heard the stories connecting Sarah Reynolds' murder to what happened at the Cadogan Hotel?"

"I've heard them."

"And you don't believe them?"

"I don't know."

"Aren't you even curious?"

"Sure. I am curious. But that's all I am."

Elmore said, "I don't understand."

"I held no affection for Sarah Reynolds. That went ages ago. If you're expecting to appeal to my sense of grief, forget it."

Katherine said, "I don't believe you."

"Well, it's true. I disliked her." Robert saw the looks his comment provoked and laughed acidly. "But not *that* much!"

Robert watched Abraham and saw anxiety in the way he shifted in his seat and how his eyes darted nervously around the room, rarely settling on anything for more than an instant. When their eyes met, it was always Abraham who averted his gaze.

Abraham was thinking about Seven of Hearts. He pictured Robert coming between him and the girl. The hands were on the shoulders, restraining him. *Take it easy. Why don't you sit down and have a drink?* His innards had been ice. *If you feel half as ill as you look, maybe you should have an early night.*

Robert answered the questions that were put to him but declined to join them in further investigation. "Thanks, but no thanks. I'll leave it to the police."

"They're not going to get anywhere," Chris told him.

"And you are?"

"Perhaps, yes."

"I may be an amateur at plenty of things, Mr Lang, but not at detective work. Besides, I said I was curious. I didn't say I was obsessed. Sarah's dead. Nothing's going to change that, is it?"

Robert saw them up to the pavement and then resumed cleaning the Mercedes. He watched the foursome walk out of Lennox Gardens, past St Columba's Church and into Pont Street.

Stephen Abraham waited until they were out of sight, at the junction of Beauchamp Place and Walton Street, before saying, "I've seen him before."

He stopped the other three dead. Chris said, "Are you sure?" and Abraham nodded.

"He was in a nightclub. Seven of Hearts."

Elmore said, "He's not the one though, is he?"

Abraham looked suspicious. He shook his head cautiously. "No."

Elmore had been watching Abraham while they talked to Robert Stark and his behaviour had again been unusual. So then he had studied Stark, but he displayed none of the signs that marked out Abraham and his kind.

"He's not the same as you, is he?"

"No."

There was uncertainty in Abraham's reply, so Elmore pushed a little. "No, but . . . ?"

"There *is* something about him. Something strange. Something I haven't come across before."

Elmore felt a warm glow in his belly. This was the general area he wanted to be in. "You don't recognize it, and yet it feels almost . . . familiar? Is there a connection, perhaps?"

Abraham put a hand over his eyes so he didn't have to squint at the old man. "Do *you* know what's wrong with him?" he asked.

Elmore shrugged. "I haven't got a clue. But I'd somehow been expecting something like this. When we met at your house, your confusion was unusual. I got the sense it was something connected, but something which you hadn't personally encountered."

Abraham nodded. "That's what it feels like," he admitted. "He knew me. We knew each other, but we said nothing. I could feel him."

"Is the killer connected to him?"

All Abraham would say was, "Well, one of the victims was an ex-girlfriend, wasn't she?"

Chapter Thirteen

She kissed him on the mouth and then he held her in his arms, pulling her close enough to feel her breathing.

"I missed you," she sighed, leading him into her apartment.

"I've hardly been away."

"I don't care," she said. "I hate it when you leave. Every time you walk out the door, it feels as though you're never coming back."

Rachel had filled a large vase with an enormous bunch of white lilies. Robert had noticed her preference for the flower. This vase dominated a table between the french windows. They were in full bloom with their fat heads drooping sadly. Rachel wore a short black skirt and a navy silk shirt.

"Did I tell you that I went to see the doctor?" he asked.

"No, you didn't. What did he have to say?"

"He is a *she*, and *she* had very little to say. It was a complete waste of time. I practically had to threaten her to get her to take a blood test."

Rachel turned round. "You had a blood test?"

"Eventually, yes. And that was only after she'd virtually accused me of having AIDS." Rachel laughed. Robert said, "I don't know why you find it funny. If I did happen to have AIDS, you'd probably have it too."

She chuckled and shook her head. "Not me."

"What do you mean?"

"I can't catch it," she said, as though it were perfectly obvious.

"I don't understand."

"Let's just say I'm immune. Something like that."

"Rubbish. No one is. We read rumours about drugs under testing, but no one's been . . ."

"I'm not talking about drugs, Robert. It's got nothing to do with that. Just take my word for it: I can't catch AIDS."

Robert said, "But that doesn't make any sense."

"Then we'll have to agree to differ, won't we?"

She bent over and picked up a violin and bow, which had been resting on an armchair. She plucked at the strings and made slight adjustments to them. Robert looked out of the window. A plume of dark smoke rose into the hazy eastern sky. Sirens wailed.

"I had a surprise visit today," he said, casually.

"Oh really?" she murmured, without interest.

"You remember the freak from Seven of Hearts?"

Rachel stiffened and turned round, as Robert said, "He appeared out of nowhere with three friends."

Her apparent indifference was usurped by an intense look which took Robert by surprise. She tried to dilute it when she saw the curiosity she was arousing. "Who were they?"

"There was an American and some fat old bloke who looked like he was on the verge of cardiac seizure. Then there was the sister of the woman killed at the Cadogan. Katherine Ross. And of course there was the weirdo. He's called Stephen Abraham."

"Stephen Abraham," she repeated, before looking up at him. "What did they want?"

"They were playing amateur detectives and wanted to know if I'd join their game."

"And you replied?"

"I told them I had better things to do."

"Did you speak to Abraham?"

"No, I didn't. We recognized each other but didn't say a word. I got the impression his friends had no idea we'd run into each other before."

"Was he behaving normally?"

Robert thought about it and said, "To begin with, yes. But when we went down to the basement, he . . ."

"You took them into your flat?"

"Well, sure. I didn't think it was the sort of conversation to be had in public. They wanted to talk about Sarah and the Cadogan killings. I thought it was better in private."

"Of course."

"He seemed very edgy to me. He was looking at me like I was some kind of . . . freak. I felt there was something between us, an invisible bond. I know it sounds absurd but I got the impression he couldn't wait to leave."

Rachel nodded as if she understood why. Robert saw her concern and felt reassured. Then she picked up the bow and started to play the violin. It was no longer a surprise to watch her brilliance at work. Her fingers danced over the strings and the bow was a blur. When she finished, her mood lightened.

"So, what do you think?"

"Excellent, naturally."

"Thanks."

"I assume that this is all down to marvellous instruction, like your cello playing and painting."

"That's right."

"And who would your teacher be? Nigel Kennedy, decked out in his Aston Villa kit?"

She smiled. "That's an interesting idea, Robert, but no. My teacher was André Perlman."

Robert was no expert on classical music. In fact, he'd never heard of the genius from Montreal until he was killed. "The guy who was murdered?"

Rachel raised her eyebrows and sighed. "That's right. I'm afraid so."

"The one who was killed with Jennifer Colson? She was a musician too, wasn't she?"

"A cellist," confirmed Rachel.

"And this guy taught you the violin, did he?"

"Yes. André was absolutely brilliant, in a class of his own."

Now that she seemed to be recalling painful memories, her face darkened a little. Robert wrestled with his next question.

"And your cello teacher, that wasn't Jennifer Colson, was it?"

Robert desperately wanted the answer to be "no". Rachel looked at him and he felt cold. "Of course it was, darling."

"I don't believe you," he said, quietly.

"Yes you do. You wouldn't have asked if you weren't already pretty sure what the answer would be. Jennifer Colson was my cello teacher. She was a beautiful woman. She had a lovely heart."

Rachel didn't seem upset. On the contrary, her face displayed marks of a smile. "It's a horrid and unfortunate coincidence, isn't it?" she said.

"What about Jacob Eckhardt? He was the guy who taught you to paint, wasn't he?"

Rachel was smiling again. "Yes, he was."

"Is he dead?"

She nodded. "As dead as stone."

Rachel could see the look on Robert's face betraying the thought process behind it. "I know what you're thinking. Two's a coincidence but three smacks of conspiracy, right?"

"Well . . ."

"Well nothing. Jacob Eckhardt was a very old man, Robert. He wasn't butchered in a hotel room like the other two."

Robert's strands of thought started to gel together. Names floated in his mind, gently bouncing off one another, forming momentary bonds. Jennifer Colson, André Perlman, Jacob Eckhardt, Katherine Ross, Stephen Abraham . . . and Rachel Cates. It wasn't random. He could feel there was method, but the over-view was still too confused to allow even a hint of clarity. The newspapers said there was a link between the murder of Sarah Reynolds and the double killing at the Cadogan Hotel. Harold Daley had denied it, but he was wrong. There *was* a connection. Robert was looking at it, as it reached for the buttons on his shirt.

He took hold of Rachel's wrist and shook his head. She

looked terrified, as though he'd pulled a knife on her. Her eyes seemed larger than ever and she opened her mouth to say something but couldn't get it out.

"I need to clear my head," Robert told her.

Rachel was too stunned to respond. She never anticipated this. She had been so sure of herself that this wasn't even a consideration. Her consternation appeared to fortify his resolution.

"Why?"

"I think you know the answer to that."

"But we were made for each other, Robert. Can't you feel it? You can't leave me. Not now."

"I need time to think."

"No," she cried, moving towards him as he made for the front door.

"There's something wrong here, Rachel. We both know it. You're hiding things from me. I'm not even sure if I want to hear them, but I've got to have time to consider."

"You've got to stay, Robert. You have to."

"I don't *have* to do anything," he told her, curtly, "unless I want to."

He didn't return to his flat. That would have been too claustrophobic. Instead, he hurried into the street, feeling some of the burden disappear as he ripped himself away from Rachel.

He drifted through the city like a spectre, largely unseen by those he passed. Couples walked to expensive restaurants, strolling past the tramps and mental defectives who tried to score for food in dustbins. They bedded down in shop doorways and on benches, even on the smartest streets. Every night they reappeared, huddled beneath their cardboard blankets, a curious form of metropolitan furniture.

Robert passed a pub full of drunks singing football songs. They fell about laughing, spilling beer over football shirts made from a material that crackled between the fingers, working up an electric charge.

He ambled down the Fulham Road. Fifteen-year-olds

crowded a pizza parlour. The girls wore too much lipstick and the boys took care not to disturb the astounding architecture of their hair. They smoked enough to shroud the back of the restaurant in a grey fog. Somebody passed by in an open-top jeep with Van Halen's "Running With The Devil" filling the night. Couples spilled out of the MGM cinema, lying about how much they enjoyed Woody Allen's latest film.

He slipped into a pub for a pint of beer. The place was hot and packed. On a small, wooden stage at the back of the main room, a young man slouched over a battered guitar was singing "She's Already Made Up Her Mind" by Lyle Lovett. He hung his head over the microphone so that his hair fell in front of his face and blanked out his eyes. A solitary spotlight incarcerated him in a narrow tube of light. He mumbled a gruff word of thanks before playing something by Tom Waits.

Robert leaned against the bar and considered buying a pack of cigarettes. He hadn't wanted one this badly for ages. He had no idea what he was going to do about Rachel. His suspicions were serious. He knew what he ought to do, but his heart wouldn't permit that. At closing time, he left the pub with the stragglers and walked to Fulham Broadway, hoping to catch the last train home.

A gentle breeze blew down the platform and cooled him. He saw distant pinpricks of light growing in the dark. The District Line train rumbled into the station and squealed to a halt. Robert boarded a carriage that was almost empty. There were a couple standing by one end, locked in a fervent kiss, oblivious to the stare they drew from a drunk who was crumpled in a seat close to them. His head lolled to one side. Halfway along, an elderly black woman sat clutching a large bag on her lap. She looked distrustfully at Robert as he passed by. Litter dirtied the floor and there was a dark stain on the seat opposite him. Someone had scrawled a swastika with a black marker pen on the window, with the words "kill the fucking yids" written underneath. The doors hissed softly as they primed themselves to shut. Just as they moved, Rachel stepped into the carriage, coming in through the same door he'd used.

Robert thought he was imagining things. He caught her in the corner of his eye and had to double-take. She looked around the carriage and then strode purposefully towards him. Her face was determined.

"What are you doing here, Rachel?" he hissed.

She stopped and looked down at him coldly. "You can't leave me, Robert," she said. Her black eyes looked as dead as a shark's.

"Will you stop telling me what I can and cannot do. Besides, all I said was that I needed time to think."

The train lurched as the wheels began to turn and it moved out of the station.

"I won't allow you to leave me."

Robert rose from his seat and matched her look of stony determination.

"You shouldn't have followed me," he told her, his mouth just inches from hers. "That was a mistake."

He turned away from her and reached for the door to the next carriage.

"Robert, listen to me."

He looked back at her and said, "Don't follow me, Rachel. I've got nothing to say to you right now."

"But we have to speak."

"No, we don't."

Robert stepped through the gap and into the next carriage. He pulled the door shut and didn't look back. He kept walking. There was a fat red-faced man with grey hair who was reading *Fear of Flying*. Further down the carriage, Robert's nose was filled with the unmistakable stench of urine. There was a damp pool by one of the doors. He reached for the next inter-connecting door.

"Robert, stop! Please!"

He turned round and shouted down the carriage, "I meant it!"

A weary looking man with a double chin coated in silver stubble sat between Robert and Rachel. He watched their exchange, his bloodshot eyes slowly turning left, then right.

There was a young man in a psychedelic T-shirt munching on something that was mostly concealed in a brown paper bag. Robert moved into the next carriage and hoped Rachel would not follow him. There were four people in there.

"Oi! You!"

He wore tight black jeans, a white shirt and a tanned leather jacket. He had a gold crucifix on a chain around his neck. His short hair was dyed blond.

"What?"

"Where d'you think you're going?"

"Into the next carriage," said Robert, looking round to see if Rachel was pursuing him.

"No you ain't!" he sneered. "Fuck off back where you came from!"

The train started to slow. Robert knew they weren't at Earls Court yet. He pushed past the stranger but one of the other three rose from his seat and blocked the gangway. He had a scalp that was virtually shaved. His biceps fully tested the elasticity of the white T-shirt he wore. Robert looked around. There was a black guy in a black and scarlet tracksuit. The fourth was a stocky man with olive skin and long, black hair. He boasted a vicious scar on his left cheek. Robert's skin prickled and he backed off, raising his hands meekly.

"Sorry. My mistake."

The man in the leather jacket said, "Oi, Gary, this turd says he's sorry. Do you think he means it?"

"You know, Lee, I don't think he does," said the muscular figure, cracking his scarred knuckles.

The bleak night scenery began to slow. The filthy brick walls supported a mass of insulated cables. They passed a junction box. Robert looked for Rachel coming through the door, but there was no sign of her. Lee patted his neat, dyed blond hair and pulled at the sleeves of his leather jacket.

"It's too late for sorry, mate," he snarled.

Robert began to panic and said, "What do you . . . ?"

Lee lashed out with his left foot and cracked Robert on the knee. A sharp pain shot up his thigh. Lee rushed in with a blow to the stomach, using his leg as Robert slumped onto the filthy floor. The train ground to a halt. Its metal wheels whistled on the rails. The lights in the carriage flickered. Robert groaned. As he tried to raise himself from the floor, another foot caught him in the side, blasting all the breath from his body and knocking him sideways against one of the seats. He caught his right temple on a sharp corner. For a moment, he was too stunned to even raise his hands in protection. One of them was laughing. The black guy spat on him.

"What do you want?" Robert whispered. "Money?"

"I don't want your money, fuckface! I got plenty of money! Do I look like a fucking tramp to you, eh? I want what I'm owed. You come in here and ignore me. That's no good, is it?"

There was a pause. Robert didn't answer and felt another searing jab in his ribs. His head throbbed.

"*Is it?*" bellowed Lee, who stood over Robert, his chest and chin jutting forward with aggressive confidence.

"No," mumbled Robert, almost inaudibly.

Lee muttered, "I want respect, you bastard!"

The lights flickered again and Robert heard the mechanical drone close down. All that was left was a soft buzzing, until it was over-powered by a voice.

"Respect has to be earned."

It was Rachel. All four men turned to the source. She stood in the doorway to the previous carriage. Robert lifted his face off the floor fractionally. If she was scared, it didn't show. Her eyes were glittering. Gary let out a contemptuous snort of laughter when he saw the intruder was female.

"I beg your fucking pardon, darling?" said Lee, who was standing over Robert's prostrate form.

Robert mustered a shout. "Get out, Rachel!"

Lee looked down at Robert, wide-eyed with fury. "One more word and Gary'll cut your fucking tongue out!"

"Respect has to be earned," said Rachel again, very coolly. Her tone recaptured Lee's attention. "Fear and respect are not the same thing."

"What the fuck are you talking about, love?"

Lee was astonished at her nerve. Robert glanced up at her. She was striking in her silk shirt and short, dark skirt, with her legs set slightly apart in a posture of defiance.

"Let him go."

"Let him go?" he scoffed, putting his hands on his hips, constantly milking approval from the other three with looks of startled amusement.

Rachel stepped out of the doorway and strode down the aisle. Robert could see her long limbs moving with customary elegance. Her face was unflinching, her eyes blazing like jewels in a fire. Lee was no longer grinning. He aimed a finger at her, as though it were a loaded handgun.

"I'm warning you!" he growled through clenched teeth. "Now fuck off, bitch!"

"If you don't let him go," she said, in a calm, reasonable tone, "I'll kill you." She looked slowly at each of them. "All of you."

Lee was momentarily silenced. Then he produced a knife from the pocket of his tanned leather jacket. He hit the switch and six inches of gleaming metal appeared with a click. He reached down and held the tip a few inches over Robert's face, while Gary grabbed him from behind and held him steady. Rachel stopped. The olive skinned man slipped off a seat and stood behind her.

"Is that right?" said Lee. "We'll have to see about that, won't we? You've got a fucking nerve coming in here, I'll give you that. But it don't make you brave, darling, just makes you stupid. Know what I mean?"

Lee smiled through clenched teeth. Rachel remained unmoved by his words or by the movement of the Latin-looking one behind her. Robert saw the man's eyes gliding over her backside and legs.

"You come waltzing in here with some fucking shit about respect. You don't know what you're talking about, darling. But don't worry . . . I'll teach you what respect is."

Robert screamed "Get out!" and was punched in the throat by Gary. For once, Rachel's expression changed, from blank into pain. She recoiled as Robert clutched his neck and gasped for air.

Lee hissed, "When I've finished playing noughts and crosses with your boyfriend's face, I'm going to . . ."

By now, Rachel wasn't even paying attention to Lee's hysterical rant. She looked down on Robert with love and pity, hurting at seeing him in fear and pain. Robert looked up, still swallowing gingerly, and saw tears swelling in her eyes.

"And if you ask nicely," Lee said, "old Vinny might stick it somewhere different, for a bit of variety! He likes that, does Vinny!"

They all laughed. Vinny, the Latin-looking man with the scar and the long dark hair, was still admiring Rachel's behind. Her chin puckered and she looked as though she was about to cry.

"She got a nice arse, Lee. Maybe I'll . . ."

Rachel spoke to Lee in a quiet voice, more fragile than before, cutting off Vinny in mid-sentence. "Take the knife away from his face and let him get up."

"Hey, bitch!" protested Vinny, strutting his machismo behind her, shifting his weight from one foot to the other, bristling with male pride. "Don't fucking interrupt! I was speaking to . . ."

She turned round to address Vinny, who was a couple of inches shorter than she was. Robert was still being suppressed by Gary's hands of stone.

"That's the trouble with little men like you," Rachel said to Vinny. "You talk too much and never listen."

Vinny was outraged. He took two strides forward. Rachel's body was blocking everyone's view but suddenly there was a crack and Vinny's feet cleared the floor by six inches. He didn't cry out. He stayed in the air for a moment and then he was crashing onto empty seats. Robert saw an arc of blood following him.

The black guy was rooted to the spot, slack-jawed with amazement. He reached for the rusty blade concealed in his tracksuit, but hadn't even withdrawn it by the time Rachel struck. From where Robert was looking, it seemed to be nothing more than a firm punch to the body. But her hand disappeared for a fraction of a second and when it reappeared it was purple and slick, dragging all manner of meaty objects out of the wound she created. The initial strike sounded like a rifle shot to Robert, followed by a chorus of cracking, like heavy boots moving over frosty twigs. The man's feet never moved until he was on the way down.

"*Jesus Christ!*" gasped Lee.

Rachel looked him in the eye and said, clearly, "Now let him get up."

But Lee had already dropped his knife in a moment of shock and was scrambling towards the far end of the carriage, pushing past Gary. There was a groan from the engine and the carriage shuddered as it inched forward and began to accelerate.

Gary released Robert and stood upright. Robert was unable to tear his eyes away from the swelling lake of blood and the crater in the black guy's chest. Rachel stopped in front of Gary, her right hand drenched in blood up to the wrist. There were splashes on her dark shirt and skirt, and on the naked skin of her legs, but considering the damage she had inflicted, Robert was surprised by how little.

"That's far enough!" barked Gary, his muscles rippling in anticipation. He was ready for a square fight. He'd never backed out of one before and he wasn't about to start. It was years since a single person had taken him on. And as for it being a woman . . .

Robert saw Rachel had the shark eyes again. They lacked any life or compassion. When Rachel took a step forward, Gary threw an enormous punch at her face. He had a huge fist, backed up by an arm like an oak tree. Robert saw his body muscles pumping beneath the stretched T-shirt as he put all his weight behind the blow. It didn't even reach Rachel. Her far smaller hand stopped his fist in mid-air. She gripped it with her slim fingers and squeezed. His clenched hand exploded like a melon under a sledge-hammer. He was too stunned to make a noise. He clutched the stump of his wrist with the other hand and simply looked at it. And just as he started to lurch forward, fishing a scream from deep within his lungs, Rachel delivered another of her lightning strikes to the body. Robert was close enough for the cracking of the breastbone to fill his ears. There was a whistle as her hand moved in a scarlet blur, tearing out his heart before she casually dumped it on a seat. Gary toppled forwards and crashed face-first onto the floor. She stepped over him and ignored Robert.

Lee was at the end of the carriage, wrestling with a locked door. It was useless. He clawed at it, now sobbing frantically, tearing his fingernails on the metal lock in desperation. As Rachel approached, he faced her, pressing his back to the door, scouring the floor for the knife he'd dropped. She was now between him and the precious blade.

Rachel showed no pity when she said, "To use an appropriately railway-orientated cliché, it looks as though you've come to the end of the line."

"Please, I didn't mean it," he wailed.

"Whether you did or didn't makes no difference. Your threats mean nothing to me."

"What do you want?"

"From you? Nothing. You have nothing I could possibly want. You're worthless."

Lee was too paralysed to move, even to defend himself. He looked as though he might faint. The train was pulling into Earls Court Station. Lee's final yell was silenced before it had been made as Rachel's fingers scissored into him. There was a wet thump as the heart hit the floor. Robert saw it quite clearly but couldn't believe it. The fingers moved through the breastbone like bullets through a cobweb.

The train was slowing. With one hand behind his body, Rachel propelled Lee against the window on the opposite side of the carriage to the platform. He hit it face first and went straight through it. There was no obvious resistance. He disappeared onto the track, where another train was about to pull in. Rachel turned round and walked back to Robert. She crouched by Gary's corpse and ripped the back of his white T-shirt off him. She started to clean the worst excesses of the blood from her hands.

Robert started to stumble away from her, but she pursued him, tossing the dirty material onto the floor. He was babbling incoherently. Temporary insanity. Rachel saw it and kneeled before him.

"I'm not going to hurt you, Robert. But you have to listen to me."

He nodded feebly because his voice was too fractured to speak. She stood up as the brakes squealed and the train came to a halt. She loomed over him, suddenly appearing like a giant as she extended an outstretched hand towards him. With her other hand, she hit the square panel which was bordered by a red light. There was a hiss as the door opened. She spoke firmly to him.

"If you want to live . . . come with me."

Chapter Fourteen

Her outstretched hand was still bloodstained, even though she'd wiped the worst of it off. She hauled him to his feet.

"Pull yourself together," she said, "and follow me."

"We'll never get . . ."

"Yes, we will."

She stepped onto the platform and headed for the steps, which rose towards the exit. Robert took one brief look back at the carriage. He could see a splash of blood on one of the windows. His legs were hard to control; the muscles felt soft and formless, quivering beneath the skin. But somehow he followed Rachel, who strode purposefully towards the ticket barrier.

The first scream was a single high-pitched screech which outclassed every other noise in the cavernous hall. By the time they passed through the exit, the solo gave way to a chorus; peals of horror. Those around the entrance instinctively turned towards the noise, their fearful curiosity swelling, as Rachel and Robert stepped onto the Earls Court Road.

"Keep walking," she commanded him, curtly.

Robert's head was hijacked by hysteria. He found it difficult to control himself. They were in Harrington Gardens when he slumped against some iron railings. Rachel turned round and came back to him, checking for onlookers.

"What the fuck are we going to do?" he wailed.

"Breathe deeply," she instructed him, crouching low and holding him by the shoulders. He was light-headed and unable to combat the shaking.

Rachel looked in his face and saw the concussion of shock. His eyes were on the pavement. She raised his chin with her hand and said firmly, "Look at me!" He did, in a feeble way. "We'll sort it out," she assured him. "I promise."

"*Sort it out?* How? Jesus Christ, Rachel! What the fuck have you done?"

She brought him back to his feet. They stayed arm-in-arm and, from afar, looked like ideal lovers as they ambled towards Lennox Gardens. Robert had no idea how he stayed upright.

Back at her apartment, she left him in the drawing-room, saying, "I'm going to get this blood off. You know where the alcohol is."

Robert took a heavy crystal-cut tumbler and poured whisky with a trembling hand. He paced anxiously, occasionally peering down into the street through the french windows, as if he somehow expected the police to pull up at any moment.

He saw Lee flying through the train window. And the black guy leaking blood from the bunker in his chest. He couldn't close out the multiple cracking of Rachel's hand carving through the bones. The crunch of her fingers blowing them apart, showering the carriage with skeletal splinters. The wet smack of blood lashing the filthy floor. The weepy pleas for mercy before she sliced them apart. The dead look in her eyes.

Rachel seemed to be taking an eternity. When she finally reappeared, she wore a long dressing-gown and was drying her hair with a towel. She looked surprised.

"I half-expected you to have gone," she explained.

"Oh, I considered it," confessed Robert. "But sometimes I'm like a well-trained dog. I get told to stay put and I do, faithful to my command right up to and beyond the point of absurdity."

She brought the whisky bottle over to Robert and held it over his glass.

"No, thanks," he said.

"You're going to need it, believe me."

He withdrew his hand and she half-filled the glass. She

replaced the bottle on the tray and stayed on the other side of the room, leaning against the table, blocking out her favourite lilies.

"Before I get in too deep, there's something I have to say."

Robert couldn't equate the figure in the dressing-gown with the one that killed. She saw he was still avoiding eye-contact.

"I'm in love with you, Robert," she said, plainly.

This caused him to look up at her for a moment, but his face remained blank. Then he looked away. His skin was white.

"I'm more in love with you than I've ever been," she continued. "I love you so much it's killing me."

He flinched. He cupped his tumbler with both hands and took a long sip from it.

"I love you too much to live without you," she said.

Rachel didn't look at him. She kept her eyes trained on her feet, allowing some of her wet hair to fall forward. She dug her toes into the floor.

Robert relived the terror. The blade an inch above his eye. The boisterous threats that Lee kept making. And then Vinny's feet weren't on the floor. The splatter of hot blood and he was in mid-air.

Rachel said, "Robert, I've loved you from the very first moment I saw you."

Much of what she'd said had washed over him, but now she had his attention at last.

"The point is," she went on, "that I was in love with you before you even knew I existed." Robert thought he must have misheard. "I was in love with you before I ever came to live here. You were the reason *why* I came to live here. By the time I moved into Lennox Gardens, I knew you better than you can imagine."

"What are you talking about?" he croaked.

She ignored him and carried on. "I'd been waiting for you for so long I'd come to believe I'd never find you."

Rachel might have been speaking in tongues. She knelt in front of him and put her hands on his knees. She looked into his face with a kind smile. Then she said, "I killed them all, darling.

Not just the four tonight, but the others, too. I killed Jennifer Colson and André Perlman at the Cadogan Hotel. And then I killed Sarah Reynolds at her flat."

Robert was numb. He succumbed to emotional paralysis. The words registered but he couldn't feel any more shock. It was all used up. He just sat there, staring into her beautiful eyes with distance in his own. She was telling the truth. She watched his eyes clouding over.

After an overlong pause, he mumbled, "I don't understand."

Rachel moved closer to him. "I know."

"What does this mean?" he asked.

She looked lost in thought. Robert finished his whisky, as she moved away. She smiled awkwardly.

"I'm not quite sure how to go about this," she said.

Her confession echoed in his skull. She'd admitted killing Sarah. It was unbelievable and yet he'd seen she could do it. Easily.

Rachel had wanted it to be so different. In her mind, there was a careful way to break him in softly. This was the instant she had worried about most. Countless hours had passed while she considered how to tackle it. But the night had destroyed all her designs and now there was no option but to meet the problem head on.

"How old do you think I am, Robert?" she asked.

"What?"

"How old am I?"

Robert looked up at her and tried to guess. "Twenty-five?"

"Higher than thirty," she assured him.

"Higher than thirty?" He was genuinely surprised. "Thirty-five?"

"More."

"More than thirty-five? Forty?" he suggested, although he knew it was ridiculous. You only had to look at her to see that.

This brought a sly smile to her lips. "A lot more than forty. How many people have you come across who are more than two hundred years old?"

He was entering a realm where sanity was an irrelevance,

an optional extra. But he'd already witnessed enough in one night to know that wasn't an impossibility. Not at all.

"I don't understand," he told her.

Rachel nodded sympathetically and said, "It's very simple. I was born in Lyon on the second of January 1789 and I cannot die."

Detective Chief Inspector Harold Daley stood on the platform and lit a cigarette. He turned to David Smith.

"Where's the fourth? I only saw three in the carriage."

"Well, some poor sod got tossed out the window on the other side. There's not much left of him now. There was a train that pulled in about thirty seconds after this one did. Chewed him up really bad. He's got a hole in him that you could park a car in."

Daley thought he smelt burning rubber. There were wisps of smoke rising from the Warwick Road exit to the station. Several ambulance men hung around the kiosk. All the medics had done was treat bystanders for shock.

"We've taken statements from as many people on the train as we can. We'll try and track down the rest, as soon as possible," said Smith. "Two people in the next door carriage say they never heard a thing. He passed through their carriage and into this one."

Daley's face lit up. "We got a description?"

"Not as good as we'd hoped for. You know how it is on trains like this, everyone avoids eye-contact, don't they? They're frightened of staring. But there was one thing, though."

"Oh yeah?"

"He had a girl with him. Very beautiful, apparently. She was following him. They were arguing. She called out his name. These two can't remember what it was, but if we interview some of the others who were there, one of them might."

Daley frowned. "That doesn't sound right, Dave. I mean, I can't see our boy running off for an evening's ritual slaughter with a beautiful girl on his arm, can you?"

"No. But it must have been him, though."

"How's that?"

"Well, they were seen entering that carriage and they were also seen stepping out of the train by people on the platform. It must have been the same pair because the connecting door at the other end of the carriage is jammed. They couldn't have moved on."

Daley nodded. "Anything else?"

"Yes," said Smith. "They both got on at Fulham Broadway. This train didn't stop at West Brompton, although it did pause just before it pulled in here. They were seen going into the carriage and we know they couldn't have moved on. No one else came out."

"Two of them," Daley whispered to himself.

Police photographers took shots of the carriage. Their flashbulbs sent a ricochet of white light off the windows and walls. Daley took another look inside. This was the worst yet. He tried to imagine how this much destruction could be inflicted on four young, strong men with such speed.

Smith reappeared. "More bad news, I'm afraid," he said.

"Oh?"

"The press have got wind of it. They're buzzing around both ends of the station like flies round dog-shit."

"That's all we need," groaned Daley.

"They want a statement from you."

"They would."

Daley stood by the open carriage door. A man in a boiler suit with "Police" stencilled across the back was examining a spray of bloody drops that marked the carriage ceiling. There was an advertisement for a secretarial college which was so bloodied that only a third of it remained legible. Lee's gold crucifix lay on the floor in a sticky pool, beneath the broken window. Gary still lay face down. His bulky shoulders were visible through the hole in his T-shirt. The torn patch lay by the door, screwed into a soggy ball, apparently discarded as casually as the collection of hearts. Someone had found half a fingernail wedged into the metal lock in the door at the end of the carriage.

Try as he might, Daley couldn't imagine how it happened. Nothing made sense. It must have been quiet, because no one in the other carriage heard anything. It must have been quick because it happened between stations, even allowing for a pause near West Brompton. It must have been clinical because there were no obvious signs of a struggle. A couple of knives were found, but it didn't look as though they'd been used.

The body-bag team arrived. One of them looked in the carriage and asked Daley, "Where's the fourth? There are only three in here."

"On the other side," he told him. "Got hurled through the window and went beneath an oncoming train."

Smith looked down at the bags and shook his head gloomily. "These won't do much for him," he said. "You'd be better off with a strong hose."

There was nothing intelligent that Robert could say. As for Rachel confessing to Sarah's murder, he really wasn't surprised to find himself numbed by it. His emotions were too exhausted to respond. Ever since Rachel moved into her first-floor apartment, Robert had spent plenty of time speculating. Who was she? What did she do? Where did she come from? Lack of answers had given rise to a multitude of possibilities, many of them apparently ridiculous. But what could match this for absurdity?

"Don't you have anything to say?" she asked.

She peered down at him and wanted to clean the graze on his temple, which he'd picked up from the edge of one of the seats in the carriage. But in his uncertain mood, she didn't risk touching him. She reached for the box on the mantelpiece, took a cigarette out and lit it.

Robert said, "Your memories must be spectacular. Two World Wars, for starters."

"And much more," she assured him. "Where mortals have scrapbooks for memories, I've got a library's worth."

Rachel exhaled a stream of blue smoke and tried to keep her

anger suppressed. Normally, it would have been an easy task, but her anxiety led her to frustration and that eroded her patience. Robert wasn't sure where to head.

"Tell me more about your . . . old age? Immortality? Whatever you want to call it."

He was thinking about murder and police interrogation, courts, judges and juries, jail sentences spanning decades. Sooner or later he would wake up and the shaking would stop.

"There is a metamorphosis, and once this is finished the subject never ages. The body remains physically locked into its condition at the time of the transformation's completion."

"And if I chopped off your finger?"

"It would regenerate."

Part of him wanted to laugh. "Bullshit!"

"I can show you, if you like," she said, with the crazy look in her eyes again.

He dismissed the idea with a flick of the hand and said, "Some other time, perhaps."

She let his cynicism slide and said, "The body is just a vehicle for the spirit."

"What? You mean you can change it, if you like? Trade it in for a new registration?"

"Don't be facetious, Robert!"

"Don't be *facetious*? You're fucking kidding me!" he shouted, rising out of his chair, suddenly reanimated. "So far this evening, you've butchered four strangers on a train, you've confessed to killing an ex-girlfriend of mine – not to mention a host of other people – and now, to cap it all, you tell me that you were born when the nineteenth century wasn't even a twinkle in Father Time's eye! I have earned the right to be anything I fucking well want!"

She took a step back. Robert didn't know why. If he lost his temper and tried to slap her, she could quite easily rip his hand off and squash it into a fleshy pancake. She took another nervous drag from her cigarette.

"I'm sorry," she said, in a frail voice.

"You owe me a lot better explanation than some horseshit about being immortal. Even if that were true, it doesn't mean you can run around killing people, does it?"

She frowned. "But they were hurting you. They would have really injured you if I hadn't intervened. You know that. I couldn't let that happen."

"So you murdered them? You ripped their fucking hearts out, Rachel!"

"I lost control."

"No shit!"

Robert walked away from her, running his hand through his dark hair. It was important to keep calm, he told himself. Hysteria wasn't going to help. He thought it was best to keep the conversation focused on her, for the moment. It would buy him time to consider what he should do.

"We're not perfect," she said.

"Wait a minute! *We?*"

"Sure. I'm not unique. Others exist. Not many, but there are a few of us, mostly behaving like the rest of you, for the purposes of social assimilation."

Robert shook his head. "*Behaving* like us? What do you mean by that?"

"I mean that I don't need food for fuel. My survival doesn't depend upon a regular liquid intake. Sleep is a choice, not a requirement. I have none of your fragility."

"So you go through the motions simply for . . . *social assimilation*?"

"That's right. We go through the motions – as you put it – so that we can live among you. It's better to blend in. Or sometimes it's because we like them. But they are certainly not a necessity."

"This is ridiculous!"

"It's the truth."

"Well of course it is! How unreasonable of me to have ever doubted you!"

The sooner he could slip away and find a telephone, the better. Maybe the police would show him leniency. On the other hand, maybe they wouldn't believe a word he was saying if he told them the truth.

"I understand your reluctance, naturally. But it's true. Anyway, I don't need to tell you this. You'll see for yourself soon enough."

She wanted to run her fingers over his skin, trace his cheekbones and feel his eyelids. She wanted to kiss his shoulders. He was shaking his head.

"What the hell are we going to do, Rachel? We've got to call the police."

"And say what?"

"Just tell them what happened, for God's sake!"

"Don't be absurd, Robert. You know we can't do that."

"We can't do *nothing*!"

"For the moment, that is precisely what we'll do. Nothing."

He looked at her and her expression reminded him of the moment before Vinny became her first victim. She wasn't flustered by what she'd done.

"What about the killing?" he asked, alert for any inconsistency he perceived in her answers. "I just don't understand how you did it, or why or . . . *anything*!"

Rachel would have preferred to have dealt with it later, but knew that it would be unwise to avoid answering his questions now. After all, he was still there and that was something. She wouldn't have been surprised if he'd tried to storm out of her apartment far sooner.

"There's a very simple reason for killing," she said, "which has nothing to do with what happened on the train. That was different."

"From what?"

"When we kill, we can, if we choose to, digest everything the victim has to offer."

"*Digest?*" Robert frowned. "What do you mean?"

"There is a way for us to inherit all their experiences and capabilities. We can absorb the memories, the talents, the fears, the strengths and weaknesses, adding them to our own, and to the others we have collected."

Robert was still squinting incredulously at her. "So what did you learn from the men on the train?"

"Nothing. I chose not to. I doubt very much that any of them had anything to offer that I would have found beneficial."

Robert drained his glass and moved over to the bottle for a refill. "So what do you have to do to . . . *digest* them?"

Rachel had hoped he wouldn't ask. "That's a detail for later."

"Why not now?"

"Later," she insisted.

He let it drop and screwed the cap back onto the bottle. Rachel finished her cigarette and ground it into a stone ashtray. She was completely insane. No court could send her to prison. It would be a straitjacket and drugs for Rachel. But he'd *seen* what she could do. That was cold reality, no exaggeration of a warped fantasy.

"You make it sound like you're some type of goddess stranded on the earth."

Rachel thought about it and said, "Well, if that's right and I'm a goddess, then you'll soon be a god."

"You've lost me."

She smiled at the irony of his reply. "On the contrary, darling. I've found you and I'll keep you. Forever."

Rachel was thrilled just by hearing herself say it. The prospect was utterly enthralling. She wanted to kiss Robert and took a step forward. He retreated.

"No fucking way!" he snapped. "You know what I think? You don't need me. You need a long stay at Broadmoor. You'd have a good time there, Rachel. They've got plenty of people who think they're Napoleon or Julius Caesar. You'd all have lots to discuss. God knows, they're probably already friends of yours!"

"That's not funny, Robert."

He nodded and put the glass down on a side-table, not allowing her to get closer to him. He'd seen how damaging that could be, especially when she was annoyed.

"You know something? You're right. This isn't funny at all.

It's sick. *You're* sick!" he said, before heading out of the drawing-room and storming down the hall.

Rachel followed him.

"Talking of sick," she called out, "how are you feeling?"

He stopped, but didn't turn round.

"Once you leave me, are you going to start feeling ill again? Those cramps and aches will torture you, make you feel like your insides are on fire. A cold fire. It's not getting any better, is it? In fact, you're getting worse, aren't you?"

"Maybe."

"You haven't spoken with your doctor since you saw her, have you?"

"No," he admitted, still facing the front door.

"I didn't think so," said Rachel. "You would have been to see me, if you had."

"Why?"

"Your doctor's got a big surprise coming. And when you go to see her, so will you."

"What have I got?" he asked, turning round. "What's wrong with me?"

Rachel moved a fraction closer to him. "Well, put bluntly, what you've got is a bad case of decay."

What did that mean? Rachel stood in a pool of light down the hall. She looked into the drawing-room and then back at him.

"What kind of decay?"

She smiled sadly and replied, "The worst kind, I'm afraid, my dear. *Terminal* decay."

Robert didn't believe she was over two hundred years old, so why should he believe her claim that he was dying?

Rachel was saying, "Except that it'll turn out to be the best kind. Best for both of us."

"You're lying."

"No, I'm not. There's no going back for you. You won't ever get better. Remember how we swapped blood in bed?"

Robert nodded cautiously.

"That started the process," she said. "Think back. You weren't ill until after that exchange, were you? The reason you were sick then was due to a reaction with your blood, a chemical protest on your body's behalf."

"A reaction to what?"

"To what I gave you."

"And what was that?" he whispered, hoarsely.

"The greatest gift I could ever give you, darling. Nothing less than eternal life."

Robert remembered the crucifix blade and the flash of blue metal as she sliced him in the night. He pictured the sheets the following morning, stained with blood. Then there was the illness and the dream. The jaws of steel had destroyed his chest just like Rachel had destroyed the chests of the men on the train.

"But you just told me I was dying."

"As you understand life, you are. You'll have to relinquish your current fragile mortality."

"And supposing I choose not to?"

"The process has started. You're withering away. If you won't complete the transformation, you'll continue withering away until you die a painful, undignified death."

"And if I go through with this, then what?"

She smiled. "Then we live together. You and I. Forever."

"And that's all there is to it?"

Rachel almost admired his attitude. His bravado was laced with sarcasm and she recognized the symptoms. Fear could do that to people. She could have told him there was much more to it than that, given him a detailed account of what would happen, but that would only petrify him further, so she said, "Yes, that's it. Either you complete, or you die. There are no other options."

Robert lost his temper. *"Jesus H. Christ!* You really *are* insane, aren't you?"

"I sympathize with you," she said, opening her arms to him. "Honestly, I do. Your natural inclination leads you to dismiss everything I've said. Logic demands it, doesn't it? It tells you it's crazy, but at least part of you suspects there's something in what I'm saying."

She was right and Robert hated it. He was still there, after all. As for logic, that had taken a beating by what he'd witnessed in the train carriage.

"I know I've been unfair," Rachel said, "but I really couldn't help it. I never gave you a chance. You never had the option. I saw you, I fell in love with you and I had to have you. I never gave you any say in the matter. And if you don't see it through, my hunger for you will be responsible for killing you. And then I'll have to live with that . . . *forever*."

She looked like a ghost down the hall and despite himself he felt sorry for her. He wanted to comfort her, to go back in time a bit, to erase the night and return to rapture.

Rachel looked determined when she said, "If I can't have you, no one else will."

Even if everything she'd said was untrue, and she was simply a lunatic, the quadruple slaughter on the train had been real. That wasn't a dream, no matter how much he wished it to be one. He'd seen the hearts dropping onto the floor with a wet squelch, heard the bones splintering and the last strangled gasps of the four victims. With or without her, he was doomed.

Worst of all, she might be telling the truth. That really upset him because what she said was certainly crazy. Did that mean *he* was going mad?

Fatigue and confusion finally swamped Robert. He leaned against the wall and buried his head in his hands. He squeezed his eyes shut and tried, in vain, to blank everything out. "I don't have a clue what's going on."

He should have been marching out of her door, down the street and into the nearest police station. But, instead, he gratefully accepted her arms as they encircled him.

"I love you," she whispered. "I'll always love you."

"This isn't right," he said.

"For us, it is."

He broke free of her comforting clutches and made for the door. Rachel took hold of his arm. He shook her off and she grabbed him again. This time she jerked his arm back and spun him against the wall.

"Stay with me!"

"No, I won't. Not after what you've . . ."

She grinned wickedly and said, "Yes, you will, my darling."

Robert's temper snapped and he was throwing a slap at her, his right arm rising from his side in a wide, lightning arc. It stuttered and stopped by her ear and she was suddenly holding him by the wrist. The abrupt halt jarred his shoulder. Her fingers were as unforgiving as any handcuff. Robert winced and his eyes widened with fear. He saw Gary's hand exploding and the way he'd looked unbelievingly at the gooey, claret stump that remained.

"Please, don't do it."

She said, "I could never hurt you, Robert."

Her thumb was digging into the underside of the wrist, massaging his pulse. Her face was expressionless. He couldn't tell whether she was going to kiss him or kill him.

"We have to stick together," she was telling him, as sleep began to creep up on him. "You and I only have each other. The rest of the world is against us."

The thumb's rhythmic pressure brought on a curious sensation of comfort. An inviting, warm glow ebbed through him, begging him to lie down, to submit to sleep. Rachel softly pressed her body against his, still soothing his pulse. Her lips brushed his lightly, their eyelashes clashed gently.

"Stay with me."

Rachel led Robert to bed, taking care not to let him see her gloating. She was triumphant, at least until morning. She expected more trouble once he was revitalized by sleep. But for now, this was a victory. She held his wrist and continued to massage his pulse, cloaking him in sleep. She slowed his heart.

"It's going to be fine, darling," she murmured into his ear, before kissing it. "You'll complete the process and we'll be together. We'll be in love and have eternity for ourselves, not just a few painful years like those who age and crumble, heading for a damp coffin and a cracked tombstone. We'll be equal. You'll be the only one to stand up to me, the only one who can question my immortality."

Robert's slide into sleep was almost complete, but those last few words pricked his thoughts just enough for him to ask, in a voice thick with the onset of slumber, "What do you mean?"

Rachel had no hesitation in telling him. She was sure it was the right thing to do. "If you were immortal, we could kill each other."

"How?"

"You already know how. By tearing out our hearts. Immortal lovers can break the law that others can't even bend."

Chapter Fifteen

When Chris woke up, he found her sitting on the edge of the sofa-bed, shaking his shoulder. Her anxiety reminded him of the stewardess who had interrupted his nightmare on the flight from Los Angeles. Katherine said, "Are you okay?"

Chris looked around and then propped himself up on an elbow. "Sure. It was just a dream."

"I could see that. A pretty bad one, by the look of it."

The girl with the dirty blonde hair had encircled his body as gently as mist, wrapping her arms around his head and pressing her cold palms over his eyes. The worn, shining leather rubbed against his cheekbones. He heard the shouts, the cracking, the crashing, the thump and trickle. And the paralysing silence that always followed. Then the hands came away and before she led him into the room, Katherine had intruded.

Her flat was the first floor of a reasonably sized house in a quiet street off the Bishop's Bridge Road. There was one bedroom, a small bathroom, a smaller kitchen and a decent sitting-room, which had a bay window that looked onto the road. On one side of the blocked fireplace there was a small TV and a VCR that belonged in a museum. There was a Turkish rug on the floor, in front of the fireplace. She had a pair of cheap Miro prints on the wall opposite the bulging bookcase. Beneath them was a small desk, piled high with writing paper and a large collection of unopened envelopes. Katherine rose from the sofa-bed and picked up a coffee cup from the top of the television. Chris looked at his watch. Five to eight.

"Thanks for dinner last night," he said. "It's the first good thing I've eaten since I got here."

She smiled warmly. "Thanks. That's the first time anyone's been polite about my cooking."

Initially, she'd been nervous at bringing a virtual stranger into her home; it ran against her instinct. She was sure he must have noticed how edgy she was. What would he think?

Chris talked about California and a childhood that Katherine could only envisage in terms of what she'd seen in too many American films. Orange groves, azure skies and a booming Pacific surf. Cars like whales trundling down broad highways. Crazy Californians with clean and salty air between their cosmetically perfected ears. Chris described it like an outsider, with an air of detachment that went from amused bewilderment to the hungry jealousy of the excluded.

Clashing glances made her blush. Their eyes would meet when they laughed and Katherine wondered what he was thinking while having her own risky thoughts. It left her confused. This was not her territory.

As a child, Katherine had been quite gregarious. It was only when boys started to take a keener interest in her that she had become shy, losing her confidence in their company, going to extraordinary lengths to avoid exposing herself to the potential embarrassments of early sexual encounters. Katherine was not interested in being taken to a Robert Redford movie if she had to get roughly fondled somewhere in the back row for the privilege. They left her cold with their tedious, clumsy experimentation. Those boys didn't know the difference between a caress and a karate chop. But, in one sense, that naïve age of discovery was preferable to the adult version: the era of committed relationships.

New complications brought new pains. Fidelity, commitment, jealousy, deceit. The machinations of her lovers confounded Katherine. In the end, she supposed she was too open-hearted – too stupid, even – to compete successfully in the evil games that lovers played.

Her last experience left her so miserable, she decided to opt out because it was easier. He lied so much to her she never knew what was true. He said he was an advertising executive. He wasn't; he sold advertising space for a motor magazine. He said he'd never been married. Apart from the two failed marriages he forgot to mention. He told her he loved her and that they would get married. Until he ran off with a girl whose only claim to fame was that she'd once bared her balloon-like breasts for a tabloid.

Chris was slowly starting to stir thoughts within her that had been so successfully buried they now felt quite alien. They weren't startling and passionate – nothing so dramatic – but they were nice and appeared as memories, as much as anything that was happening in the present. When she went to bed, sleep wasn't easy. Her head was filled with saccharin thoughts. If he decided to come into her room, what would she do? Resist or submit?

And while she was entertaining these vaguely erotic notions, a siren voice harangued her for her insensitivity. He was only there because Jennifer was dead. That was why they were thrown together and Katherine was uncomfortable with the idea of trying to milk the situation for something more. Eventually, the only thing she submitted to was sleep.

Now it was daylight. She went over to the bay window and drew the curtains. Explosive sunshine filled the room. She looked onto the street. The pavements were dusty. Chris shielded his eyes from the sudden brightness and watched her coming back towards him.

"Breakfast?"

"Just coffee, thanks," he said.

Katherine went into the kitchen while Chris dressed. She'd seen his nightmare. That wasn't just a bad dream. He'd been thrashing around as though he were having a fit. His flailing hands had smacked against the coffee table by the sofa. The contact was bringing up a small bruise across the knuckles. But the blow never woke him. She'd had to shake him to cut through to the conscious.

She found him curious. As soon as she discovered something she felt comfortable with, something else presented itself which left her on edge. Katherine was attracted to him. She liked his looks; he had a kind face. But she'd never seen such a haunted look as in those first few seconds after he awoke. The flashes of darkness which erupted and vanished were made more vivid by his general air of composure. She handed him a mug of coffee.

"So what are we going to do today?" she asked.

"I guess we should have another stab at Robert Stark."

"What about Abraham?"

Chris shrugged. "I don't know. The guy's losing it, that's for sure. Whether he actually knows who did it . . . who can say? He certainly can't. Or at least that's what he says. And if that's the case, then he's of no use to us. My inclination is to leave him out of this."

"Is he really going to die?"

"We're all going to die," said Chris, before taking a sip. "But he's going to do it sooner than most."

Robert looked up into Rachel's face and saw an angel. She was sitting on the bed, looking over him with a shocking halo of sunlight around her head. For one exquisite moment, the night never existed. Her black eyes sparkled.

"Do you feel better?" she asked.

His memory stirred and he replied, "Less hysterical."

She smiled and put her hand on his forehead, softly brushing the graze on his temple. It was another scorching day.

"What about you?" he asked.

"I'm fine. I spent the night watching over you."

"All night?"

"All night."

He nodded. "Sleep's only for . . . *assimilation*, right?"

Fragments drifted aimlessly. Purple hands and cracking bones. Screams. Dizziness. 2 January 1789. Her thumb massaging the wrist. The leaden pulse. Sleep overwhelming protest. Immortal lovers breaking the law that others cannot even bend. Rachel was speaking again.

"All night I was thinking about you. It was sad."

"Why?"

"Because I was imagining how I would be if I had to watch you waste away and die."

Robert spied her crucifix on its chain. It was lying on her bedside table, just by the clock. It was after nine in the morning.

She went into the kitchen and Robert tugged on his blue jeans. There were dark flecks on the material. He went onto her balcony. A lady with bomb-proof mascara was walking her horrid terrier, which tugged at the red leather lead. Her face was powdered white and clashed with her ruby lips. A milk van floated around the gardens, buzzing like a bee. A British Airways 747 drifted overhead in the sandy haze, its engines grumbling as it descended towards Heathrow. Robert went into the kitchen, where Rachel was scooping ground coffee into a filter.

Daylight gave him composure. Panic threatened but, for the moment, he had a rein on it. He pictured Lee clawing at the jammed metal lock at the end of the carriage. The horrible realization that he was going to die spread over his face, the new expression mutilating his features.

"You must have some stories," Robert said, leaning against the sink and folding his arms. "Tell me something."

She looked up to the ceiling for a moment and then broke into a smile as she placed the filter cone over the pot and reached for the kettle.

"I knew the Romanovs. I was in St Petersburg in 1915. In those days I was Sophia . . . a duchess, no less."

The way she said it made it sound like she was referring to a regular family in the next-door street. She was scanning him for a reaction. Robert was thinking about police interrogation.

"Nice people, were they?"

"Too nice. I remember waking one morning, after I had

dined with them. Alexandra summoned me and when I arrived she was examining the gold figurine I brought for them. It was from the ancient Incan city of Cuzco. They seemed intrigued by it, as I'd hoped they would. A very humble gift, of course, but they were extremely gracious.

"She asked me how I came across it and I described to her the journey I took through Peru and Bolivia. While I was talking, we were looking out over the city as the cold silver rain fell to earth. She suddenly turned to me and said, 'I'm so jealous. Here am I, the Tsarina, and yet a prisoner to the nation. We can do with this country as we please. We rule the people absolutely because our bloodline is God-given and it is that which chains us. That is why I know we will never escape.' I still sense that moment."

"And that was in 1915, was it?"

"Yes."

"Not bad. A Tsarina who can foresee the future," said Robert, flippantly. "A neat idea."

The look on her face confused Robert because he didn't believe her story. But her reaction looked real. She broke the moment with a fragile smile because she didn't want to dwell on that memory. So she clutched another, something that would distract Robert.

"I met Jack Kennedy once."

"As in President Kennedy? That Jack Kennedy?"

"None other. It was before he became President, though."

"You're making fun of me."

"No, seriously. He tried to seduce me."

"You and the rest of the world," said Robert, making no attempt to disguise his disbelief.

Rachel expected nothing less. "To be honest, it wasn't seduction. It was virtually rape . . . or at least it would have been if he'd had his way."

Robert laughed loudly.

"It's true," she insisted, permitting herself a smile, as Robert wiped his eyes. "It was at the Waldorf-Astoria in New York City. When I told him to take a walk, he said he had the power to persuade me." Rachel looked into the middle-distance for a moment. "I have to confess that when he threatened me, I toyed with the idea of killing him. With hindsight, it might have made for an interesting twist on today's history."

"Oh sure! But then you would have robbed Lee Harvey Oswald of his fifteen minutes of fame!"

"Quite. Jack Ruby too. Suffice to say, I dissuaded him firmly enough."

Robert pictured her grabbing JFK's wandering hand and squeezing until it exploded like Gary's fist. He said, "I can imagine!"

"I enjoyed my years in New York. I was sad to move on."

"So why did you?"

"I had to. That's part of the problem with my existence. I never age. After a while, people notice."

Rachel refilled the filter cone and produced a mug from a cupboard next to the fridge.

"Immortality is lonely, Robert," she said. "We have to keep moving. We can't have friends. Nothing is permanent except our continued existence. Even if we chose to make friends, it would hurt too much to watch them decay and die in what, to us, is the blinking of an eye. We all seek the one individual who we can hold onto forever. We crave love.

"In the past, it was easier to live without fear of repercussions. Today, technology reaches everywhere and makes anonymity much harder. I used to enjoy the highlife, but I left that all behind when I left New York in 1967. Since then, I've led a far quieter existence. Wherever I am, I'm now something of a recluse. I suppose I was a little naïve back then, but who could have predicted how the world would change, just since the war, let alone since the middle of last century, for instance?"

Robert had to admire her story. "Hold on a moment," he said, when Rachel looked as though she was about to continue. "There's something I don't understand. You said that you never physically age."

"Yes."

"You're sort of fixed at a physical point of development?"

"That's right. You stay at the same physical age as you were at the moment the transformation was completed."

"So the way you look now is just the way you looked when you were immortalized, right?"

Rachel tossed her hair over her shoulders and then tugged at the bottom of the large T-shirt, which almost fell to her knees.

"Yes."

Robert took his coffee cup and held it beneath the pot as she filled it. Then she stood on her toes and kissed his cheek.

He said, "Rachel, this is a great story. Really! I mean it. Naturally, I'm not buying a word of it, but I have to confess you've done a marvellous job."

She nodded. "Okay. Let me ask you something. Why do you think I killed André Perlman and Jennifer Colson?"

Robert shrugged. "I've no idea . . . that is always assuming you did actually kill them, of course."

"Of course. You want proof, don't you?"

Rachel went back to the bedroom and Robert followed. He didn't need proof that she could kill; he'd already got that. It was indelibly etched on his brain. She opened the windows fully to the sound of the waking city.

"In the immortal state," she said, climbing onto the bed and sitting with her legs bunched beneath her, "there are choices to be made. It's perfectly possible, for example, to drift through the years mimicking mortals as closely as possible, moving on to new places and fresh faces from time to time, but never progressing in real terms. But I've always believed that's a criminal waste when there is, in fact, an alternative way to exist. We can consume people."

He vaguely recalled her mentioning it in the night, but he'd been too frazzled to focus on it. There had been too many demands on his imagination and faith. The look on Robert's face made Rachel laugh.

"Don't worry!" she said. "I'm not talking about cannibalism.

Not literally, anyway. What I mean is that by killing people in a certain fashion, it is possible for us to consume a victim in a way that a cannibal could never aspire to. We can inherit everything they were: all their experiences, every last thing.

"To give you an example, I might retain an author's literary prowess but dispense with his fear of failure or hatred of homosexuality. All the desired qualities can be absorbed, as though they were our own, constantly compounding."

Robert was struggling with the concept. Rachel leaned forward.

"Don't you understand, darling? I am not just me . . . I am the sum total of the best parts of everything I've ever killed and devoured."

The speed and strength she had displayed in the train carriage had definitely been unnatural. Robert saw the astonished look in Gary's eyes as he stared at the stump where his fist had once been.

"Which brings us back to the question," continued Rachel, "why did I kill André Perlman and Jennifer Colson?"

"From what you've said, I assume it was so you could absorb their musical skills."

"That's right. And the same goes for Jacob Eckhardt."

"But you said you didn't kill him."

"No, I didn't. I just said he was an old man and that he wasn't butchered in a hotel room like Perlman and Colson. He *was* an old man. Actually, I killed him in his house."

Rachel paused and looked away from Robert, lost in a distant memory. She snapped out of her reminiscence and seemed momentarily confused.

"Antwerp was a struggle. I don't know why I stayed for so long. Anyway, that was where Jacob Eckhardt lived. He was a first-class forger and his talent was only matched by his ingenuity. What he taught me about ageing a canvas remained priceless until relatively recently. These days, technology makes it much harder to successfully pass off forgeries. But he was the best of his time, one of the best of *all* time.

"When I killed him, I took a forgery from his home. It was a wonderful copy of a small painting by Vermeer. I sold it, along with its perfectly faked provenance, at auction in Geneva in 1984. It fetched over five million Swiss francs. Isn't that funny?"

"Hilarious," said Robert, flatly. "And did you do Jim Morrison too? There seems to have been quite a lot of speculation about his alleged death."

Rachel giggled and shook her head. "No, I didn't. Given the musical and writing talents that I've already inherited, I really don't think Jim Morrison could have broadened my mind much."

"Perhaps his powers as an amateur chemist might have been worth investigating?"

"Perhaps. It's an interesting idea, I have to admit. Maybe I should have killed Elvis Presley, just to learn about criminal dress sense and chronic obesity."

"You know, Rachel, this is all very amusing, but I still don't believe you. I know what I saw last night, but don't ask me to accept that it's got anything to do with immortality or eating people, or whatever the hell it is you do to them."

She was scratching her elbow. "What about Sarah?"

"What about her?"

"I killed and absorbed her. Why did I do that?"

"That's not funny, Rachel."

"Why did I do it?" she asked, more forcefully.

He didn't say anything.

"Well, I'll tell you," she said. "I did it so that I could find out as much about you as possible. I'd already done as much as I could, in a general way, but I needed a lot more."

Robert felt his anger growing. Sarah would be backing away and Rachel must have been smiling. The fist would plunge through the breastbone and then what? How did the absorption take place? The consumption of spirit. He shuddered.

Rachel said, "I needed more than I could get from observation and discreet enquiries. Sarah was ideal. She was your most recent girlfriend, a partner from a passionate love affair that had lasted long enough for you both to know each other's innermost secrets. I couldn't have asked for a better candidate."

"Stop it!" shouted Robert. He was appalled by the pleasure he saw in Rachel's eyes. "You can't talk about her like that! It's . . . it's . . ."

"Don't be tiresome. You didn't even like her. Remember?"

He looked indignant. "I know!" he snapped. "But all the same, you shouldn't . . ."

"Speak poorly of the dead?" she interrupted, before snorting contemptuously. "*Please!* Don't burden me with your tedious notions of decency."

Her disgust shocked him. She looked genuinely revolted by the concept. She said, "I know things about Sarah that you probably don't even know yourself."

"*Rachel!*"

"What about Sardinia?"

Caution crept up on him. "Sardinia? What about it?"

"Did you know that the reason she was so angry was because she suspected you were having an affair with Clara Martin?"

An affair with Clara? Robert blushed. He hadn't had an affair with Clara, but they had flirted dangerously on several occasions. She had a talent for infuriating women, by flirting with their men. Had Sarah really believed he was having an affair with Clara?

"Clara Martin *was* on that holiday, wasn't she?" asked Rachel.

"Yes, she was," said Robert, his temper humbled. "But that doesn't prove a thing. You could have found that out somehow else and then . . ."

"Yes, I could have, but I didn't. You're still resisting me, aren't you?"

"Do you blame me?"

"Not really, but I've got to convince you and since I haven't, I'm afraid you don't leave me with any choice. This is going to sting a bit, darling, but just remember, it's all in the past." She looked a little remorseful and it made him anxious. "Did you know that Sarah was unfaithful to you?"

Robert breathed a sigh of relief and answered, dismissively, "Of course. Anthony Baker. She went out with him for . . ."

"No. Not him. Before that."

Robert tried to convince himself there was no reason to believe what he was about to hear.

Rachel said, "You were at dinner with Jonathan Stainger on the night Miriam Menzies split up from some accountant she was dating. You and Sarah had a row at the table. You left, much to everyone else's embarrassment. Jack Clark gave Sarah a lift to that flat of hers in Earls Court . . . the one where I killed her. She was upset and they had a couple of drinks and . . . you can guess the rest."

Robert stared at her. "*Jack?* No way. He wouldn't do that. Not to Sarah. Not to *me*!"

She shrugged. "He would and he did. Only once, as it turned out, but not for lack of trying. He wanted to repeat the indiscretion, but Sarah wouldn't have any of it."

Robert was adamant. "You've got it wrong. Jack's not like that. He's one of my best friends. We've been through . . ."

"You can never tell about people, Robert. Not until you get to know them like I can."

He muttered, "That is enough! I don't want to hear another word. You've gone too far and . . ."

"Well, you're going to carry on hearing it until I've convinced you," she insisted. "What about the Blackbridge Hotel? You and Sarah stayed there for that dirty weekend in Oxfordshire. Do you remember? You laughed yourselves stupid about the names you were going to give to your children. If the first one was a boy, you were going to call him Boris and, if it was a girl, she was going to be Bertha. Do you remember that? And after the bath, you went into the bedroom and you blindfolded Sarah for the first time, before making love to her. Is any of this ringing a bell?"

Robert was reeling. The blows were stunning. He was too dazed to respond.

She said, “When you and I first made love, I said you could hurt me if you wanted to. Why did I say that?”

He shook his head dumbly.

“Isn’t it true that Sarah actually *liked* limited violence on occasions, and that it turned you on as well?”

“No!”

“You’re lying, Robert,” she said, flatly.

“No. I’m not. I’m really not!”

He sounded desperate. She cooled and considered this for a moment. She cocked her head to one side and then the other. “Well, maybe you’re not. Maybe you genuinely didn’t know. But *she* liked it, that’s for sure. Take my word for it.”

“I can’t.”

“You mean you don’t want to. But believe me, Robert, *you will* take it. Let me give you something else to think about. There was that night when you were in her bed at Earls Court. You thought she was fast asleep when you whispered into her ear, ‘Will you marry me?’, didn’t you?”

The memory hurt despite everything he thought about Sarah.

“She was awake, Robert. She heard you and made a vow to herself that if you actually woke her up properly and asked her, then she would say ‘yes’ to you.”

How could Rachel possibly know these things? He couldn’t argue with her any more.

“You’ve made your point,” he told her.

Rachel held her thumb and forefinger just fractionally apart. There was cruel delight in her eyes, as she said, “You were that close to marrying her, darling.”

Chapter Sixteen

"Robert? Robert?"

Cassie looked like the ghost of the Mrs Lorenzo that Robert had become accustomed to. The blonde hair was bedraggled. The delicate skin around her eyes was red. The eyes themselves were watery and anxious.

"Do you think you could help me?"

He feared the worst. "Of course. What is it?"

"Our luggage. Would you bring it down? It's rather heavy."

She was shaking. Her shoulders were rounded like an archer's bow and she was stooping. Normally, Cassie carried herself in an athletic, confident fashion. The woman in front of Robert looked exhausted to the point of collapse.

Robert had his own crisis and didn't need another one. "You're leaving him?" he asked.

There was so much to consider. Murder and immortality. Sarah and marriage. Had he really been so close to engagement? There was no proof any more, but Rachel became harder to disbelieve with every revelation.

Cassie looked up at him and said, "He tried to hit the children this morning. He made terrible threats and I just couldn't . . . I just couldn't . . ."

"Where are the children?"

"In the apartment," she said, between deep, gulping breaths.

What would the police be doing? He wondered how far their investigation had proceeded, how long it would be before the metal handcuffs snapped around his wrists. When the moment came, would he deny everything or would he confess, in return for a vague promise of clemency?

Robert heaved the cases into the lift. She took one last glance at the apartment and then slammed the door. When they reached the ground floor, Cassie ordered the children to wait for her in the back of the waiting cab. She watched them settling in, before turning back to Robert. She was more composed now, adjusting her sunglasses.

"Thank you, Robert. Thank you for everything. It couldn't go on. You of all people should understand that."

"Of course."

She brushed some imaginary dirt off the blue blazer she was holding. Then she peered over the top of her sunglasses and said, "Are you feeling okay?"

"Yeah. Well . . . sort of."

"I don't want to sound rude – especially after the kindness you've shown me – but you don't look too hot."

"I'm okay," he lied. "So, where are you going?"

"I'd rather not tell you, Robert."

"I understand."

"And if Vernon questions you, maybe you'd say . . ."

"I'll tell him I never saw you."

She managed a smile. "Thanks for everything."

"You're making the right decision," he assured her.

Robert watched her joining Kevin, Melissa and Nixon in the back of the black taxi. They waved at him, as the cab pulled away.

Harold Daley held his creased jacket folded over his forearm and took a drag on his cigarette. Normally, at this time of the morning, the station would have been packed with commuters but not today. The bodies were gone. The train remained at the platform with its doors open. The Underground strike meant there was no particular hurry. But the forensic team were finished and there was little more to be gleaned from examining the carriage. It would soon be removed and taken away for a thorough cleaning.

Bryon O'Sullivan stood close to Daley, drinking lukewarm coffee from a plastic cup. Daley felt drained. His forehead was damp and his shirt sucked the skin on his shoulders and back. He looked at the carriage. Black streaks of blood marked the dirty windows and dark pools had dried on the ribbed floor. O'Sullivan took another sip from his coffee and then spilled the remains onto the filthy platform. He crushed the cup and chucked it onto the rails. Daley flicked his cigarette butt in the same direction.

"I'm going back," he told O'Sullivan. "Want a lift?"

They found Smith by the ticket machines. Daley collared him and they pressed through the small crowd gathered around the Earls Court Road entrance to the station. The sun beat down on them through the haze filter. The air was dirty. The traffic was a nightmare. The transport strike had encouraged people to use their cars, so the city was jammed.

Several drunks congregated by a newspaper vendor, waiting for the off-licence to open. They counted their copper coins and wondered whether there would be enough for a cheap two-litre plastic bottle of cider. A queue started to form outside the Post Office. Daley walked into a man who was munching a hamburger which leaked melted synthetic cheese onto his shoes. He was scouring the sports page of a tabloid. He muttered something through his greasy mouthful and moved on, eyes cast down, as he left a trail of shredded lettuce and tomato ketchup behind him.

A uniformed officer handed Daley a large, padded envelope as they climbed into a police car. The driver pulled out into the traffic. The flashing blue light was of little use in combating the vehicular paralysis.

"What's in the envelope?" Smith asked.

"Security-video from the new set of platform cameras they've been testing."

The car finally reached Kensington Police Station, at the top of the Earls Court Road. They walked into a room where the light was dim and the air was soured by tobacco smoke. In one corner, the harsh glare of a computer screen cast a sickly green glow over a collection of dirty cups and an overflowing ashtray which had been stolen from a pub.

Smith was thumbing through some of the statements. "It seems as though they both have names beginning with R. Robin, Richard, Robert. Something with R."

Daley nodded. "That's right. And two of the witnesses on the train said they heard him calling her Rachel."

There was a knock on the door and a uniformed officer entered the room and handed Daley a piece of paper.

"What's this?" he asked, preferring to hear it, rather than read it.

"The check on the Cadogan."

"And?"

"There were two who remembered. We've interviewed both of them again. There was a bellboy who actually put it in his original statement and he's just confirmed it for us. And there was a woman who was working on the reception desk. She remembers it quite well, but didn't include it in her original statement because she didn't think it was relevant.

"She was on duty at the time and got a good look at her. Physically, she seems to match. She never spoke to anyone, so far as we can tell. The woman on the desk just assumed she was meeting someone and knew where to go."

"Smart," conceded Daley. "Listen, I want you to get hold of Lang."

"Lang?"

"The Yank. The one staying at the Monarch, down in Pimlico. Remember?"

"The vampire-hunter?" asked Smith, incredulously.

"I know, I know! I think he's a fraud too, but he seems to know more than he should. Maybe now would be a good time to talk to him in more detail, don't you think?"

Smith shrugged. "Whatever you say."

Daley looked at the uniformed officer and nodded towards the door. "You can show them in now, if you like."

The young man opened the door and the officers who were waiting outside slowly filed in. Daley tore open the padded envelope and took out the video-cassette. There was a large television on a raised stand in one corner of the room. He slipped the cassette into the video-player.

"Before we have a look at this," he told the assembled congregation, "I'd like you to fill me in on any developments."

Smith flicked through several sheets of paper that were fastened to the clipboard on his lap. Daley counted another dozen people crammed into the airless office. Four were standing, while the others sat unevenly around the table. Smith looked up and addressed a man with closely cropped ginger hair. "You got something, didn't you?"

The officer nodded eagerly and turned in his seat to address Daley directly. "That's right, sir. From the Reynolds place."

Daley perked up, as he removed the plastic outer wrapper from a new packet of cigarettes. He pulled one out and lit it. "What was it?"

"Someone saw our girl there. One of the residents. His name is Roger Quick and he lives in flat thirty-one. Forty-four years old. An economics lecturer at King's College. He was on his way out and saw her in the hall looking for a name on the board, so he asked if he could help. She ignored him. Didn't say a word, apparently. She just walked right by him – close enough to brush his sleeve, so he says – and went upstairs."

Daley looked around for Malloy and, when he couldn't see him, asked, "Where's Kevin?"

"Last I heard he was checking out some freak who walked into Paddington Green this morning. Confessed to everything. Complete bullshit, as usual!"

"How many is that now?"

"About a dozen."

"*Sick!*" muttered Daley, bitterly.

By one wall there was a narrow table with three computer terminals. Daley leaned against one, resting his elbow on top of the computer closest to the television. The room was a mess. It stank of cigarette smoke and if human fatigue had a smell, then it reeked of that as well.

There were several other people missing. Callaghan was cross-checking vehicles. Rosie Marsh was one of four who were continuing to interview people from Earls Court Underground.

Daley said, “It looks as though it's the girl we want. We're pretty sure there was no male at either the Cadogan or at the Reynolds place. Where he fits into the picture isn't clear.”

Daley moved away from the computer and slowly started to circle the room. He stretched his back and then scratched the bristles on his cheek.

“The other thing we know is that she doesn't appear to have used a weapon. On every occasion she's been seen, she's had no baggage of any sort and has usually been dressed in clothes that couldn't conceal a sheet of tissue, let alone some kind of instrument for carving people to pieces. She's not selecting weapons from what's available at the crime scenes, either. The wounds are too uniform for that.”

He turned on the kettle and spooned some granules into a plastic cup. There were four opened cartons of milk on the table. Three were off. He poured milk from the fourth, added sugar and then hit the “play” button on the machine.

It was a large screen. The camera had a fixed angle from above the platform. In the bottom right-hand corner white digits gave the date and time. There were pockets of passengers clustered together, punctuated by a few strays. There was a group who were clearly drunk. The train arrived, pulling up slowly to the platform. Most of the figures were bland and indistinct, but everyone in the room recognized her when she stepped out of the carriage. Watching the soundless images was eerie. Suddenly there was a commotion. Two or three stunned onlookers formed a group which quickly became a small crowd. They were pointing into the coffin carriage. Then there was a silent hysteria.

At Daley's request, the uniformed officer replayed the sections that showed Rachel. He managed to get a close-up of both the man and the woman, but the more he focused on detail, the more clarity was sacrificed.

He caught himself wondering what they would have heard if the pictures had been accompanied by a soundtrack. The screaming would have filled the cavernous hall. Echo would have made the cries louder.

Daley asked for a freeze-frame. The image burned into everyone's mind and he touched a light-switch to brighten the room a fraction.

"I know what you're thinking," he told them. "I can see it in your faces. This bitch is in complete control of herself. You're all wondering the same thing I'm wondering: how the hell does she do it? How can she possibly be so detached? What the fuck is she?"

When Chris and Katherine reached Lennox Gardens, they went down the tradesman's steps to the basement, just as Rachel was coming out of Robert's flat.

Chris said, "Is Robert Stark in?"

Rachel was wearing a pair of loose blue cotton trousers and a large white T-shirt. Dark sunglasses concealed her eyes. She placed Katherine immediately. Jennifer Colson's younger sister. She smiled at their mutual memories. The other one took a little longer, but once she made the connection, she was surprised.

"No, he's out," she told them.

"Will he be back soon?"

She shrugged. "I don't know. Can I help?"

"I'm not sure. Who are you?"

Rachel smiled. "His nearest and dearest. Rachel Cates. Who are you?"

"Chris Lang. This is Katherine Ross."

Katherine felt something stir within her. The woman looked vaguely familiar. Rachel ignored Katherine and looked at him. "Lang? Really?"

"That's right."

Rachel thought about this for a moment and then nodded. Now she understood. She said to him, "Did you two come here before, to see Robert? With the other two?"

Chris nodded. "That's right. Richard Elmore and Stephen Abraham."

"Abraham?" she murmured. "As in the sculptor?"

"Yes. You know him?"

This seemed to amuse her. She wore a crooked smile. "Sort of. I know some of his work. He's overrated."

Chris inclined his head to one side and said, "I couldn't agree more."

Katherine watched the exchange and felt her earlier suspicion growing stronger. She wrestled with dates and names and places.

Rachel looked Chris up and down. He was tall and broad with thick hair that was quite curly. His dark eyes had an attractive sleepy quality to them. Rachel noted that Katherine was not dissimilar to her elder sister. Jennifer had harboured plenty of unspoken jealousies regarding the woman who stood on the steps. Rachel wondered if Katherine ever guessed as much. There was one way to find out and the possibility amused her. Sisters would be a rare coup. Katherine had the same dark straight hair and pale skin. Rachel could see she made more of an effort than Jennifer had. Katherine stood behind Chris and looked anxious, wishing she could see the eyes behind Rachel's glasses.

"Could we go inside and talk?" he asked.

Rachel looked up at the sky. "I was going for a walk in the gardens. The flat's too gloomy for a day like this. You're welcome to join me, if you wish."

All three of them rose to pavement level and crossed the road to the central gardens. They walked beside the railings until they reached the entrance. Rachel produced a key from her pocket, unlocked the gate and ushered them in.

"You live here?" Chris asked.

"The first floor," she said, turning round and pointing at it. "The one with the french windows opening onto the balcony."

Katherine said, "And you and he are . . . ?"

Rachel turned round. "Are what?"

"Well, you know . . . it's a little unusual."

"Resident and caretaker? Yes, I suppose it is. But you can't legislate for love, can you? I'm sure that's something your sister understood."

Rachel was pleased to catch both of them off-guard. Jennifer Colson had been desperately in love when she died.

"What do you mean?" asked Katherine.

Rachel considered dropping the whole load, but in the end restrained herself. "As I understand it, she was seeing André Perlman, a violinist who was considerably younger than she was, a man with a reputation for emotional volatility, whereas she was usually regarded as a very traditional woman. That's what I mean. Love chooses unpredictable targets sometimes."

Chris took a pack of cigarettes out of his breast-pocket and offered Rachel one. She refused. An Indian girl was leading her Alsatian around the path. Rachel stepped onto the burned grass. There were only a few feeble patches of green left on the scarred lawn. Pigeons flapped around the upper branches of a tree.

"Are you aware that Robert's ill?" Chris asked, before bringing a match to his cigarette.

"Of course."

"Do you know what he's got?"

Rachel nodded. "I know exactly what he's got. Do you?"

Chris frowned. He wondered how she could be so certain, assuming his own suspicions were correct. He sounded unsure when he said, "I think it's some sort of blood disorder."

Her snort of laughter was dismissive, almost contemptuous. "A blood disorder? It's more serious than that."

A thought occurred to Chris. He recalled what Abraham said about his dark feelings for Robert Stark, when he first came across him in the night club and then the second time, when the impression had been stronger. He said, "You've encountered Stephen Abraham before, haven't you?"

"Maybe."

"At Seven of Hearts. You were there with Stark, weren't you? What happened when you ran into Abraham?"

She smiled. "Very good. Two and two are finally beginning to make four, aren't they? Tell me something, where is Abraham today? Did you forget to ask him?"

"Why do you suppose I would have asked him at all?"

"You tell me. Why was he here in the first place? Just for the hell of it? I don't think so."

Rachel was toying with him. Chris had rung Stephen Abraham earlier in the morning and asked him to come with Katherine to Lennox Gardens. He refused, citing preparations for his Breaking Skin exhibition as the reason.

"He was busy."

"Oh, I can imagine!" she scoffed.

"He has an exhibition coming up and . . ."

"Don't patronize me. I know you've been using Abraham as your canary in the coal-mine."

Katherine suddenly made the connection. "You're the private commission!" she exclaimed.

Chris looked lost. "What?"

Rachel grinned and nodded.

Katherine turned to Chris. "The private commission at Abraham's house? Don't you remember? The work that he said wasn't part of the exhibition. There were sketches tacked to the wall for the marble sculpture."

"A crude block of stone from which you no doubt saw me emerging," remarked Rachel, brushing hair from her eyes.

Chris recalled the work. "Jesus Christ! He was right, wasn't he?"

Rachel continued to find humour in the situation. She said to him, "You still don't recognize me, do you?"

He furrowed his brow. "What?"

"We've met before. Don't you remember me?"

Now he was completely surprised. His memory couldn't turn up a face or a name. The thin rasp of a cheap radio was just audible from a car on the kerb. The driver hung his arm out of the window and drummed the door panel in time with the music.

Chris said, slowly, "I don't think so. You've made a mistake."

"No, I haven't. Think again."

He did. Katherine bit her lip and disliked the direction the conversation was taking.

"No," he said. "I can't place you."

"Let me give you some assistance then, Mr Lang. Except you're not Mr Lang, are you? That's not your name, is it?"

"Yes, it is," he said, without conviction.

Rachel said, "I think your surname is Martin."

"No!" he whispered.

"You might be Lang now, but you weren't always, were you? I think you were born into the Martin household."

Katherine couldn't believe how quickly skin could lose its colour. Chris looked winded.

"Your father was Dr Andrew Martin, wasn't he?"

Chris glanced at Rachel in horror. She slowly removed her glasses, so he could see the glitter in her gaze. Katherine reached for his arm and held onto it.

"And your mother was Margaret Martin. I believe her maiden name was Forbes. You have a sister called Julia. Right?"

Chris felt dizzy. His knees were weak and he really believed he might collapse. "She . . . Julia's . . . dead!"

Rachel looked serious for an instant. "Julia's dead? I didn't know that. I'm sorry." She raised an eyebrow and cocked her head to one side. "What happened to her?"

He just shook his head sadly. Katherine held him more tightly and said, "Please stop it! Leave him alone!"

Rachel smiled cruelly. "Well, well! I hadn't realized! It didn't occur to me that you two were . . . I must be losing my touch!"

"How do you know this?" he asked.

She appeared to ignore the question and said, "Lang is your adopted surname. It belongs to your Californian uncle . . . from

San Francisco, as I recall. That's where you and Julia went to live, wasn't it?"

"How do you know this?" he repeated.

"Do you remember me now?"

"No, I don't."

"What were you doing on the day President Kennedy was assassinated?" she asked him, still smiling. "Everybody remembers that, don't they?"

Chris was shaking and sat down on a nearby bench, suddenly old and infirm. Katherine looked at Rachel and couldn't understand what they were talking about. Had he been lying? Was Rachel lying? And what was she doing talking about the day Kennedy was shot? If she'd been alive at all, she would have been gurgling in a cradle in 1963.

"What happened on 22 November 1963?"

"Kennedy."

"Not Kennedy. What happened?"

He looked up at her. The blistering sun formed a blinding halo around her head and forced him to squint.

"No, not you!"

She nodded. Katherine was completely lost, looking from one to the other and learning nothing.

Rachel said, "I was going by another name, in those days. You might remember me as Marilyn . . ."

"Webber!" he cried.

She smiled slyly. "That's right. Marilyn Webber. Different hair colour, different haircut, *definitely* different clothes. I was Marilyn Webber."

"That's not possible!" he exclaimed. "You couldn't have been . . ."

"Julia was in the house that night, wasn't she? I knew you were both there. I spied you through the crack in the door. She blocked your eyes and tried to shut out the noise, but she saw and heard everything, didn't she?" Rachel allowed a pause for it to sink in, before adding, "Did that experience have something to do with the fact that she's no longer with us?"

He was in shock. Katherine looked up at Rachel and whispered, "What the hell's going on?"

She ignored her and continued to address Chris. "I've aged rather well, don't you think?"

He said, "I don't think . . . it doesn't look . . . like you've aged at all."

This amused her. "That's a more accurate observation than you probably realize, Chris Martin. In fact, I haven't aged a single millisecond since that night." Then her good humour vanished. If Chris had been in Robert's place in the London Underground carriage, he would have recognized the deadly look which clouded her face.

"I don't understand."

"I don't expect you do, so be wise."

She put them both in temporary shadow. Chris had dropped his cigarette. It was burning a black patch on a piece of brown ground.

"What do you want?" asked Chris.

"I want to be left alone," she said. "I'm not going to be around here for much longer, but while I am, I'd like it to be peaceful. There's been too much violence already. Just leave me alone, and I'll leave you alone. In a day or two, I'll be gone forever and all this will be committed to memory. That's the safest place for it, believe me."

She took a step forward and looked down on the humble pair. She stretched her hand out and ran her fingertips slowly across Chris's cheek. Katherine never moved.

Rachel said, "I could kill both of you in the blinking of an eye, right here, right now, and I'd be so quick that the old fools looking down at us from these surrounding buildings wouldn't even realize what they'd seen. I don't want to do it, but I won't think twice about it if you give me a reason."

Chapter Seventeen

They were sitting outside a pub, at one of several wooden tables which were on the pavement. Chris was staring into the double whisky she'd bought him. She thought the fog of shock was at last beginning to clear. He'd been almost incoherent in the gardens, as they watched Rachel Cates disappearing.

"Let's start with your name," she suggested. "What is it?"

"Legally, it's Lang. But I was born Martin. Like she said, I went to live with my aunt and uncle in San Francisco. They adopted us."

"*Us?* I assume you're talking about Julia."

"Yes."

"You told me you didn't have any brothers or sisters."

"I know."

"So why the lie?"

"Because it was easier than the truth. I didn't want to dwell on painful memories."

"Your sister's a painful memory?"

Chris shook his head. "No, but she features in plenty of them. She's the star."

"I don't understand."

"Of course you don't. How could you?"

She was caught off-guard by the snap in his voice. When she looked at him, he averted his gaze and she felt guilty, although she did not know why. Perhaps her phrasing had been too jokey, but his reaction was still too serious. For a moment, he looked back at her and said, "I mean, when you think of Jennifer what comes to mind?"

Katherine was shocked by the question. It seemed insensitive to the point of brutality. "What do you mean?"

He showed no remorse for the verbal stab. On the contrary, the look on his face was pure determination. Either he hadn't considered whether the enquiry might sting, or he didn't care. "I'm talking generally. I'm not talking about her death, but before that. What are your memories of her?"

She was still floundering. "Well, I'm not sure. Her cello playing, perhaps. She was at her best with her music. I think of the holidays we had as children, or her dreadful dress sense, the things we laughed at . . ."

"That's right. Happy times."

"Not all of them," she insisted. "I remember how upset David used to make her. The phone calls we had which stretched into the night. The times she came to stay and . . ."

"Happy times and sad times," Chris corrected himself, "but normal times. Normal memories, right?"

"I suppose so," she agreed with a curious frown.

"You know what I think about when Julia's in my mind?"

There was bitterness in his tone, but Katherine couldn't decide whether it was due to anger or desperation. "What?"

"I think of her standard issue nightdress, made out of some sort of medicated paper. I can smell institutional disinfectant. I hear pistol-size keys turning in locks and see wire-mesh covering the windows. Her eyes look jaundiced; the whites are yellow, dry and dead. I look at the leather restrainers around her forearms – they're like vast wristbands – and I'm glad they're there because they cover up the jagged scars made by the scissors."

Katherine flinched at the severity of the image which filled her mind. Scissors and skin. Chris looked away from her as he dredged up further horrors from his memory.

"The scars . . ." he murmured, almost drawling. "There were too many to count. All bright and pink and shiny. They crossed over each other, corporal intersections. It looked like a really bad street-plan for a crowded city; highways and byways of cauterized skin. I think it's the scars more than any other thing that really get to me. More than the drugs she was made to take, more than the hospitals she was sent to, more than what Marilyn Webber did.

"There are other memories, of course. Good ones, like you have about Jennifer. But they're never the ones that spring to mind. I have to struggle past all the worst ones before I can remember anything good about her, and even then, the image is stained. I still get nightmares about it and . . ."

"I know."

Chris looked back at her, evidently surprised. "You do?"

"At my flat? Or was that about something else?"

He smiled sadly at the recollection. "No, it wasn't. It's never about something else."

His venomous attitude suddenly vanished. He bowed his head slightly and she saw some of the tension in his face ease. He took a deep breath and looked as though he were about to speak, before sighing and gently shaking his head.

On instinct, Katherine found herself saying, "I'm sorry."

"Don't be. I'm the one who should be sorry. There was no need for me to jump down your throat."

"Maybe, but under the circumstances, it's understandable. I shouldn't have been so flippant about equating your sister with painful memories. It just slipped out, a cheap quip."

He nodded and looked deep into her eyes. "They always let us down, don't they?"

A police car cruised slowly by and Katherine, keen to change the subject, said, "So tell me something about Rachel. What is she?"

He shrugged. "I wish I could tell you."

"What about this 1963 business? She couldn't have possibly been around then. I mean, she might have been a baby or something, but . . ."

"I know. It's crazy. But that's not the worst of it. She knows things she couldn't possibly have known unless she'd been there."

"Where?"

"At home, on the day Marilyn Webber murdered my parents."

Katherine mouthed the word "murder", but Chris didn't see it. He took another drag from his cigarette.

"It's peculiar to think about it now," he said. "It's so long since the event, and I've thought about it so often it really doesn't seem that real any more. It feels like something I saw on a screen. I guess if you replay something enough – if you analyse it to death – then it just loses its potency."

"What happened?"

"She came to our house. My father was very excited about it. My mother wasn't, but that was her style, you know. I asked Julia what was going on, but she didn't know – or didn't care. I thought my mother's coolness might have been jealousy. Marilyn Webber was pretty to look at and my father was excited, so you know . . . you add it all up."

She smiled. "Natural enough, I suppose."

"About one-thirty in the morning I was woken by the sound of shouting. I got up and went across the landing to Julia's room. We sat together for a while, wondering when it would finish. Then we ventured downstairs and as we got closer, the sound got clearer.

"Julia and I were huddled together in the corridor outside the living-room. The door was partly open and we could peep through the narrow slit by the hinges."

Chris's eyes were unusually intense as he dug into the memory bank. Katherine wondered how much of the past's reality had been embellished by years of painful imagination, transformed from fearful fantasy into fact.

"Julia played the big sister. She covered my eyes with her hands and encircled my head with her arms, trying to shut out the noise. But she only dimmed it. The screams were indistinct to me, followed by a sequence of the most bizarre sounds I've ever heard. It all finished in an explosion of glass. Julia saw and heard everything. Once it was over, she let me go and we tiptoed into the living-room and there it was."

Chris stopped for a moment and swallowed, avoiding eye-contact with her. Katherine felt the hairs stand up on her arm.

"They were on the floor and their . . . their hearts were like . . . they were next to them. Torn out. Blood everywhere. Broken furniture, broken bones. I don't remember even being that upset. It was just too much, the mind was overloaded, the fuses blew, nothing registered."

"The hearts?"

Chris nodded. "Yes."

"Like you said happened to Jennifer?"

"Like I said *might* have happened to her."

Katherine nodded. "And Marilyn Webber? Where was she?"

"Gone. Through the living-room window. I don't know what she did, but the whole thing was shattered. Not just the panes and glass, but the whole structure. She damn nearly blew a hole in the wall. Julia and I were standing there, up to our ankles in family blood, too dumbstruck to do anything."

Chris finished his whisky. He wore a blank expression, like he was talking about somebody else's tragedy. Katherine plucked the glass from the table and went inside for a refill, glad to break the moment. He sat in the sun and smoked his cigarette. When she returned, he seemed relaxed.

"How come Marilyn Webber came to be at your house in the first place? Where did your father meet her?"

Chris thought about it for a moment. "To be honest, I'm not sure how he first heard of her, but when he actually tracked her down and met her, she was terrorizing a small mining community in the Appalachian Mountains of Virginia. These people were poor and desperate anyway but, from what I've learned, she made their lives before her arrival look like some kind of prize.

"Burrows was this godforsaken little town, cut off from the rest of the world in every sense. A backwater that existed only to service some crummy mine that was about to go out of business, a real third-world pocket. To the outside world, it was the sort of community that was nothing more than an embarrassment. The kind of people who lived in Burrows were considered half-crazy in the first place. The underclass. So no one paid much attention when they started claiming they were being victimized by some monster who roamed the mountains that loomed over the town.

"But that was *exactly* what was happening. Marilyn Webber was living above Burrows, among the woods which covered the hills. She was an animal of the wild."

There was an awkward silence. Chris was thinking about Rachel's threat. He had no doubt she was serious. Katherine was contemplating everything Chris had just told her. She could barely believe she was even listening to this, let alone accepting it.

"When I was a little older, Josef Koptet approached me himself, offering assistance and fatherly advice – *surrogate*-fatherly advice, I suppose. At that time, Koptet had just set up the institute in Seattle, but he was based in Los Angeles, which was the headquarters for Koptet Pharmaceutical, his money-making machine.

"I was pretty hostile towards him at first, as if I somehow blamed him for what happened to my parents. But he persevered and I mellowed, gradually becoming more interested in what my father had been doing. Up until that point, I'd always just assumed he was a regular doctor – I was too young to know better. But I became intrigued by his research and that, as much as anything else, dictated the course I was to follow. In the end, it was neither an accident nor a surprise that I wound up working for Josef at the Koptet Institute."

"Jack Clark phoned me this morning," he told her. "I could barely hold a conversation with him. Every time I opened my mouth, I wanted to ask him whether he slept with Sarah."

Rachel sighed. "I regret telling you about that. I should have kept quiet."

"You had to convince me. Or at least try to. But all you've

done is confuse me. Jack's one of my oldest, closest friends and all I really wanted to do was punch his lights out! I just couldn't get the idea out of my mind."

"I'm sorry, darling."

Rachel approached him slowly. When she looked at him lovingly, her innocence seemed incontestable. She intoxicated him. Every shimmering touch and blistering kiss left him light-headed. Those who say that physical beauty's only skin deep, that it never lasts, are wrong. With Rachel, it was guaranteed forever. No decay and no change. Besides, her beauty went far deeper than the skin.

They went for a walk. The sun was climbing high into the sizzling mustard sky. Pont Street was choked with cars and buses. As they passed the Cadogan Hotel, on the other side of the road, she pointed at the building.

"See that window on the first floor? That one there, the one that's slightly opened?"

"Yes."

"That's Room 114. That's where I learned to play the cello and the violin."

He looked up at the window, set in the red-tinged brick. What she meant was, that was the room where she tore two musicians to pieces. She made it sound so virtuous and she enjoyed it. Robert tried not to look shocked.

"You haven't got long, darling," she said, evenly.

"What do you mean?"

"I've seen the signs in you. Your skin is losing its colour. The flesh is dying. Your eyes are getting duller. This morning I noticed how poorly the pupils dilate. They try to change with the light but their reactions are slowing."

"I don't feel markedly worse."

"Trust me, I've seen it before. You don't have much time. You're going to have to make up your mind very soon."

They bought a litre carton of chilled orange juice and some french bread before entering Hyde Park. People played football on the beige grass, using piles of shirts as goal posts. Cyclists in Lycra shorts and multi-coloured racing vests weaved in and out of slow pedestrians, who ambled along the irregular network of inter-connecting paths. Robert and Rachel left the baking tarmac and strolled across the firm earth.

"What's going to happen?"

"We must exchange blood again. Just as the initial transfer is killing you – *has* killed you – so my blood will save you. You have to die and then . . ."

"*Die?*"

"And then my blood will give you life again, just as it's taking it away from you right now."

"I die?"

She stood in front of him and flicked some hair out of his eyes. "Don't worry, darling. I'll be there. It'll be fine."

Robert felt panic. "You never said anything about dying, Rachel. Jesus Christ! I don't want . . ."

"In return for immortality?" she interrupted. "You know what you're giving up? A gradual decline into old age, a death of decrepitude. That's what you're forgoing. And what do you get back? Not just immortality, but the ability to ascend to a higher plane of existence altogether."

He heard what she was saying but couldn't get the notion of dying out of his mind. She held him and stared into his eyes.

"You'll be like a god compared to these people. Dying's going to be a minuscule price for what you'll be." She kissed him. "I'd say it was the bargain of all time, wouldn't you?"

They reached the Serpentine. The notion of his own death was swimming in Robert's mind. They crossed the bridge. He took a swig from the carton of orange juice. The ducks and swans at the water's edge seemed to resent the human intrusion.

He said, "What is it that makes me feel better around you?"

"The energy I'm giving off."

"But you don't have the same effect on everyone, do you?"

"No. Only you are affected because of your condition. It's rather like radio transmission. You're receiving the signal because you're tuned into the wavelength on which I'm broadcasting."

Some riders were working their horses along the sand track. The thundering hooves sent up explosions of dry sand. The horse sweat foamed beneath the saddles.

"And even though I feel better in your presence – because of this energy field – I'm still going to die?"

"You are."

"So when this is all over . . . what will I be?"

"Be? You'll be immortal. You'll live forever."

"But what will it be like? What will I feel?"

"It's pointless for me to go into detail because it won't mean anything to you now. One thing's for sure, though: once you've grown accustomed to the changes, and to the reality of your new condition, you might find things you currently regard as sacred no longer seem that important."

"Like what?"

She said, "Human life, for example," in a way which suggested she had picked it out at random. But he didn't think it was as spontaneous as she made it appear. "I'm not saying that immortality makes the mortal lives of human beings worthless. It merely puts them in their rightful place."

There were a couple lying on a tartan blanket. They held each other in their arms and kissed, much to the amusement of a group of children who sat nearby. Two dogs ran round in circles, each chasing the tail of the other. A fat man lay on his back, fast asleep, with a copy of the *Daily Mail* over his face.

"Why me, Rachel? If everything you've said is true, you could have had anyone you wanted. But you chose me. That doesn't make sense."

Rachel smiled sympathetically and said, "Love isn't logical. I don't know why it turned out to be you, darling. But the very first time I saw you, I knew. I felt it. You exploded in my heart. Do you believe in love at first sight?"

Robert laughed a little. "Can't say I do."

"Nor did I. When you've been lonely for as long I have, it gives you a healthy sense of scepticism. But the moment I saw you, it changed. Love at first sight. It happens."

The distant wail of an ambulance siren stood out against the background hum of a labouring city. A mother was calling back her daughter from the water's edge.

"After all the painful years, it was obvious in a moment."

Robert asked, "How did it happen?"

"I saw you in a restaurant. I was there with a very tedious banker, organizing the purchase of a house in the south of France."

"Very nice, I'm sure."

"It is. You'll find out for yourself soon enough. We'll go there when this is finished. Anyway, I was looking around the room, while pretending to listen to what he was saying, when I suddenly caught sight of you. There were four of you at the table, but you were the only one I truly saw. You looked so sad and . . ."

Her voice drifted into silence. Robert waited for her to resume but it didn't look as though she was going to.

"What happened?"

"It's hard to find words that are adequate. I suppose it was like being shot. This enormous sensation – it was almost painful, it *was* painful – erupted inside me. The shock made me dizzy. I looked across the dining-room once more and it was as though you were highlighted in a tube of brilliant light, while everyone else was forced into the gloom of heavy shade. I was powerless to do anything about it. It was the first time I'd ever experienced that complete loss of control.

"Anyway, I made my excuses to leave. It was raining. I crossed the street and stood beneath the canopy of a jeweller's store, trying to gather myself. I was shaking with excitement and confusion. Two centuries of emptiness brought to a shuddering end in one casual glance! I could barely stand up!

"To begin with, I thought I must be wrong. It couldn't be! But I waited all the same and when I saw you stepping out of the restaurant, it hit me again. That was when I really knew.

"I followed you home and discovered where you lived. I was careful not to rush. Everything had to be correct and thorough, but it was difficult not to let my enthusiasm get the better of me. My research was painstaking and wonderful. Every little detail I learned set me alight. I was obsessed. The countless hours I spent watching you passed as quickly as seconds. My appetite for you grew greater and the more I absorbed you, the more it confirmed what I felt in that first moment: you were the one I crossed two centuries for.

"But I couldn't spend all my time looking and learning. After the hopeless years, I was impatient to move closer, to actually have contact. When the first-floor apartment at Lennox Gardens became available, I bought it immediately.

"You ask me why it turned out to be you? I don't know. I don't even care."

A father was trying to demonstrate the art of kite-flying to his restless son. There wasn't even a hint of a breeze to help him. Someone whistled by them on a skateboard with earphones clamped tightly to his skull. A young man with long greasy hair sat on a bench with his legs stretched out across the wooden slats. His attention was focused on the pages of a worn copy of *Jamaica Inn*. Not far from him, a fat middle-aged man stood barefoot by the water, smoking a cigarette and looking vacantly into the distance.

"Where did you first see me?"

"I told you. In a restaurant."

"Which one? Can you remember?"

She smiled. "*Can I remember?* How could I ever forget? It was Villa Manzari."

Robert cast his mind back. Villa Manzari. It took a few moments, but then he recalled the time and the place. There had indeed been four of them and Robert remembered feeling outraged at the prices which the other three took for granted.

"That was well over a year ago," he pointed out.

"I'm aware of that."

"You mean you've been scheming all this time and . . ."

"*All this time?*" she laughed. "For me, it's barely been time to blink when you consider how long I waited for you."

They were back at Katherine's flat, as afternoon conceded to night. Chris appeared to have conquered the shock of phoenix-like memories rising from the ashes of his past.

She asked him, "What are we going to do about her?"

"I don't know," he confessed. "I really don't."

"Do you believe she was Marilyn?"

Chris smiled. "You've seen her. If she was Marilyn that would make her at least fifty now, probably closer to sixty. Does she look like a sixty-year-old to you?"

Katherine was drinking a glass of wine. She dipped a finger into the chilled liquid and replied, "Of course not. But you said she knew things she couldn't have known without being there."

"I know. And I stand by that. Which means we find ourselves with a problem that doesn't have a logical solution."

There was something Katherine wanted to discuss, but she felt awkward about raising it. He'd skirted the issue earlier on, but she wasn't sure whether it was by design or by circumstance.

She asked, "What happened to Julia?"

Chris dropped his eyes for a moment. The flinch was over in half a second, but Katherine noticed and said, "You don't have to answer if you don't want to. I was just a little curious and . . ."

"It's okay."

"I know you said you don't normally talk about it, but . . ."

"Julia committed suicide." Chris took a deep breath. "What happened to our parents screwed up both of us. *Obviously.* You can't imagine what that does to you. There's no way I can adequately convey the horror of what we saw.

"After that night, Julia changed entirely. I mean, I changed too but, after a while, I reverted to something close to what I was before. But Julia changed into somebody quite new.

"For one thing, she became a serious introvert. And as far as the killings were concerned, she became a mute. She never spoke about it. Not to the police, the doctors, the psychiatrists, her relatives, her friends. Julia was the only person who really knew what happened. I never saw a thing because she was shielding my eyes. She never once told me, despite all my requests. I mean, I saw what the result was – which was enough – but she wouldn't tell me how it happened.

"Before that time, Julia had been very open and gregarious. She loved childish pranks. You know the sort of thing – lacing the dog's water-bowl with gin to see if we could get it drunk. Stuff like that.

"Once we were out in California, she was under the care of a string of doctors and psychiatrists. The more they studied her, the more she closed up. They put her on expensive drugs, some to keep her calm, some to try and draw her out of her private world – shit, I don't think they knew what they were giving her half the time. They alienated her – I could see that – using her as a guinea-pig for their mind-bending drugs.

"I guess a suicide attempt was inevitable. She took an aspirin over-dose but was discovered just in time. A stomach pump took care of most of the damage. They hadn't had time to dissolve and work their way into the bloodstream."

Katherine was beginning to wish she hadn't been so inquisitive. Chris turned round. "It was six months before they let her out of the psychiatric hospital."

There was no escaping the bitterness in his voice. He was upset, but trying not to show it in front of Katherine.

"She seemed a little happier, you know. She got herself a boyfriend called Paul, a saxophonist in a band. He had an offer for some session work back in Philadelphia. Julia chose to go with him. None of us thought it was a good idea, but we were just so relieved that she was behaving normally again, we didn't want to upset her in case . . . I don't know."

"In case it triggered something bad?"

"I suppose so, yes."

Katherine really wanted to say something to comfort him, but couldn't find the words. He came away from the window and pulled out his wallet. He reached inside and withdrew a dog-eared photograph which he handed to her. Katherine looked at a smiling girl with sun in her blonde hair. Time had faded the colour in the print.

"She was pretty."

"That was taken the day before she left for Philadelphia with Paul."

Katherine handed the shot back and he inserted it into his wallet once more. He didn't say anything. Katherine watched his eyes darting here and there, settling on nothing.

He stubbed out his cigarette and paced anxiously around the room. When he was back by the window, his hands were clasped behind his back. She wondered whether he realized how frantically his fingers were fidgeting, tying themselves into temporary, tight knots, leaving marks on the skin.

"About a month after I got back to San Francisco, I got this call. It was five in the morning or something. A friend of Paul's . . . telling me Paul and Julia were both in hospital."

"Both?"

He looked her in the eye. "She attacked him with a pair of scissors. Tried to kill him. And when she thought she'd done enough, she used them on herself."

Katherine felt a lurch in her stomach.

"Paul recovered," Chris said, "but was horribly scarred. Said he never knew why she did it. They didn't argue. There was nothing wrong, no tension, no pressure. He'd just been getting up in the morning, doing his teeth in the bathroom and suddenly, there she was. He said she came tearing through the doorway and managed to stab him five or six times in the back before he even knew who it was."

He shook his head and swallowed the rest of the sentence. Katherine said, "Please, Chris!"

"As for Julia . . . well, she had scars like roads on a map. All over her arms. Even on her throat. Can you imagine that? You try to kill yourself by scissoring open your neck? Jesus Christ!"

Katherine rose from her seat and was about to go over to him, but he raised a preventative arm. She stood still.

"So Julia came back to California and they locked her up in this hospital. Except it felt like prison, you know. I don't know how many times I visited that place. Enough for my mind to be permanently stained by it, that's for sure. The bars, the hard floors, the lock and keys, the stench of disinfectant. I can't get rid of any of it.

"When I think about her, she doesn't wear blue jeans and an all-American smile. She wears a paper nightdress and leather restrainers connected by chains. Every time I went to visit there were more needle marks in both arms. They were pumping all sorts of medication into her – some to keep her down, some to pep her up. Made Keith Richards look like Julie Andrews," he said, laughing bitterly. "The skin toughened up so much they had to start jabbing her in different places. She had veins like leather."

Katherine winced. "How long was she in there?"

"Eight years."

"*Eight* years?"

"Eight, yes. She came out on a warm May morning. I was there, with my aunt and uncle and a couple of other relatives. She really did seem okay. A little subdued and shell-shocked of course – who wouldn't be after eight years? – but essentially a lot better. Anyway, it was all over in less than twenty-four hours."

Katherine was stunned. "What?"

"She used the scissors again. But this time, she did it properly. A hot bath and deep lines along the arteries."

This time, Chris didn't prevent Katherine from approaching. He sank into the nearest armchair, as shocked by making his first confession as he'd always feared he would be.

"She left me a note," he croaked, looking up at Katherine, who sat on the arm of the armchair and placed her hands on his shoulders. "It was in my bedroom. I only discovered it later. She must have placed it there while I was asleep."

"What did it say?" whispered Katherine.

"I never read it. I couldn't. I just . . ."

She leaned forward and kissed him softly. "It's okay, Chris. Don't say any more."

Rachel paced. The tentacles covered a large portion of the

floor. She traced her fingers along the emerald satin sheets. Her temper simmered.

Stephen Abraham had promised to be here, but she'd detected the uncertainty in his voice when he made the assurance. Nevertheless, she thought she'd made herself clear. He was not to leave his house until after she'd seen him. There had been no answer when she rang the bell so she crushed the lock on his back door and let herself in. She scoured the house from attic to cellar and found it empty.

Now she circled his studio, considering her next move. She ran her hand over the roughly hewn block of marble from which her form was escaping. He'd never finish it now. Her anger spilled over and she hit the stone with the base of her hand. The top third exploded into fragment and dust.

She let her rage off the leash, destroying everything she could find. She set light to the sketches he'd made of her, watching the growing flames lick the wall and pool on the ceiling. She squeezed the soapstone horse's head until her fingers fractured the sculpture into half a dozen large chunks. She demolished all of Breaking Skin.

Where was he?

Chapter Eighteen

There was some embarrassment afterwards. Katherine couldn't remember feeling so deeply unfashionable. It wasn't supposed to be nineties behaviour, but then she'd never considered herself to be *en vogue* anyway. They lay in each other's arms and she laughed lightly.

"I feel as ridiculous as a teenager."

He laughed too. "I'm glad you said that. I thought it might just be me."

She thought she'd left these scenarios far behind. Her kisses of comfort had developed into something keener and despite his precarious frame of mind – or maybe because of it – Chris had responded. They made one fleeting gesture to propriety. It was a pathetic attempt, really, more of a passing nod at restraint rather than a serious consideration of it.

"This isn't right, Katherine," he'd mumbled through his kisses, as she moved round from his side to face him.

"Sure it is," she'd replied.

"Not through sympathy."

"This isn't sympathy, Chris."

And that was it. They stumbled into the bedroom. Their thoughts were similar: it didn't feel right, but it was what they wanted, so why not? Neither could honestly shake the fact that their desire was coloured by an awkward sense of the self-conscious, but it wasn't strong enough to hold them back.

Making love was clumsy. It wasn't the cinematic glimpse of heaven that Hollywood traded in, but Katherine thought it was nice. Given her most recent sexual history, it was a welcome and refreshing change. It was honest and clean and she couldn't remember feeling like that. Usually, the aftermath was tainted by an emotion that was more menacing than soothing.

Chris said, "I feel like someone's going to walk through the door and scold us."

"I know what you mean," she said, before kissing him.

"I'm not sure what I think about this coming on the back of my confession."

She didn't want the moment spoiled so she put a finger to his lips. "There's no need to think anything about it. Too much thinking can be dangerous. I should know."

Her forehead was damp and hot. He brushed some of the hair out of her eyes. They lay together in comfortable silence until Chris rose from the bed and dressed.

"How long will you be with Elmore?" she asked.

"I don't know. Not too long, I hope. He wants to discuss Abraham's future, but what's there to say? He doesn't have one."

He kissed her and walked out of the door. She pulled a striped cotton shirt around her shoulders, one of the few relics from her last relationship. The sleeves drooped off the ends of her hands, the tails hung to the backs of her knees. She sauntered into the kitchen and prepared some coffee, sensing shame and delight in equal measure. There had been no scheme, no premeditation at all. It really had been spontaneous. That was what she liked most about it. What she liked least was the timing.

It felt a little shabby to hear his story and then to end up making love to him. But she tried to shake this thought off. It happened. That was all there was to it. Instinct isn't a slave to reason.

The buzzer rang. She assumed Chris had forgotten something and opened the door. Instead, she found Stephen Abraham before her.

"Jesus!" she cried. "*You!*"

He was leaning against the wall in the hall. His skin was grey and gleamed beneath the central overhead light, damp with perspiration.

"Did you pass him?" she asked.

"Who?"

"Chris. He only just left."

"He isn't here?" Abraham sounded desperate and pressed the heel of his left hand against his temple, squeezing his eyes shut for a moment. He was in a black suit with a maroon silk shirt that he'd buttoned up to the throat.

She shook her head. "No. He went to see Elmore."

"Shit!" he snapped.

Katherine swallowed and found herself clutching the front of her shirt, as if that would make it more secure. "What do you want?"

"Oh, you know, the usual things," he said, airily, with a casual flick of the hand. "World peace, an end to global warming, a cure for AIDS, your head on a plate."

She reached for the door and tried to swing it shut, but he stretched out, blocked it and forced it back. Katherine was mugged by panic. She started to back down the hall. Abraham clutched his head again, grinding his teeth and moaning. The chaos had physical form. It was more than voices. He could feel grating inside his skull. Instruction and counter-instruction. He hadn't slept for . . . how long? It was impossible to tell.

"You're not over-dressed, are you?" he said, before running his tongue over his meaty lips. "Am I to understand that you and Lang are . . . *better acquainted* than when I last saw you?"

His phrasing amused him and, for a moment, the torture ceased. He looked smug.

"You can assume what you like!" said Katherine, curtly, in a rare moment of courage. "Now get out!"

Abraham snorted. "What kind of hospitality is this?"

"Take one more step and I'll scream."

He was annoyed. "I'm disappointed in you, Katherine. I'd rather hoped we could get together in an amicable sort of way but, ultimately, it . . ."

He slumped against the wall. She watched in horror as he grimaced and cried out. His eyes were lifeless islands in dark seas. She backed away from him, retreating into the bedroom, the only avenue left open to her. She scanned the room for some weapon with which to defend herself. Abraham was babbling incoherently, protesting to a crowd she couldn't see.

". . . Alone, for God's sake! . . . I won't . . . I can't . . . I . . ."

Katherine saw the hand out of the corner of her eye in the very last instant before it cracked against the side of her face. The blow came without warning and she had no time to avoid it. She smacked against the wardrobe cupboard, crushing half a dozen wooden slats, before falling away. Her legs buckled.

Abraham had tears streaming down his face as he staggered across the bedroom floor like a drunk. He looked as though he had two black eyes.

"What's going on?" he wailed. "*What the fuck is happening to me?* Why me?"

Her head ached and her vision was blurred. She felt nauseous, but couldn't tell if it was from the blow to the head or from sheer panic. She curled into the foetal position on the floor. Abraham paced back and forth at the foot of the bed, looking down at her hatefully before turning his disgusted face away.

"What the fuck am I supposed to do?" he roared to his invisible audience.

Katherine was trying to think. Notions of escape had gone for the moment. She felt too weak and battered to mount a serious challenge to his physical superiority. Now it was a matter of survival.

"Stupid bitch!" he shouted, his voice high enough to sound like a girl's. It was a scary screech. His teeth were clenched and his lips seemed bloodless when he parted them. "You stupid bitch! I told you . . . I . . . where is he?"

Katherine put her hands over her head, partly to drown the sound and partly to protect herself against any further blows. Abraham turned away and thumped the wall.

"I need help!" he yelled. "Where is he? He's got to help me!"

She tried to sort through her options and found she had none so long as she was dazed and temporarily powerless. A sickly voice murmured, "So, let's see what you've got on under this preposterous shirt."

The tone had changed completely. All the anger was gone. She looked up to check it was still Abraham. He loomed over her, appearing as ill as ever, but with intent in his eyes. His new composure frightened Katherine more than his hysterical ranting had. He reached down, grabbed her by the shirt and tossed her onto the bed. Her head swam.

Abraham was shivering. Through pain and pleasure, he felt detached from his body, no longer in control of it, completely at the mercy of his uninvited guests. The reluctant host. His eyes ached and his throat felt dry.

She looked up at him with eyes that flickered uncertainly. She didn't want any tears. Abraham looked at the graze on her right temple and ran his fingers over it.

"This isn't my fault," he told her. "You do see that, don't you? I can't . . . I won't . . ."

His voice faded while he ran his forefinger down the side of her face, over her throat and to the top button of the shirt, which he unfastened. He pulled the cotton away slightly and pressed his hand against her flesh. He leaned forward until his face was just inches above hers, gazing into her petrified eyes before pressing his mouth down onto hers. She pursed her lips as he squeezed his into a bruising kiss. Katherine tried to minimize her revulsion, not to protest too vigorously, but Abraham was so vile, she couldn't prevent herself from resisting the force of his mouth when he tried to part her lips with his tongue.

She had to get him in a vulnerable position and then make one devastating strike, a blow that would incapacitate him long enough to allow her a guaranteed escape. Anything less and . . . she tried not to imagine the consequences.

"Such lovely skin," he murmured thickly, almost swooning with the dizzy pleasure of his anticipation. His voice sounded utterly alien. His pain was gone, torment replaced by delight.

Katherine closed her eyes and cringed, feeling the traces of saliva his mouth left upon her. She kept screaming in her mind, *Be brave, be patient, be . . .*

They both heard it. A distinct noise. Several clunks. The front door. Movement in the hall. Footsteps. Katherine's hopes soared. Abraham lifted his head from her body and wore an expression of utter bewilderment, as both of them looked over to the doorway.

"Chris!" she cried out. "In the bedroom! Chris, help me!"

Rachel wore a summer dress. It was a loose fit; cool for humid days. Her shoulders were mostly bare and she wore her hair gathered back into a pony-tail. She looked at Abraham, who was now on the other side of the bedroom, by the window that looked onto the street. All his fear had returned as she fixed him with a scathing stare. Katherine's head hurt. She closed her eyes and felt dizzy. Rachel was content to stay in the doorway. She looked down at Katherine.

"As far as you and I are concerned, this is a coincidence. I'm only here because of him."

"You've been following me?" he spluttered.

"I told you not to leave the house."

"I . . . but, I . . ."

"You were stupid enough to leave clues in your wake. I had no idea you were so taken by Miss Ross. But then I found the sketches you'd been making of her and thought you'd probably come here. They were really quite good."

"*Were?*"

"That's right. Were. Unless the Fire Brigade have broken some kind of speed record."

"Fire?" he gasped.

She nodded. "I torched your house, your work, everything. You're all that's left."

Abraham stumbled over an overnight bag that was on the floor by a wooden chair. He fell onto one knee and made no attempt to get up. The perspiration that rambled down his neck was starting to stain the collar of his shirt. He tugged at it with two fingers, as if it had suddenly shrunk and become too tight. Rachel regarded him dispassionately.

"Who are you?" he whispered, hoarsely. "What have you done to me?"

"The important thing is not who I am. It's who you are. It's *what* you are. I knew you the moment I saw you. A little man who'd sell his soul to the devil."

Rachel leaned over Katherine and pulled her shirt back across her chest, covering the flesh he'd exposed.

"We don't want him getting more excited than he already is, do we?"

Katherine didn't respond. The closer Rachel moved to Abraham, the further he backed away, until he had nowhere else to go. Katherine heard his breathing quicken. He sat on the floor and bunched his legs up close to his body, holding his hands up in a protective fashion, similar to the way Katherine had when he'd stood over her.

"What do you want?" he whimpered. "Please tell me. What do you want?"

Rachel blew a strand of loose hair out of her eyes. "I want you to know what I am and what you are, to be aware of the differences between us. I want you to realize how worthless, how insignificant you are compared to me."

"I know!" he wailed. "I know!"

"No. You do not know. Not yet. When Robert and I were at Seven of Hearts, I felt your pathetic presence before you even made an approach to us. You didn't really recognize me, did you? Despite the fact that you've sketched me and that I've commissioned a sculpture portrait from you.

"I knew you as soon as I saw you. You thought you were so magnificent – so much *better* – compared to most people you'd ever come across, but look at you now. You're nothing before me. Too small to handle even a sliver of the gift I gave you. Your arrogance exceeded your potential, Abraham."

She leaned closer to him and he winced, as though in real physical pain, even though she wasn't yet close enough to touch him. He bowed his head.

"I was amused to watch you lurching through Seven of Hearts when you felt my presence. You've no idea how comical – how foolish! – you appeared. Everyone thought you were drunk. It would have been better for you if you had been. I didn't know whether to laugh at you or to kill you."

"*What . . . what is . . . he*?" mumbled Abraham.

Rachel beamed. "Confused? I'm not surprised. Robert is something very unusual. He's a . . . *chrysalis*. That's what he is. He's changing."

"Into what?"

"Something magnificent. He'll be what I am soon," said Rachel, before looking at Katherine. "Do you understand this?"

"I don't understand anything."

"But . . . but what . . . is it?" spluttered Abraham.

"Something so fantastic I don't expect you to be able to wrap your little mind around it. He'll be immortal. Like me."

Rachel's words echoed in Katherine's skull. *He'll be immortal. Like me.* She put her fingers to her temple and when she withdrew them there were delicate crimson traces on them. The dizziness and the nausea were starting to pass.

"This is what I wanted you to know. I am immortal. I will live forever. You think you're special, but by comparison, you're nothing."

She took another step closer to him, but didn't touch him. Pain crucified him anyway, except this time it was far worse. He cried. Katherine was mystified and appalled to watch him writhing on the floor, wrapping his arms around his body, grinding his teeth against the need to howl. Rachel peered out of the window.

"You're dying," she told him. "I gave you a glimpse of eternity – a gift you sold yourself for – and I saw you crack. You've insulted me. So now, like casting a small fish back into the water, I'm casting you back."

He looked truly confounded. "But . . . I don't understand."

Rachel smiled and said, "That's okay. You don't have to."

She moved and he screamed. He summoned all his reserves

of energy and self-control for one final effort at salvation. He tried to leap across the bed, heading for the door. Katherine cried out, when it looked as though he'd run right across her. But he didn't because Rachel intercepted him. She took his arm and brought him crashing to the floor. He grunted loudly. Then she reached down with her left hand, dragged him to his feet and hit him with the right. His body was propelled through the doorway into the bathroom. Katherine could scarcely believe her eyes. His feet didn't touch the ground until he smacked against the far wall and collapsed onto the floor.

Rachel turned round. Katherine edged away, nervously looking for implements with which to defend herself. She found herself wondering why. If it came to that, there would be no contest. Rachel's single punch had thrown Abraham ten feet. Katherine wasn't going to combat that with anything short of a bazooka. And if what she said about immortality was right, the bazooka would be a waste of time too.

Rachel said bluntly, "You know I killed your sister, don't you?"

Katherine edged a little further away. "I . . . I wasn't sure."

"But you suspected?"

Katherine bit her lip.

"Little minds have little thoughts," sighed Rachel.

The telephone rang. Both of them looked at it and then Katherine looked at Rachel, who said, "Leave it." It continued to pierce the air with its shrill peals. Rachel ran her hand across the sheets and looked at the two dented pillows. "Jennifer would have been happy."

The phone stopped as Katherine said, "*What?*"

"She wanted you to find a lover. She worried about you. That last guy – the one who was always lying, the one who said he'd never been married – he was no good. She didn't like him at all. A lying bastard. But she would have liked Chris. She *does* like Chris."

Rachel was smiling but Katherine looked horrified. The phone started again and this time Rachel just shook her head in answer to Katherine's gaze. When it stopped, she reached over to the bedside table and removed the receiver from the cradle.

Then she said, "You know, Chris and you both have something in common. Apart from a recently acquired taste for sharing beds, that is."

"What?" asked Katherine, unsure of whether she wanted to find out.

"I've killed and absorbed people you've both loved."

There was a full ten seconds of silence before Katherine said, very slowly, "Absorbed? What does that mean?"

Rachel ignored the question. "What about all those excuses Jennifer dreamed up when she was fending off persistent boys for you? Do you remember? Katherine can't go out with you because she fancies your brother!" she said, in a sing-song voice. Rachel smiled at the memory that had once been Jennifer's memory and was now hers. "She always knew you didn't approve of David and once they were married, she always wished she'd listened to you. Did she ever tell you that?"

Katherine's eyes glistened with tears. Her chin was trembling when she whispered, acidly, "You should know."

Rachel nodded and smiled sympathetically. "Yes, I do know. And she didn't say a word to you. There were many things she wanted to tell you. André was just one of them. It was fear that held her back."

"But she told someone else," said Katherine.

"I know. Caroline Taylor. But she felt guilty about not telling you first."

Katherine was reeling. "Why?" she gasped.

"She didn't want to tell you until she was sure."

"I thought they were in love?"

"They were. Intensely. Believe me, Perlman was hopelessly in love with her, but you know what Jennifer was like. Her self-doubt and lack of confidence always lingered. She couldn't believe someone like Perlman would fall for her, just like she couldn't believe it when Colson first fell for her. And she didn't want to make the same mistake twice. She was scared, Katherine. But she needn't have been. The point is, she wanted to be sure when she told you."

"So how come she told Caroline Taylor?"

"It slipped out by accident."

Katherine frowned. "I spoke to her. It sounded like they had quite a conversation about André."

Rachel shook her head. "They didn't. I think Mrs Taylor's been exaggerating, Katherine. It slipped out in conversation and Jennifer asked Caroline Taylor to keep it a secret, fearing that she wouldn't. Quite rightly, as it turns out."

Katherine felt better knowing that Jennifer hadn't confided willingly in Caroline Taylor. And suddenly she realized what she was doing: accepting Rachel Cates for what she claimed to be. The realization sobered her.

Rachel said, "If it's any consolation, Jennifer had no doubts by the time I visited her. They both knew they were wholly in love. They died in bliss, Katherine."

Rachel's eyes looked ready to judge. Katherine tried to steady herself. There was so much to consider. A low groan emanated from the bathroom. Both women turned to see Abraham shifting minimally. Despite crawling back towards consciousness, he wasn't about to go anywhere.

"Why did you do it?"

"For their talent. I only collect the finest. There's no reason to go for anything less. They were both exceptional and to find them together at the same place – and in love too! – well, it was just too good to . . ."

"Stop!"

"If I had the cello here, I'd play something that would touch the strings in your heart."

Rage and despair waged war inside Katherine, neither yet prevalent. Rachel smiled at Katherine in her baggy shirt. Her sister had been wearing a loose-fitting dress when Rachel ripped her heart out. The entertaining possibilities were endless.

She asked, "What are you thinking?"

Katherine wiped the dampness of misery off her cheek with

the back of her left hand. "Whether you're for real or not. Whether you killed Jennifer or not. And if you did," she muttered through bitter tears, "then I'm thinking about how I can kill you."

"You can't. The only one in this flat who's going to do any killing is me."

Katherine froze. Rachel was grinning. Katherine edged away, kicking at the sheets as she scampered towards the other side of the bed. But there was nothing there for her, except a short stretch of carpet and a solid wall. She was trapped and Rachel was moving across the bed, eating up the distance between them.

Chapter Nineteen

Robert lay still, at the centre of the sitting-room floor, curled into a tight ball with his arms across his stomach. Laura took another look, rubbing her fingers across the window and clearing away a patch of dust and grime.

"Robert!" she cried.

Nothing.

"Robert!"

She went round to his door, which was shut, and so returned to the window. "Let me in," she shouted through the dirty glass.

But anxiety got the better of her and she didn't wait for a response. She scoured the alley between his flat and the damp storage rooms and found an old broom, whose bristles had been worn down to the chipped wooden head. She took a firm grasp of the handle and rammed the head through the window, sending a shower of glass over the sitting-room floor. Robert flinched and looked up from the carpet to see Laura brushing the larger pieces out of the frame, before climbing through the gap.

Her feet hit the floor and the soles of her shoes crunched little shards of glass into dust on the carpet. Her palms were grazed by small glass fragments on the frame.

The worst of the attack had passed. Robert was left in the cold aftermath of the spasm. The pain had been sensational, unlike anything he'd ever known. It completely overtook him, preventing him from any muscular coordination. His brain couldn't cope with the messages it was trying to send. It was too busy receiving distress calls from every nerve-end in his body.

"What's wrong with you?" she asked urgently. She couldn't believe how dreadful he appeared. He didn't look as though he was dying; he looked as though he was already dead. His skin was grey.

"The cramps."

"Cramp? Cramp did this to you?"

"Yes."

"Bullshit! I'm calling an ambulance. You need some . . ."

"No."

"This isn't cramp, Robert. You know damn well it's got nothing to do with cramp. You've got to . . ."

"No ambulance!" he insisted.

"Then I'll get the doctor."

"No."

"Don't be stupid!"

Robert uncurled himself slightly and then slowly drew himself up into the kneeling position. He took a deep breath and let it out gradually. He felt relief at the absence of serious pain. The attack had passed, but how long would it be before another one persecuted him? They were coming in waves. It was like being in labour. Perhaps that was what it was; the first stages of his rebirth.

"Please see the doctor, Robert," said Laura, in a less confrontational tone.

"I did and she was useless."

"Well, we'll go back and get her to do her job properly. Or we can go to another one."

"I will."

"Yes, I know you will," she said. "Because I'm going to make sure you do."

She had never seen anyone look so wasted. It was all she could do to look him in the eye without showing her distaste.

"Did you have to break the window?" he asked.

"I was worried about you!" she protested, upset by the

remark. "Goddammit, Robert! You could have been dead for all I knew! What was I supposed to do?"

Robert's skin was sagging, bereft of any tautness. His eyeballs looked almost . . . *dry*. He frowned.

"Why were you here in the first place? We didn't have an arrangement to meet, did we?"

She avoided his gaze and looked down at her hands. "No."

"So how come you suddenly showed up?"

"For the same reason I broke your window."

"Because you were worried?"

She thought about it for a moment. "Indirectly, yes. Anyway, let's go. We can still make the surgery, if we hurry."

Robert frowned. "I don't follow."

She was looking for her car keys. "It's why I was worried that counts."

Robert smiled uncertainly and confessed, "I think I'm missing something."

Laura overcame his facial disfigurement and kissed him lightly on the lips, before saying, "It's been on my mind recently."

"What has?"

Robert hoped he wasn't going to get another lecture from Laura on the state of his health.

"It's been driving me crazy. I can't shake it."

"Shake what?"

"The fact that I love you." She let out a deep breath. "*There!* I've said it. It's out in the open, okay? Can we go now?"

Robert never expected to hear those words from Laura. Her dark brown eyes were cruising his face for an expression. He was confused.

"I . . . I don't know what to . . ."

"Forget it, Robert," she muttered, shaking her head and tugging his arm. "Don't say anything."

He slumped in his seat and thumbed through a tatty back issue of *Motor* magazine. Laura sat beside him, fidgeting furiously.

She absentmindedly took out a packet of cigarettes and had to be restrained from lighting one by the receptionist, who pointed at the "no-smoking" sign and looked at her with an air of moral superiority.

Robert knew the other patients were stealing furtive glances at him, all wondering which cruel disease he had. He looked at Laura and thought about Rachel. He was being unfaithful to somebody, but it was difficult to tell who was the victim and who was the co-conspirator.

"Mr Stark?"

How could he feel so ill and still be alive? Laura nudged him gently. It hurt and he winced.

"Mr Stark?" said the receptionist again, leaning over her counter to get his attention. Robert looked up at her. "Dr Foster is free now."

Dr Rebecca Foster wore a pair of nasty brown trousers and a cream blouse. It didn't look good against the avocado and grey of her surgery. She couldn't disguise her shock at his appearance.

"I'm a friend," said Laura, preempting the doctor's inevitable question.

"Take a seat," she said to both of them, quickly looking away, buying herself moments to find her professional composure.

Robert knew what horrified her. He'd seen it in the mirror. The skin was dead. It seemed to hang off his face, peeling away from the aching bone structure beneath. His eyes were sunk deeper into his skull. He could feel the beads of sweat on his forehead. One or two trickled down the side of his face. Another spasm made him sit upright, but he was determined not to show too much. Laura reached over and put her hand on his, squeezing it softly.

"So, did the blood test tell you anything? Or didn't you bother to run a test on it?" Robert wondered.

She looked cross. "I resent that. Whatever else I may be, Mr Stark, I'm professional."

"Perhaps qualified would be a better word." Robert leaned

forward and drummed a finger on her desk. "You didn't think there was anything wrong with me! You said rest was what I needed. Well, I've had plenty of rest and look at me!"

Foster flushed with embarrassment. She looked at Laura and was met with a gaze of equal hostility. Robert felt his flesh crawl like a soaking shirt in a gale. Foster watched his disintegration with undisguised awe.

"We did do some tests," she mumbled indistinctly.

"And?"

"And they were inconclusive."

"*Inconclusive?* What does that mean?"

"Precisely that," she retorted. "But that's not important right now. The main thing is to get you into hospital straight away."

"What about the blood test?" he insisted.

She screwed up her face with frustration at her inability to steer him away from the subject. "Like I said, it was inconclusive."

"But there's a difference between what you say and what you mean, isn't there? You *say* my test was inconclusive but that's not what you *mean*, is it?"

She clasped her hands together and placed them on her desk. "I'll be blunt with you, Mr Stark. You should be hospitalized until we discover what's wrong with you."

"I'm not going to hospital."

"I'm not just thinking about you. I'm thinking about the people you come into contact with."

"I'm not going."

"I insist."

"You can all insist all you want, Dr Foster, but I don't have time to hang around in a hospital."

Laura patted him on the arm. "Robert, listen to her."

Robert leaned across the table and grabbed Dr Foster by the wrist. Laura tried to pull him back but he was too determined. He looked as though he might threaten the doctor. Instead, he whispered, seriously, "Tell me the truth about the blood test."

She jerked in her chair and replied, in a trembling voice, "There was a mistake. That's all."

"What kind of mistake?"

She looked fearfully at him and shook her head. "It doesn't matter. It was void."

"What was it?" he asked, more ferociously.

"Well, according to the blood test, you're already dead."

Laura looked surprised. Robert didn't. He released Dr Foster's hand and she started to massage the white pressure points, clearly shaken by his aggression.

"Thank you," he said, "that's all I need to know."

The two women looked at each other momentarily, as confused as each other. Robert rose from his chair.

"Where are you going?" asked the doctor.

"I don't know."

"For God's sake!" cried Laura. "Just look at yourself, Robert! She's right. You must..."

"Like I said, she's already told me everything I need to know. Going to hospital isn't going to solve anything."

"But the blood test was void. It was clearly a mistake. The result was ridiculous. The fact that you're here proves that."

"No, it doesn't. The result was correct."

Robert opened the door and Laura followed him out into the corridor. "Please stay!" she begged. "She's right! Without help, you'll..."

"Stay away from me, Laura!" he shouted, pointing a finger at her. "You can't help, so go back home!"

"No! I won't! I won't let you..."

"You don't have an option."

He pushed her back against the wall, grabbing her chin in his hand and squeezing it so that her mouth crinkled into a twisted pout, a terror kiss.

"Please, don't do this," she wailed, her voice distorted like the shape of her mouth.

"Leave me alone!" he hissed, when his lips were almost brushing hers.

* * *

Chris stood on the landing by her front door and examined the lock. It hung at an angle. There were several splinters on the floor. He pushed the door open.

"Katherine?"

He stepped into the dim hall and gently closed the door behind him. His fear was coloured by caution. He saw the blood in front of him. It was on the floor and at the base of the wall. The picture which had hung on the right was now on the carpet, its frame fractured, its glass shattered. The kitchen door was closed. The wet scarlet traces disappeared beneath it.

Chris took hold of the handle and paused. He could barely twist his wrist. The feeble action rolled back his life to Connecticut again, standing with Julia by the door into the living-room, waiting to investigate the eerie silence that had descended on the house. He shuddered at the comparison. The door didn't open fully. There was something blocking it. He put his shoulder to it and forced it open.

Stephen Abraham was lying face down on the tiled floor. Blood blossomed beneath him, forming a smooth pool. Little crimson rivulets ran in the tiny gullies where individual tiles kissed each other. Chris had been bracing himself, expecting to find Katherine as the victim.

There were drops of blood fanning out in a film of spray across the kitchen table, over one wall and a chair. Chris refused to look into the sink, to discover what was lying with the dirty plates and cutlery.

"Katherine?"

She was in the bedroom, sprawled across the bed. Chris faltered in the doorway, trying to catch his breath. The sheets were crumpled and torn. One of the bedside lamps was on the floor, its shade broken. The mirror on the dressing-table was smashed. He looked back at the bed. Katherine lay on her front. There was blood on the sheets.

"Oh Christ!"

He touched her. She stirred. Her tiny movement ran

through him like an electric shock. "Katherine!" he gasped. "Katherine, are you . . . ?"

"Chris," she mumbled, "Chris, is that . . . you?"

She blinked and he stroked her hair. She gradually moved a hand to her face and rubbed her eyes. He saw the graze on her right temple.

"Katherine, are you badly hurt anywhere?"

She swallowed and shook her head. "She . . . she was here."

"Who?"

"Rachel Cates."

Chris's mind sparkled. Abraham's mutilated body. Blood. 22 November 1963. Julia and her scissors. André Perlman and Jennifer Colson. And Rachel Cates.

"Why?" he asked, as Katherine slowly began to move.

"Abraham . . . she was following Abraham."

He lifted her into his arms and she looked around the bedroom She glanced into the bathroom and said, "He's gone. He was here. In the bathroom. Stephen Abraham was lying in the bathroom. She knocked him unconscious with a single blow. I swear he was here."

Chris said, softly, "He still is."

She clutched him tightly. "He tried to . . . to . . . Rachel arrived just in time to stop him and . . ."

"Abraham's dead, Katherine. He's in the kitchen."

A look of confusion slowly spread across her face. "She was coming across the bed towards me. I was backing away, kicking out, scratching at the sheets. I really believed she was going to kill me. When I was in the corner, she got off the bed and I tried to run. She caught me. I fought, struggling like an animal, but she . . . I'm not sure, but then I was on the bed and she had me by the wrist and I remember this hot point of pain just here."

Katherine pointed to the spot on her wrist, but there was no mark.

"What was she doing?"

"She was rubbing it and it felt hot. It spread right through me and it was like an anaesthetic. I started to feel sleepy, even though I was continuing to struggle against her. After that . . . I don't remember a thing until just now."

Chris hugged her and kissed her forehead. "Thank God you're all right."

"I was so scared, Chris. I thought Abraham was . . ." Her voice trailed off and for a couple of minutes they held each other in silence. Eventually, she asked, in a fragile voice, "What are we going to do?"

"We've got to get out of here."

Katherine turned her face up to Chris's and said, "She saved me, you know. Rachel saved me. Abraham had me in here, pinned down and powerless. He was responsible for this," she said, pointing to the graze on her right temple. "I was weak and dizzy, I couldn't stop him."

He looked at the dried blood around the small, parallel cuts. Katherine turned her head away. "She arrived just in time, and as soon as she did, he changed. You should have seen him. It was pathetic. He was squirming in the corner. She was incredible, really fired up, screaming at him."

"About what?"

"How worthless he was compared to her. She told him she was immortal. When she got too close he appeared to be in unbearable pain. There was no physical contact, but she was crucifying him anyway. He was crying like a baby. Then he tried to escape and she stopped him. With one blow she knocked him from here to there."

Chris looked in the direction Katherine was pointing. There were several small red stains on the far bathroom wall.

"He flew. His feet never touched the ground. And once he was unconscious, she turned to me." Katherine nodded to herself and then said to him, "She knows things."

He squinted at her. "What do you mean?"

"Like she knew things about your sister and your family. She knows things about me that only Jennifer knew. She's telling the truth, Chris. She is what she says!" Katherine had a fanatical urgency in her eyes. "I'm telling you, she knows! Jennifer was in love with Perlman and . . ."

"Katherine, listen to me. We have to get out of here. *Now*!"

But she wasn't paying attention. "She's going to immortalize him," she murmured, as the realization flooded back.

Chris stopped thinking about getting out of the flat and said, "What?"

"She's going to immortalize him. That's what she said."

"Who's she going to immortalize?"

"Robert Stark. That's what she's waiting for. Remember she told us she wasn't going to be around for much longer? That's why."

"You sure about this?"

Katherine nodded. "She was explaining to Abraham. She called Stark a chrysalis. She's changing him into what she is."

Chris whistled. "What are we talking about here? Immortal lovers?"

"What are we going to do?" asked Katherine. "We've got to do something."

"Right now, you've got to get dressed," he told her. "When we're safe, we'll consider what our next move is."

She nodded lamely. He helped her off the bed and guided her into the bathroom, where she washed, touching the graze gingerly. He saw her wince when the cold water splashed onto it. She was unsteady on her feet. When she was finished, she moved back into the bedroom and looked for clothes. He lit a cigarette.

Judging by the spilled blood, Abraham was hurt in the bedroom, but not dispatched until Rachel got him into the kitchen. That was where the bulk of the blood was. Why had she removed him from the bedroom to kill him? Why had she apparently changed her mind about taking Katherine?

Katherine suddenly sat down on the edge of the bed and put her head in her hands. Chris moved over to her, sat down beside her on the bed and put an arm around her shoulders.

"I thought I was going to die. It wasn't just a possibility. I was certain of it. I really believed she was going to kill me."

They sat together for a few moments, until she was under control. Then she rose stiffly, like an old woman, and finished dressing. They stepped into the hall and she stopped, her eyes caught by the bloody lines sliding beneath the kitchen door.

"Oh God!"

"Come on," said Chris, curtly.

She stepped over the worst bloodstains. When she reached for the kitchen door, Chris took hold of her arm and shook his head. "Not a good idea, believe me."

"Shouldn't we call the police?"

"And say what? The dead body is in *your* flat, Katherine. We're in enough trouble already."

"But . . ."

"You're going to be a suspect, so what are you going to tell them? The truth? Can you imagine how far that's going to get you? Nowhere. And if not the truth, then what? Once you start lying to them, they'll catch you out."

"But it's not right."

"I know, but it's the position you're in."

Robert was gone. In the few moments it had taken Laura to regain her composure, he'd fled from the surgery. By the time she ran out after him, he'd vanished. She returned to Lennox Gardens, but he wasn't in his flat. The only other likely option was Rachel Cates. She hammered her front door and as Rachel opened it, Laura said, "Is he here?"

"Who?"

"Robert, for Christ's sake! Who else would I be . . . ?"

"You're Laura, aren't you?" said Rachel, coolly. When Laura looked at Rachel, she checked herself. The eyes were the opposite of Robert's lifeless ones. Rachel was wearing a black shirt with a stiff collar and a skirt which accentuated her slim waist. Her hair was still damp from the shower she'd had on returning from Katherine's apartment.

"Is Robert here?"

Rachel admired Laura's fabulous curly hair. She had fair skin, as most redheads tend to. Rachel imagined she would burn easily in the sun. "I'm not sure I understand," she told Laura. "Why do you think he'd be here?"

"Because you've got something to do with his illness. You know what it is. I mean, the doctor doesn't have a clue, but you do, don't you?"

"The doctor?"

Laura nodded. "I've just been with him to the surgery. He got the result of a blood test she took. Guess what it was?"

Rachel shrugged. "I have no idea," she lied.

"It said he was already dead. I know that's ridiculous, but you should have seen him. He didn't look that far off it."

"Perhaps you should come in," she suggested. "And then we can discuss this properly."

Laura hadn't expected civility. She assumed she'd be asked to leave. She stepped into Rachel's apartment. The air was cool in the dark hall, creating a sense of stillness. Rachel led her into the drawing-room. Laura gradually turned a full circle, taking it all in. When she was finished, she was standing in front of Rachel, who asked, "Would you like something to drink?"

"No, thank you."

She could easily understand how Robert fell for Rachel. She was a wealth of beauty surrounded by a wealth of beauty. No wonder he couldn't see what she was doing to him; a love this dazzling could easily blind. But Laura had her feet firmly on the ground and if Robert couldn't look after himself, Laura decided she was going to do it for him. She tried to compose herself.

"What's it all for? I've got eyes and I'm using them. Whatever's happening to him is to do with you."

Rachel raised her eyebrows. "Do you have any evidence?"

"No," admitted Laura.

"So how do you know?"

Laura was struggling to keep her temper under control. "When I came to see him today," she said, "I found him in a ball of agony on the floor. Something's tearing him apart. What is it?"

Rachel's facial expression never changed but her eyes flickered momentarily. "Is he all right?"

"No, he isn't. I think he's dying."

"Where is he now?"

"I don't know. He ran out of the surgery, saying he needed to be left alone, and that was the last I saw of him." Laura averted her gaze. "He needs hospitalization. I've never seen anyone look so awful. You can help him, I'm sure. I need you to do what you can."

Rachel looked genuinely puzzled by the change of tone in Laura's voice. "Why are you telling me this?"

"Because I love him."

Once the words were out, silence reigned while their impact settled upon both of them. Rachel nodded slowly and then murmured, "I see."

"No, you don't! You don't see at all! I really do love him. And in his own way, he loves me too."

Rachel smiled gently. "You're quite sure of that, are you?"

The heat flushed in Laura's cheeks. She fumbled for a packet of Camel and dropped them on the floor. She bent down to pick them up and felt faint. Rachel watched her and saw the anxiety in her eyes. Laura was squeezing the Camel packet out of shape. Rachel felt truly sorry for her. Her own heart was heavy. Love could be appallingly savage sometimes.

"I'm sorry, Laura, but I can't help you. I can't stop something I no longer have any control over."

"You started whatever it is, so you can stop it."

"No. I cannot."

Laura watched Rachel's face harden towards her. "But you must!" she pleaded.

"I can't. And even if I could, I'm not sure I would. You say you love him, but how do you know I don't love him also? How can you be sure that I haven't waited for him and yearned for him for far longer than you? How can you know that your feelings are stronger than mine?"

"I know what I feel and I . . ."

"Yes, but you have no idea what I feel, do you?"

"If you loved him so much, you wouldn't be hurting him."

"I'm not. I'm not hurting him at all." Rachel stood barely a foot in front of her. "Now I think you should leave."

"No way!" snapped Laura, through clenched teeth. "I'm not leaving this flat until you promise to . . ."

"You know I won't do that."

Laura's right hand was travelling through the air in an arc, a blur as her open palm cut through the stillness towards Rachel's cheek. But suddenly it stopped. Laura's eyes widened as she saw Rachel holding her by the wrist, but still looking deeply into her eyes. The grip was as strong as a powerful man's and made her cry out.

"Let go!"

Rachel's black eyes burned deeply into Laura, making her squirm with a discomfort that went far beyond the physical. Laura tried to yank her hand free but the grip was solid. The pressure made her wince.

"For God's sake, let go! You're hurting me!"

But none of her pleas made any impact on the deadly face that stared back at her.

"You think crushing my wrist is going to stop me from seeing him? No way! You can break my bloody arm if you like, but I'll still love him!"

Rachel's mouth seemed to harden, like her eyes and her grip. She struggled to stop herself from doing what she most wanted: to crunch Laura's fragile bones and tear her heart apart. The urge to kill grew stronger, its scent becoming quite thrilling. But there had been too much blood already. That had been one of the reasons she resisted the delicious possibilities offered by Katherine Ross. She would have been a luxury.

So Rachel ignored the desire to gut her rival for Robert's love and raised her free hand to Laura's throat. She dug two fingers into the pulse and worked them in tandem with the pressure she applied to the wrist. Before Laura could even register what was happening, there was a patch of pain in her throat, which left a peculiar numbness. She felt anger and energy flooding out of her. When Rachel let go, she was dazed.

"Where did he go, Laura? I have to find him if I'm to help him. And I'm the only one who can do it. He's my blood."

Laura shook her head wearily, unsure of what she was hearing. "I'm not . . . I don't know."

Rachel took a step forward, cupped Laura's face in her hands, and kissed her on the mouth. Then she broke away and said, "We may both love him, but only I can have him. He's beyond you now. So go home, Laura. There's nothing for you here."

Chapter Twenty

The picture on the screen was blurred. Robert sat in the back row, bent over two seats, changing his position as the pain moved around his body in a weird rotation. The gormless hero of the picture crashed through a stained-glass window and rolled across the floor of the Gothic cathedral.

Robert had staggered through London's streets, hoping that his relative isolation would bring enlightenment. But it hadn't. He had the information he wanted from Dr Foster and all the pain and confusion he could handle. But he couldn't go home. He needed to be away from Rachel and Laura.

If it turned out Rachel was right, and she really could change him, then he had to be clear in his thinking before he committed himself to her. An eternal marriage was what she proposed.

The pain was relentless and felt as though his ribs were razors, cutting into everything surrounding them. His head throbbed with the unceasing thump of his pulse, which boomed as loud as a bass drum in his skull. It nauseated him.

The hero rescued the feeble heroine, who was tied to the altar, ready for some obscene sacrifice. They hijacked a car and tore through the town, pursued by yet more thugs.

The dreadful heat and humidity had finally forced Robert off the streets. He opted for the cinema, on account of the air-conditioning. The ticket girl eyed him warily when his fingers pressed several grubby coins beneath the window. The auditorium was shabby. The red seat covers were faded and torn. There were brass ashtrays attached to the seats, despite plenty of "no smoking" signs. The walls were covered in the type of garish, red and gold flock wallpaper more usually associated with cheap curry houses.

There was a colossal explosion as an office block collapsed into a pile of smoking rubble. The hero dragged his grateful girl from the wreckage in a ludicrous display of resilience. The camera cut to a bedroom, where the girl was offering her gratitude in the fashion she knew best. The end credits began to roll and the house lights came up.

Robert waited for as long as possible before leaving. The foul stench of the street rose up and made him grimace. The filth was ubiquitous. He choked on the poisonous dust which is the city's air; particles of burned rubber, decayed dog-shit, grease-proof wrappers, rotting vegetables, cigarette butts, vomit, diesel fumes and a million other items of metropolitan excreta. Robert belonged with it all, down in the sewer.

The humidity surpassed itself. It was impossible to prevent perspiration. Even the buildings seemed to sweat, their rotting brickwork weeping with the green slime of a century's accumulated filth. The air was liquid and carried a taste. The hazy sun of the early morning had been ousted by a brigade of charging clouds which rumbled across the city. The sky was purple and black. Thunder rumbled. The clouds looked as though someone had dropped a collection of dark inks into a pool of swirling waters. The city shuddered.

The fire came again. This time he recognized it as some invisible hand lit the touch paper in his chest. Drops of sweat erupted all over his clammy skin, staining and soaking his clothes. He felt dizzy and his lungs took in less sour air with each shallow breath. In the past, he always kept the fear at bay, narrowly avoiding the plunge into total insanity. But not this time.

The people around him were devils. The paving stones moved beneath his feet and Death was standing casually by, waiting for him. He couldn't collapse in front of all these strangers. If he was going to die, he wanted a degree of privacy. The alien humanity terrified him.

He ducked into an alley between a sleazy cinema complex and a decaying building with shops on the ground floor and grim rented accommodation on the upper floors. The sky grumbled ominously as he stumbled forward, bouncing off one filthy wall onto the other. The alley was filled with rusting dustbins that had been discarded and never emptied. There were crushed crates and packing cases, rotting cardboard boxes and litter tossed from the windows above. He smacked blindly against an old fridge which lay on its side without a door. He fell to the ground and rose uncertainly to his hands and knees. He found he was unable to stand. Instead, he resorted to crawling through the dust and dirt.

He could feel the evil darkness closing in on him. Its powerful black fingers wrapped themselves tightly round his brain as his vision began to shut down, like an old-fashioned TV. The picture went and the light faded to a central bright spot, which gradually died. His last pain-induced scream was reduced to nothing by the roar of thunder from the bruised clouds.

"What are you doing here?" asked Elmore, as they stepped out of the storm and into his hall, shaking the rain from their drenched hair.

Chris said, "We're in deep trouble."

"How deep?"

"Fathomless."

They went up to Elmore's small apartment, where he broke out towels and whisky. "I'm glad you came," he explained. "I've just had sad memories for company this evening."

"I don't think we're about to improve the atmosphere much."

Elmore handed Katherine a glass and said, "Try me."

Chris gave an account of what happened at Katherine's flat and when they were finished, Elmore just nodded sagely, while he fiddled with one of his roll-ups.

"The question is, do we believe her?" He looked directly at

Chris. "After all, she flies in the face of everything we've been trying to establish. She goes right off the other end, if she's legitimate."

Chris nodded. "I know. We've spent our adult lives trying to prove that people like her only exist in crap films. But she's offered me incontrovertible proof. Whichever way I cut it, I can't argue against it. Not any more. I've tried to find a rational explanation for some of the things she knows, but there isn't one."

"You're really convinced she was Marilyn Webber?"

He sighed in exasperation. "I just don't have any other options."

"Which means you're buying into the immortality theory?"

"I know it sounds ridiculous, especially for someone like me, but I can't help it."

Elmore stroked one of his chins and looked at Katherine. "And you're sure you heard her correctly, when she was talking about Stark?"

Katherine nodded and Chris added, "She told us in the gardens she wouldn't be around for much longer. We figure that must be the reason: she's waiting for him to complete his metamorphosis and then they'll be off."

"That's definitely what she's intending," said Katherine, "and it's going to happen soon. But whether that means days or hours – or even minutes – who knows?"

Chris reached for the bottle and refilled his glass. Elmore said, "So what are we talking about?"

"What do you mean?"

"Well, you two come here in the night, leaving a dead body in Kathy's flat, seeking sanctuary from me – which is fine – but where's all this leading?"

Chris said, "I don't know."

Elmore turned to Katherine. "And since you believe Cates killed your sister, that means you've both got a grievance."

Chris said, "Sure, but there's nothing we can do about it. If she's telling the truth about those killings – and with the proof she's offered us, she has to be – then she's probably also telling the truth about her physical state. Take it from me, she doesn't look a day older than Marilyn Webber did on that night."

Katherine was watching the rain hammer the window, making it shudder in its rotting frame. She ran the towel over her soaking hair.

"The question is," said Elmore, "what would you do if she was a mortal?"

"If she was a mortal, she'd be about sixty by now."

"It's hypothetical. Supposing Cates is just as she is now, physically speaking, and that she had done everything you think she's done . . . but she was also mortal. What would you do?"

"I'd kill her," said Chris, flatly.

Elmore raised an eyebrow. "It wouldn't even occur to you to call the police?"

"No. Well, it might, I guess . . . after I'd killed her."

Elmore nodded to himself. "Well, I suppose it's easy to say that since it's hypothetical."

"You don't believe me?"

"I'm not sure. It's one thing for us to talk about it, but if the situation arose, could you actually force the blade in?"

"The blade?"

"If she looked you in the eye, do you really think you could do it?"

Chris took a little time to answer. Eventually, he said, "Yes, I could. When I think about my parents, the answer's not so clear. That was so long ago and I was so young it almost seems like someone else's memory. But when I think about Julia and her scars and the years she spent rotting away in a medical fog . . . the answer's definitely yes. In fact, I'd want the bitch close enough so I could feel her last breath on my skin."

Elmore pinched the end of his handmade cigarette and took another suck from it. He nodded at Katherine. "What about you?"

"I'd want her dead too," she said. "A prison sentence wouldn't be justice, no matter how long."

"Richard, what's all this about?" asked Chris. "This doesn't feel hypothetical."

He smiled limply. "Of course."

Chris and Katherine looked at each other as the old man hauled himself out of his armchair. He puffed out his cheeks, as he shifted his weight forward and straightened himself.

"There is a way to kill her," he told them.

Chris shivered. "She is immortal and she isn't?"

Elmore dropped his cigarette into a clay ashtray and said, "That's right. Left to their own devices, those two could live forever quite happily. But they do possess an Achilles heel."

Katherine said, "You knew about this all along?"

"No. Absolutely not!" he replied, adamantly. "In fact, quite the opposite."

"I don't understand."

"I've spent years trying to put this aside, to cast it off as an absurd aberration. Folklore and legend, that's what I tried to pretend it was. But I've known about it since . . . since Josef and I came across it in . . ."

"Koptet knows as well?"

Elmore raised his hand. "We didn't *know* anything for certain. That was why we got into this game. But we've seen the results of it and, for years, we tried to find logical – scientific, even – explanations for it. But we had our suspicions."

Chris said, "You mean you believed in this?"

Elmore took a moment to answer. "We couldn't disbelieve it. And the more we discovered . . . the more we were forced to shelve our sense of logic. You have only confirmed what we suspected, but could never prove . . . and since we couldn't prove it, we tried to bury it."

"Why?" asked Katherine.

"Because without proof, it was a hindrance to our work. It was difficult enough getting anybody to take us seriously without proposing fantastical theories for which we could offer no evidence."

Katherine pictured Rachel moving across the bed towards

her. The struggle. The pressure on her pulse, the warm numbness. Then Chris was calling her name and when her eyes flickered open, she wasn't sure if she was alive. Elmore was still talking.

". . . and it's so rare, too. We only came across it a couple of times and after a while, as the memory fades, it becomes easier to dismiss. You find yourself thinking you must have been mistaken at the time. And then you two come along and not only resurrect it, but substantiate it."

Chris lit a Marlboro. "So how do we do it?"

Elmore went over to the bookshelf and came back with a bound album. He flicked through many leaves until he found the one he wanted. He handed it to Chris who set it down on the floor, in front of Katherine, who was sitting cross-legged by the fireplace. She recognized it immediately. It was the desperate crowd looking up at the handsome dagger which was held aloft by one of the congregation. They were standing in front of the peculiar looking church, with the slats blown off one side of the stumpy steeple. The trees were dead and weak. She couldn't imagine them bearing leaves in even the most tender spring.

Chris looked up at Elmore and said, "You're kidding! You've got to be!"

Elmore looked deadly serious. "No, I'm not," he said, flatly. "That is the way. The only way."

Katherine ran her finger over the plastic which covered the photograph. "A dagger in the heart?"

"Yes."

"How do you know?"

"The same way I know that you're telling the truth. I've been there. Those people in the photograph have had to live with what you discovered for generations. It was never news to them, like it is to us. It was part of life itself, a permanent threat like the risk of a fatal epidemic, or a great storm, or any other ungodly phenomenon. The dagger in the heart was the only way they knew to combat it."

"But not just any old dagger, right?"

"That's right. It has to be a special one, made specifically for the purpose."

"I don't believe I'm even listening to this," said Chris.

"Why not? You seem happy enough to accept that Rachel Cates and Marilyn Webber are the same, so why not the dagger?"

He held out his hands in an exasperated gesture. "I don't know, it's just so . . . so *ridiculous*! You know? Straight out of the cheapest film and into our lives? It just doesn't feel right."

"Under the circumstances, what would?"

"Yeah, I know. But a dagger in the heart? It sounds more like Christopher Lee's territory than Christopher Lang's."

"I can't argue with that," Elmore conceded. "But it's the truth. And now that this is reality, let's go back to my question. Could you really do it? Could you be the one to stick the blade in? Do you really want her last breath on your skin?"

The humour evaporated. Chris looked Elmore in the eye and said, "Absolutely."

Elmore hadn't anticipated such a firm commitment. He nodded in an awkward fashion and looked at his watch. "Fine. Well, it's late and . . ."

"How are we going to get hold of a dagger, Richard? I don't think we have much time."

He replied, "I've got an idea, but . . ."

Chris said, "I'm serious, you know."

Elmore looked at him for a moment and then nodded sadly. "I know you are. And I'm serious about the dagger."

Rachel stood in Leicester Square. Above her, the sky snarled, baring its lightning teeth. She looked at all the shocking neon which surrounded her. Filmgoers filed in and out of cinema complexes, while Steven Seagal and Jean-Claude Van Damme leered at the public from grotesque billboards; smug grins two yards wide with perfect white teeth the size of paving stones. Tourists meandered in London's cinematic heart; productive carcasses for the pickpocketing vultures. The homeless wandered aimlessly, as hopeless and lost as the looks in their eyes.

The first few fat drops of rain hit Rachel's shoulders. Robert was near. It was a miracle. She'd believed she might have lost him for good, but now she could feel him close to her. At first, she thought it was an illusion. She assumed her imagination had conjured up hope where there was none. But now she knew it was true. She closed her eyes and felt her heart thumping. In time with his. He was very weak. Death was lurking, hungry and hopeful. She didn't have long. The signal was frail and fading. The raindrops grew into a steady drizzle and then erupted into a sudden downpour.

Laura had revealed the name and address of Robert's doctor. The surgery had been shut when Rachel arrived, but the scent lingered. She picked up the trail, abandoning herself to the inherited tracking instincts of animals far better suited to the task than humans. She knew Robert wouldn't go home. She knew the symptoms. Even those with a strong desire to live, inevitably shunned familiarity as death beckoned. She'd seen it before, the sick animals limping off instinctively to the graveyard. She followed him as best she could, a hunting animal on the scent of prey.

She lost him in the West End. She was sure he'd been there – all her tracking senses told her so – but suddenly the trail died and she couldn't understand why. That was when she became frantic.

It occurred to her that he was already dead. She found it hard to keep that terror at bay. It seemed too spiteful; two hundred years of yearning, halted by a slither of promise which would turn out to be nothing more than a cruel deception, followed by a hollow eternity . . . was that how it would be?

The downpour matured into a storm. A whiplash wind drove the rain into a slanting attack. Rachel stood still and felt his fragile pulse flickering. The tears that ran down her cheeks were hidden by the rain. The cold wind howled in her ears but she could still hear the incessant beat. She had no idea why she had suddenly picked up the pulse. She offered her trust to instinct and started to walk.

The cinema lobbies were crowded. Diners filled a steak

house, apparently oblivious to the gale outside. Five minutes ago, empty taxis had scoured the streets, competing for trade. Now they were set for a busy night. Nearly everyone had deserted the area, even if it was only to huddle in the inadequately protected doorways of shops. Rachel's concentration sharpened and she homed in on the pulse.

She turned into the alley and couldn't see him, but she knew he was there. The torrential rain hammered at the series of rusty fire-escapes, which clung precariously to the crumbling wall on her left. It was dark, having no illumination other than the weak light that came from lamps at either end of the alley, and from the tiny quantities of light that filtered down from the dim windows above her. The right-hand wall belonged to the cinema complex and had no windows at all. The wind seemed stronger in the alley, as it squeezed into the narrow channel and compressed.

"Robert?" she called out.

Rachel stepped over splintered crates and the jagged glass of broken bottles. Wet rubbish has a smell unique to itself and she sensed it now. London had been full of vile odours for weeks, but this hadn't been one of them. But now that the rain was back, the stench made a triumphant return. She had just passed an old broken fridge which was lying on its side without a door, when she saw him.

Robert lay across the filthy ground. He looked dead. The sight reduced Rachel to tears. She lifted his head out of a pool of black mud and held it to her chest, her soaking shirt sticking to his cheek.

"Oh God, Robert!" she moaned.

She felt the pulse in his throat. His eyes blinked rapidly in the wild rain.

"Rachel!" he whispered.

"I love you."

"It's too late," he insisted, feebly.

"Please, Robert! You can't leave me!"

"I love you, Rachel."

He managed to raise his arm and bring it across his chest, so he could touch her hand. He coughed painfully. She looked down at him and said, "I won't let you die. It's not fair. If you die, I want to die, and without you, I can't."

". . . I love . . . you . . ."

Rachel reached up to the stiff, black collar of her shirt and ripped it open. She undid three buttons and reached inside, pulling out the slim silver chain which she was wearing around her neck. Her fingers found the tiny scabbard and pulled it away from the blade.

Robert looked up at her with his dying eyes. Rachel tore the sleeve of her shirt and kept her eyes firmly fixed on Robert, telling him, "Don't leave me, darling, don't leave me," as she plunged the brilliant blade into her wrist. It wasn't a delicate slice. She stabbed herself, working the silver into the flesh, twisting it in the wound, making it broad and ragged. Hot blood spurted over her fingers and splattered her wet clothing.

"Save yourself," she told Robert.

"I can't," he croaked.

"Then save me."

Although the rain pounded his body relentlessly, he could clearly feel the hot wash of her blood on his chest. She was moving her wrist towards his mouth. The blood was splashing onto his neck and then his chin. It sizzled against his cold, soaked flesh.

"I love you, Rachel."

"Then save me."

She steadied his head and clamped her wrist over his mouth, just forcing his lips fractionally apart. He felt the hot liquid leaking onto his chattering teeth and stinging his tongue.

"Drink!" she begged.

Then he opened his mouth, moving it over the gushing wound and the blood flowed freely down his throat. He swallowed clumsily at first, then slickly.

Rachel felt the rush. It was incredible. She slumped against the wall until she was sitting down, holding his head in her lap, while he sucked the blood out of her torn wrist. The draining buzz made her giddy. Robert was drinking greedily now, so she reached down and took his right hand. He was on a complete high, drunk on her life-giving fluid. He never flinched when she thrust the blade into his wrist. She watched the crimson rivers flow down the underside of his forearm. She placed her own mouth onto his cut and started to draw upon it.

The two strains of blood mingled and flowed from body to body. The rain came in sheets, propelled by the steel breeze. The sky crackled with thunder.

Rachel let go of Robert's arm and tore her own wrist away from his hungry mouth. She reached down for his face, but he was already halfway up to meet her. Their bloody mouths clashed. Drops of blood spilled over their lips and off their chins. Rachel's heart was racing. She gathered his head in her arms, as he sucked on the tender skin of her throat. The blood seeped out of her cut and ran down his face, while she ruffled his hair and pulled his head as tightly to her as she could.

"Make love to me!" she gasped into his ear.

Robert frightened her. His energy was horrifying. His body shook as new life burned through him. Quivering fingers clumsily scratched her drenched clothing and Rachel tensed with painful pleasure when his bloody mouth sucked her soaking skin. Her own fingers reached for his clothes, ripping them when they became too awkward for her impatience.

They made frantic love in the filth, on a bed of grime and mud and beneath a blanket of rain and thunder. It made it better, more visceral and, therefore, more appropriate, as they pressed against each other by the weeping wall of the rented apartments, or while they moved together on London's vile mattress. Robert rolled over broken glass and felt the shards splintering beneath their combined weight and slicing into the skin of his lower back. One of Rachel's legs smacked against a rusting dustbin and sounded like a cymbal. Robert grazed his knuckles against the crumbling wall when he hit the back of his hand against the weak brickwork in an unguarded moment of pleasure.

Rachel drew yet more blood when she bit her lip, as Robert pressed her against the wall. She turned her face up towards the heavens, looking at the raging skies through the metallic filter of the fire-escapes above them. Robert felt divine to her, and as she shuddered with delight, her teeth sunk into the ripe flesh of her lower lip. His hot mouth slid over her and she welcomed the free fall of icy rain on her face. The ecstasy made her light-headed. Rain ran through her hair and over her forehead. The blood from her lip was diluted by the rain and ran in pink streams down her neck and between her breasts, over Robert's busy mouth.

When they were finished, they creased and slid by the wall. Robert's energy surge had taxed him too greatly and he passed into sleep, as she had anticipated he would. Rachel clutched him tightly and tugged her torn, soaking shirt around her naked shoulders. Her heart was overcome and she cried again. It was here; everything she had searched for and dreamed about, the one thing she had started to believe she would never have. She was content to be in the storm, holding onto him.

Rachel felt complete and perfect in the silver rain.

Chapter Twenty-one

The dream came to him again. He felt the steel jaws and the hurricane wind which burned everything it touched. The hooks pulled at his flesh. Rachel watched him, her head bowed in the storm, with her wet hair falling over his face. She saw the black puddles growing broader and felt the splatter of waterfalls which spilled from gutter overflows. She listened to the harsh cacophony that the rain orchestrated. When he awoke, she was staring lovingly into his eyes. She kissed him on the forehead.

"I love you," he murmured up at her.

"I love you too."

Robert's eyes betrayed his uncertainty. She could hardly believe it herself. Two desperate centuries had drawn to a close. The future was no longer a thing of dread. It seemed too fortunate, after all the misery which had gone before. Part of her was exhilarated and another part was terrified that something could yet threaten her bliss.

"No more pain?"

"No," she said. "Can't you feel the difference?"

Robert thought about it and replied, falteringly, "I don't think . . . I can feel anything at all."

The harsh wind sent black waves through her soaking shirt. A sheet of torn plastic was trapped between the nearest fire-escape and the wall. It flapped furiously, smacking repeatedly against the brickwork with a wet kiss.

"How long was I out for?"

Rachel looked at her watch. "It doesn't matter."

"I'm sorry."

"Don't be. I was happy."

"Sitting in all this filth, with the icy wind and rain?"

"With you in my arms, and in my heart, with everything in front of us . . . yes, I was happy. Happier than I've ever been. The rain was an advantage. It hid my tears."

Robert looked at the grime around them and then up into the leaking sky. To a casual onlooker, it would have been a pitiful sight. They might have appeared as two assault victims, left beaten and robbed in a back alley, scratching in the slick dirt for what remained of their belongings and dignity.

Robert looked down the alley. Despite the deluge and the lack of light, he could see everything clearly. He could even see minute details well beyond the end of the alley, details that should have been blurred by the storm. Some were shrouded in shadow and would have remained invisible to him before. But now everything had astonishing clarity.

When they returned to Lennox Gardens, Robert checked himself in her bathroom mirror. Was it really him? It looked close to what he remembered of himself, but there was something different. He couldn't tell whether it was an addition, or whether there was an element missing. Certainly, the flesh colour had returned. Perhaps he was paler than he tended to be, but the skin had never been so flawless as now. The cadaverous grey had gone and it was once again fresh and tight over the face, and not like a mask of old chewing-gum that sagged off the crumbling bones beneath. The eyes burned brighter, with brilliant whites surrounding dazzling pupils. His entire body seemed to have been reconstituted. The musculature returned to the condition it was in before he first made love to Rachel. There were no signs of the decay which had afflicted him since that night. All the wastage had been reversed. If anything, he looked in better shape than he ever had.

But he lacked a quality. It irritated him that he couldn't identify the change in the mirror. He was more than he had ever been, physically improved, cleansed of imperfections and marks of character. The upgrading robbed him of humanity. Presumably, that was the point.

"Are you beginning to believe it now?" she asked, standing naked behind him and running her fingers over his shoulder-blades and down the spine.

Steam from the hot shower began to cloud the reflection. He turned to her. "Slowly and with reservations," he admitted.

She smiled and said, "It's just the beginning."

They showered together and then went to the bedroom. Rachel opened the windows and said, "I love the sound of the rain."

They made love. Afterwards, in each other's arms, they were content to lie quietly and reflect. Robert still expected fatigue to make a claim on him once in every twenty-four hours. He couldn't shake the idea that eating two or three square meals a day had suddenly changed from a healthy necessity to a pointless luxury. If he never cut his hair again, it would never grow longer than it was now. If he cracked the teeth in his mouth, they would mend.

"How do you feel?" Rachel asked.

"Hungry."

"No, you don't. You just think you do. It's conditioning and it'll take some time to purge it."

Robert smiled and shook his head. "I'm not finding it very easy to swallow this, if you'll forgive the pun. When we got back here and I was looking at myself in the bathroom mirror, I didn't really recognize myself. I wasn't sure I was real. I'm not sure *this* is real."

Rachel nodded. "In the alley," she reminded him, "I sliced apart both our wrists."

She held hers up for inspection. There was no cut, just a tiny scar.

"Go on," she encouraged him. "Take a look."

He thought of how he sucked the life-giving blood out of the gash she carved in her arm. The hot rush flooding into and filling his mouth, burning his throat, igniting his stomach. He looked at his own wrist. The blemish was identical to hers. "Regeneration, right?"

"Right."

"I'm still not sure, though."

"Naturally. But you should trust your instinct and leave notions of logic and laws of nature for those who understand neither."

"I still can't get round that. I mean, I'm still me, Robert Stark, the same guy as I was yesterday."

She shook her head. "No. Yesterday's Robert Stark is dead. You died."

"I was still alive when you found me."

"Not in any conventional sense. If you'd been in a hospital, they wouldn't have picked up any vital signs."

"But I spoke to you. I drank your blood."

"I know, darling." She seemed genuinely amused. "Remember, you're never going to get anywhere if you keep using mortal logic as a yardstick. Trust me. The man who was Robert Stark yesterday is dead. You and I are different beings altogether. We're not shackled by the physical restrictions which afflict men and women, and we shouldn't be chained by the limitations of their thoughts, either."

A WPC brought two cups of milky tea from the kitchen. Harold Daley handed one to Anne Chaucer and took one for himself. He sat down on a small wooden chair in front of her. She was perched on the edge of an armchair, maintaining perfect posture despite being badly shaken. Daley asked, "Do you mind if I smoke, Miss Chaucer?"

She shook her head. A small woman with curly grey hair, she dressed neatly and soberly, trying to maintain the casual appearance of a woman from a wealthier station. She nervously fingered the string of pearls around her neck.

"How did you discover it?" he asked her.

"I took her mail up."

"You do that every day, do you?"

"No, but recently I've taken to doing it. Just a little

something to help out since . . . well, since what happened to her sister."

Daley nodded. "Jennifer Colson, yes."

"A terrible thing!" declared Anne Chaucer. "Kathy was devastated, you know. It was awful. So I tried to help out here and there. Just little things to ease her day, really. And I suppose I got into the habit."

"I see. So what happened?"

"The door was partly open. I could see the lock had been broken. It was hanging at a peculiar angle. I called out her name and when there was no response, I pushed the door open. That was when I saw the blood. My first instinct was to run, but I went in to see if she was there. She wasn't, but I saw the state of her bedroom and then . . . in the kitchen."

"You saw who was in the kitchen?"

"I saw that it wasn't Kathy. That was when I came down here and dialled 999."

"And you heard nothing?"

She shook her head. "Not really."

"Not really?"

"Well, I heard muted voices and footsteps. But the sound wasn't very clear because of the rain."

"Did you recognize the voices at all?"

"Well, I know Kathy's. But as for the others . . ."

"More than one?"

"Yes, I think so. I'm pretty sure. One of them might have belonged to her gentleman friend, but that was a little later."

Daley perked up. "She has a lover?"

Anne Chaucer frowned at the phrase. "She's had a guest. A nice man."

"But not the guy you saw in the kitchen?"

She shook her head. "No. Definitely not."

"And you think his was one of the voices you heard?"

"Yes. It's quite distinctive."

"How?"

"He's an American."

Daley tried not to let the surprise show in his face. He took a slow drag from his cigarette. "Have you seen him? Do you know what he looks like?"

Chaucer tilted her head to one side as she remembered. "Very tall and broad. Strong-looking with dark eyes and dark curly hair. He might have a scar on his chin, I'm not sure. Crudely handsome, I suppose."

Lang, thought Daley, before picturing Katherine with him. They had been at Kensington Police Station at about the same time. Daley hadn't seen the two of them together and so never thought about it afterwards. Both their presences coincided too neatly. Perhaps they ran into each other outside the station. Maybe Katherine Ross had witnessed his confrontation with Lang from some concealed vantage point. However it had happened, they were together now.

Daley had asked someone to contact Lang at the Monarch Hotel. It transpired he'd checked out. The fat, stubble-coated slob who passed for a manager said he'd been with a woman when he paid his bill. The description had been improbably vague – in that kind of hotel, the management never went out of their way to offer descriptions of guests and their friends – but now, with hindsight, such sketchy details as had been provided roughly correlated with Katherine Ross's appearance.

"Does the name Christopher Lang mean anything to you, Miss Chaucer?"

"No."

The door opened and Daley turned to see David Smith. "Sorry for the intrusion, but could I have a word?"

"Excuse me for a moment, Miss Chaucer," said Daley, setting his cup and saucer on the fragile table before rising from the wooden chair.

The two men moved into the cramped entrance hall and then out onto the pavement. The rain bullied them while uniformed officers cordoned off the entrance to the street from the Bishop's Bridge Road. Daley turned up his collar, took another drag from his cigarette and exhaled into the storm. "What's the news, Dave?"

"It's awful messy up there."

"Another member of our 'lonely hearts' club?"

"Yeah, I'm afraid so. Found it in the sink with the remains of a Chinese takeaway."

"Charming."

"His name's Stephen Abraham, lives in Notting Hill. He's a sculptor. At first glance, there's no obvious tie-in to Ross."

"Well, maybe we ought to cross-check him with Lang."

"Lang? The American?"

Daley nodded. "None other. It turns out he's been staying here. That's why we couldn't find him after he left the Monarch."

Smith whistled. "She's sure?"

"Heard his voice."

"What are you going to do?"

Daley finished his cigarette and flicked the butt into someone's soaking rose bush. "I want them both arrested. Get it on the TV and radio, and in the papers. We need to know what those two are up to. If they weren't here when all this happened, where were they, what were they doing and what were these other people doing in her flat? And if they were here, why did they suddenly take off like fugitives?"

Laura dialled Robert's number and there was no answer. She lowered the receiver back to the cradle. The room had a warm, rusty glow to it which was at odds with the gale outside. A small spotlight illuminated an enlarged print of an old black and white photograph of the Duomo in Florence. A work lamp cast a yellow pool across her untidy desk. Unpaid bills, unread letters, Cellophane-sealed junk mail, postcards with the smudged ink of illegible handwriting. A photograph of Laura and Robert together, laughing in front of a sapphire sea. The roasting overhead sun cast thin, sharp, vertical shadows. Mediterranean midday. She picked up the photograph and held it beneath the light for closer inspection. Robert was milk chocolate. He never burned or peeled. His hair was shorter than he wore it these days and he looked . . .

Where was he? *How* was he? Laura had never seen anyone look so awful as he had in the surgery. His grey skin had been damp. He was repulsive to her touch. She tried Robert's number again. Still no answer. Perhaps he was with Rachel Cates. Laura hoped not, but knew better. She shook her head and smiled sadly to herself. How could she expect to compete with such wealth, such beauty, such *aura*?

What had the fingers done? They had pressed into her throat and dug into her wrist. She'd felt the fury flooding out, against her own will. The recollection was a little hazy, but the bitter aftermath lingered. It was mean and hollow. Laura hated Rachel's firm assurance that she could not have Robert, that there was no way she could challenge for his affection, because she knew it was the truth. So when Rachel told her to go home, she did.

She'd had a couple of glasses of wine, while she prowled from one room to the next, waiting for her troubled mind to drop anchor. But it didn't. She thought of the first moment she saw Robert after Sarah Reynolds dumped him. Why that airhead had opted for Anthony Baker over Robert remained a mystery to Laura.

Her casual relationship with Robert was a mockery. They might pretend they were friends who occasionally fell into bed together, but the reality was different. She was in love with Robert, plain and simple. And since she was being honest, she supposed she might as well accept that it wasn't something new. She couldn't determine exactly when it started but if jealousy was some sort of bench-mark, then it hailed back to the era of Sarah Reynolds. Laura loathed her for having a hold on his heart.

She was surprised to feel a solitary tear staining her cheek. Although alone, she was embarrassed. She wiped it away, reached for a cigarette and lit it, blowing a thick cloud into the centre of the low amber-lit room. She regarded the evidence of her lover, the trinkets of sentiment which accrued almost unnoticed while time slipped by.

On the back of a chair hung a worn pair of Levi's which she

had borrowed from him and never returned. They were sacred, torn and faded to the point of disintegration and yet more precious now than ever before. Every day she chanced across reminders of Robert. Old counterfoils from restaurants, scraps of paper with badly-scrawled notes on them, cassettes that were exchanged and forgotten, photographs of holidays and weekends shared with friends. She flicked through a copy of *Perfume* by Patrick Suskind. Robert gave it to her, but she'd never got round to reading it. At the back of a drawer of old postcards and bound letters she found two ticket stubs for a U2 concert at Wembley Stadium.

She tried his number again and there was still no answer. She rang Directory Enquiries to find Rachel's number. She was ex-directory. Laura looked down at the photograph of her and Robert in the sun. There was no point in waiting for him to answer her calls. Inaction threatened her sanity. She kissed him, pressing the snapshot to her lips, and whispered, "I love you," before dropping it back on the desk and reaching for her car keys.

"Bitch!"

"*No, please!*" she wailed, but it was too late.

The knuckles caught Cassie on the cheek. Vernon swung through on the backhand and his wife was driven against a small table of lacquered wood. It fractured beneath her body, as she fell to the carpet.

"How dare you try to steal my kids from me!" he shouted, leaning over her and jabbing his chest with his right forefinger. "They're my fucking children!"

"I . . . I wasn't stealing them, Vern. I just . . . they needed a little . . . time to . . ."

"Shut up! Just shut your goddamned mouth!"

He stood up straight and turned away from her. The way she'd crept into the apartment nauseated him. It was deceitful, breaking into their home like a burglar, assuming he'd be out.

The flat was in chaos. He'd rampaged through it since she left with Kevin and Melissa – she'd even taken the dog! –

tearing at the wallpaper and fabrics upon which she had wasted so much time and money. The kitchen floor was showered with the shattered wine glasses that had been so carefully selected by her. The fine china plates now looked like the world's largest jigsaw puzzle.

Cassie was sobbing. He had to find out where his children were. All other priorities were secondary. Vernon put his hands on his hips and considered what would be the best way to squeeze this priceless information out of his wife. So far, she'd proved resistant to verbal threats and to violence itself. Her bleeding and bruised body looked pathetic and broken, as she wiped her red eyes.

"Where are they, Cass? Tell me now and we can stop this."

"I hate you," she whispered, bitterly.

"*Where are they?*" he screamed.

He reached down and grabbed her by the hair. She yelled with pain and fright. He ignored several weak blows which she directed at his face, but which mostly landed on his chest and shoulders. He was speaking gibberish now, dribbling as his mouth ran away with itself.

"Stop it!" commanded the voice behind him.

Vernon turned round to see Robert standing in the doorway to their drawing-room. When he saw who it was, he stood up straight and leered at him. "Well, look who it is! My wife's best friend! How the hell did you get in here, you dumb fucker?"

Robert had had to break the lock on the Lorenzos' front door to gain access, but he'd found it remarkably easy. When his fist shattered the wood and blew the metal lock into the hall, he'd barely felt it. There were no marks on his hand. He looked around the drawing-room. Everything sparkled.

"Let go of her."

"Get out of here, Stark!"

"Please, Robert!" pleaded Cassie. "Help me, I . . ."

"Shut up!" Vernon ordered her, shaking her roughly by the handful of hair that he still clutched.

From Robert's point of view, it wasn't clear whether Vernon intended to injure her or kill her. It didn't make much difference to him.

"Back off!" Vernon warned him.

Robert took Vernon's wrist and twisted it sharply. He winced and his fingers sprang open. Cassie scrambled away from both of them.

"What's going on?" Robert asked Cassie.

Husband and wife looked at him and marvelled at his condition. His pale skin was smooth, like a girl's. His eyes glittered. His dark hair was rich and shiny.

Vernon started his own version, saying, "This bitch came . . ."

"Be quiet!" said Robert, with absolute authority. "I'm talking to Cassie."

"Don't you talk to me like . . ."

Robert took Vernon by the throat, cutting off his protest. It was an automatic reaction. Then he turned back to Cassie and said, "Go on. Tell me."

She was sitting on the floor, trying to tug her skirt back into place and brush the hair out of her face. Vernon was still clutching his neck, gasping for breath and trying to massage some life back into his stunned vocal cords.

"I came back to get some extra things for the children. I thought he'd be out."

"Fucking typical!" rasped Vernon.

"And when I wouldn't tell him where we're staying he started to . . . he started to . . ."

"Leave here now," Robert told Cassie.

"Wait a goddamned minute!" protested Vernon.

Cassie looked uncertain, her anxious gaze moving back and forth between the two men.

"Leave here!" said Robert again, more firmly than before. "And don't come back!"

Robert's stomach contracted. His blood pumped the muscles, priming them against his greater will. He was unable to tell whether he felt an emotion, like fury or sadness or hate, or whether it was a purely physical sensation. In any event, he felt the pressure crushing him, as though his mass would be reduced to the size of a pinhead.

"Go on!" he shouted, as she rose unsteadily to her feet, with the awkward clumsiness of a foal.

Vernon made a move for her as she staggered towards the front door. Robert intercepted him, just a yard short of his wife. And then Cassie was gone, sprinting down the hall towards the door, never stopping to look back at her miserable husband.

Robert pinned Vernon to the wall, planting his hands on both shoulders and forcing the body back. Vernon grumbled, "Jesus Christ, Stark! You're making a big mistake!"

"Stark isn't here. He's gone."

Vernon frowned. "You're out of here, man! *Finished!* You got that?" he spluttered, trying to palm his dirty hair back over his head.

"You can't run around treating your wife like that," said Robert, speaking softly as he started to stalk his prey across the carpet.

"She's *my* goddamned wife! I'll treat her how I want."

"No, you won't."

"Yes, I will!" he hissed, suddenly turning to lunge at Robert.

Vernon was well built and in good condition for a man on the verge of his fortieth birthday. He was strong and he knew it, but he was no match for Robert. He was staggered by the younger man's speed and strength. So was Robert, who stepped aside and thrust his outstretched arm into an upward swing that caught Vernon in the throat and dropped him to the floor. He was clasping his neck when Robert reached down and took hold of his collar, dragging him to his feet. Robert felt free of compassion when he hit Vernon in the face. The blow was accompanied by the sharp crack of a breaking cheekbone.

Robert stood over him and watched with fascination. Vernon looked up from the floor. Blood streamed from his nose into a sticky pool on the cream carpet. Robert had the desire but his sense of logic resisted. Vernon moaned pathetically and clamped a hand over his horribly depressed cheek, feeling the free-floating fragments of bone beneath the skin.

Robert felt her presence before he saw her. He turned round and waited. A moment later, she appeared in the doorway, looking firstly at him and then at the figure on the floor.

"I warned you about this," she said.

"I know, but I couldn't help it. And once it started, I couldn't control it."

"I'm not surprised. It was bound to happen, but it would have been better if we could have waited until we were safe."

Her voice registered with Vernon, who shifted his body with a painful groan and looked up at her. He stretched a raised hand in her direction, but she never even looked at it. Instead, she put a hand round the back of Robert's neck and kissed him keenly.

"I love you," she whispered.

"I'm sorry," said Robert, "but I had to."

"You should see this through," she whispered, running a finger over his ear and down the side of his face. "Drink his blood."

"*What?*"

"Drink it and see what happens."

"Is this how . . . ?"

Rachel nodded.

Robert wasn't sure whether he wanted to. "How?" he asked.

She said, "The way you feel is right."

Robert pulled Vernon up again, pushed him against the wall and looked into his eyes, which danced with the horror of the unknown. He tried to raise his arms for protection. Robert closed his own eyes for a brief moment and tried to calm the storm inside. It scared him. Then he took hold of Vernon's shirt-sleeve, ripping the cuff and yanking it back to the elbow.

"No!" Vernon pleaded, pathetically, "Please God, don't! *Please!* Don't hurt me! Listen, we can . . ."

Robert paused for a moment and then plunged his teeth into

the softer flesh on the underside of the forearm. He instinctively found himself drawing the blood into his mouth. It rushed like a river and he swallowed it. It was hot and sticky and it disgusted him, but despite this, he drank fully. The sizzling liquid leaked from the corner of his lips and ran down his throat.

Vernon started to scream like a baby. Robert slapped a hand across his mouth to muffle the sound. His protests were easily restrained and then he lapsed into the silence of severe shock. Robert continued to drink until Rachel said, "That's enough!"

He lifted his bloody mouth from the wound, panting like a dog in the sun. Rachel was delighted, quivering with the pleasure it brought her to watch him.

"That's excellent," she told him. "And now you must finish it."

"How?"

"You've seen me do it."

"And that's it?"

She saw his doubts and kissed him on the cheek. "Don't resist what's in your heart," she murmured into his ear, "and there'll be no resistance from his."

Robert was over-flowing with contempt for Vernon and then thought about Cassie, and how she had endured his cruelty for the sake of their children. His hate was all-consuming, stoning him like a drug. These thoughts cooked in his mind when he drove his fingers against Vernon's chest. The savage desire to kill – just as viciously as Rachel could – was overwhelming and Robert submitted to it completely.

There was a crack and suddenly his hand was wet to the wrist. The blood scalded him. Vernon's eyes bubbled with shock. Robert allowed his fingers to probe and prod, while he studied Vernon's extreme facial contortions in the last few moments of his life. The sound of cascading blood was like flimsy crystal cracking on jagged rock. Robert closed his hand into a gooey fist and yanked it backwards, dragging a collection of purple, bloody organs out of the colossal wound he had created. There was a sickly slurp as he hollowed Vernon, who fell face first into the expanding lake of his own blood. Robert regarded the heart in his hand and then dropped it. Rachel stood close to him and looked into her lover's eyes.

He said, "Now what?"

"Now you wait."

"For what?"

She said nothing and merely smiled, as the rush hit him like a hammer on the heart.

Chapter Twenty-two

Robert is making love to Cassie. She is choked with happiness. Her hair is blonder than usual, brightened by the sun. She seems slimmer than Robert is accustomed to. He can hear the sea crashing onto the beach, just outside the window.

The flash of blue-white light temporarily blinds and stuns Robert. When the shockwaves recede, he's holding Cassie's hand and she's crying out in pain, her skin dripping with perspiration. Robert is wondering about Kevin, who is staying with Cassie's parents, at their house out at Easthampton. In five minutes' time, Melissa will be in the world.

Rachel looked down at her stunned lover. It had to happen sooner or later. She wasn't going to allow Robert to tread water through the years. Right from the start, she wanted an equal. Or something better. Robert was right for the role, but in the early stages there were barriers to overcome. It would be difficult to conquer the asphyxiating effects of a life of conditioning. All those tedious delusions of morality had to be destroyed. They belonged to the fragile, those who lived on borrowed time and worried about not waking up in the morning. The property of mortals.

Robert and Kevin are walking through so many lines of parked cars that it seems like the entire planet has parked outside the Meadowlands Stadium. It's the child's birthday and this is the first time Robert has taken him out to New Jersey to see a game. The boy is still wide-eyed with the shock of the spectacle. He cheered fanatically as Lawrence Taylor handed out a severe lesson to the Redskin offence. Robert took pleasure watching the boy, mouth agape, cheering on the New York Giants as they stuffed their divisional arch-rivals from Washington. Now they are on the way home and when they get there, Kevin will babble non-stop to Cassie about every magical detail.

Killing Vernon had not been a good idea. Rachel wouldn't have planned it this way, but the moment had presented itself. She and Robert had been in her bed, lying in each other's arms, playing gentle games. They both heard the crash from the floor above.

"What was that?" he'd asked.

"What was what?"

He gave her a you-can-do-better-than-that look and then there was another thump, followed by the muffled sound of a desperate cry.

"What was *that*?" he said, as he sat up and swung his legs off the bed.

"Where are you going?"

"To see what's going on. It's my job."

Rachel was momentarily speechless. In the light of everything that had happened, how could he possibly be worried about his job?

"Don't go," she said.

"I have to."

Several more muted sounds filtered down from the Lorenzo apartment and she chose to follow him. She passed Cassie on the staircase. When Rachel arrived, it was really too late. Robert was already hitting Vernon, amazed by his new strength and speed. He was losing control. There was a very good chance he would have slaughtered Vernon anyway. She only hoped it wasn't too soon for him.

Everything was already in motion. They didn't have to wait for long. All the arrangements were made. Tomorrow they would bask beneath a Mediterranean sun, while they decided where their future lay.

* * *

Robert hammers the accelerator on the Mercedes, pulling out of the traffic and gunning the engine as he speeds down a lane reserved for oncoming vehicles.

Cassie sits in the back and screams, "Be careful, honey!"

"I know what I'm doing!" he shouts, so as to be heard over Melissa's ear-splitting cries.

Her hand hangs loosely at the wrist, from an arm that looks staggered like a staircase, with several vicious breaks to the forearm bone. The skin hasn't been breached but already the swelling has started, bringing black and blue bruising.

It'll be a long night for Robert and Cassie, until Melissa is wheeled out of the surgery, with her arm repaired and set, ready for recovery.

She would give Robert the options. The first five to ten years should be his. It could be Madeira or Madagascar, Seville or Shanghai, the Netherlands or Nepal. Rachel didn't care where they were, so long as they were together. She would never be lonely any more and that was all that mattered to her. He was her equal, her reflection, her very heart.

Robert finishes hitting Cassie in the bedroom. He goes into their bathroom and makes sure his slick hair is in place. The kids eye him cautiously when he steps into the kitchen. They didn't see what was going on, but they've got that frightened look in their eyes. He knows that when he's gone, she'll compose herself before appearing in front of them, and that they'll no longer be convinced that anything was the matter. Robert had been careful to avoid the face. He'd only hit her there on a couple of occasions and it was a mistake.

Robert wears a shirt that's allergic to creases, and a blue tie with small white dots. A gold tie-pin keeps it in place. It's another sizzling day, as he walks into the entrance hall and out towards the dazzling sun. He sees the caretaker, Robert Stark, polishing the brass intercom plate. Robert hates Robert Stark because he suspects that the young man is sleeping with Cassie. If he ever proves this, he'll thrash her to death's border. Until then, he's content to antagonize the caretaker, on the off-chance of provoking an incriminatory response.

"Happy?" he asks Robert Stark.

"What?"

Robert squints at him and says, "What the hell are you doing here, Stark? Why don't you get a proper job? Haven't you heard? People aren't reading any more. They watch films and take drugs. Jesus!"

Then Robert walks off, leaving the caretaker to look at him with a raised arm shielding his eyes from the sun.

Robert's eyes opened and darted anxiously around the room until they came to rest on Rachel. She was leaning against the door with her arms crossed, smiling warmly on him like a gentle sun. He was inclined to smile back at her until he saw Vernon. He had a purple face. His arm was twisted and there was a gaping cavity halfway between wrist and elbow. As for the chest . . .

The room resembled an abattoir. Vernon Lorenzo's choicest cuts were on the floor, Robert was lying in his cooling blood. The crimson shimmered in front of his eyes. He tried to catch his elusive breath. It was hard to imagine a human form so brutalized by hands alone, but there it was. And the hands that had done it were his. He held them up in front of his face. Vernon's blood was drying, staining his skin, crusting in the narrow ravines across his palms and on his fingertips.

Murder filled his mind. He couldn't get rid of it. Vernon's perfect white teeth were bared in a horrible sneer. Some of them were speckled with delicate scarlet drops, tiny petals of his blood. One of his hands had made a claw of itself, as if it had been clutching life like a rock, at the very moment it had been snatched away from him. Robert gradually picked himself up from Vernon's corporal slime and rose to the kneeling position. He saw the heart. The torn valves, the punctured ball.

Rachel made no effort to move towards him. She watched

the horror – the terror of realization – spread slowly across his face. He examined everything around him in minute, agonizing detail. His clothes were soaked. He could feel the slickness on his thighs, coming through the drenched jeans. Robert shook his head. Murder.

He said, "He was cheating on Cassie."

"Not any more."

"He was seeing this young French woman, who's living in a flat in Egerton Gardens which he's been paying for and . . ."

"There's no need to justify it, Robert. There's no point in trying because you can't. And besides, you don't have to. Not to me."

"But . . ."

"And I'm the only one who counts."

". . . it's murder!"

Rachel sighed. "No. It isn't. *We're different!* For them it may be murder, but for us it's . . . well, we can call it what we want."

"It doesn't make it any better, though, does it?"

"Better? Worse? Than what? Why compare? You and I are not the same. Don't allow us to be judged by . . ."

"I murdered him!"

"No!" she replied, adamantly. "You did not."

He looked down at the butchered proof on the floor, then back at Rachel. "So what did I do?"

"You did what you were created to do, you did what was natural, what was *right*."

"Killing is right?"

"We are animals that hunt and feed. It is our nature. We feed on flesh and we feed on the memory of those we slaughter. It is what we do. Our prey are not the same as us, they are a different species altogether, something weak and inferior. You know this is true. What you have just done proves it beyond all doubt.

"So be reasonable, darling, and just accept what you already know. They were *your* fingers that went through his breastbone like it was rice-paper. It was *you* who inherited everything he's ever been, consuming him, absorbing him . . . *taking* him. You've got it all. So if you still believe you're the same, tell me I'm wrong."

Robert looked down at the corpse. He knew he wasn't the same, but murder was still murder, whatever clothes you dressed it in. He was repulsed by what he'd done, but not enough. He wanted to feel more disgust, as though that would somehow prove his humanity.

Instead, he looked on his first victim and worried more about Vernon's memory than his heart. He looked at Rachel and felt his own heart surge in a way that no mortal could know. She was more beautiful than ever.

He said, "I was making love to Cassie fifteen years ago. It was strange. It really was me. I was him."

Rachel nodded. "I know." She peeled dirty hair from his forehead and asked, "Was it good?"

"Yes, I think so."

"That's how he remembered it."

"You know what the weirdest thing was?"

"What?"

"I discovered why Vernon was so unpleasant to me. He thought Cassie and I were sleeping together."

"And were you?"

"No, of course not. It was just his paranoia. But there was one aspect of it which really blew me away."

"What?"

"Seeing me. I was Vernon and I came downstairs and saw me – Robert Stark – and spoke to him. Does that sound insane?"

"Yes, it does, but I know what you mean." She kissed him on the cheek, her lips picking up a faint trace of Vernon's blood.

"What are we going to do about him?"

She looked down at the body. "Nothing."

"We can't just leave him here."

"What would you suggest?"

"Well . . ." started Robert, before petering out into silence.

"This time tomorrow we'll be in another country, darling.

Cassie won't be back tonight, that's for sure. So who's going to find him? No one, so why risk trying to get rid of him?"

Back at her apartment, he showered. When he reappeared, with a towel around his waist, she asked him, "Were you scared?"

He nodded. "Terrified. When I looked up at you, I could tell you knew what was about to happen. In that second between seeing the look on your face and feeling the hit . . . that was terror on a new scale."

Rachel kissed his collarbone. "I didn't bother trying to explain what it would be like. Nothing I could have said would have prepared you adequately."

"You're right. It would have made it worse."

"It's quite a sensation, isn't it?"

"Unbelievable. Really amazing. It's some kind of supernatural rush. It's an all-time high."

Rachel stood on tiptoes, kissed him on the mouth and said, "An all-time high? I like that. That's precisely what it is. An all-time high."

Katherine kissed Chris on the neck and said, "A penny for your thoughts?"

He was looking down onto the rainswept street. The piles of dead brown leaves which had spiralled from the trees during the heat-wave were now reduced to soggy pulp. The wind sent shivers through the puddles. Chris took a sip of whisky.

"To be honest, I'm scared."

"So am I," she said.

"I never believed it could happen, so I never seriously contemplated this. I mean, occasionally I fantasized about what I'd do if I ever met the person who killed my parents – the person who was responsible for Julia's death – but I never thought it through."

Elmore was on the phone in his bedroom. When they were silent, they could just hear his voice, but not what he was saying.

"I feel like a fool," Chris told Katherine. "For years I've

been preaching a gospel that's suddenly been discredited. And now . . . *this*!"

He took another sip.

"She killed your mother and father."

"I know. And your sister, too."

"You *do* believe that, don't you?"

He nodded. "Her evidence is incontrovertible. I'd love to dismiss her as a fraud, but I can't."

"So you'll kill her?"

"I guess so."

"You don't sound very sure."

"I'm sure I want to," he told her.

"But you're not sure you can do it?"

"No, I'm not."

Katherine frowned. "And when will you decide? When you've got the blade halfway in?"

Chris shrugged. "I don't know. How can I tell?"

She was about to protest, when Elmore appeared. He held a mug of tea in his left hand. He saw he was breaking into a tense moment and lingered in the doorway for a second until Chris engineered a slim smile and said, "You've been running up quite a phone bill."

Elmore took a sip. "It's at the cheap rate in the middle of the night."

"Just as well, really."

"We have a problem."

"What?"

"I can get a list of daggers and their owners. I can find out when and where they changed hands, and for how much. I can even get a list of those who might sell, if the price was right. Josef could wire us the money and we could purchase the weapon straight away."

"So what's the problem?"

"I can't get the list until tomorrow."

Chris looked at Katherine and then back at Elmore. "So? Tomorrow sounds good. I'm impressed you can get it together so quickly."

"Tomorrow will be too late." Elmore swilled the cooling tea around his mug. "Rachel Cates is booked on a British Airways flight to Nice, first thing tomorrow morning. She'll be in the south of France before I even get hold of the information."

Katherine saw the shock in Chris's face. She said, "Are you sure about this?"

"Yes. I checked. She booked it yesterday. And guess who else is on the passenger list?"

"Robert Stark?"

"None other."

Chris looked crestfallen. "She can't be allowed to get away," he murmured.

Elmore said, "She can't be stopped. There's no alternative to the dagger."

"There must be."

"There isn't."

Chris lit a cigarette. Katherine and Elmore glanced at each other for several seconds, while Chris paced back and forth by the window. Then he stopped and looked over at them. "I'm going over there," he told them.

"What? *Now?*" exclaimed Katherine.

"Of course. She'll be gone in a few hours."

"And what are you going to do when you get there?"

"I don't know. Something. *Anything.*"

"There's nothing you can do," said Elmore.

"I've got to try."

Katherine laughed in exasperation. "And what are you going to use? Foul language? Without the right dagger, you don't stand a chance."

"I can't just do nothing."

"She'll tear you in two. You've seen what she can do and you've heard what she promised."

"Katherine's right," said Elmore.

Chris replied, "I'm going anyway."

Katherine looked irritated and then sighed wearily. "In that case, I'm going with you."

Elmore looked astounded. "What?"

"If he insists on going, I'm going too," she explained.

Elmore was furious. "Just because the two of you fell into bed together, it doesn't mean you have to die for each other, does it?"

"Excuse me!" protested Katherine.

Chris said, "As far as I'm concerned, it's got nothing to do with that. Now, are you coming with us?"

Elmore shook his head. "No, I'm not. I like both of you too much."

Robert flexed the fingers of his right hand, stretching the digits which had ram-raided Vernon's rib-cage, looting his innards. The shower had cleansed him of visible traces, but the flesh still felt contaminated.

Sometimes he was so in love with Rachel his own heart ached, as though her fingers were wrapped too tightly around it. And sometimes he was repulsed by her on a scale he'd never encountered. Her lack of compassion and her overwhelming sense of superiority were hard to stomach. Even worse, he could feel those same characteristics blossoming within himself. It was a curious sensation, rather like the beginning of a cold; he felt the onset of the early symptoms and could tell that the condition would worsen.

He saw her in the mirror, as beautiful as ever, a flawless vision. She said, "Darling, she's here."

He turned round. "Who?"

"Laura, of course. Who else?"

Robert was taken aback. "*Here?* Laura?"

"She's downstairs, in your apartment. I saw her arrive."

He looked down at his hands, still moving the evil fingers. Rachel watched him for a moment and then said, "Are you going to see her? It might be your last opportunity."

She waited for some fiery protest, but there was nothing. She guided him out of the bathroom and into the bedroom. Clean clothes lay on a chair by one of the windows.

"What's wrong?" asked Rachel.

"I . . . I'm not sure."

"Is it Lorenzo?"

He looked up at her. "I suppose it is, yes."

Rachel had worried that it was too soon, but there had been no other way, no genuine alternative once he'd started. She nodded pensively.

"It's not the same thing," she assured him. "Don't compare yourself."

"I can't avoid it. However I try to look at it, it's still murder."

"Hi, Laura."

She turned around. He was standing in the hall, shrouded in shadow. Rachel was behind him. Laura tried to rise above her jealousy. He stepped out of the shade and took her breath away.

He was perfect. In all the years she'd known him, Laura had never seen Robert look so healthy, so strong, so . . . *magnificent.* At any time, it would have been a shock, but to compare the creature standing before her with the miserable, infected animal of just a few hours earlier . . .

"Robert? It *is* you, isn't it?"

"Can't you tell?"

She slowly shook her head. "I'm really not sure."

Rachel peered at Laura over his shoulder. The two of them locked gazes. Laura was expecting a sneering, victorious look but didn't get it. She wasn't sure what she saw in Rachel's oil-pool eyes.

"Could I speak to him alone?" asked Laura. "Please."

Rachel didn't like the idea much, but didn't want Robert to see her being too possessive of him, so she faked a look of casual composure and nodded. She kissed him on the cheek and said, "When you're through, come upstairs, darling," before leaving the room.

Laura fumbled for a cigarette with awkward fingers that lacked coordination, as though they were numb from cold. Robert stood motionless on the other side of the room, his mind still consumed by Vernon's last moment of life, an instant of pure terror. He must have felt Robert's fingers working inside him, exploring the wet, virgin territory. What had gone through his mind in that last fragment of a second before Robert's fingers contracted into a fist and retreated?

Laura leaned forward and whispered conspiratorially. "What did she do to you?"

He frowned. "I'm not . . . I don't . . ."

"Dr Foster said you were going to . . ."

"She doesn't know anything. She doesn't understand."

"Understand what?"

"What I've become."

"And what is that? It's something to do with her, isn't it?"

He was like a statue, still and silent.

"*Isn't it?*" she repeated, more forcefully.

"Yes."

There was no satisfaction for Laura in the confirmation. She took a sip from the vodka she'd poured for herself.

"Are you going to stay with her?" she asked.

Robert saw the body tumbling forward. The thump and squelch as Lorenzo ploughed into the drenched carpet. The heart in his hand, dribbling blood between his fingers as he held the organ up like some ludicrous Yorick's skull. *Alas, poor Vernon. I knew him . . .*

Never were those words more appropriate. Robert *did* know him. He knew everything Lorenzo had ever known, inherited every tiny experience from birth to death. He was a man with a rotten soul, which now festered inside Robert's head. But just because Vernon was corrupt in spirit, that didn't make killing him an act of virtue.

"I feel tired," he told her.

She moved over to him and took hold of his arm. His eyes were brilliant. The whites were as pure as virgin snow, sparkling and sharp. When she focused on the pupils they seemed endless, like a vast tunnel into which she was inexorably sucked. His skin was so smooth she almost disliked it. She resisted the urge to trail her fingertips across it to confirm it was real. She kissed him lightly on the lips and took a step back.

"I love you, Robert."

His heart stirred, but he couldn't identify the emotion that caused it. There were too many things making a claim on his attention. A fresh declaration of love from anyone was the last thing he needed. The fact that it was Laura only confused him further. Love and murder.

"It's not . . . not possible . . . for us."

She said, "Why not? I mean, do you love her?"

Robert's brow furrowed. "Of course, but that's . . . not it. I just can't . . . you and I . . ."

"What are you talking about? Listen, it's simple. I love you and I want you. Now if you can tell me, in clear English, that I should leave, then I'll leave."

"I don't want you . . . to go."

"Do you love her?"

He bowed his head so that his chin touched his chest. "Yes."

"I don't believe you."

Robert looked up at Laura. "I do."

"Leave her."

"What?"

"Leave her. Come with me."

"It's not possible!" he snapped.

She issued a dismissive snort of laughter. "Nothing could be easier! We just say goodbye and walk out. In fact, we don't even need to say goodbye."

"I love her!"

The words smacked Laura and she smarted.

He said, more slowly and calmly, "I am deeply in love with her. Do you understand that?"

Laura's shoulders sagged. For a moment, she thought she'd sensed hope, picking up its heady scent in the bleak undergrowth of despair. She'd followed it wildly, abandoning caution. And now her recklessness had brought her humiliation.

"I'm sorry," she whispered, meekly.

Then she did the thing she despised most. She cried. In the hierarchy of reactions she hoped to avoid, crying was king. But there was nothing left inside her to prevent it. And once the first fragile tears trickled over the brim of the tear-duct, she couldn't even be bothered to try to contain it. Her steel streak melted. Robert watched her fall apart at the seams. He was pricked by guilt and compassion, but both were perverted by indifference. He hated that. Just like he hated the fact that he'd felt remorse after killing Vernon, but not nearly enough.

"There's something else," he told her. "I'm not who I was, Laura. You're not in love with me. You're in love with somebody else. A different Robert Stark. He's not here. He's gone."

He couldn't tell whether his words were getting through. She avoided eye-contact. She took a sip from her drink. Then she picked up her cigarette from the stone ashtray.

"I am different. That is why it wouldn't work for you and me. I know you don't believe it, but . . ."

"I don't care," she wailed.

"If you understood, you would."

For the first time since the tears started, she looked up. "No, I would not! I love you and . . ."

"If you knew . . ."

"*I don't care!* How many times do I have to say it? *I don't care!* Don't you get it? My love isn't conditional, Robert. I don't give a fuck what you are or what you've done. I love you unconditionally."

Laura thought of all the missed opportunities she'd had with Robert. And now it came down to this. If she hadn't been crying, she would have been laughing. And since her dignity was in shreds and everything else was in ruins, she figured she might as well go the whole distance. She took a deep breath and said, "I'll commit myself to you right now, if you want. For life."

Robert looked at her coldly and said, "For life?"

"That's right."

"What do you know of life?"

Laura could barely believe she'd heard him correctly. He sounded callous and cruel in a way she couldn't identify with the man she knew so well. He saw her bewilderment giving way to resentment.

"This is what I've been trying to tell you, Laura. Life. It's not the same thing for you as it is for me."

Her eyes were slightly red, the rims of the eyelids a little raw. She sniffed.

"It doesn't matter," she said, in a weak voice that lurched with her uneven breathing.

"Don't say that any more. It *does* matter. Until you understand precisely what I'm trying to . . ."

"No. It does *not* matter, Robert. *That* is the point. There is nothing you can say which will make me change the way I feel about you. You can tell me you hate me, and I'll still love you. You can tell me you'll marry Rachel, and I'll still love you. You can tell me you'll never see me again, and I'll still love you. You can tell me you killed someone, and I'll still . . ."

"No!"

"*Yes!*"

The phone rang but Daley was in too deep a sleep to be roused immediately. Too many sleepless nights had generated fatigue on a massive scale. His sleep was like winter hibernation, deep and impenetrable. So it was his wife, Alison Daley, who awoke, reached across her husband and picked up the receiver.

"Yes?" she snapped.

"I'm sorry to wake you, Mrs Daley, but this is Detective Constable Malloy speaking. Could I have a word with your husband?"

"Do you realize what time it is?"

"Yes, and I wouldn't have called unless it were absolutely necessary."

It took several seconds of prodding to withdraw Daley from the warm, comfortable cocoon of deep sleep. Alison pressed the receiver to his face. "Yes, what is it, Malloy?"

"It's blown wide open, sir."

He was lost for a moment. "What has?"

"The case. The standby firearms unit has been put on full alert and there's a car on its way to you right now. Smith's in it. He can brief you on the way back. The vehicle should be with you in three to four minutes. We're waiting for your instructions and . . ."

But Daley had already put the phone down and was getting out of bed, reaching for his clothes.

Chapter Twenty-three

Rachel took a bottle of champagne from the fridge. In a few hours she would leave Lennox Gardens forever, which was a sadness to her, despite everything there was to look forward to. In the early morning, they would fly to Nice and then drive to her villa up in the hills. They could pass time there, looking onto the distant sea, while Robert became fully accustomed to his brand new reality. She imagined them on some Caribbean island, or strolling through perfected Parisian boulevards on an impossibly idyllic spring day. That was what she craved. That fantasy would soon be real and the wait of two centuries would finally be vindicated.

She moved through the dark halls of her apartment. The wind howled outside, begging to be let in. She stood in the doorway to the bedroom and looked down at the bed, reliving the first time she made love to him, doused in some astonishing emotion. The blue blade in a flashing arc, his sizzling blood in her mouth, the ecstasy as she sliced apart her own flesh, her blood on his lips.

She had wanted him to avoid killing until she had him safely hidden away at the villa. Its relative seclusion made for an ideal private school, where she intended to gently introduce him to the stunning possibilities for both of them. The messy situation with Vernon Lorenzo had occurred through an unfortunate series of coincidences. Rachel worried that it might undermine her careful orchestration.

Robert's shock and self-disgust were both natural and irritating. Had there been a suitable period of grace between his metamorphosis and his first kill, the aftermath would have been different. He would not have been burdened by such petty delusions of morality.

Rachel was in her drawing-room when the doorbell rang. She opened the door and found Chris Lang and Katherine Ross standing in the hall, where she had expected to see Robert. She eyed them warily and took a sip from her glass.

"What a pleasant surprise," she said, in a voice which unmistakably suggested it wasn't. "You'll excuse me for not offering you a drink, but I can't imagine this encounter lasting long."

She had been enjoying her solitude, moving from room to room on a tide of nostalgia. This kind of intrusion was a thing she neither anticipated nor desired. She led them to the drawing-room.

"I had to see you before you left," Chris said.

"So you come to my home in the middle of the night? Is that how people are behaving in America these days?"

"You told us in the gardens that you were leaving soon."

"I also told you that if I ever saw either of you again, I'd kill you."

She went over to the fireplace and reached for a silver box on the mantelpiece. She withdrew a Turkish cigarette and lit it. Katherine felt her skin tingle when Rachel looked deeply into her eyes and said, softly, "Coming across you in my pursuit of Stephen Abraham was an unfortunate coincidence, Miss Ross. It didn't count. This, however, does."

What were they going to do now? Rachel exhaled blue streams of smoke. Chris tried to picture her as Marilyn Webber. He couldn't recall the face of 1963, so the image remained agonizingly incomplete.

Rachel said, "What's on your little mind, Chris Martin? Do you want to ask me awkward questions? Do you need to know whether your father was faithful to your mother? For the record, he wasn't."

Chris swallowed. "He wasn't?"

Rachel shook her head. "No. He had an affair with a woman called Lorraine Hunter. She lived in Queen's and they saw each other for three years, until she moved west to San Diego."

"Lorraine Hunter?"

"Yes. A rather unspectacular dyed blonde. A secretary for Pan Am, as I recall. An uninspired choice, if I may say so. And what about you, Miss Ross? What are you . . . *dying* to know?"

Katherine's mouth moved but nothing came out.

"Would you like to know which sexual acts your sister and André Perlman favoured?"

"No."

Chris said, "Why did you kill my parents?"

Rachel geared her grin back into a smile. "I took your father because I wanted to know everything he'd discovered during the course of his research and, frankly, it was pretty unimpressive. Too much trust in science, I'm afraid. Logic shut off the avenues that he should have been investigating. Too much time wasted looking for non-existent diseases. He should have paid more attention to the hysterical legends. As for your mother, well . . ."

"Well what?"

Rachel looked maliciously at Chris. "She was there, so why not? And at the time, I knew that you and your sister were watching. The idea was intriguing: what kind of effect would it have on you, watching something like that? I've thought about it quite often since then."

Julia had seen everything and it had, ultimately, been the death of her. The suicide had its roots in what she witnessed. And here was Rachel chatting about it casually, wondering, in an offhand sort of way, what kind of reaction her destruction provoked. Chris tried to control his rage, knowing that to strike out, as his heart wanted, was pointless.

"Supposing we'd tried to intervene?" he asked.

"If you'd actually come into the sitting-room?"

He nodded, the blood flushing in his cheeks. "Yes. If we'd tried to stop you."

She looked bored by the notion. "Who knows? We probably wouldn't be having this conversation. You'd probably now be a very tiny part of my memory."

"You . . . you bitch!"

Katherine tried to defuse the situation by asking, "What did you do to Abraham?"

Rachel looked almost embarrassed. "He was an indulgence. A game to kill time. A cheap amusement."

Katherine was exasperated. "He was a human being, for God's sake. *A life!*"

The humour vanished from Rachel's face. "Precisely. A life. Singular. One solitary existence and nothing more. No big deal."

Chris was as horrified as Katherine. "What did you do to him?"

"I showed him the accumulated experiences of dozens of people from the last two centuries and it quite literally blew his mind. It went up in smoke like a cheap fuse."

"Why did you do it?"

"I wanted to see what effect it would have on him. He agreed to let me show him."

Chris was amazed. "He agreed? He actually believed you?"

She grinned. "No. Of course he didn't believe me. He thought I was trying to seduce him."

Katherine shook her head in disgust. "And Robert Stark's next on your hit list, is he?"

Rachel froze and turned to her, slowly. "I could never kill him," she whispered, icily. "I could never harm him. *Ever.*"

"Why not?"

Katherine had never seen such venom in a stare. "Love. That's why. A pure love. Something neither of you would – or could, I expect – understand. Love on a fatal scale."

Katherine thought Rachel might attack both of them in that instant, but she didn't. She took a small sip from her glass and then drew on her cigarette and said, "It's a pity neither of you will ever know perfect love."

* * *

The flashing blue light worked in tandem with the siren. Harold Daley clutched his armrest and asked David Smith, "How did this all happen?"

"Pure luck, sir. A cab-driver heard the descriptions we put out over the radio and they matched a fare he'd just dropped off. Derek Fowler's his name. He's making a full statement at the moment. He picked them up and . . ."

"Where? Bishop's Bridge Road area, near the Ross woman's place?"

"No. Caledonian Road, up by King's Cross."

Daley pulled a face. "Any thoughts on that?"

"No. According to Fowler they were walking along the pavement when they flagged him down. He heard the descriptions in a news bulletin on one of the FM channels just after he'd dropped them off at Lennox Gardens."

Daley muttered, "Well, we've earned a little luck."

"Anyway," continued Smith, "we showed him a couple of photographs of Ross and Lang and he's confirmed them. Plus he heard them talking and said that the man spoke with an American accent."

The shot of Lang which the NYPD had faxed over to them was particularly poor. Daley was surprised that anyone could make a match off it.

"So what's the link with Lennox Gardens?"

"Robert Stark."

Daley frowned and took a heavy drag from his cigarette. "No. I can't place him."

"He was interviewed by Marsh and Malloy in the aftermath of the Reynolds killing. Apparently, Sarah Reynolds was an old girlfriend of his. According to Fowler, he dropped Lang and Ross off at the same building where Stark lives."

The driver straightened out at the top of Park Lane and gunned the engine. Sluggish vehicles crept to the kerb, creating a free channel. Daley found himself thinking, rather curiously, of how Moses had parted the Red Sea.

"It sounds a bit slim, Dave. Just because he lives at the same place, doesn't mean he . . ."

"There's something more. Stark's the man in the video from Earls Court."

"What?"

"That's right. He was the man who stepped out of the carriage at Earls Court Underground with our girl Rachel."

"Who made that identification?"

"Marsh and Malloy."

"They what?" spluttered Daley.

"They've seen hundreds of faces, spoken to hundreds of nobodies, taken hundreds of pointless statements. They were only with him for a couple of minutes. A lot's happened since then."

Daley ran a hand over the thinning remains of his hair. "I suppose so."

"But when he was fingered earlier on – and when everyone started to focus on him – they matched him with the face on the video."

Daley nodded. "What about the girl? Any leads on Rachel?"

"Nothing yet."

"Well, let's take one thing at a time, eh? Once we've nailed him, who knows what we'll turn up?"

Robert directed Laura into an armchair and then knelt at her feet. He held onto her hands and said, "I'm sorry."

"Why? What's there to be sorry about? It's not your fault. It's mine. How could I . . . ?"

"Don't be silly."

". . . have been so foolish?"

She turned her face away. He let go of her hands and rose to his feet. It was hard to believe that he could inflict genuine terror on anyone. But that was precisely what he'd seen in Vernon Lorenzo's eyes, in the final moment before his life came to an abrupt end. Robert feared the dark storm clouds which gathered at his mind's horizon.

Laura said, "I feel so stupid, Robert. I mean, you and I had an arrangement. No strings attached, no complications, no messy separations. That was the point, wasn't it? We were supposed to avoid all this, weren't we?"

It was true. He nodded. "Even the best laid plans . . ."

"But I guess we were just kidding ourselves," she said, before dropping her eyes to the carpet and adding, in a gloomier tone, "at least, I was."

She looked up and waited for a response, hoping for some confirmation that he felt the same way. But Robert was staring out of the window with vacant eyes and, so far as she could tell, might not have heard her at all.

"At first, I didn't want to accept it. I liked the set-up we had. I really didn't want anything to screw it up. But I couldn't ignore what I felt. And I thought that since I was kidding myself, maybe you were too. How naïve!" she said, before permitting herself a bitter laugh. "Just because I love you, why should you feel the same about me, right?"

"Laura, please."

"Oh, what?"

"Don't do it."

"Make a fool of myself? Jesus Christ! What difference does it make? I can't feel any worse than I do right now."

Robert kissed her. At first, she tried to back away, arching her back against him and turning her face away. But he pushed his mouth onto hers and she offered diminishing resistance. He released her hands and she threaded them around his back. Her tears burned their cheeks. When he broke away from her, she ran a hand across her forehead, blinked and said, "Well, you've got me truly confused now."

"It's possible to be in love with two people at the same time, Laura. In different ways. After all, no two real loves can ever be the same. A real affair is as individual as a fingerprint."

She cleared her throat. "Yes, I know," she admitted, in a tone coloured by resignation. "But I'm just greedy. I won the lottery, but the prize had to be shared and I wanted it all for myself. Greed's a killer."

"I understand."

She shook her head. "No, you don't. Not really, Robert. I mean, what am I going to do without you?"

He smiled. "You *will* get over me."

"I won't get over you."

"This may seem brutal now, but one day you'll thank me for this. When enough time has passed to allow you to think about this dispassionately, you'll find . . ."

"Dispassionately?" she interrupted. "How am I going to think about you dispassionately, Robert? *I love you, for God's sake!*"

"You won't always love me."

She wasn't sure whether she was going to laugh or cry, so she turned away from him. "I'm not just talking about love!" she protested. "I can't deny that I do love you – and I wouldn't want to deny it, either – but that's not the whole picture. You're more than that, Robert. You're my best friend too. You think I'm going to get over that in a hurry?"

Robert dropped his gaze to the carpet. "Our futures are incompatible. She waited for eternity for me."

Laura frowned and assumed he'd got his words in a muddle, and had meant to say, "She waited for *an* eternity for me." She shrugged and said, "This is more than lust and desire. You're as vital to me as blood."

Robert squirmed. The more intense her declarations, the more uncomfortable he felt. Shame seemed like a suitable price to pay. He took a deep breath and said, "Okay, Laura, I'm going to tell you something and I want you to hear me out. Do you think you can manage that?"

"Sure, why not?"

"You'll see why not."

Robert looked around his sitting-room, a small damp dungeon in the bowels of the building he serviced. In a few hours, he would be clear of it forever.

He said, "Robert Stark died earlier tonight. He passed away in a filthy back alley when the storm broke. What stands before you is a different creature altogether. The identical name and similar appearance are misleading. Don't be fooled. The man you say you love – your best friend – is dead.

"I had to die to escape from the chains of mortal reality. I had to relinquish the stifling handicaps of man's physical being to become what she wanted and needed, to become what I am now. The fact of the matter is, I had to die in order to live forever.

"Some say that when the body dies, the spirit lives on eternally. If you believe that, then it's not such a leap of faith to accept what I have become: the physical embodiment of that spirit. I am immortal."

He allowed a digestive pause. Laura didn't laugh or shout or even raise her eyebrows. She just murmured the word, "Immortal?"

Robert nodded. "I will live forever. Rachel was born in Lyon on 2 January 1789. She's been searching for a perfect lover, the ideal mate, for two centuries. And I'm the one she found.

"Don't ask why it turned out to be me. I don't know. *She* doesn't even know! But that's the way love works, isn't it? It seemed ridiculous to me at the start, but not any more."

He admired her composure. She wasn't giving anything away. The tears dried and her gaze was locked onto him.

"What can you be thinking?" he said. "You saw me fall to pieces, decaying in front of your eyes and now – just a few hours later – I'm in better condition than you've ever known. You don't know what to think, and I certainly wouldn't expect you to believe what I've just told you, but you're wondering how it happened, aren't you?"

"You got better because you died?" she asked.

He ignored her query. "There's something else I'd like you to know. You've read the papers so you know about the murder of André Perlman and Jennifer Colson. Well, I'll tell you something you didn't know: Rachel did it and she killed Sarah too."

Still Laura wouldn't give him the satisfaction of a protest, or even a forceful enquiry. He wondered what she was thinking.

There was a way to find out, of course, but he dismissed that as soon as it occurred to him.

"I'm the same as her, Laura," he said, flatly. "I'm an animal that hunts and kills, feeding off my prey in my own way, just as surely as if I ate the flesh itself. That is what I have become and..."

"Robert?"

He stopped mid-sentence. She still looked as austere as before. "Yes?" he said.

"Shut up and kiss me again."

Rachel left them alone in the drawing-room for a minute. When she returned she asked Chris, "Do you appreciate beauty?"

He was caught off-guard by the question. He glanced at Katherine and shrugged. "Sure, I guess."

"What do you think of this?"

Rachel raised her right hand. She was clutching a dagger with an eighteen-inch blade. Chris and Katherine instinctively backed away towards the french windows. Rain exploded across the clear glass. Rachel moved slowly towards them.

"It's as sharp as a surgeon's scalpel," she assured them, running a forefinger lightly along one cutting edge. "It's a real work of art, manufactured according to a set of specific instructions, for a *very* specific purpose. But I don't really need to tell you that, do I?"

Chris said, cautiously, "Under the circumstances, I'm surprised to find you in possession of it."

"I collect things of beauty, Mr Lang. Its added significance only heightens its value."

Chris and Katherine were cornered. Rachel had cut off their only exit channel. She tapped the tip of the dagger against a marble ashtray on a small side-table. Katherine watched light dancing on the moving blade.

Rachel smiled when she looked at Chris. "You know what you remind me of? Your father. He had that same look in his eyes, when I first met him in Burrows, Virginia. It's part fear, part excitement and you're not sure which is which, or which is stronger, are you?"

Chris edged in front of Katherine and put a protective arm across her. This gesture amused Rachel.

"How touching," she said. "What a pity you chose to come here. You might have had quite a future together."

"What were we supposed to do? Just accept what you've done and let you walk away?"

"If you think I'm moved by your notions of propriety, you're wrong. I don't care how you feel or what you think. All I'm saying is, you were foolish to come here. Your sorrow doesn't shame me, it doesn't sadden me at all. I have no guilt. I'd just as soon kill both of you as light a cigarette or take a look out of the window."

"I don't believe you!" protested Katherine, in an unguarded moment of nervous anger.

Rachel's eyes blazed. "You don't?"

Chris stayed mute. He and Katherine were at Rachel's mercy, which was the most precarious position to be in. She retreated to the french windows.

"I love the sound of the rain," she told them, before opening both sets to the elements.

She returned to where Chris and Katherine were standing, the dim light casting a warm glow over both of them. She turned the dagger around, holding the end of the blade in her hand. She slowly extended her arm, edging the handle towards Chris.

"I'm sure you'll be interested in examining this more closely. Go on," she whispered, "take it, but remember this: if you're of a mind to use it, you'll have to be quick. Quicker than me."

Rachel grinned as he wrapped his fingers around it. She let go of the cool metal and took a step back. He had no doubt she could move like lightning, if she chose to.

The blade was brilliant: two tapered silver sides, each flawless. He gently touched one of the cutting edges. It was laser sharp. Held upside down, it looked like an ornate crucifix.

The handle was wood and ivory with tiny figures carved into the stem. They were tortured souls, hideously stretched and painfully thin. Where they were clothed at all, they were draped in rags. Some of the figures were more than malnourished; they were skeletal. They pressed uncomfortably into the flesh of Chris's hand when he tightened his grip on the instrument. He looked up and Rachel was watching every fractional movement.

Chris kept the tip of the blade pointed in her direction. The wind was banging the french windows against their stressed hinges. Rain stained the Persian carpet. He said, "You're still a murderer, whatever else you might claim to be."

She was angered by his classification. "That is an irrelevant detail. If your mind can't be any more flexible than that, perhaps it would be better if I had it, rather than you."

Chris raised the dagger in a threatening fashion, but they both knew that in a contest of speed, she would win. He'd probably never even see her hands until they were dismantling him.

He said, "Having assimilated so much, I'm surprised you don't have a stronger sense of compassion. Or was callousness a prerequisite of being one of your victims?"

Rachel smiled. "Well, you should know! Were your parents callous people? Was Jennifer Colson a callous cellist? All I was ever interested in were the qualities which made them interesting to me in the first place. I have too much to consider without allowing clumsy human sentiment to clutter my thought process."

"I notice that doesn't extend to Robert Stark."

"Indeed not. But then again, who can legislate for love? No mortal I ever met could deal with it. At its most intense, it has always been far too powerful a force for the fragile human mind to control. Love is more than just one of the players on the emotional team. Love is the star."

Chris wasn't sure. It had never struck him that strongly. Behind Rachel, the curtains billowed as the gale filled the drawing-room.

"My love for Robert is something you could never appreciate. You will never know what it is to commit yourself to someone forever, and for forever to mean exactly that: *forever*. When a man marries a woman, they're lucky to get fifty moderately happy years together. Robert and I will share a passion which will never diminish with time. Anything which tried to interfere with that would be criminal, wouldn't you agree?"

"You're insane!"

"No. I'm in love."

Over the desperate scream of the wind, thunder growled. There was a lightning flash.

Chris's lunge wasn't planned. Instinct took over, a heady brew of fury and madness. He threw himself forward and planted the blade in her breastbone, throwing all his weight behind the assault. She never moved, making no effort to avoid his charge or prevent the metal from piercing her. His bulk and momentum should have sent them both tumbling to the floor. Instead, he bounced off her as though she were a stone pillar. His grip on the dagger loosened. The left hand came away but the right was clamped to the instrument by her smaller, slimmer fingers.

Katherine watched in silent astonishment. Chris saw the shining metal protruding from her chest, the blood spilling freely from the wound. And he saw her face, which bore no trace of pain.

She said, calmly, "Did you really think you could do that to me? After all your years of careful research, you were that eager to lose yourself to some ridiculous piece of mythology? You should be ashamed of yourself!"

The pressure from her delicate fingers began to increase. The ornate carving on the handle started to cut into the flesh on the palm of his right hand. Chris clawed at her grip with his left hand but it was futile. He started to wince.

"But if it's not the dagger," he gasped, trying to prevent himself from crying out, "then how?"

She smiled when she said, "For you, there is no 'how'.

There's nothing you can do. All the worst rumours you heard about my sort are true, and all the best were nothing more than fiction born of hope; a child of desire, not reality. A triumph of fantasy over fact."

She squeezed much harder and broke all the fingers on his right hand. Katherine choked in horror at the popping of knuckles and splintering of bones. Chris found his lungs robbed of the air with which to scream. Then Rachel slowly started withdrawing the crimson blade, still grinding the fragmented remains of Chris's hand onto the handle. She sucked in every drop of his pain, making herself giddy on it. Then she flicked her hand in a rapid arc.

There was a crack which seemed as loud as the thunder above them, when Chris's right wrist snapped under the pressure. The dagger clattered to the floor. The colour drained from his face. Rachel let go and his trembling legs gave way. Katherine sank to her knees beside him, trying to be courageous and not let her fear show. Rachel loomed over the pair, oblivious to her own injury and concentrating instead on their sweet misery.

She said, "Once I'd found him, did you ever really – *honestly* – believe there was any chance that I'd allow someone to threaten our union? You can't appreciate what a discovery he is for me. He's my salvation from damnation."

She was shaking with rage, her eyes burning, her lethal fingers twitching. Katherine held on tightly to Chris as Death took a step closer to them.

"It's quite something to experience genuine fear, isn't it?" she whispered. "That's what it is to stare into the bleak abyss of eternal solitude. That was how I lived for two centuries, with no reason to believe I'd ever be delivered."

She gazed upon the pitiful pair. They accepted their fate. She saw it in their pale faces.

"You would find many of the things I've done . . . *questionable,*" she told them. "But many have been extraordinary, too. I met Tsar Nicholas and I met John Kennedy. I have the minds of the most gifted people you could imagine; artists, linguists, scientists, professors, criminals, soldiers, musicians . . . there's virtually no occupation I haven't touched in some fashion.

"When I consider an argument, I can balance it with a thousand measured opinions, taking any side I want with conviction. I have a library of collected memories that is so extensive it could be eternally nourishing without my ever having to add to it. I have trodden on the moon. I have taken decisions which killed thousands of innocent people. I've attended world premieres for my work. I have been revered and vilified. I've been a rape victim and a rapist. I have fought in wars, on opposing sides at the same time. I have acted as cruelly and as indiscriminately as a foul pestilence. I have acted as sweetly as a saint, devoting myself to the helpless and hopeless. I am a Muslim fanatic and a Zionist terrorist. I am a prostitute, a mother, a father, a Nobel scientist.

"As surely as time passes, I am a proper chronicler of it. I am not just a brief chapter in it. Since my birth, I have been as constant as Time itself. Time and I will finish in a dead-heat.

"Do you now understand how absurdly insignificant you are to me? In my story, the two of you don't even represent a sentence, let alone a chapter. You're an expletive; a minuscule outburst which comes to a very abrupt end."

Chapter Twenty-four

Robert kissed Rachel. His fingers trailed down the flimsy material of her shirt to the blood-drenched tear.

"What happened?"

"Lang and Ross, remember them?"

He nodded. "Yes."

"They made a mistake."

"And now?"

Rachel smiled mischievously. "And now they've paid for it."

Laura swallowed anxiously. While Rachel was away, she'd listened to what Robert told her. All his talk of immortality was ridiculous, but she'd never seen him so sincere. She found herself wanting to accept him, to do anything he asked of her, but to believe his story demanded too much of her faith. Between heady kisses and the gloom of promised separation, Laura found herself utterly bewildered. She clutched at stability where she thought she glimpsed it, but never ended up with anything.

Since Laura had started her final, passionate plea for a chance at a future together, Robert had descended into broody silence. Even when Rachel reappeared, he continued to be shrouded in gloom, drifting through his own sombre thoughts, entirely cocooned from what was happening around him.

Laura fumbled for a cigarette with shaking fingers. Robert and Rachel were still in a clutch. It crucified Laura to admit that they looked magnificent. They had an aura about them which almost glowed, like some giant halo. They were perfect physical specimens, bonded by blood and soldered at the heart. Their dazzling eyes looked merciless and beautiful, appealing and appalling in equal measure. To Laura, they seemed vicious and wonderful in the same instant.

Nothing could possibly match them for their excellence. Each of them was the beauty and the beast. They were glittering savages.

Rachel said to Robert, "Darling, I want you to have her. She is my wedding present to you."

He appeared to have receded into the fog of his depression again. His expression was troubled. "What do you mean?"

She turned towards Laura and said, "I look at the two of you and I see . . . well, I see that you're more than just friends."

Neither Robert nor Laura would confirm it.

"If I hadn't appeared in your life," she went on, "maybe you would have fallen in love with her, the way she has obviously fallen in love with you."

She allowed a little pause for her words to sting Laura to the maximum.

"What a waste it would be if all that potential were lost."

Laura wondered whether he was even listening to Rachel. His stare was almost catatonic.

"That's why I want her to be my present to you," said Rachel, softly. "She can be more than a mere memory. She can be part of you forever."

Rachel was almost licking her lips at the prospect of watching Robert accept her gift. Laura felt like a prime cut of meat being eyed by a hungry tiger. Robert's face remained a picture of beautiful confusion.

"Take her. Let her be a part of you, permanently inside your heart and head. It's what you want, isn't it?"

Laura sucked on her cigarette. Robert slowly lifted his gaze to meet hers. He frightened her. His eyes were dead. She slowly started to shuffle along the wall, feeling her way with trembling hands, while Rachel encouraged Robert.

"Please, darling!" she implored him, now kissing him on the face, working herself into a frenzy of lust and anticipation. "Do it! *Here and now!*"

Robert turned to her slowly and said, "I love you, Rachel. I always have and I always will."

Her smile was pure joy. For a magical moment, she looked more radiant than ever before. He kissed her again. Laura continued to move along the wall, constantly fearing the inevitable instant when one or other of them would halt her. She tried not to imagine what would follow. Rachel wrapped her arms around Robert, as he pressed her against the wall. She sighed ecstatically between eager kisses, plugging her fingertips into his back, urging him on. Laura stopped moving altogether, too engrossed in her voyeurism to even consider her own escape and safety. The cigarette slipped from between her fingers and started to burn a hole in the threadbare carpet.

It was insane. Rachel started to claw at the buttons on Robert's shirt. Both of them seemed to have allowed their sense of purpose to dissolve in lust. Laura couldn't avert her gaze or move her body. She felt disgusted by the spectacle, and yet addicted to it. She watched Robert run a hand between Rachel's thighs, disappearing beneath the skirt. Rachel unfastened enough of his shirt to expose a shoulder. She started to kiss the flesh, running from collar-bone to throat. Robert slipped his fingers into the bloody tear of her shirt and yanked the material to one side. It ripped easily.

His mouth moved over Rachel's wounded breastbone, licking the bloody traces which stained her pristine skin. She panted, encircling his head with her arms, running her fingers through his long dark hair. As he worked his way slowly upwards, she tossed her head back and gasped, "I love you, darling. With all my heart."

"I know," he mumbled, before plunging his teeth into her throat.

Rachel's body went into spasm. Her hands jerked backwards and slapped the wall, cracking the plaster into powder. Her feet tried to kick against him but his grip was unrelenting.

Robert drew on the wound with all the energy he could muster, diving into the richest blood source of all. The boiling liquid gushed into his mouth too plentifully for him to cope. He took down as much as he could, sucking and swallowing as if he intended to drown himself. It scorched his throat and stomach. Rachel hammered at his shoulders, but he had her pinned into a position where retaliation was pointless. Her will and strength began to diminish.

In the first instant, Laura assumed she was imagining what she was seeing. Rachel's body tensed and flexed, and suddenly there was protest in place of passion. She saw Robert's lips firmly planted on the throat. A torrent of blood started to seep from the corners of his busy mouth, streaming over her pale skin and showering onto the floor.

Rachel shivered as the river flooded out of her. Darkness loomed. She could feel it closing in from every side. But she felt no pain or fear, just sadness. *Why?* It was the word she couldn't air. Two centuries were streaming through her veins and arteries towards Robert's receptive mouth. But then he stopped. She felt his lips leaving her throat and the wound suddenly felt cold. She wanted him to continue. He held her lovingly, lowering her gently to the floor.

Robert was crying. "I'm sorry, but only immortal lovers can break the law that others can't even bend," he whispered. "I had to. I love you, Rachel. I always have and I always will."

That was all she wanted to know. She forced what she hoped would appear as a smile and said, weakly, "I love you, Robert. Please . . . please . . . kill me . . ."

He nodded and kissed her, cutting her off mid-sentence. She would never know why. Robert knew it was better this way. There would be no time for sorrow and no need for debate. The last thing he wanted was to prolong her misery any more than necessary. So he'd elected not to say anything, but just to act during a moment when she was supremely happy, bringing her to an end with as little warning as possible.

He drove his hand through her breastbone, reached for her heart and killed her in an instant. That was when Laura started to scream hysterically.

A second later, Robert was overwhelmed by the rush and collapsed across Rachel's body.

When Laura regained her self-control, she inched slowly towards the two motionless lovers on the carpet. She leaned forward and said, in a very frail voice, "Robert? Can you hear me? *Robert?*"

In the distance, over the howls of the storm, she heard police sirens.

Epilogue

The cold rain fell softly. The mountains rose steeply on either side of the winding road, the taller ones losing their peaks in the slate grey clouds. Katherine drove the rented car past a slip-road which had fallen into disuse. Chris peered down it and saw a set of large, rusting gates, secured by padlock and chains.

"That's the entrance to the mine that got shut down," he told her. "So just round the next corner, we should . . ."

A rotten wooden board said "Welcome to Burrows, Virginia, population . . ." There had been a number once, but the figure was now obscured by a single spray-canned word: *insane*. Population: insane.

They cruised slowly into the town, a collection of decaying wooden shacks on either side of a short stretch of bad tarmac. She parked by what had once been the general store. Katherine took hold of his good arm and helped him out of the car. His broken wrist was still in plaster. The doctor in London had told Chris that further surgery would be required. It was impossible to say whether the fingers would make a full recovery. Their reconstruction was still at an early stage.

Katherine looked at the ramshackle buildings which surrounded them. The wood had rotted, turning soft in the wet. The garage forecourt had greenery sprouting up through cracks in the concrete. The old-fashioned pumps had been vandalized.

Chris assessed the menacing hills which rose above them. The pines looked black.

"Can you picture it?" he asked Katherine.

She wiped her glasses dry. "Yes, I'm afraid I can."

As Chris lit a cigarette, a figure appeared out of the rain. He approached slowly, walking with a limp, using a stick for support. Chris supposed he was in his seventies.

"Can I help you?" asked the stranger, as he came closer.

"Just looking."

"Burrows ain't never been no tourist attraction."

"Do you live here?"

This brought mirth to his wrinkled face. "Shit, ain't nobody lives here no more! I'm from Baker's Bridge, about five miles down the road. If you're looking for gas or food or some place to stay, that'll be your best bet. You won't find nothing in Burrows."

"Since when?"

"Since the mine closed down in 1975. There was a few fools who lived on for a while, but there ain't been no one here since '78 or '79, I suppose."

Chris offered the man a cigarette and he accepted one. As he gave him a light he asked, trying to sound as casual as possible, "Were you around this area back in 1963?"

The man puffed on the cigarette and said, "What crap you been reading, then? Monsters in the mountain, I'll bet. Let me tell you something: don't believe a goddamned word you read about this town. Not one frigging syllable!"

"Why not?"

"Because none of those assholes bothered to come down here and check it out! Nobody knows what went on here. We're only five miles away in Baker's Bridge and *we* didn't know."

Chris looked at the decay around him. Burrows must have been a miserable enough place in which to live, without the additional hell of coping with Marilyn Webber. They must have wondered what their crime was to deserve such punishment.

"Have you ever heard of anyone called Marilyn Webber?"

"Can't say I have."

"Rachel Cates?"

"No."

"Or Dr Andrew Martin?"

The man shook his head.

"Well, do you have any theories about what happened here?"

"Nope. I just saw the results. Poor diseased bastards! We got a few straying into Baker's Bridge, but it didn't make no difference, though. They were crazed out of their minds and then they died," he said, wistfully, looking across the road to the disused church. The wooden slats had been blown away from the chubby steeple by ferocious winter winds. Years of neglect had contributed to the disintegration.

"And no one knew the cause?"

"A few had ideas. State authorities said it was a virus, but they've always been full of shit. Then there was some who thought it was some kind of beast living up in the mountains," he said, nodding at the dismal peaks which loomed over Burrows. "Some vicious predator type. One or two even said it was human!"

"Human?"

"Sure. There were a couple of real asylum cases who said a woman was responsible. A beautiful *naked* woman. Wishful thinking, that's what I said."

Chris and Katherine looked at each other. Marilyn Webber, Rachel Cates, now Robert Stark. Somewhere.

"A beautiful naked woman doing all that stuff?" he cackled. "If that ain't proof of their insanity, I don't know what is!"

They watched him walk back into the rain, merging with the grey as he reached the far end of town. Katherine tugged Chris's arm more tightly and then kissed him on the cheek. "Let's get out of here," she suggested. "It's too cold and wet and . . ."

"And depressing."

They got back into the rental car and left Burrows, Virginia. They passed through Baker's Bridge, where life still continued, and half an hour later joined the road to Winston Salem in North Carolina. It was Katherine who broke the gloomy silence when she said, "I still don't understand why she didn't kill us."

Robert finished swimming and climbed out of the pool. The sun blazed overhead. He looked down towards the sea, a thin strip of turquoise, just where the sky died. Rachel's villa was beautiful. He wondered what time it was. He was due in Nice at two for a meeting with Rachel's lawyers, when he would sign for everything she had ever possessed. The men who handled it had come down especially for the meeting from Lyon, her birthplace. They'd instinctively recognized him straightaway, and treated him reverentially.

He wondered where Chris Lang and Katherine Ross were. To his amazement, he discovered that Rachel had spared them. She'd seen that they *knew* they were going to die, that they'd accepted their fate, and that was a sufficient price for Rachel. She'd almost been compassionate.

Laura had been too shocked to speak when he conquered the rush, just in time to leave the building before the police arrived. His farewell never registered with her.

A gentle breeze drifted in from the sea, taking the edge off the stinging heat. He saw the old gardener in animated conversation with the cook. The villa was staffed by four locals. Rachel had lived luxuriously, wherever she was.

Robert still found it hard to accept what he'd done. It had been morality's last stand, but it was only after the event, after he'd inherited all of her, that he understood the enormity of what that represented.

As he shook off his humanity, like some wretched hangover, he'd still believed that his respect for mortal life would prevent him from becoming quite like Rachel. He'd felt genuine horror at what he'd done to Vernon. He couldn't kill Laura, and the prospect of butchering countless victims in the future appalled him. He couldn't allow himself to become like that, and therefore wouldn't allow Rachel to perpetuate her own reign of slaughter. So in one passionate moment, he killed the one he loved.

But now that she was part of him, he recognized his true nature. He understood how Laura represented the most generous gift Rachel could have ever given him. He accepted everything and knew he'd kill again. He was born to stalk and slay. It was absurd to regard human life as sacred; it was a plane of existence so inferior to his own that he found it hard to place any value on it at all. She had been right about everything and now she was gone, he felt compelled to live by her code. He would make her spirit proud. Rachel's collection of souls would pale into insignificance next to his. It was stunningly obvious and he welcomed the ceaseless rampage ahead, which only served to emphasize the horror of what he'd done to her. In one dreadful moment of mortal frailty, he'd damned himself needlessly.

Now Robert faced the bleak horror that Rachel had been forced to confront for two centuries. The prospect of eternal solitude left him cold. But at least he hadn't lost her. She was part of him forever. They could never be separated now.

As he looked out over the mirror sea, Robert lit a cigarette, a habit he'd recently resumed. Like Rachel had, he tried to make it an act of pleasure, not desperation.

MARK BURNELL

FREAK

DO YOU BELIEVE IN MIRACLES?

An astonishing gift is about to transform Christian Floyd's life: the power to perform miracles, to heal the sick and save lives. A power that makes him a freak.

Bewildered by his new talent, he suddenly finds that everyone wants him. He's sought by the sick, exploited by opportunists, hounded by the media . . . and haunted by a maniac.

It seems the only life he can't save is his own . . .

NEW ENGLISH LIBRARY PAPERBACKS